after
hours

APHRODISIA BOOKS are published by

Kensington Publishing Corp.
850 Third Avenue
New York, NY 10022

All Kensington titles, imprints, and distributed lines are available at special quantity discounts for bulk purchases for sales promotion, premiums, fund-raising, educational or institutional use.

Special book excerpts or customized printings can also be created to fit specific needs. For details, write or phone the office of the Kensington Special Sales Manager: Kensington Publishing Corp., 850 Third Avenue, New York, NY, 10022. Attn. Special Sales Department. Phone: 1-800-221-2647.

Aphrodisia and the A logo are trademarks of Kensington Publishing Corporation.

Kensington and the K logo Reg. U.S. Pat. & TM Off.

ISBN 0-7582-1480-4

First Printing: April 2006

10 9 8 7 6 5 4 3 2 1

Printed in the United States of America

after
hours

jodi lynn copeland

APHRODISIA

APHRODISIA BOOKS

www.kensingtonbooks.com

CONTENTS

Night Moves

1

There was something to be said about the way a woman danced. Between her body-hugging, short red dress and the arousing way she twisted her sleek curves, the woman who currently held Brendan Jordan's attention seemed to be saying "do me" loud enough to be heard halfway across the hotel reception hall.

He glanced over at Mike Donovan, his one-time college roommate and the newest victim of matrimony, then nodded toward the blonde.

From his seat next to Brendan at the head table, Mike followed Brendan's gaze. His grin turned from one of newly married idiocy to that of male understanding. "Pretty incredible, isn't she?" he asked loudly, to be heard over the blaring music.

Drool-worthy was a more suitable way to describe her. Only, Brendan didn't drool over women. If anything, the situation was reversed. They gave him the hot, hungry, fuck-me looks that made it clear what they wanted even before they approached. And, if they were lucky, he gave it to them.

The blonde wasn't drooling over him. Judging by the dreamy

expression that tugged her slightly too wide mouth into one of the sexier smiles he'd seen, she wasn't even aware there were other people in the room.

Brendan was aware, however. Aware of how damned long he'd been sitting there ogling her. Looking away, he took a long pull from his beer. He set the bottle back on the table before nonchalantly asking, "So, who is she?"

Mike's eyebrows rose. "You haven't met Jilly?"

"That's her name?" Brendan gave the woman an assessing look. Jilly didn't sound right. With breasts plump enough to fill his hands and a curvy ass that had the bulk of his blood firing straight to his dick, she deserved a far more sensual name.

"I'd just assumed with your new jo—"

Brendan glanced back at Mike. "My what?"

Mike's gaze clouded over. After a few seconds, his grin returned—a little too deviously, in Brendan's mind. Mike used to grin like that back in college, just before he pulled the kind of shit that ended up getting both of them in trouble.

"Never mind what I was about to say." Mike pushed his chair back from the table. "Let me do the honors of introducing you."

Brendan pushed back his own chair and stood. The blonde might not be eyeing him over the way he felt various other women doing, but that didn't mean he needed Mike's help in getting her to talk to him. There was a reason he'd earned the title of "The Midwest's Most Eligible Bachelor" from *People* magazine. That reason wasn't due to shyness around women, knockouts or otherwise. It was because of his money and heritage and, more than that, his business savvy. He'd opted to take a break from the financial aspects of business and try his hand at the advertising end of things less than two years ago. Already he was rising up the corporate ladder with relative ease.

"Thanks for the offer," he said to Mike, "but I can handle things from here."

"Sure thing. Just let me know when you need help."

Brendan laughed at the absurdity of the statement. They might share a passion, and even wisdom, for success, but they sure as hell didn't for females. Mike's knowledge of women could fit into a thimble. If it hadn't been for Brendan literally pushing him in his new wife's direction, the man would still be single.

Single, free and happy.

Guilt edged through Brendan, quickly fading when he noted the nauseatingly doting smile Mike shot his bride's way. Nothing to feel guilty about there, just as there was nothing to be learned "The day I need help with women from you, Donovan, is the day I'll have truly sunk to an all-new low."

Mike glanced back at him, humor lighting his eyes. "Hey, whatever you say, man. Just remember you said that come Monday."

What was Monday? The day he started in on his latest career venture with the high-power, Atlanta-based advertising firm Neilson & Sons, but what did that have to do with the she-devil working her magic on the dance floor?

Whatever it was, it wasn't important enough to stay in his mind and, therefore, not important enough to worry over.

With a last look at Mike, whose attention was again on his wife, Brendan started across the room. He stopped on the edge of the light-brightened dance floor where a mass of females and a handful of males worked their bodies in a number of interesting moves. None quite so interesting as Jilly's, however.

Her profile was to Brendan, but he could still make out far more than he'd been able to back at the table. Honey-blond hair framed an expressive face and hung midway down her back in loose waves. Full breasts pressed against the snug bodice of her short, sequined dress as her nicely rounded ass swayed seductively in time with the music. Black high-heels streamlined long, slender legs encased in sheer stockings. While her eyes were closed, the sultry look on her face said plenty.

So did the arousal in his tuxedo pants that turned his cock from slightly hard with simple interest to rock-solid and throbbing.

There was something about her. Something he needed to discover before this night was over, or, at the very least, something he needed to uncover by way of removing the layers of silk, sequins and nylon that hid the lush body beneath.

Not about to stand by and wait for her to open her eyes, Brendan moved onto the dance floor and through a sea of thriving bodies to the one he ached to touch.

Jillian Lowery's pulse went from a happily fast beat to all-out chaos in two seconds flat. A hand settled over her belly—a hand that she didn't need to look down at to know was large and masculine. If the sudden throbbing between her thighs that came with the hot breath caressing her neck and the languorous movements against her backside were any sign, the owner of that hand knew exactly what he was doing.

She should stop his highly suggestive and far too intimate moves, whoever he was. Any other day she would. Today wasn't a normal day. Today was the first time in a very long while that she wasn't surrounded by colleagues and clients alike who'd come to respect her cool, professional demeanor. Today the subdued wilder side of Jillian had a chance to come out and play. After today, that Jillian would have to go back into hiding until some unknown time in the future.

She should stop him, but she wasn't going to. Not yet anyway.

Summoning nerves she'd forgotten she possessed, Jillian covered the stranger's hand with her own and ground her bottom against her dance partner's groin. The hand tightened at her waist and a low growl drifted to her ears. The animalistic sound would have been enough to bring too-long-denied hunger swelling to life. The length of an erection pressed against her buttocks was more than enough. Wetness gathered in her panties and her pulse threatened to beat out of control.

The hand beneath hers slid lower, down the sequined silk of her dress, and his palm turned and molded itself to the slight curve of her mound. The breath snagged in her throat. Perspiration gathered on her flushed skin. Her hips reacted out of instinct, grinding against that hot, weighty touch.

Restlessness screamed through Jillian, further moistening her panties with the juices of arousal, making her want in a way she hadn't experienced in years. Maybe ever.

Need egged her on, shut out all thoughts of their surroundings, of the flashing lights and thundering music. Jillian tightened her hold on his hand, urging it to press harder, silently begging him to go farther. To push her dress aside and sink his fingers deep into her aching pussy, thrusting them in and out until she cruised past the limits of ecstasy and there could be no stopping her mindless screams of release.

He pressed the slightest bit harder. Her clit throbbed. She mewled deep in her throat. "Oh, yes. God, please . . ."

She wanted so badly.

Wanted to forget about being the consummate businesswoman. Wanted to let go and be the fun-loving, carefree woman she'd left behind four years ago. Wanted to experience satisfaction once this decade that didn't have anything to do with landing another prestigious client en route to obtaining her dream job.

"I'd love to please you, Jilly, but we're on a dance floor, sweetheart. As crowded as it is, the song's going to end soon and everyone's going to see where my hand's at."

The thickly spoken words drifted to her ears, reflecting appetite as well as humor. Jillian heard both, but it was the truth that pulled her from the sensual haze, the truth of how much she'd allowed herself to forget the mistakes of the past and let herself go. Panic assailed her, tightening her limbs and tamping back the raw desire coiled to life in her belly and burning like a wildfire of need deep in her core. Her grinding moves came to an abrupt halt as judgment returned to taunt her.

Oh, God, what the hell had she been thinking?

She had to stop this. Had to explain that she'd allowed the music to carry her away and act completely shameless with a man she had yet to set eyes on.

But how?

And did she honestly want to?

Anxiety ate at her, but so did the scintillating thrill of doing the kind of daring thing she hadn't done in years. The kind of thing she would never do with or around those who knew her as Jillian the Professional.

The magical hand that had spun warmth and wetness in her with barely more than a touch lifted away. The discontented whimper that broke from her lips answered her earlier question. She didn't want to end this. Only, judging by the fact that her dance partner had let her go, he did.

Dejection filled her for one gloomy second, and then he caught her hand in his and twirled her. She landed awkwardly against a wide, hard chest and swallowed back a breath of mixed shock and elation. He wasn't dismissing her, just changing course as the music dictated.

The flashing overhead lights gave way to the soft glow of candles arranged throughout the reception hall. A slow melody drifted from the front of the room, a mesmerizing song that had nothing on the gripping heat in the stranger's eyes.

They were dark—maybe brown or deep blue; Jillian couldn't tell in the dim lighting. She could tell other things, like his build. He had a good six inches on her five-foot-seven frame, and, if the feel of his body against hers was any sign, he was both muscular and lean. Thick, dark hair framed an angular face that sported a touch of five-o'clock shadow. Full lips hovered over hers as if they might advance at any moment.

Her mind cleared with that last thought and a fresh dose of heat coursed through her. He was yummy, but he was also vaguely familiar. From the wedding party, yes, but for some other reason. Some reason she prayed had nothing to do with business.

"You're a friend of Mike's?" she asked.

He twined her arms around his neck, then placed his own at her waist as they fell into a slow dance. A lazy smile tugged at his lips. "From college, yes."

He was educated, whoever he was. Not that education mattered for what she wanted to do with him, but . . .

What she wanted to do with him? What did she want to do? Okay, have a night of wild and kinky sex—that much was a given, from the shockingly hard points of her nipples to the cream that seeped between her thighs—but did she dare? Not without a little more information.

Jillian didn't want to know him well, just as she didn't want him to know her well. Too much information could lead to potential future problems. A few details were important, though. For starters, if he was married.

But, no, he wasn't married. Mike might only know Jillian through his new wife, Molly, but he still wouldn't allow a married man to come on to her. "What would Mike say if I asked about you?"

The stranger's smile kicked higher. His fingers began a rhythm at her waist that was both featherlight and amazingly distracting. "That I love a good challenge and know how to leave a woman with a smile."

The cockiness of the answer probably should have made her have second thoughts. Instead, she laughed and smiled back.

God, how she missed bantering for the hell of it. "So, you're a womanizer?"

"Is that what it sounded like?"

"Is that how it is?"

Seconds ticked by, and Jillion anxiously waited for his response. It came in actions instead of words. His fingers moved higher, along her thinly clothed sides, to graze the outer swell of her breasts. He applied the slightest bit of pressure and her nipples pulsed for his touch.

That dangerously sexy mouth of his curved once more. His eyes showed amusement that ensured he knew the effect he was having on her. It was tempting to turn away and reject him and the arrogance he gave off as far as his sexual appeal was concerned. She might have, too, if at that moment his thumb didn't reach out to stroke the underside of her breast, the pad moving in a leisurely circle that had every one of her nerves at attention.

She bit back a sigh that he would move inward, closer to her straining nipple. There was no need to sigh, no need to beg. She could feel his swollen cock cradled against her belly. He wanted her. All she had to do was say she wanted him, too, and they would be out of there and in some place far more private.

Heat speared through her with the thought of how quickly they could be away from there, their clothes stripped away, limbs tangled, naked and sweaty. Those strong, very capable-looking lips of his on hers, his tongue stroking her flesh with damp, lazy licks. The hot, hard length of his shaft pushing between her thighs and deep into her sheath.

Oh, yes, she wanted that. Wanted to let go and just feel.

If only the circumstances were right. . . .

Jillian struggled to mask her eagerness. That he knew Mike didn't bother her. Once they returned from their honeymoon, Mike and Molly would be moving halfway across the country. The only things that mattered here were that she wouldn't be seeing or hearing from this man after tonight and that her actions with him couldn't return to harm her. "Where are you from?"

The slow movement of his thumb along the underside of her breast paused, starting again with his reply. "Chicago."

Anticipation jetted through her, pushing her building desire to new heights. He wasn't from around here, and the more she looked at him, the more certain she was they'd never met. Those two factors combined were an even greater stimulant than his potent grin. They meant the circumstances were right. And that meant she was going to have the one thing she'd craved these last four years even more than the loud, slightly tacky outfits that used to make up her wardrobe.

She was going to have no-holds-barred, *kill the composure and give into the thrill* sex. Hallelujah!

"What about a name?"

She didn't bother to mask her eagerness and he clearly took note. His penis jerked against her belly and his expression became one of urgency. "Brendan," he said, the calm tone belying his hot look.

"Just Brendan?"

"That would all depend. Is it just Jilly?"

Jillian managed to stop herself from correcting his usage of her childhood name. It was immature and completely removed from the capable, commanding woman she'd transformed herself into. But, for tonight, it was perfect.

Smiling, she moved her hands from his neck to coast over his sides. She thanked the glasses of wine she'd had with dinner, and moved her hands lower still. Her fingers reached his tuxedo pants and, through the thin material of his dress shirt, she caressed the virile flesh just above his waist.

His breath rushed in and his cock jerked once again.

Her smile growing with the distinctly female power that assailed her, she brought her lips to his ear. The spicy tang of aftershave and something far more intoxicating filled her senses as she whispered, "Just Jilly, and so you don't have to waste your time asking, the answer is yes."

For a second or two when Jilly had swiveled around and stared up into his eyes, her own filled with desire as much as what appeared to be hesitancy, Brendan had thought he'd made a mistake—that she wasn't the hot-blooded vixen her invigorating dance moves, and the bold way she'd ground her mound against his hand in a room full of people, seemed to indicate. Then her cautious look had faded and she'd snaked her palms down his chest and breathed one very warm and willing *yes* into his ear.

Coincidentally, it was the same word leaving her lips now, as they stood twined together inside his hotel suite's doorway. They hadn't made it any farther.

He leaned into the softness of her body and ran his tongue over the spot on her neck where her pulse beat erratically. Her hands buried in his hair, short nails biting with just enough pressure to have the blood screaming to life in his veins.

Jilly squirmed, and the hard ridge of her pubic bone brushed over his rigid shaft. Shuddering with the need the simple caress brought forth, he turned his teasing licks to fervent nips.

She shivered in his arms and tossed her head back. "Oh, yes. Yes. Yes!"

Brendan stopped his nibbling to grin at that last ecstatic one. If she made this much noise when all they'd manage to accomplish so far was a little necking, what would she be like when they got around to the main event? Not that he was complaining. He happened to be a big fan of a woman who wasn't afraid to let her love for sex show.

She lifted her head and met his gaze. Her hands moved to cup his ass. She tugged him closer yet and rotated her pelvis against his. "I want you, Brendan. I want you now. Right now!"

Had he actually thought her the cautious type for a second

or two back downstairs? Fuck, no, nothing cautious about this one. She was all fire and impatience. And sex, he added with a short laugh he let flow into his words. "Now? No patience, sweetheart? No buildup? Just get to it?"

"I had my buildup on the dance floor. I don't need more."

"What if I do?"

Wariness flashed through her moss-green eyes, then was gone as one of her hands released his buttocks to cup his dick through his pants. An impish smile curved her lips. "I can feel. You don't need any more buildup, either."

Jilly's fingers clasped tighter, pumping his stiff cock. He groaned. If she kept up with the squeezing, he also wouldn't need to bother with taking his clothes off or locating a condom. He'd be coming right here by the suite's entrance.

Not that it was a bad idea. In fact, it was a very good idea.

Moving too fast to allow her the time to digest his actions, Brendan jerked from her hold and slid his hands down the front of her dress and under the short hem. Elation filled him as his fingers met with the crotch of her panties, making it clear she wore the type of stockings that were hooked to a garter belt and ended at the tops of her thighs.

He pushed past the damp lace and speared through the curls beneath to finger her slit. With a shallow gasp, Jilly released a hot stream of breath into his face. He liked the sound of that, of her losing control. From the way she'd taken over their sensual dancing to her agreement to have sex even before he could ask, he took her as the type who had to be on top and in command, both in bed and in every other facet of life. It was time she learned change could be a good thing. "You're wet."

"Yes."

"But not enough."

"What?"

He moved his finger, stroking the swollen lips of her juicy cunt, but going no farther. He wanted to build this up the way she said she didn't need. He wanted to make her come undone completely, until she was thrashing in his arms and screaming with her climax.

Her breathing grew shallower with each caress of her pussy lips and finally he allowed himself to go farther, to rub at her engorged clit. She shuddered with that first touch and his entire body vibrated with the unguarded look on her face.

Damn, she was stunning when she let herself go. Not more stunning than other women he'd fucked, just different, that something different that had convinced him to break from the norm and be the one to do the approaching.

Brendan stilled his teasing and skewered one finger deep inside her warm, slick sheath. Her eyes flared wide and then shut.

"Open them, Jilly!" In the past he'd never cared about watching the excitement in his lover's eyes—only pleasing their bodies. This woman he wanted to feel and see everything with. Maybe it was because she didn't seem to recognize him and want him for his money or legacy, the way so many others did, or maybe it was something else. It was a maybe he'd ponder later; right now there were far more pressing matters at hand.

Jilly opened her eyes. He added another finger to the first, plunging in and out of her drenched cunt, rubbing against her clit with each deep thrust. He reveled in every whimper, every throaty sigh, and the awe of rapture building on her expressive face. "I want to watch your eyes when you come. And you will come. You want to right now. I can feel your pussy contracting, begging to be let free. Come for me, Jilly. Let go."

"Not like . . ." The muscles of her sex compressed, pulling at his fingers, hardening his cock to the point of explosion. "Wasn't . . . supposed to . . . be like . . ." Her eyes slammed shut. She snapped them open again as her pussy clenched around him, contracting tighter, tighter, then all at once letting go. "Oh, God. . . ."

Hot cream poured over his fingers, showering his palm and

forcing him to mentally stop himself from responding in kind. This moment was for her. There was plenty of time for him later. "That's it, sweetheart. Just let go."

Brendan pulled free of her sex and brushed his fingers across her clit. Jilly's body let loose with another round of tremors. She bit down on her lower lip and her cheeks blazed with vivid pink. Her eyes stayed focused on his. Focused and so damned green and direct they seemed to see right through him.

"Fuck, you're so intense. I love watching your face when you come. It makes me want to see how many different expressions I can bring out. How you'll look when I take you with my mouth, my tongue. When I fill up your sweet cunt from behind. I want to see it all, Jilly, but I don't think one night will give us enough time.

"Once I move here permanently, we'll meet again. Wherever you want. Once more, or twice. However long it takes to see—"

A squeak slipped past her parted lips, cutting him off short. She closed her mouth and took a step to her left, dislodging his fingers from her body. Her head whipped around, coming to a stop facing the opposite wall. "Oh, my God, would you look at the time! Ten forty-five already."

"Like I said, we won't have time for everything tonight, but we'll still have time for plenty."

Jilly continued to stare at the wall clock another few seconds and then looked back at him. Determination filled eyes that moments ago had been dark with ecstasy. "No. We don't. I—I have to go. Now!"

"*What?*" Brendan took a step back. Was she fucking kidding him? Things were just getting good and she had to go?

"I was supposed to be home by ten."

Yeah, she had to be kidding him. Who in their right mind went to a wedding reception with the intention of leaving by ten o'clock? A kid, or maybe a ninety-year-old. Neither of which she happened to be.

Feeling irritation made all the worse by the restless ache in his pants, he smirked at her. "And this is because of your Cinderella complex?"

She frowned. "She could stay out until midnight."

He almost laughed with the irony in the remark, only he wasn't up to laughter at the moment. "My point exactly. What the hell's the rush? Mommy and Daddy have the curfew reins held extra tightly tonight?"

Fine lines marred Jilly's forehead. She wrapped her arms around her waist and stared at him like she'd just reentered her body and didn't like what the person who'd taken over in her absence had done. Unfolding her arms, she moved to the door. "I—I'm sorry. I have to go. Ginger needs me."

"Ginger?" As in her daughter, maybe?

"My . . . she just needs me." She opened the door and slipped through to the other side, closing it behind her.

Brendan stared at the door, uncertain of what he was feeling. Shock. Anger. Disbelief. Maybe a combination of them all, over the unlikelihood of what had just happened.

Women never walked out on him. Sure as hell not without a good-bye or an explanation to their abrupt departure. And for damned sure not seconds after he'd given them an orgasm with the intention of supplying several more. But then, women generally knew who he was. Jilly hadn't and she'd wanted him all the same, at least for a small amount of time. That made her one among the masses. Having left him with a major hard-on or not, it also made her a challenge he couldn't resist, not when he'd yet to taste that slightly too-wide mouth of hers.

"You left to feed your dog, and that doesn't strike you as odd behavior?"

Jillian frowned at her friend Tawny, who sat next to her in the boardroom, waiting for the Monday morning meeting to start. They were keeping their voices lowered, but she was still far from comfortable talking about her personal life around her coworkers. "I knew she'd be hungry. I always feed her before I go to bed and I always go—"

"To bed at ten thirty," Tawny finished with a knowing look. "That you live by a hard-and-fast schedule these days is clear. What's also clear is that your leaving had nothing to do with a schedule, but the fact that you were scared."

"*What?*" The word came out loudly. She cast a surreptitious glance around, thankful to find no one paying attention.

"You were afraid of letting go enough to have a little fun."

"I have plenty of fun and I wasn't scared."

"Uh-huh, right. The hard-nosed persona and black-widow wardrobe might have the rest of these people convinced, but, girl, I know you better. I know the real you. I also know that, outside of your brief lapse Saturday night, the last time you let the real you come out to play was four years ago when we got drunk off Jell-O shots at the company New Year's party."

And Jillian had subsequently proceeded to ring in the New Year by kissing every guy in the place on the mouth whether he was single or not. Every guy including the husband of a major hotel chain proprietor with whom she'd been in the throes of signing a grand-scale deal. The deal had gone belly-up fifteen minutes later and the job Jillian loved had come damned close to going right along with it.

Heat raced into her cheeks with the far-from-pleasant memory and she focused on her portfolio on the table in front of her. She wasn't afraid of letting go of the cool and composed professional image she'd spent every day establishing since that fateful night. But she also wouldn't screw it up. She'd worked too hard to get here, on the cusp of taking over the role as senior advertising account executive when Donaldson retired next month, to jeopardize things over one night of fun—even if the mere thought of the fun currently under discussion had her sex growing moist and tingly, and her pulse picking up.

She pushed the sensations aside and glanced at her friend. "Fine, I'm not exactly the life of the party on a routine basis. I lived that life once. I don't want it anymore."

Tawny's hot-pink lips curved upward, and amusement glimmered in her eyes. "Kinda like the way you didn't want Brendan Saturday night?"

"I never said I didn't want him. I just . . . didn't have time."

"Right. Because you had to rush home to feed Ginger."

"Because I don't have time to deal with a relationship." Jillian just managed to hold back her laugh. The last thing an admitted bad boy like Brendan had been after was a commitment. He'd suggested they meet for another night or two of sex. She was well aware that was all it ever would have been.

Tawny tipped back in her chair and frowned. "If it's one night of fun you're after, then you missed your chance. By the sounds of things, this Brendan guy wasn't after anything more than a few minutes of exploration time in your pants. That being the case, it brings us back to my original point. The only reason you didn't finish what was started on that dance floor is because you were scared."

"For the last time, I was *not*—"

"Good morning, everyone." Larry Neilson, CEO of the advertising agency, entered the boardroom, his booming voice silencing her. "I'd like to kick off today's meeting by introducing you to Neilson's newest employee. Not that I think with his track record, he needs an introduction. . . ."

She was *not* scared. . . . Jillian continued her tirade silently while Larry droned on about the new hire. If Brendan hadn't brought up the fact that he was moving to the area, she would have gone through with things in a heartbeat. She was way overdue for some excitement of the sexual kind. Given how quickly he'd had her abandoning her better judgment and crying out her bliss as he brought her to climax, he definitely could have done the job.

Maybe Brendan was no longer a candidate to relieve the carnal hunger Jillian had been denying for too long, but there had to be plenty of others out there. She would simply find one to see to her needs for a night or two. So what if he didn't have Brendan's talented hands and sexy smile? She didn't need a man of his caliber to satisfy her. She just needed someone who was anatomically correct.

All right, so a decent face wouldn't hurt when it came to getting her heated up. She closed her eyes as that face began to take shape. Dark eyes were always good, the kind that seemed to look right through you and into your darkest, deepest, most intimate secrets. He might as well be tall and have dark hair.

Mmm . . . Nice, full, sensual mouth. A tongue that

Tawny's elbow nudging into her side dissolved the developing face of Jillian's fantasy lover. She opened her eyes to glare at the other woman, but never made it past the man who stood twenty short feet away—the tall man grinning at her with amusement in his sinfully dark eyes. The man who had the breath wheezing from her lungs and her heart beating so hard it was liable to come out of her wide-open mouth.

Larry's spiel drew to a close. He added in an elated tone, "Everyone, give a warm welcome to our newest account specialist and a man who's already assured me he's in the running for the senior advertising account executive position once Donaldson retires, Brendan Jordan."

2

When he'd first walked into Neilson's boardroom and spotted the woman cloaked in dowdy black with her hair pulled
back into such a severe knot it was a wonder her head didn't explode, Brendan had felt a sense of déjà vu. It wasn't until her
mouth flopped open and she'd shifted uncomfortably in her
seat that recognition set in. Then all he could think of was one
thing: What the fuck had she done with the knockout he'd met
Saturday night?

Jilly could hide her delectable body all she wanted, but the
striking beauty of her face and that too-wide, too-tempting
mouth would still be there for all to see. They were sure as hell
still taunting him. One look at those dark red lips and his body
was back to the state it had been in when she'd walked out on
him two nights ago—hard as hell and ready to gather up the
woman responsible and remedy the situation.

If the fish-face look were any sign, Jilly had no plans to let
that happen. If the sudden glowering were to be believed, she'd
be happy if he turned back around and pretended he'd never

stepped foot in Neilson's boardroom, let alone knew her from another far more enjoyable time and place.

"Why don't you take a seat while I go over this week's updates, Brendan?"

Brendan nodded at Larry, and started along the wall that stretched out beside the elongated conference table. There were two open chairs—one across the table from Jilly, and one a seat away. He'd just as soon be sitting beside her—under her would be even more preferable—but he settled for the chair one away.

A redhead in a cleavage-baring orange top sat between them. She raised an eyebrow, her Day-Glo-pink smile wide and warm. Quietly, she asked, "'Brendan.' Now, why does that name seem so familiar? Hmm . . ." She glanced in Jilly's direction. "Jilly, do you have any idea why Brendan might seem so familiar to me?"

"I don't know," came a blasé reply from Jilly.

Brendan leaned back in his chair to see past the woman's head. Jilly sat facing the front, appearing as if she weren't aware she was being spoken to, certainly not about him. Her rigid posture suggested she wasn't nearly so oblivious.

The redhead laughed, pulling his attention back to her smile. It reminded him a lot of the smile Mike had shot his way right before Brendan had approached Jilly at the reception. The one that now made it clear Mike had known that Brendan and Jilly would soon be coworkers, and that he couldn't be more amused that Brendan wanted her. Mike had also made it sound as if he thought she'd turn him down.

Was that her MO, to get a guy hard and aching and then run? If so, she was in for a surprise. He might have let her walk away temporarily, but he had no plans to do so long-term. Sure as hell not until he got some answers—to both her reason for leaving him and to his own for thinking about her since.

"You'll have to forgive Jilly," the redhead said in a hushed voice. "She's suffers from SMD. By the way, I'm Tawny Madison."

"It's a pleasure, and what exactly is SMD?"

"Selective Memory Disorder. Nasty little thing." Her smile grew and the amusement he'd detected spread into her eyes. "Once upon a time Jilly was this fun-loving woman who was the life of the party, but then she was bit by a dark and nasty bug and—"

"Oh, God." Jilly turned to glare at them. "My name is Jillian, not Jilly," she hissed out, "and I was not bit by a dark and nasty bug. Now would you please knock it off already and pay attention to the meeting?"

"And miss filling Mr. Tall, Dark, and What the Hell Were You Thinking When You Left Him to Feed Your Dog? in on the Jilly in witch's clothing. Sorry, girl, no can do."

Brendan managed to hold back his laughter at the implication in Tawny's words. If that was on Jilly's MO—get the men hard and aching, only to leave them high and dry so she could go home and feed her dog—she seriously needed to work on her routine. "That wouldn't happen to be Ginger, would it?"

The pink he'd spotted in Jilly's cheeks when she'd looked up and seen him smiling at her returned. She closed her eyes and inhaled audibly. She reopened her eyes and annoyance shot from her gaze in waves so heavy and lethal a lesser man would have cowered. Her lips parted and Brendan waited for the barbs she would fling his way. He wasn't a lesser man, but he must have been a deranged one because the passion behind her anger only added to her appeal.

"That's it for this morning, folks," Larry said from the front of the room, cutting off whatever she'd been about to say. "Thanks as always."

Jilly glared a moment longer, then looked away and pushed back her chair. She stood and grabbed her portfolio, clearly planning to make a break for it. Larry appeared at her side before she could go anywhere. "Since your positions are so similar, Jillian, I thought you'd be the best person to show Brendan around."

"Lovely."

She'd muttered the word, but not quietly enough. Brendan fought a smile while Larry asked, "Pardon me?"

She glanced over at Brendan, her gaze returning to its narrowed state for an instant, then back at Larry, and smiled. "I said . . . lovely. I was hoping you'd ask me."

"Excellent." Larry turned to Brendan, and Jilly made a beeline for the door. "Brendan, you're in great hands with Jillian Lowery. She's one of Neilson's best, not to mention your biggest competitor for Donaldson's position. Shame there isn't a need for both of you up that high. With her experience and your reputation, you'd make a great team."

So that was the reason her look had gone from fish-faced to pissed off in the midst of Larry's introduction. His presence here gave her competition that concerned her.

"From the little I've spoken with her so far, I'd have to agree with the whole 'great hands' theory." Great hands, great mouth. Great ass. He glanced over at her retreating rear end in the loose-fitting black slacks and, though he couldn't see a thing that resembled a feminine curve, his cock responded with an impatient throb.

As if she could feel his stare, Jilly glanced back. For just a second he caught a glimpse of the fiery woman behind the dowdy clothes and fierce hair knot, and then she masked her expression, turned her head back around, and walked out the door.

Brendan smiled as he again regarded Larry. He listened absently to the man while the bulk of his thoughts focused on Jilly. He might not understand what it was about her that stayed in his mind, but he planned to figure it out, and soon.

* * *

"Why do I get the impression you aren't happy to see me?"

Jillian looked up at the too-familiar, too-knowing, too-damned-sexy-for-its-own-good-voice to find Brendan standing in the doorway of her office. With an inward groan, she came around to the front of the desk and crossed her arms. "Perhaps because you're intuitive. Now, can I help you with something?"

After closing the door, he walked toward her, stopping a few feet away. "You're mad about Saturday night, because you left?"

She'd been about to tell him to back off and quit invading her personal space with his impossibly tasty scent. The arrogance in his words had her gasping instead. "Why would I be mad about my own leaving?"

Jillian shook the question away, paced back behind her desk and sat down. She needed distance from his earthy scent before it began to cloud her reasoning. She'd already let that happen once, and look where it had gotten her—not only with opposition for a job she'd believed was hers, but fearing the opponent in question would use his knowledge of her weekend antics to his advantage. "Forget it. It doesn't matter. What does matter is that you realize that . . . that person you met Saturday night wasn't me."

Brendan looked thoughtful for a moment, then, "You have an evil stepsister who looks exactly like you? Or maybe you *are* the evil stepsister. The woman I met on Saturday didn't feel the need to hide behind ugly clothes or a crass attitude. She knew she had a killer body, and wasn't afraid to use it. She also had enough finesse to make me break my personal mantra."

And what was that?

Jillian hadn't known who he was on Saturday, but she knew now. Knew his bad-boy reputation as much as she knew his background. He was the only child of a wealthy financier, born with a silver spoon in his mouth and living life as he pleased ever since. The way he'd acted toward her at Mike and Molly's wedding fit perfectly with his standard procedure. He was goading her by suggesting any differently, trying to get her to admit she was still interested.

She wasn't interested—at least, not the logical portions of her. The parts of her body that had reacted to the heat in his eyes in the boardroom were another story. They were also something she could take care of all by herself with a strategically placed vibrator.

"I didn't mean that it wasn't me you met. I meant . . ." What? That she was usually a coldhearted bitch, or at least close enough to one that she didn't even compare to the woman who'd shown him? It wasn't true, but maybe if she allowed him to believe it, he would keep his distance. "Look, Brendan, I don't plan on liking you. I also don't plan on helping you. This is a tough business, so good luck."

His mouth twitched and then broke out into a grin. "Well, gee, Jilly, tell me how you really feel."

"Jillian. My name is Jillian!" And why did his grin have to affect her so physically? He smiled at her rudeness, and all she wanted to do was climb across her desk and attack him with her mouth. Jillian the Professional did not attack.

Brendan's grin disappeared. He rounded the corner of the desk and sank his hip on its edge. He was too close to her again. His scent was working its magic on her senses, not to mention every other part of her. Good God, it was like her nipples were dowsing rods, and he much-sought-after water, with the way they were pointing at him.

She should push him off her desk. Having a woman put him in his place was bound to do wonders for his inflated ego.

"Funny,"—his hand reached out and cupped her face before she could stop it—"I expressly remember you telling me it was Jilly. Just Jilly. Remember?" He released his hold on her face to caress her cheek. The intimacy of his touch made her feel like she was dressed in another short, red dress and thigh-high stockings instead of her current witchy wardrobe. A defiant part of her wanted to be dressed that way again, now. It was that part she blamed for sinking under his touch.

"As I recall," Brendan finished, "it was right before you ground your pussy against my hand and begged me to fuck you."

The magic of the moment burst. Jillian jerked from his touch and narrowed her gaze. She should have knocked him on his ass while she'd had the chance. She would still do it if it she didn't need to get his promise to keep silent about her Saturday night behavior.

Curbing her impulse to lash out at him, she drew a deep breath and said as calmly as she could manage, "I am honestly not this cold, but I'm also not the woman you met on Saturday. I'm a professional. If you're willing to forget about what happened and treat me as a coworker, then I'll try to like you. I won't help you. At least, not for the next few weeks."

"Ah, so the truth comes out."

"What's that supposed to mean?"

"You're afraid I'm going to steal your job."

"Please. You know nothing about the way this company runs. Besides, there is plenty enough work for the both of us."

"I meant Donaldson's job. The one you're salivating over."

She winced at how close he'd hit on the truth. Brendan might be silver-spoon-born and -bred, but he was also intelligent. He'd used that intellect to make his mark on the finance industry and now was barely into his midthirties and already becoming a well-known name in advertising.

"Don't worry, Jilly, I won't steal your job. I plan to earn it, fair and square." Once more he reached out to her and once more she missed the opportunity to move away until he was caressing her cheek. The heat returned to his eyes, rendering their dark brown shade nearly black. "Just as I plan to make you see what a mistake your leaving on Saturday was. A mistake I'm willing to let you remedy."

Jillian bit down hard on her lower lip and quelled the desire building within her with each of his lazy strokes, making her belly tight and the need to pinch her thighs together almost unbearable. That he could make her want so thoroughly with nothing more than a touch was not a good sign. It was all the more reason to make sure he never got this close again.

She jerked away and stood to round the opposite side of the desk. "It will never happen."

"You're forgetting how much I love a challenge."

And that, even more than his IQ, was probably what made him a success. He went after what he wanted even if he knew it wasn't available. He might have been victorious in the past, but he wouldn't be now. He couldn't. Not when she'd wasted the last four years of her life acting like a merciless workhorse to attain her dream job.

Oh, God! She wasn't a merciless workhorse. She loved her job. Maybe she'd turned a bit cooler over the years, left behind certain facets of her personality and life she'd once considered among the better, but there was a need for it. She was still warm inside, still the real Jilly when time allowed.

That time wasn't now. "I realize you're used to getting your way, so let me be the first to assure you this is one challenge you're not going to win."

"I guess we'll have to wait and see about that." Brendan turned and started for the door.

Jillian breathed a sigh of relief, aware that while she might be able to keep up the collected facade for a while, she couldn't do so permanently. Not when his physical presence and the scintillating tang of his aftershave bothered her more than she'd ever realized possible.

He stopped halfway to the door, and turned back. "By the way, you left something at my hotel suite."

"What could I have left? I didn't have anything with me but that ridiculously tiny purse and I know I didn't leave that behind."

Brendan's grin returned. He was standing in front of her before she'd even realized he'd moved. "Actually, I was referring to this."

Jillian let out a gasp as he pulled her against the hard warmth of his body. And that's all that got out before his mouth was on hers. She froze, determined to fight off the demanding kiss he was sure to give her. Only, the kiss wasn't demanding. It was slow, sensual, impossible not to fall into.

He nibbled at the corners of her lips. Moving gradually inward, he brushed her mouth tenderly, almost without any pressure at all. He continued that way, rubbing, caressing, moving with featherlight weight. Slowly he parted her lips and sank his tongue between them. He stroked with languorous licks and teasing darts and thrusts, inflaming the interior of her mouth even as the rest of her body exploded with warmth. Blood pitched through her limbs at a frenzied pace. Her pussy grew liquid with longing, her nipples rock hard. She responded in kind, licking, sampling, stroking his tongue with welcoming fervor.

Brendan's hands lifted from her arms to slide along her back. His fingers kneaded through her jacket and top, gradually coasting downward to grip her ass through her slacks.

Oh, yes, this felt so good, so right. So like everything that was missing in her life.

The daring part of Jillian was back in full force and she burned to keep going, to give herself over to him completely and continue where they'd left off Saturday night.

As if he knew her thoughts, he pulled her closer yet. The hard length of his cock pressed against her belly momentarily stilled her. Then she was moving again, coaxing his tongue, sliding her hands toward his tight buttocks. Just when she would have made contact with his ass he broke the kiss, released his hold on her and stepped back.

Brendan smiled down at her through eyes dark with lust. "As much as I hate to leave when you're just starting to see things my way, I promised Larry I'd let him take me out to lunch."

The words splintered through Jillian's racing thoughts, splashing like ice water over her heated body. She reflexively jerked away from his touch, only to realize he'd already released her. In fact, he was already leaving.

Brendan reached the door and she opened her mouth to stop him, but she couldn't say the words. Mostly because she didn't know what the words were. She was feeling too much right now. Anger, jealousy, like she wanted to rush across the room, toss him to the floor and screw his arrogant brains out. Speaking wasn't a good idea, so she just let him go.

Jillian took a last look around for eavesdroppers, then moved into Tawny's corner cubicle and whispered, "All right, you win. I'm scared."

Her friend swiveled in her chair from the ad layout on her computer screen to shoot Jillian an *I told you so* look. "I take it Brendan stopped in to see you?"

"Larry asked me to show him around." Which she'd never gotten around to doing, since the moment he'd stepped into her office she'd gone on the defensive, then subsequently turned into a puddle of mush. Her pussy tingled even now, just thinking about the feel of his delectable lips on hers. "My talking to him isn't what I'm scared about. Neither is the effect he has on my body."

"But you admit he has an effect?"

"Do I look dead?"

Tawny laughed. "No, and you'd have to be to miss the way he looks at you."

Jillian had hoped to avoid talk of Brendan—at least, the attraction that existed between them—but now that Tawny had brought it up, she had to hear more. "How does he look at me?"

Tawny rolled her eyes. "C'mon, like you can't tell."

She could. She'd been hoping others couldn't. "I don't care. That isn't what matters. He wants my job, Tawny."

"You mean Donaldson's job?"

"Yes!" She grimaced at the outburst and quieted again. "With his track record you know they're going to give it to him. Larry's already taking him out to lunch. He's never taken me out to lunch once in the six years I've been working here."

"Larry wasn't CEO when you signed on," Tawny pointed out, "his father was. And I don't think his taking Brendan out to lunch has anything to do with favoritism. Larry is fair. He'll promote the best person for the job." Her lips curved in a playful smile. "Now, about this way Brendan looks at you. What do you plan to do about it?"

"Absolutely nothing."

Her smile vanished and she sighed. "That's what I was afraid you'd say."

"We work together. Not to mention he's my competition." Not to mention Jillian had already done more with him than she should ever have allowed.

She had to quit thinking with her hormones! What if someone had come into her office when she'd been wrapping herself around Brendan? She never would have lived it down, professionally or personally.

"Not to mention he's majorly hot for your bod," Tawny added. "So hot that when he saw you sitting in that boardroom, he didn't let the frump look turn him off, but zeroed in and made his intentions clear to everyone there."

"He most certainly did not."

"Oh, yes, he did, girl. There's already an office pool going on how long it will be before the two of you hook up."

Damnit! She could not have this. She depended on people thinking of her as levelheaded and the woman to go to when things needed to get done. She relied on their respect and the knowledge she would never let her outside needs come before her work ones. "I already told him I'm not going to sleep with him."

"He's already asked?"

"Yes. No. Oh, hell." Why was this happening to her? She'd stepped out of her carefully constructed professional box for one night, and as a result everything she'd worked so hard for was going up in smoke.

"Don't be scared, Jilly. You're so overdue for some fun. With Brendan's reputation—don't think for a second I don't know it—he's perfect for the job. And if you happen to learn a few insider tips on the secret to his success and how he might or might not plan to leverage Larry in his direction, well, that can hardly be your fault."

Jillian sobered with the words, not quite believing the other woman. They'd been best friends since college almost a decade ago and never once had Tawny proposed anything so ludicrous. "You're suggesting I sleep with him to learn how he plans to get Donaldson's position?"

"I'm suggesting you indulge in sex with a man who was made for the act. He wants you bad, Jilly. At the same time he isn't going to risk losing the position. Use that knowledge to your advantage. Make things work for you. Just don't be scared. You're too smart, and you deserve fun in your life too much to be frightened away by the hottie who's hungry to give it to you."

"Just do it," Jillian ordered herself as she stood outside Brendan's closed office door late Friday afternoon. "If you don't do it now, you never will."

And maybe that would be for the best.

Only, she couldn't forget Tawny's words. Even her friend knew how much Jillian was in need of a little fun, how it had been so long since she'd indulged her wilder side that some days she thought she might explode with the need to cut loose.

She had to give into her needs before they took her over. As much as she hated to admit it, Tawny was right about Brendan being the perfect man for the job. He came without strings where the long-term was concerned, and she already knew he could have her panting in seconds. Then there was the matter of reliability.

She'd been scared he would tell others about her staged personality and that she wasn't the collected businesswoman she'd led her associates to believe. Since that first morning when he'd come into her office and kissed her until she was weak in the knees and damp in the panties, he'd treated her with as much professionalism as anyone could. He hadn't so much as passed her a smile that could be deemed flirtatious.

That didn't stop her from being physically aware of him.

If anything, it made Jillian want him more. Made her ache to barge into his office and demand to know why he'd stopped pursuing her. She wasn't going to barge in. She was going to walk in calmly and lay her offer on the table. And he would accept. He would agree to her rules. He had to. Exploding on the job was not an option.

"Jilly?"

She jerked her head up to find Brendan standing two feet away in his office doorway. The top two buttons of his shirt were undone to reveal a sprinkling of dark, curly hair over suntanned flesh, and his laptop bag's strap was slung over his shoulder. Wonderful. He was leaving. "Uh . . . oh . . . hi."

"Did you need something?"

Did she ever. She needed to stop stammering like an idiot and move close enough to run her fingers over that deliciously exposed stretch of skin, to sink her tongue between those lips that with a brush could ignite her internal fire. She needed to say the words. "Uh, can I speak with you in private?"

"I was about to head out for the week—"

"In that case, I can come—"

"—but I'm really not in that big of a hurry." His expression neutral, he stepped back from the doorway and into his office. "Come in and make yourself comfortable."

She bit back a laugh. Comfort was the last thing she felt. Nervous. Wary. Like she might just explode on the job after all. Comfort? Not on his life.

Brendan made his way across the office, set his bag on the desk and sank down on its edge. Jillian closed the door but remained where she was. She ached for him. Had been thinking of very little else but laying her hands all over his leanly muscled body since Monday morning. Okay, if she were to be honest, since Saturday night. But she had to maintain a certain level of finesse here. One that didn't include following her baser urges and attacking him where he stood. First there were words to be said. If she could get those words out.

"So what is it you wanted to discuss?" he asked.

She glanced around the room at the various painting and art mock-ups that lined the soft-beige walls. "You have good taste. Better than what I'd have guessed."

Brendan tried to hold back his smirk at the surprise in her tone. The way he'd found Jilly standing outside his office, muttering to herself about getting it over with, he knew one wrong move or word on his part and she'd be hightailing it out the door—after she reopened it.

He wondered why she'd closed the door. Had even ventured a guess as to what she thought a closed door might indicate, but then quickly passed it off. She'd been nothing but coolly polite to him this week. To think she'd come here now, ready to take him up on his offer of sex, was implausible. Even if she had, it was too late.

He'd told himself he had to find the reason why she stayed in his mind when all those before her had come and gone in days, if not a single night. He'd believed the best way to obtain those answers was to get closer yet, until he was skin deep. That had been on Monday. He'd gotten to know her this week—not personally, but her office demeanor. This company was Jilly's life. While he had no intention of lying down and letting her have the senior ad exec position, he also wouldn't jeopardize her chances any more than her professionalism by making further advances. He would keep his distance, just the way she wanted.

But if that's what she wanted, why had she closed the door?

The question niggled at Brendan. He stood and crossed to her. She drew more rigid with each of his steps. Her breathing quickened. Nervous. Interesting. He stopped a few feet away and smiled. "Thanks for the compliment, but I get the impression that isn't what's on your mind. Whatever it is, spit it out. We both know you're not one to lack for words."

She glanced at the door as if she might leave. She surprised him by looking back at him and stepping forward. She set her chin, and that sudden proud gesture had him stifling a laugh. Maybe that she was an enigma was really all there was to his attraction. The women in his past had all been fairly similar, easy to figure out, easy to guess their next move. With Jilly he had no idea what was coming next.

"I've changed my mind."

Like that, for example. That, he'd sure as hell never seen coming. He gave his head a shake, certain he'd heard her wrong. She couldn't be here asking for sex. Could she?

"You don't want to go after Donaldson's position?" Bren-

dan asked. "Too bad. I was looking forward to the competition."

"That's not what I meant."

"What did you mean?"

Pink sparked in her cheeks. She made an arcing gesture with
her arm. "I meant the other thing."

He mimicked her move. "The other thing?"

She frowned, the color in her cheeks darkening. "You know.
The *other* thing."

Un-fucking-believable. She really had come to him for sex.
He would have believed that of the Jilly he'd met at the wedding reception. With Jillian the Professional, mistress of the
butt ugly hairdo and breezy attitude, not in a million years. He
also had no intention of giving in just yet. "I'm afraid I don't
know. Can you possibly spell it out for me?"

Jilly's eyes went wide and she let out an exasperated breath.
"Oh, for the love of God, the *other* thing. S-E-X!"

Brendan chuckled heartily while the pink spread into her
ears and fanned down her neck. "You know, ugly-ass hair knot
aside, you're really stunning when you're embarrassed. I've
never been particularly turned on by women who blush, but I
find you're an exception to that rule."

Her mouth went slack, gaping far enough for him to see the
small, pink tip of her tongue. He could easily imagine that little
slip of heaven moving against his own, over his naked flesh,
sliding along the throbbing length of his erection. His cock
stirred to life with the appeal of that last thought. Seeing no
need to delay this thing between them a moment longer, he
reached for her.

His hands barely touched her sides, when she attempted to
pull away. An inferno of accusation shot from her narrowed
eyes. "You bastard, you knew what I wanted when I came in
here, didn't you?"

Not even close, but since she thought so highly of his ability to read her, why ruin the impression? Using his hold on her sides, Brendan tugged her toward him until she bumped up against his thighs. She made an irritated sound and he laughed again. "You're entirely too much fun to taunt, sweetheart."

"Then I suggest you enjoy it while it lasts," she said, teeth gritted. "If you accept my proposal, it's on the grounds that I'm in control, that you do what I ask and *only* what I ask."

Jilly pushed at his chest, attempting to get away but only managing to rub her pelvis against him. His dick hardened further, twitching against her belly. Gasping, she stilled her thrashing and looked up into his eyes.

Good, she was right where she belonged—accepting that he wasn't a man who sat back and took orders. If she wanted to make him her lover for a week or two and then toss him aside, that was fine—it worked beautifully with his plans to figure out her appeal and subsequently dislodge her from his mind—but it happened on his terms.

Brendan slipped his hands around her back and pulled her more firmly against him, grinding his shaft against her stomach, giving her the chance to change her mind. "Do I strike you as the type of man who lets his women order him around? I don't think so, Jilly. And I think you like that about me. I think that's why you're here right now."

Her mouth opened again, likely to voice denial. Before she could do so, he bent his head and slanted his lips against hers. He'd kept Monday morning's kiss gentle, showing her she had nothing to fear. This time he held nothing back, pushing past her lips, licking over her teeth, suckling at her tongue with demanding strokes, making it clear what she was up against.

Bringing his hands around her waist and upward, he pushed past her bulky black jacket. Through the thin silk of her shirt, he filled his palms with her breasts. The erect points of her nipples pressed against his fingers and his balls tightened with the reality of how long he'd been waiting to get his hands on her. He ached to shove everything off the desk and take her right there in his office, not caring who heard their mutual cries of pleasure. Instead he released his hold on her breasts, on her mouth, and let her go.

Jilly staggered, then righted herself, looking at him through eyes dark with passion. The same eyes that had beckoned to him that night in his hotel suite. The eyes that, even closed, had called to him across the crowded reception hall and made him move onto the dance floor.

Brendan had known there was something different about her that night. He knew now it was partly her contrast from the women he'd been with in the past—her many layers and the fact that she'd wanted him even without knowing who he was. But it was also more. That distinctive something he saw in her was the same thing he saw every damned time he looked in the mirror.

Hunger. Drive. The thrill of success. And, beyond that, the need to be free.

For him that need was derived from expectation. Because of who he was, he was expected to follow a certain pattern, to fall into line right alongside his highly successful father, as well as to bounce from the bed of one beauty to the next. Only, he was tired of falling into line, which was why he'd taken a break from his family's financial company and put his skills to use in advertising. As far as the bouncing beauties went, they fell into his Mission of Operation: Freedom nicely, even if their reasons for wanting him had long run thin.

His reasons for feeling and acting the way he did were clear. Jilly's weren't.

What possible reason could she have for playing the part of the sex kitten one instant and the shrewd businesswoman the next? What possible thing could she be seeking freedom from?

Brendan couldn't answer the questions any more than he

could explain the sudden anxiety that tightened his gut. That feeling told him the best thing to do would be to tell her no. To turn her down and walk away without so much as another kiss. But no matter what his gut told him, he'd tasted just enough to whet his appetite and leave him longing for more. He couldn't walk away. However, he *could* buy some time.

"If we do this, Jilly," he said, moving back to his desk, "we do it my way. I know you value your hard-core office identity, so this stays out of the office from here on out. If that becomes a problem one or both of us can't handle, we forget about it completely. As far as control, everything we do will be by my command, or at the very least both of ours. I don't take orders and I'm not into submission.

"Can you live with that, Jilly, or do you plan to run home to Ginger with your tail between your legs?"

Passion still suffused her face, but determination was also alive in her eyes. She nodded. "I can live with it."

"You're certain?"

"Yes."

"Good. Then I'll see you Monday night at your place."

Brendan saw the questions come into her eyes, the frustration over the length of time until Monday night. He wasn't about to explain his reasons for wanting time away from her before they took this thing to the next level. He wasn't even sure he understood them himself, so he grabbed his laptop bag and walked out the door before she could say another word.

3

Three days had never felt so long.

Jillian sank back against her couch pillows and sighed. Ginger, her cocker spaniel, glanced up from the other end of the couch and gave her an understanding look.

Poor Ginger. The dog could read her thoughts so well, she ought to be human. She knew when Jillian was in a bad mood—or an impatient one, as she was now.

Jillian had spent the weekend thinking of all the good reasons she should march into the office on Monday morning and tell Brendan she'd changed her mind about sleeping with him. She'd thought of several, including the big one—that maybe he hadn't been sincere about keeping things outside the office and still planned to use their intimacy against her somehow. She'd even worked up the courage to go to his office and break the news. Only, he hadn't been there.

Larry confirmed his absence. Brendan was still moving his effects to Atlanta from Chicago and he'd taken a long weekend to finish the tedious task. Larry had also let on how he planned to determine the best person to fill Donaldson's position. Neilson had been pushing their services to *the Wild Side*, a big-time costume-design firm responsible for outfitting the casts of kids' movies and various children's events for years. The time to move full-speed ahead and bring the firm onto their client list was now, and Larry planned to reward the person who devised the best ad presentation with the coveted promotion.

As much as Jillian loathed the idea of letting her softer side show—the way getting to know the faces behind the kid-targeted company would necessitate—the childishness of the firm's services gave her hope. If there was one place a manly man like Brendan would feel out of his league, it was with a firm like this one.

Brendan, whom she'd never had a chance to tell she'd changed her mind about sleeping with. . . . As she sat in her dimmed living room watching *Peter Pan* for the express purpose of research (or so she'd tell anyone who caught her in the act), she couldn't be more appreciative for her inability to do so.

It was almost ten and Jillian's body practically hummed with the anticipation of his arrival. She'd expected him sooner, had stressed over what to wear for this momentous occasion hours ago. He'd tried to taunt her into agreeing he would hold all the control. She had agreed somewhat, but not expressly, and she had no such plan to let him do the controlling. She would be the one with the power, and that meant dressing the part.

She'd dug to the back of her closet for the white lacy teddy Tawny had given her the Christmas before and, after removing the tags, had put it on. Her reflection had stunned her. The scraps of lace and mesh that made up the risqué outfit barely covered her slit, and what material there was on her breasts showed the dusky hue of her areolae as clearly as if she wore nothing at all. Thigh-high stockings and three-inch-heel pumps completed the ensemble. She looked bold, daring, like the brazen woman Brendan had first believed her to be. Like the one she once was.

Butterflies of anxiety had flitted to life in her stomach and she'd known she couldn't open the door to him wearing the outfit. Refusing to cave to her unforeseen fears completely, she'd pulled on jeans and a T-shirt over the teddy and stockings. He would see what she wore beneath her casual clothing eventually—just not the instant he arrived.

Jillian's belly tensed with nerves. She reached for the glass of white wine on the end table, determined to lower her inhibitions and get back to the impulsive woman she'd been last Saturday. She shouldn't be nervous any longer, considering the number of times in the last three hours she'd envisioned Brendan stripping away her clothes to find what lay beneath, but she was—nervous and excited by the thought of him looking upon her with raw appetite blazing in his eyes, his strong and oh-so-capable hands petting her stimulated body, his fingers thrusting deep into her sex.

Wetness pooled in her pussy and moistened the crotch of the teddy. She took a long sip of wine and blocked out the warming sensations rolling through her, refusing to get herself worked up again. Considering how late it was, Brendan probably wouldn't even show. He might not even be back in town yet. Or maybe he was and he'd changed his mind about wanting her. He'd told her not once but twice how much he loved a challenge, and she'd allowed him to win this one when she agreed to have sex. Obviously, he was no longer interested.

"Evening, Cinderella. Is your evil stepsister home?"

Jillian had been in the midst of swallowing wine when Brendan's deep voice reverberated from somewhere too nearby. She let out a squeak that had the wine going down her throat the wrong way. She slapped a hand to her thudding heart and choked. When she could breathe normally again, she turned to find him standing at the end of the couch, petting Ginger. Ginger, the traitor, looked up at him with loving eyes and shook her hind leg like she'd just found her new best friend.

Jillian shot to her feet, glaring first at the cocker spaniel, then the man. For a moment she was uncertain which of the two were more infuriating. Then the man smiled that too damned confident and sexy smile and she remembered. "Why, you no good bastard, you broke into my house."

"I believe I have my answer, Ginger, love. The evil stepsister looks to be home indeed." Brendan straightened and Ginger let out a whine of displeasure that he'd stopped petting her.

Jillian glanced back at the dog and groaned. It was no wonder the man was so confident with himself where females were concerned. Even her dog looked ready to roll over and beg for his attention. "Did you ever hear of knocking?"

"I did. You were obviously too engrossed in the movie to hear." He glanced at the television. "Interesting choice, *Peter Pan*. A personal favorite."

Yeah, right, she'd bet it was his favorite. "This is the PG version," she said dryly. "You know, the one without the S after *Peter*?"

He chuckled. "You have so little faith in me, Jilly."

She curbed the lust that unfurled with his rich laughter. Now that he was here, standing feet away, looking like he might pull her into his arms and devour her, her second thoughts swiftly returned.

What if all this backfired? What if he'd only agreed to keep things out of the office as a way to garner blackmail against her? Larry relied on her to be cool and collected. If Brendan let on she was anything but, it could ruin everything.

As much as she knew that, she couldn't get the words out or the energy up to make him leave. Instead she crossed her arms and set her chin, taking on the icy veneer she'd perfected. "Obviously I had enough faith to invite you here."

Brendan's grin faded. "That's something I've been wondering over all weekend. Why did you? What made you change your mind?"

The fear of exploding. The need to scratch an itch she could no longer disregard. The attraction that sizzled between them even when they were ignoring one another. She wasn't about to reveal any of that, just as she wouldn't tell him that in some ways she'd learned to trust him. Namely because those ways were still very uncertain. "You know why."

"I'm not sure I do. Not really."

"Because I want to . . . sleep together."

Humor glinted in his eyes. "You watched me this past week and decided I kept my distance enough that I'd suffice as your personal teddy bear?"

Jillian bit back the laughter that bubbled up in her throat. Brendan was *not* teddy-bear material. Not to say it wouldn't feel good to spoon against his naked body—she had a feeling it would feel damned good—but cuddling was not on her list of things to do with him. Whether he'd been sincere about keeping this out of the office or not, she had. Out of the office and out of her head. A hello-and-goodbye fling.

"Not that kind of sleep. You know what kind."

His grin returning full throttle, he closed the distance between them. The dark stubble that lined his jaw gave his face a dangerous appeal in the dimmed lighting, one that made her fingers itch with the urge to reach out and touch. She fisted her hands and ordered them to remain at her sides until she was 100 percent certain she wanted to proceed with this. He had no such reservations. Uncurling her fingers, he took hold of her hands and pulled her tightly against him so that she could feel the hard bulge of his cock against her belly.

She dragged in a breath and struggled to gain freedom. He could *not* have control! He couldn't even touch her until she said it was okay for him to do so.

She opened her mouth to yell at him. He spoke before she could, his words peppered with a husk that slipped into her mind and sent her senses reeling. "Maybe I do know what you mean, Jilly. To be sure we're on the same wave length, do you mean the kind of sleep where we don't sleep at all? Where I pull you into my arms and slowly remove your clothes?"

He sank back on the couch and released her hands. Some part of her knew she was free, but that part wasn't what controlled her feet. She remained rooted in place, frozen by anticipation, trapped by a hunger she didn't fully understand.

Brendan moved his hands beneath the hem of her T-shirt. She held her breath, waiting for his next move. "Do you mean where I go down on my knees and bury my face between your breasts?" His hands slid up over the lace of the teddy, pushing up her T-shirt in the process. She sucked in a shallow gasp as his fingers connected with the puckered tips of her breasts. "Where I suck on your nipples until they're so hard they hurt with it?" He bent forward and settled his lips on the thin lace that covered her breasts. He nipped into its softness with his warm, wet mouth and swirled his tongue in lazy circles.

Lust crashed through her with that intimate caress. Her clit tingled. She squirmed against his tongue and bit back a cry.

"Where I go even farther down and slide my tongue deep into the heart of you?" He pulled back. She whimpered with the need to feel his strong tongue buried inside her, licking at her pussy, setting free her wild side once and for all.

He didn't follow up his words with his mouth. Instead he tipped his head back and looked up at her while he cupped her in his hand. He rocked his palm against her sex through the worn softness of her jeans. Cream dripped from her inner thighs. The pressure was just enough to make Jillian want to scream.

"Is that the kind of sleep you mean, sweetheart?"

"Y—yes." She was aware of the desperation in her voice, of the fact that she was giving him the control and in doing so trusting him with much more than her body. She should stop him, but she didn't want to. She wanted only to feel, to allow the ravenous lust that charged through her to be freed. To allow him into her life and her secrets completely.

"So you agreed to this simply because you want to fuck me?"

The directness of his words broke through her forbidden longing. She blinked but didn't recoil. The words were a reminder: He wasn't here to share her secrets, only her body. Her body that burned for him. The sensitive folds of her cunt were afire.

Giving him the control hadn't been the plan, but so far it was nothing to fear. So long as they kept things impersonal, everything would be fine. "Yes. That's why. The only reason."

Demand flashed in Brendan's eyes and he stilled his hand. "Say it, Jilly. If you're bold enough to want it, you're bold enough to speak the words."

He was right. She was. And saying it just kept this thing all the more remote. "I—I want to fuck you."

"You don't talk that way very often do you, sweetheart?" Smiling up at her, he lifted his hand from between her legs. He turned her and pulled her down on his lap. His cock cradled against the seam of her bottom and she jerked up out of instinct. He wrapped an arm around her waist and tugged her back down, holding her too tightly for escape.

The beat of Jillian's heart thudded between her ears with his controlling grasp and she fought against a wave of anxiety. This wasn't what she'd classify as personal. It was what she'd call intense. Too intense. Too much of him and not her. This was something to fear.

She turned and met his eyes with the intention of demanding he let her go. The depth of longing in his dark gaze stilled the words on her tongue.

His hand came up to rub the pad of his thumb over her

lower lip. Her panic passed with that tender caress. There was no malice in his expression, no desire to exploit her in any way, just need. The same desperate, hungry need she knew.

"It's hot when you talk dirty, Jilly," he rasped. "Everything's hot about this mouth of yours. I love how full your lips are, how wide. How even when you wear those ugly-ass suits and pull your hair back in a knot, these lips still give away your sensual nature. I've been thinking about them all week, about tasting them again, about feeling them running over my skin. I'm tired of thinking. I'm ready for action."

Brendan's thumb left her lip. Through the building haze of need he'd rendered with his look and the truth that seemed to fill his words, she was conscious of him scooping her into his arms and standing.

"Down the hall," she uttered before he could ask where the bedroom was. "Hurry."

He followed her direction, then stopped outside the bedroom door and glanced back.

Jillian's pounding heart came to a standstill. Why was he stopping? He couldn't mean to change his mind, not when it was clear to them both how much they wanted this to happen. Or had she been wrong about him? Was his needful look and tone an act? Had he made her ache for him and believe he ached for her, too, as a way of paying her back for running out on him last weekend?

"*What?*" she demanded when he remained motionless.

"Have you fed Ginger yet?"

Ginger? What did her dog have to do with this? "No. She doesn't eat till ten thirty. She's fine in the other room by herself. Just don't . . ." Stop. Only, she couldn't say it. If she'd been wrong about his look, his want, it would only give him all that much more ammunition with which to make a fool out of her.

"I'm sure she is and I'm sure she likes her schedule, but tonight she's not going to follow it." Brendan settled her back on her feet and brushed a quick kiss over her lips. It was reassuring in that it made her believe he'd been sincere and had no intention of leaving her, and frustrating in that it only added fuel to a fire that already threatened to burn beyond management's sake. "Go feed her and let her do her doggy business. Once we get started, neither of us is leaving the bedroom until we're finished."

Brendan never would have guessed that the dog responsible for making Jilly leave him last weekend would be the same one bringing him a moment of much needed thinking time now.

What the fuck was going on with Jilly?

He couldn't read her well, but he still thought he knew the way she'd behave tonight. Like a dominator. A control freak. A woman who would never completely succumb to a man's will, particularly one she was determined to best professionally.

True, he'd made her agree to give him the power, but he'd thought that would be all the more reason for her not to want to give in. She had put up a fight. A very small fight that lasted a few brief seconds and then faded to . . . what?

What was the word for the way she'd given into him? Not subservience. That involved a second party who was in control. The truth was, as much as she might believe it, he wasn't in control of the situation. The way she responded to his teasing words, to his subtle strokes, to the heat he knew was apparent in his eyes, made him want to give into her, as well. It made him want to know more, to ask questions about her that had nothing to do with sex and not even with work.

Brendan wasn't asking any damned questions. He couldn't.

He'd spent this past weekend in his hometown of Chicago avoiding people by the droves—women, the press, his father. All those who wanted something from him, be it his body or his time or his plans for the future. People who made him realize how much he valued the freedom his moving had rendered.

He wouldn't jeopardize that freedom because of something he thought he'd felt when Jilly looked upon him with need in her eyes. That's all it had been. Need. Of the physical kind. For whatever reason, she too valued freedom, so it would be asinine to believe it could have been anything else.

Jilly appeared in the bedroom doorway and Brendan pushed away his thoughts so he could concentrate on her clothing. She had entirely too much on. If this thing between them was about feelings, he would take great pleasure in slowly removing each article. But this wasn't about feelings and he wanted her naked now before his mind could conjure up thoughts to the contrary.

Sending her a wolfish smile, he patted the mattress next to his thigh. "C'mere, sweetheart."

She bit her lip and started over. "Sorry it took me so long. Ginger's not used to going out this time of night."

Ginger might not be used to it, but he had a good feeling the dog wasn't what had Jilly nibbling on her lip. She looked worried, as if she was having regrets. She couldn't. They needed to do this. He needed to flush her from his mind. Time hadn't worked, sex had to. The most it had ever taken in the past to get bored with a woman and want her out of his bed was three rounds. Hopefully with Jilly it would take only one.

"Her schedule, right. I hope she'll be able to forgive me for changing it. I hope you'll be able to forgive me, too."

Jilly reached the bed. Brendan caught her hand and tugged her down on the mattress. He pushed her back, straddling her hips while he took her mouth in a hot, wet kiss. Fast was the solution. Fast and frantic allowed no time to think. No time to get too involved. Fast was good.

Only, she wasn't responding fast. Her lips had parted for him, but otherwise were still. Her hands were fisted at his sides.

Regret. The word filled his head. Damnit, she couldn't have regrets. He had to make her see that they needed this one time.

Determined to get her response, to evoke the passionate woman she'd become every other time they'd touched, he stroked her tongue with his. He moved his hands along her sides and caressed the shallow dips at her waist, slid them lower to mold the rounded shape of her hips.

Finally she came alive, licking at his tongue, eating at his mouth with a relish that was too frantic to ignore. This was supposed to be fast, mindless, but suddenly Brendan wanted to go slow, to savor. Releasing her hips, he buried his fingers in the silky waves of honey-blond hair she routinely punished into submission. The weight of it sliding through his hands was intoxicating, as was the sweetness of her mouth.

Too sweet. Too much.

Jilly murmured against his lips and shifted beneath him. The hard ridge of her pelvis scraped against his dick. Raw desire jolted through his system.

He grunted and released her lips, aware of how wrong a direction the kiss was leading his mind. He couldn't think about this. He had to play it cool. Had to be the careless bad boy Jilly expected him to be. The one he'd been with every other woman he'd taken to bed.

He rose up on an elbow and forced casualness into his tone. "So, do you forgive me?"

Her pupils were dark, dilated. Her expression one of mixed demand and euphoria. She was the reckless, wild woman she'd been when they'd first entered his hotel suite the previous weekend. And that's exactly what he needed her to be.

"Yes," she breathed, "but I'll change my mind if you don't stop with the damned taunting and fuck me already."

Brendan chuckled at her impatience and the way she could change character in the blink of an eye. Then he pushed the thought from his mind—and her T-shirt up and over the swell of her breasts. The dusky pink shade of her nipples contrasted exquisitely against the white of the teddy. He brushed his hands over her breasts. The peaks strained against the lace, arching upward to meet his thumbs. His cock twitched while his mouth salivated for a taste. One more taste couldn't hurt anything.

Jilly moaned. He forced himself not to look up. If he saw the passion alive in her expressive eyes, it was sure to get his mind roaming again. He moved his hands to her jeans and tugged at the zipper, drew a nipple into his mouth through the lace.

He bit down on the aroused tip. With a throaty cry, she bowed up and gathered his back in her hands. Aware he was breaking his one-more-taste vow, he moved to the other nipple. He kneaded the erect flesh between his lips, suckling through the lace while his hands liberated her hips of her jeans. He worked his way down, tugging her pants lower on her thighs. Finally he reached the one area he'd yet to see of her.

He'd experienced the intensity of her pussy contracting around his fingers and letting loose her juices as she came. He'd never had her totally naked. She wasn't naked now, either, but the lace at her mound was so translucent with its wetness that he could easily see the dark blond thatch of curls that covered her opening.

The heady scent of her arousal filtered through his senses, obliterating his thoughts to avoid any area above her neck. As he pulled her jeans the remainder of the way down and tossed them aside, his attention went to her face.

The slight part of her pouty red lips, the flush of her face, the awareness in her dark eyes all called out to him, made him ache to say words he had no right saying.

Before he could voice them, he placed his hands on her thighs and pushed her knees up, her legs apart. Moving the damp material that covered her slit aside, he parted her curls to reveal the delicacy beneath. He shouldn't allow another single taste, and yet he had to. Just one more sample.

He bent his head and brushed his stubbled chin against the swollen, pink flesh of her cunt, then plunged his tongue deep and met with a salty-sweet nirvana that had his cock throbbing with the urge to explode.

Jilly's hands clamped tighter on his back, her short nails nipping inward. Her hips bucked up, pressing at his face. "Oh, God . . . you don't have to do that!"

He didn't have to and he shouldn't be, but, Christ, he wanted to, if only for a few more seconds. He licked at her cream slickened core, sank his tongue deep into her center, then allowed himself one tug at her clit before lifting his head and grabbing the crotch of the teddy in his hand.

He held tight to the damp material so that the wet lace clung together. He rubbed the lace back and forth over the swollen lips of her pussy, grinding it with purposeful pressure, and was rewarded with a shout of ecstasy as she arched up off the bed.

She looked at him through wide eyes. "What are you doing?"

"You like it, don't you? Yeah, I can see how much you do, smell it in the air. You're so wet, Jilly, so fucking hot right now you want to come, but you're afraid to give in. Don't be scared. Give in to the sensation."

"I'm not scared!"

The way she shouted the words, it sounded as if she'd used the same defense in the past. Brendan couldn't afford to wonder over that. Only on purging her from his mind. He concentrated his efforts on grinding the lace over her aroused flesh, pulling it tightly against the lips of her cunt, chafing her most sensitive spots and making her completely helpless, in the hopes she'd come to hate him for it. "Good, because this is how it's going to be between us, Jilly. I will always be in control. I will always be the one with the power. If you don't like it that way, all you have to do is tell to me leave and I will."

She opened her mouth. The air lodged in his throat with the idea she would do exactly as he'd suggested. He wanted her to, needed her to, but he hoped to hell she didn't.

Her mouth remained open, as if she was trying to speak. No

words made it out before her body gave in to the play of his fingers. Her limbs drew tight and her eyes slammed closed. She reopened them instantly, as if remembering he preferred them that way. Against his better judgment, he watched the myriad of expressions play out on her face, the hedonistic thrill of orgasm exploding in her eyes, and just managed to hold on to his own need to let go as she came with a scream.

Jillian closed her eyes and savored the force of her release. She could never make herself come like that, with a vibrator or otherwise. No man had ever come close. But then, no man had ever tried to make her climax in such a way. She felt boneless, like she was nothing more than a puddle of melted flesh, like she couldn't open her eyes if she had to.

Brendan's weight lifted from the bed and her eyes snapped open, disproving her last thought. "Where are you going?"

She bit her tongue at the automatic question. He'd done his duty, he was free to go. Only, she didn't want him to leave. She wanted to feel the heat of his skin beneath her hands, the hardness of his muscles. Wanted to experience the sensation of climaxing with a man buried deeply inside her just once this decade. She wanted that experience to be with this man. Between the professional issues between them and the reputation he claimed where women were concerned, he was the last person she should be so attracted to, to feel pulled to on a level beyond the physical, and yet she did, had from the moment they'd met.

He turned back to her and tugged his shirt over his head. "Nowhere. I just thought this might work better if I was naked."

She barely heard his response as she took in the wisps of dark hair that covered his tanned chest. Renewed warmth coiled in her belly and fresh wetness seeped between her thighs. He wasn't overly muscular, but he wasn't out of shape either. His body was lean and hard in all the right places.

All the right places, Jillian realized when he moved his jeans and boxers down his legs, then straightened to reveal the length and thickness of his jutting erection. His cock jerked under her perusal, pre-cum gathering on the dark head. Her pussy pulsed eagerly in response.

Brendan retrieved a condom from his jeans pocket and rolled it on. He returned between her thighs. His mouth came down on hers. He brushed her lips once quickly before pulling back and flashing a cocky grin. "You thought I was going to leave, didn't you? I told you I wasn't leaving, Jilly. Not yet."

But he would as soon as they were finished.

It was the way she'd wanted it, the way she should still want it, and yet she didn't. She wanted to talk to him, to get to know him better outside of what she'd read in *People* and heard through the grapevine. That wasn't part of the deal, and if she tried to make it part of the deal, he would end things. Or worse, he would both end things and spread the time they'd shared together throughout the office.

She couldn't let that happen. She had to play this out the way she'd planned from the start. She had to be the carefree woman who wasn't afraid to go after what she wanted, the bold one he'd first met at the reception. The one she used to be.

"I did," Jillian admitted, adding a bite to her tone. "I thought you were going to leave and it upset me. It made me very angry. It made me want to punish you." She pushed at his chest and, because she shouldn't have been able to roll him over so easily, she knew he was enjoying her moment of dominance. She came up over him and rubbed her sex against his. A fresh dose of longing spread through her at the feel of him so near and the reality he would soon be inside her.

Before she could think any further on the connection such a joining might trigger, she reached between them and moved the soggy lace covering her slit aside. "I'm going to punish you. I'm going to use your body and then I'm going to order you out."

She punctuated her words with her movements, slowly inching onto his dick, shivering with the enlivening feeling.

He groaned and grabbed hold of her sides. "Damn, you are so tight."

Warmth welled in her cheeks. She refused to blush, to act like her tautness was a big deal. "It's been a while."

"How long is a while?"

"Four years." She forgot all about blushing then and laughed at his stricken look as she sank the remainder of the way onto him. Her laughter turned to a gasp with the force of sensations that spirited through her when he was embedded inside her. "You would think I should be dead, from the way your face looks."

"Four years is a long time. A very long time."

"I can pleasure myself just fine."

Brendan's cocky grin returned and he released her sides to cup her ass. He tipped his hips and lifted her up his shaft. He moved her back down as he drove hard into her sheath. The air whooshed from her lungs and she cried out with the magnitude of need splintering through her body, building pressure deep within her pussy, making her want to come again so soon.

He chuckled and lifted her once more, slamming her back onto him so hard she was amazed stars didn't dance before her eyes. "You might be able to pleasure yourself, but nowhere near to what I can."

It was the truth, and yet she couldn't allow him to believe it. "You're so damned arrogant."

"You like it."

The audacity of his response ate at the edge that came with Jillian's stimulation. She sank back and dug her nails into the sinew of his thighs. Before, when she'd said she wanted to punish him, it had been for the sake of keeping things distant. Now she really wanted to. She wanted to hurt him for making her want him so badly, for making her yearn to know him beyond the physical, to uncover what it was that had made him approach her in the first place that night at the reception.

He'd said she made him break from his norm. She longed to know why and how, and knew that she could never ask. She could only act the same way he did, aggressive yet holding part of herself back. "Sometimes I like it. Sometimes it makes me hate you."

He stilled his thrusting and met her eyes. "You don't hate me, Jilly. You can't. Because as hard as you try, you're not the callous woman you make yourself out to be. It blows my mind that anyone could ever fall for that act you put on at the office. I mean, look at you. You're warm as they come. Warm and sexy and sensual."

She froze. He couldn't be any more wrong. She might have been that woman once, but she wasn't any longer. She was cool and callous and dowdy. A dependable workhorse that people respected. Maybe he thought differently because for a while there she'd allowed the woman of her past to come out and make her want things she knew better than to want, but that woman was no longer around. "Shut up and let me blow your mind."

She grabbed hold of the headboard and ground her pussy against his cock, riding him hard, fast, determined to end this quickly. He met her thrust for turbulent thrust, until her body was shuddering and her sex clenched tightly around his.

As if he knew how close she was to giving in, Brendan took over the frantic pace. He plunged into her again and again while he found and fingered her clit. He stroked the inflamed pearl, rubbing his thumb in circles. She was helpless from holding back an instant longer. She tightened once more and then came around him, just managing to hold back her shout of bliss. Seconds later, he found his own soundless release.

For almost a full minute, Jillian allowed herself to revel in the belonging she felt when they were joined so completely, and then she pulled free of him and rolled off the bed. A sense of loss filled her as she stood. She refused to acknowledge it with anything more than a passing shrug.

She grabbed the throw blanket that had fallen off the bed, wrapped it around her and moved to the door. She stopped when she reached it, but didn't turn back. Couldn't turn back. It was one thing to act like the cold, callous commander who didn't need anyone or anything but work in her life. It was one thing to tell herself she wasn't the woman she used to be. It was another thing entirely to believe those things. She didn't, and she knew if she turned back and saw so much as a hint of sentiment in Brendan's eyes, she would tell him so.

Forcing her emotions aside, she murmured, "I'm going to check on Ginger. Be gone when I come back," and walked out the door.

4

How could anyone go so long without sex, and why in the fuck would they want to? It was a question that had plagued Brendan all morning.

Jilly might dress like the wicked witch of the southeast for work, but what about when the workday ended? Larry and Tawny had indicated that this company was her life, but had they meant her only life? That she didn't date, or even gather with friends for an after-work or weekend drink?

If that's what they'd meant, what a waste of a woman.

She'd reverted to Jillian on him last night soon after he'd thrown up his own walls. It hadn't been quickly enough to stop him from seeing her softer and sensual sides emerge. Not nearly soon enough to stop him from spending most of last night and all of this morning searching his mind for answers to the way she acted, to the way she made him feel in return.

Son of a bitch. He'd vowed to get her out of his head and all he was doing was thinking about her more. It had to stop. He'd more or less promised that this thing between them wouldn't occur at or even be discussed on the job, but he had to have some answers and he had to have them now.

He'd spent the first hour of this morning catching up on Larry's plans for appointing a person to take over Donaldson's position. Thanks to a love for movies of all types, particularly fantasies such as the kid-oriented type he'd caught Jilly watching last night, he felt confident he could put together a great ad presentation for *the Wild Side* with little to no effort. The problem was he also felt confident Jilly could do the same. He had to be more than great. He had to be outstanding, and that would involve research. And research involved a clear mind—one thing he wouldn't have until he spoke with Jilly.

Jillian, Brendan corrected himself as he started toward her office. If he called her Jilly when someone was around she was liable to de-nut him.

He reached her office door and found it open a crack, just far enough to hear voices filtering through from the inside. Damn, she was already occupied. So much for his plan to clear his mind and move on to more important matters.

He started to turn back when his name reached him. It came from inside Jilly's office, but it wasn't Jilly who'd spoken. He knew the soft, slightly husky sound of her voice. Knew how it grew even huskier when she was wet and hot from his touch, knew the almost imperceptible mewls she made in the back of her throat right before she came.

Pushing away the thoughts and the hardening effect they had on his dick, Brendan focused on the voice he now recognized as Tawny's. Eavesdropping wasn't something he approved of, but it might be the only way he'd get to the bottom of the puzzle known as Jillian Lowery.

". . . tell me?"

"We're here to discuss my proposal for *the Wild Side*, remember?" Jilly's words were muffled and yet the irritation behind them was clear.

"Ah, c'mon. I don't even get a hint if he was any good?"

"I never said I slept with him."

"Right. Like I'm supposed to believe that big red hickey got on your neck all by itself."

"*What?*" Jilly gasped and Tawny laughed

"There's nothing there. I was testing you and you failed, so fess up, girl. You did it, didn't you? You finally let Jilly the Wildcat out to play."

The arousal Brendan had fought off moments ago returned as a full-blown hard-on with the memory of Jilly's ravenous look and the way her short nails had nipped into his back, urging his control to the snapping point. Jilly the Wildcat had a certain ring to it.

Jilly groaned. "Do you think you could say that any louder?"

"You did. I'm so proud of you."

He smiled at the unexpected sound of Jilly's laughter. What would it take to get her to laugh that way for him, so honestly, so openly, where she held nothing back? The smile fell as his thoughts caught up with him. Not that he wanted to make her laugh that way, or make any other joyful sound come out of her mouth. At least, he shouldn't want to.

Shit, what was wrong with him? He never thought about a woman this way, never wanted one this badly after having her less than twenty-four hours ago.

"If I knew that all it takes to make you happy is knowing I got off, I'd have informed you of it long ago," Jilly said.

"Right," Tawny returned. "As if you've gotten off in years."

"I have. Just not with . . ."

Brendan pushed aside his unsettling thoughts to concentrate on the turn the conversation had taken.

"A man?" Tawny guessed.

Jilly's tone returned to irritated. "Can we please get back to work?"

"If we have to," Tawny said glumly, "but can you at least tell me if he lived up to his expectations?"

He was confident in his ability to please a woman, knew how well he'd done just that to Jilly last night, even if she hadn't allowed him to stick around and make certain, and yet Brendan found himself holding his breath for her response.

"He was okay," she supplied after several long seconds.

He let free his breath with a rush and fought back the urge to bolt into the office and remind her how much better than okay he'd been. If she truly believed he'd only been "okay," then it was her own goddamned fault. She was the one who'd turned witchy just when things were getting hot.

All right, so he'd closed himself off, too. He hadn't had a choice. She'd been getting to him with her softer, more trusting side, getting under his skin and slipping past his defenses in a way that hadn't been close to a good idea. Just as standing here, listening to this conversation, wasn't. Only, he couldn't make himself turn and walk away.

"Right," Tawny said, "and so was the bagel I had for breakfast this morning. He was *not* okay. He was good. Damned good, if the color in your cheeks is to be believed. Not to mention the way you're riding that chair."

"Oh, my God! I am *not* riding the chair!"

Tawny dissolved in a fit of laughter. Brendan bit back his own chuckle and sighed. He knew he hadn't been just "okay."

"Fine," Jilly admitted. "He was good. He was very good. He made me moan, groan and scream."

"That's more like it. Do you plan to see him again?"

"I don't know."

She didn't? Why the fuck not? She'd just said he'd made her moan, groan and scream. Was this about her kicking him out? Did she think he was upset about it? Her curt dismissal had bothered him at first—more so than he'd ever imagined rejection could—but she'd done it for the right reasons.

"But you do want to see him again?" Tawny asked.

"I shouldn't."

"But you do."

"It's just sex."

"Is it?"

Hell, yes. What else could it be?

"Yes," Jilly agreed with his silent response. "He didn't even stay the night." She hesitated, then added in a barely audible voice, "I made him leave."

Brendan had just told himself her dismissal had been for the right reason, and yet hearing her admit it to someone sparked the same gut-deep reaction he'd had last night.

"Oh, God, Jilly, you aren't!"

"I'm not what?"

"Falling for him," Tawny said in a rush that turned the tightness in his gut to near pain. "He's fine for a fling, but that's all. You know his reputation. You know he's the—"

"Of course I'm not falling for him! I don't even like him."

The tightness should have subsided with Jilly's remark. Instead it grew, fanning out as fingers of ache.

She damned well did so like him. She'd tried to say she hated him last night, but he'd known it was a lie then as he did now. The fact that for even a short while she'd let loose enough to show him her "wildcat" side, as Tawny had called it, confirmed it. Maybe she didn't love him yet, but she liked him.

"Why not?" Tawny's question stopped him from worrying over his inclusion of the word *yet,* and again Brendan found himself waiting for Jilly's response with held breath.

"Because he's . . . he's . . ."

"After the job you want?" Tawny guessed.

"Yes. Among other things."

"Why do you even want it? I mean, you've never been the type to get into managerial stuff like this job would entail."

"There's more to it than that."

"The job, or your reason?"

"Both," Jilly admitted after several seconds of hesitation. "I just want it. Why can't that be enough?"

Because she didn't sound like it was enough. She didn't sound any more convincing than she had when she'd claimed not to like him, either last night or now.

"Because I know you better," Tawny said. "Up until four years ago you weren't like this—so career-driven nothing else mattered. You wanted things out of life that had nothing to do with work. Things like friends, like a family, like the same kind of lasting love your parents have. I think deep down you still want it. Maybe you've set your mind on moving up the corporate ladder before worrying about anything else, but what if your mind isn't listening to your heart? What if your heart's so desperate for attention it falls for the first guy you let into your bed in years?" She sighed loudly. "Promise me you'll be careful, girl. That you won't let him hurt you."

"No one is going to get hurt. I promise."

"I hope not. I really do."

So did Brendan, because Jilly didn't sound sure of herself. She sounded like she wanted to believe it, but might not be capable of it. Ironically, that's exactly how he felt. Like he wanted to believe he could return to her bed and at the same time keep her distant from his thoughts and feelings. Only, he wasn't sure he could. Not after hearing what he had and, subsequently, adding more questions to a growing plethora of questions. And sure as hell not after hearing there was a chance she could be falling for him.

Jillian lay in bed, petting Ginger's soft coat and wishing to God sleep would claim her. It was after midnight, and thanks to her stupid body and its even more ridiculous belief that Brendan would return, she was too keyed up to shut her eyes.

She shouldn't want him again, shouldn't want to risk her feelings becoming more tied up in things than they already were. Tawny had hit too close to the truth this morning with her thoughts that Jillian could get hurt with Brendan. She'd known it last night, and she knew it more so now. As much as she knew it, she couldn't stop herself from wanting him to return. She wanted it so badly she'd raced home from work and wolfed down a microwave dinner so she'd be ready for him if he did show up.

That had been more than six hours ago, and she still waited for him. Waited for a man who had the power to steal not only her heart, but her dream job. How pathetic was that? "You *are* an idiot," she chastised herself. "Completely hopeless."

"And *you* really should be asleep. It's well past midnight, Cinderella."

Jillian jerked upward and screeched loudly enough to send Ginger racing off the bed and out of the room. Her heart thudded against her ribs. The pounding increased when Brendan dropped down on the end of her bed and crawled up over top of her.

His dark eyes were more intense, more potent, more sinfully arousing in the dark. The shadows of night played with the strong angles of his face while his scent reached out to fill her senses and fire her longing.

"Hi, Sleeping Beauty," he breathed, lowering his mouth to nip a kiss at each corner of hers. "Were you waiting for me?"

"Yes," she responded automatically.

He chuckled. "You were?"

Her judgment returned with the rich, rolling sound of his laughter. Oh, God, she was all but falling into his arms! Fury raced through her at the witless way she was acting. This kind of behavior was exactly the type that could lead to heartache.

Refusing to set herself up for a fall, she pushed at his weight, which was trapping her arms beneath the covers, and tried to squirm free. "No. I wasn't waiting for you, you overgrown ape. How the hell did you even get in my house? I know I locked the door."

"And left the windows open. You need a security system, sweetheart."

She glanced at one of the three open bedroom windows and sighed. She had only her own negligence to thank for his presence. A presence her wriggling was not urging away. A presence that less than five minutes ago she'd ached for. Truthfully, she still ached for him—her pussy grew wetter and her breasts heavier with each wriggle—but she could never admit that aloud. Giving up her struggle, she glared. "Thanks for your concern, but this is the first time I've had any problems."

Brendan looked wounded by her response and she knew a moment's sympathy. Then his mouth tugged up knowingly. "A problem, am I? So you want me to leave?"

Of course not. "Yes."

"No, you don't. You know how I can tell, Jilly? Because you're breathing hard. And because I can feel your nipples pressing against my chest through the covers." He rubbed his upper half over her slowly, and she dragged in a hard breath as the friction worked its magic on her body. Humor glinted in his eyes. "You're excited, aren't you? Just wondering what I'm going to do next. Close your eyes and I'll tell you."

It was tempting. Damned tempting. And the absolute last thing she could do. Closing her eyes would mean trusting him with far more than her body. Silently she might be able to acknowledge she trusted him, but never out loud. "Do I look stupid to you?"

"Beautiful, sensual, pissed off, yes. Stupid, never."

The breath dragged between Jillian's lips and she fought the urge to scream. What was wrong with him to keep saying things like that? Things that she might have believed about the old her, but not now. Not when she went so far out of her way to make sure she wasn't attractive or warm. "I am *not* beautiful, and I am *not* sensual."

"And I am *not* blind," he retorted in the same angry tone. His voice gentled and he raised a hand to stroke along the rise of her cheek. "You don't have to close your eyes, Jilly, this will work just as well with them open."

"What wi—"

Her question died with a gasp as the hand on her face fell to the covers. He stripped them back and tugged her into his arms. She was on her stomach in an instant, the weight of his thighs trapping her hips in place and making movement all but impossible. She was about to shout at him when the hiss of a zipper being lowered stopped her short. Next came the unmistakable crinkle of a condom wrapper.

The breath stilled in her throat even as cream filled her pussy. "What are you doing?"

"I think you know. I think you've been waiting up for me for this very reason."

"No, I haven't!" But she had, and she knew he could hear the lie in her words every bit as much as she could.

The weight of Brendan's body moved off of her for several seconds, then returned to cover her completely. She wore only a T-shirt. He slid his hand beneath the cotton and upward. He palmed the bare flesh of a breast and squeezed the nipple. "Tell me the truth, Jilly, or I'll be forced to tease you until you're hovering on the edge of orgasm and then leave. You've been waiting for me, haven't you, hoping I'd come by and do some of those things I promised to do last night?"

His grip on her nipple tightened and the juices heightened in her sex. Her pulse beat rapidly. Her stimulated scent reached up to assail her nose. She forced her response through a dry throat—not lies; it was pointless to lie when the truth was so obvious—with words that held no emotion outside of lust.

"Yes. I wanted you to come here. I want to feel your cock thrusting inside me. I want you to make me come."

"Awful needy little thing, aren't you? That's okay, because I want that, too. I want to feel your mouth on mine, to feel your cunt contracting around me. It's all I've been able to think about since last night, Jilly. Having you. Again and again."

The mixture of annoyance and wonder in his words filled Jillian's mind with questions, with panic, with the tiniest seed of something she hated to recognize was hope. Then Brendan came up on his knees, freeing her naked bottom to the cool lick of night air rushing in through the nearest window, and her mind emptied of everything but sensation. He pulled her up on her knees, as well. The warmth of his hand on her belly was startling in contrast to her suddenly chilly flesh. His cock prodded at her buttocks as he found her damp opening and sunk a finger inside.

She moaned with the pleasure that came with penetration. He murmured his satisfaction. "You're wet, sweetheart, but I knew you would be. Were you wet today at work, knowing how close I was, how you could come into my office and ask me to take you and I'd never have been able to say no? I wouldn't have. I'd have had you on my desk and been inside you in a second."

The heated words he whispered, the feel of his warm breath sliding along the sensitized flesh of her neck, the intimacy of his shaft cradled against her ass, were all too much to deny. Jillian melted against the persuasive stroke of his finger. The pressure and wetness built. His finger began to retreat and she followed its course, trying to pull it back inside her pussy, desperately needing him to continue.

He pulled out of her completely and kissed her ear. "Relax. I'm not done yet."

And he wasn't. Not even close, she realized, as he tipped her hips and pushed his dick inside her. He breathed a growl into

her ear, a sound she mimicked as sensation a[...]
tion spiraled through her. Then he stilled his m[...]
turn his hand to her belly and grip her tight. [...]
went to her front, tangling in the curls of her [...]
teased over the lips of her pussy, stroked her clit.

Jillian knew he preferred her eyes open and was thankful he couldn't see her face, because keeping them open in this position, when he filled her so completely from behind, wasn't an option. Neither was withholding her emotions. She felt so much as he drove deep into her sex, his balls slapping against the rear of her—intensity, desire, trust, possession. And then she felt nothing at all but ecstasy as he turned up the pace, fingering her clit with teasing pressure, thrusting his cock fast and hard into her slick core, and then letting go of her waist to cup a breast. His fingers plucked at her erect nipple. His hot, wet mouth suckled at her neck. She gasped for breath as her heart pounded recklessly beyond control.

From somewhere Tawny's voice came to her, telling her to be careful, telling her not to let her heart become involved. From that same place came Jillian's own voice, telling her to keep the control, to maintain the power. The words were fleeting and then forgotten with the first tremors of orgasm. Her thighs shook, her arms felt ready to collapse. She couldn't stay in this position a moment longer.

"Oh, God, I'm going to fall. I'm going to—"

"Shh. . . ." Brendan whispered, letting free her nipple to again grasp her waist and help support her. "You can trust me. I won't let you get hurt. I won't let you fall. I can't keep this up any longer, though. You're too tight, too damned sweet. I've wanted to come since the second I entered you. Hell, from the second I got in my car and started over here. We're both going to go now. Come for me, Jilly. Come . . . for . . . me. . . ."

His words tapered off as his thrusts grew harder, deeper. His fingers moved faster, stroking that spot where their bodies joined. She couldn't hold back a moment longer. Her pussy tightened and the shudders of climax spilled through her, taking her beyond thought but that of Brendan and the feel of him finding his release.

When the tremors subsided, he mouthed something inaudible near her ear and slumped against her. Jillian had barely been able to breathe before; now she couldn't in the least. She didn't want him to move, knew the moment he did he would be out her window. But he also couldn't stay.

He was saying too much. Saying he'd wanted her since the moment he'd left last night, saying she was all he'd been able to think of, saying she could trust him. He was acting as if he felt as close to her as she did to him right now. He couldn't feel that way—he wasn't that kind of man—and even if he somehow could, she couldn't afford to acknowledge it.

"You're crushing me," she squeaked out.

He rolled off of her, but didn't move any farther. She glanced over at him and he sent her a satiated smile. The look speared through her, warmed her in places she'd forgotten she possessed. Her heart gave a bump. The breath snagged in her throat while anxiety lurched in her belly. She pushed the uncomfortable feelings aside. The bump had been nothing more than exertion, or possibly a tremor of lust brought about by his scrumptious smile. Nothing more. Nothing to panic over.

She forced her own smile. "I take it it was good for you?"

He chuckled. "*You* were good, sweetheart. Beyond good."

Good enough that he wanted her again? Is that why he was still lying on her bed, smiling at her that way?

"Who are you, Jilly? Who are you really?"

"*What?*" The anxiety returned to Jillian's belly in a fit of roiling waves. A chill shook through her. She grabbed for the covers, suddenly feeling overly exposed.

Why in the hell would he ask who she was? Not only was he not a man who got to know the women he slept with, but why did he think she was anything but the cool, calculated woman she presented herself as?

She sat up and glared, desperate to set this right, to prove she was who she claimed to be, to get his smile out of her head, her heart. "You know who I am," she snapped, "what I am. Don't look for anything more, Brendan. There's nothing to find."

His lazy smile slipped away. He sat and moved to the side of the bed, standing in one fluid motion. His gaze pinned her for an instant, the complete look of a moment ago replaced with something dark, something that told her his words would sting even before he turned his back on her and uttered, "You're such a goddamned liar. There is more. A hell of a lot more. I can feel it when I touch you. I can see it in your eyes, in the way you decorate your home, the way you love your dog. You're not the hard-ass you pretend. You're someone different, someone so much better. What I don't know is why the fuck I cared enough to ask who that someone is."

The covers were no protection from the bittersweet accuracy of his words. She didn't know why he'd asked either. What did he expect to gain even if she told him the truth? The only possible answer was he thought to somehow use what she'd tell him against her to win the senior ad exec position. And if that was the case, then it also had to be the reason he'd come back here tonight. It had to be why he'd acted as though he'd missed her and had been thinking of her all day.

His back still turned, Brendan disposed of the condom in a Kleenex and dropped it in the wastebasket by the bed. His stance was so inflexible, it hurt her to look at him. But his stance didn't match his motivation. If this was just about the job, it shouldn't show in his body.

And if it wasn't about the job . . . She'd already determined it the only possibility, but what if it wasn't? What if he really had missed her? She shouldn't ask, shouldn't cross that barrier, and yet she ached to know. "Brendan—"

70 / Jodi Lynn Copeland

"Don't waste your breath with orders, Jillian. I'm leaving. I was just taking a minute to get my bearings." Without another look in her direction, he went to the far corner of the room, climbed out the window and vanished into the darkness of night.

Jillian lay back and pulled the covers tightly to her neck. She hadn't missed the way he'd used her full name, and knew that the chill that stole through her had nothing to do with the crisp night air. It was directly related to that bump she'd felt in her heart and the ache that had come into her chest with the hurt in his parting words.

God, how she wanted to chase after him, to share every last one of her secrets with him.

She couldn't do that. She'd worked too hard and long to risk her heart on a man with his reputation, let alone her chances of winning her dream job. And so she called Ginger back to the bedroom and soothed her restless soul by lulling the dog to sleep.

Stick to the task at hand. How the fuck hard was that?

Prior to meeting Jilly it hadn't been all that difficult at all. Since meeting Jilly it seemed a damned impossibility.

Brendan had sneaked into her home almost a dozen times in the past two weeks. Though he hadn't spoken more than a few words other than those meant to stimulate her, the need to uncover her secrets was like a living thing. He still had no idea what it was about her—the enigma of her night-and-day character shifts? The fact that she never failed to keep him guessing? Or something else completely? Whatever it was, he wanted to go back again and again and again.

Christ, he'd never wanted to leave her in the first place.

He'd never experienced that with another woman, the desire to stay behind and hold each other, to kiss her for no reason at all but to see her eyes light up and a myriad of emotions pass over her expressive face.

It was a damned bad thing that he was feeling it now.

As much as he knew that, he also knew he wasn't ready to end his nights with Jilly. If nothing else was to be said for these last weeks, he had managed to accomplish a good deal of work, and had made several strong connections with major players at *the Wild Side*. Unfortunately, so had Jilly. It was foolish trying to compete with her. They should be tackling this thing together. But that wasn't an option any more than it was an option to spend the night with her. She didn't want him in her home, her bed or even her mind for any longer than it took to have them both climaxing. He shouldn't, either. That he did was something he wasn't going to waste any more time worrying over. There was no reason to worry so long as Jilly felt the way she did.

He was late again.

They were two and a half weeks into their affair, and Jillian had decided Brendan kept her waiting on purpose to aggravate her, which in its own twisted way stimulated her. And made her edgy, and think about things she had no right thinking about, like how badly she wanted him to ask about the real her again. When push came to shove, she might not have what it took to tell him the reasons why she acted the way she did, but she wanted the opportunity to try, wanted to ask him questions in return and discover what he felt toward her, if anything.

A scraping sound at the bedroom window had her gaze whipping to the opened sill and her heart beating with expectancy. A branch from a neighboring tree rapped against the side of the house, brushing at the window's frame.

She sighed. Not Brendan, just a branch.

An hour later, Jillian accepted the truth. He wasn't coming. It was too late. Almost two already and he never came so late.

He wasn't planning on coming over again, period.

It shouldn't be a shock. She'd always known he bounced

from one woman to the next without regret; Tawny reminded her of that fact on a daily basis. But he'd come back to her so many times. Not once since the night he'd asked who she really was—when she'd retaliated with nastiness—had he attempted to voice the question again. He didn't need to ask, because the wonder was in his eyes every single time they touched. Between that question and the cautious, almost reverent way he'd held her the last few nights, she'd nearly convinced herself he could feel something for her.

It was a senseless idea, knowing what she did about him. Still, hurt pressed at her chest. The bumping that had become increasingly familiar and harder to pass off as exertion returned, knocking at her ribs. She squeezed her eyes shut and blocked out the sensations, refusing to accept heartache where he was concerned.

So he didn't want to sleep with her any longer. So what? Yes, she did want a family eventually, wanted someone to love and be loved by in return. There was plenty of time for that and scads of men more suitable for the task than Brendan. Right now her focus needed to be on work.

She'd finished her marketing presentation for *the Wild Side* that afternoon and planned to turn it in to Larry tomorrow. The tangible part done, she would dedicate the next few days to schmoozing until the new senior advertising account executive was appointed. It wasn't her style to suck up, but it would be well worth the sweet victory of grabbing the job out from under Brendan's arrogant nose. It was a comforting thought, and the one Jillian clung to as she drifted to sleep.

5

The worst day of his life was about to begin. If not the worst, then it was a damned close second.

Larry had pulled Brendan into his office as he was heading out for home last night and proceeded to congratulate him on his new position as senior advertising account executive. The news had sunk in slowly and was bittersweet as hell. The advancement and healthy raise that came with it put him in a position to stay with Neilson & Sons for as long as he wanted, which in turn meant staying in Atlanta—a city where he wasn't known as his father's son, or expected to perform a certain way simply because his heritage and reputation dictated it. At the very least, the expectations weren't so high here. They left room for him to breathe comfortably.

Almost comfortably.

Son of a bitch. If he'd known Larry would make up his mind before giving Jilly's proposal adequate consideration, he never would have turned his in so early. He would have waited until the last possible second, so at least he felt like she'd had a fighting chance.

Not that it would have made a difference.

According to Larry, he knew both Brendan and Jillian were more than competent to take over the position. It was Brendan's relaxed, team-player attitude that swayed his decision. While Jillian was a great asset to Neilson, her stiff nature and the formality she treated the bulk of her colleagues with made it hard for him to promote her to a role that would require staff management. Larry had made it sound as if he were saving her from herself by not giving her the job.

What he wasn't doing was saving Brendan from Jilly.

She was going to hate him after this. She would find a way to blame him for certain. In a way, it was his fault. Had he not come to work for Neilson & Sons, she would have been the natural choice for the position. At the same time, if he hadn't come to work here he never would have met her, never realized that sometimes freedom wasn't the answer. Never acknowledged he could care about a woman on a level other than a physical one.

He cared about Jilly.

Too much to have Larry deliver the news to her. Brendan had taken that task upon himself. Initially he'd planned to go to her house last night and tell her there in an attempt to save her from making a scene in the office. But then he'd realized how bad of an idea that was. She would have thought he was there for sex. And given the way she'd started to anticipate his arrival, the way she'd meet him at the door or the window or whatever route he might use to get inside her house, he never would have gotten the words out. He would have taken one look into her moss-green eyes, seen the passion alive in their depths and jerked her into his arms. He wouldn't have let go again until he was buried hilt deep and experiencing the soul-bending connection he longed to share with so much more than her body.

Going to her place hadn't been an option, and so he'd opted

to tell her first thing this morning. The news was supposed to be kept secret until the official announcement on Friday. Since Larry had already had his personal assistant place the costume order for the party that would be held as part of the marketing campaign, Brendan wasn't counting on that secret enduring.

Dragging in a frustrated breath, he punched in Jilly's phone number. He had one duty here and he had to get the words out if it killed him. Or, in this case, if Jilly did.

She appeared in his office doorway a few minutes later and bit out, "You wanted to see me?"

Yeah, he wanted to see her. He wanted to haul her into his office, tear off her baggy black wardrobe and see every inch of her beautiful body. Only, that wouldn't be happening, today or ever again. He knew better than to think she'd still want to sleep with him after this. He'd be lucky if she spoke to him. She sure as hell wouldn't like him.

"Come in and close the door."

She frowned, obviously hearing the guilt he hadn't quite been able to keep from his voice. "What's wrong?"

"Close the door and take a seat. Please."

She shut the door and crossed the room, dropping down in a chair across the desk from him with concern etched on her face. "You never say please, Brendan. Not even ... you know, outside the office. Tell me what's wrong."

Faster was better. The sooner he got the words out, the sooner he could fix things. And he would fix things. Jilly was the first woman to make him want her for longer than a few days, to want her even when a bed or a couch or a table or any other conveniently flat surface wasn't involved. To want her on an emotional level as well as a physical one. He'd accepted it these last few days: Jilly was simply "the one." The one he'd never expected to find, let alone want to keep around.

Brendan sat forward and, leaning his elbows on the desk, bridged his fingers. Remorse turned his gut as he watched the anxiety building in her eyes. "I . . . don't know how to say this."

"You're not the type to be at a loss for words."

She was right; it was one of many things they shared in common. Normally it was, anyway. This situation was hardly normal. They weren't normal coworkers, as they weren't normal lovers. They were something else, had been something else from the moment he'd first spotted her. "I'm sorry, Jilly, but—"

"Hey, this must be for Jillian. Whatcha think?"

The loud male voice from somewhere outside Brendan's closed door cut off short Brendan's announcement. He glared at the door, then back at Jilly's anxious look. He started a second time, only to be cut off again.

"I'd say Brendan's taking care of that frigid complex of hers just fine. She actually smiled at me this morning and said hello. I didn't know she knew who I was."

"Frigid complex?" Jilly mouthed, the color leaving her face.

"I wouldn't get used to it, man. You know his rep. It's only a matter of time and he'll be moving on. And Jillian the cold-hearted witch will be back to stay."

Brendan's stomach clenched at Jilly's expression. She blinked at him and looked away, but he'd still seen the way her eyes watered, the hurt the out-of-line words rendered. He was around the desk and tugging her into his arms before he had a chance to consider his actions. "Don't listen to them, sweetheart. They don't know you. Not like I do."

For an instant she was still, barely audible sniffs the only sound to be heard, then she pushed from his chest and out of his grip. She took a step back and jutted out her chin. A vivid pink painted her cheeks. "Don't you *ever* do that again! If someone were to have come in—"

"What, Jilly?" Shit, he was so sick of this pretense. Sick of hiding things between them. Sick to death of her allowing others to believe the worst about her. No matter how she might try to deny it, she was nothing like the callous woman she pretended to be. She was warm and kind and gentle. The way she held him, kissed him, the way she decorated her home in bright shades and comfortable, well-loved furniture, the way she took care of her dog as if it were her child, all spoke to the truth.

He had no idea why, what happened to make her think she had to hide who she was, but it was well past time she stopped. "What do you think would have happened if someone had come in? You heard what they were saying. They already know about us, or at least they're speculating. I care about you, sweetheart. Too damned much to stand idly by while some assholes who don't have a clue what they're saying cut you down."

An unnamable emotion passed over her face, giving way to icy determination. "You're wrong, Brendan. They do know me. I *am* a coldhearted witch, and I'm not sorry about it. It's gotten me where I am today."

"Disliked by most of your coworkers?" No matter how truthful the words, he regretted them the moment they left his mouth.

Jilly flinched. She quickly recovered, steeling her gaze. "I don't care if they like me. I don't even care if they hate me. I just want their damned respect."

"The two come hand in hand."

"Not always. Not where I'm concerned. Whatever you brought me in here for, it's going to have to wait. I need to find out what it is that's so perfect for Jillian the Frigid."

"Goddamnit, you're not frigid!"

She'd opened the door in time for his shout to leak out and attract the attention of the two men standing several feet away. They looked to Jilly, then Brendan, then back at Jilly, neither saying a word.

Jilly glared at the man—Frank from the mail department, Brendan recalled. Frank held a large box of colorful clothing Brendan recognized as the costumes for the party this coming weekend; he'd obviously been on his way to deliver them. Jillian turned to the other man, jerked the shroud of black from his arms and held it out in front of her. Any other time the wicked-witch costume and the fact they'd associated it with Jilly would have made Brendan laugh. Now it pissed him off beyond compare.

Jilly cast the men a smile laced with bitterness. "Thanks, Keith, Frank. You're both true gems."

Keith shook his head. "I had no idea you were around."

She lifted a shoulder and murmured, "Don't mention it."

It was amazing she could manage a calm tone when Brendan knew how upset she was. Even more amazing was the casual way she turned and walked away. The men stood there with Brendan, watching her go until she disappeared around the corner, and then they looked at him. The tightness of their expressions made it clear they knew he wasn't done.

He didn't let them down, but pierced the man Jilly had taken the costume from with a deadly look. "You had no idea she was around listening, is what you really meant, isn't it, Keith? You might want to keep in mind that even if she hadn't been around, I was. Since it would seem it's my job to heat up her cold heart, it's also my job to see that everything that's said about her gets back to her.

"Just for the record, she isn't cold. She's warmer than any-one I've ever known, and you have my approval to share that bit of gossip along with everything else I'm sure is being said about the two of us." He jerked the box from Frank's arms, then before he could say or do something he'd live to regret, stalked back into his office and slammed the door.

Jillian wanted to stay home, lumped on her couch with Ginger's gentle snoring for her only company. Her conscience wouldn't let her. Neither would her self-conceit.

Rumors traveled fast at Nielson. She'd heard the way Brendan had stood up for her. She'd also heard that he'd said she was warm.

Warm!

What in the hell had he been thinking? He knew how much she valued her cool office persona. Maybe Frank and Keith didn't appreciate it, but she knew others did. Larry did. Had. By now Larry would know the truth. He would know she was nothing but a two-bit sham. A gentle, caring woman in a callous, unfeeling witch's clothing.

God, she wanted to kill Brendan.

He'd given her the perfect opportunity to do it. He'd left her a sealed envelope at Neilson's front desk. Inside had been an address and the words *Wear the costume*. She had no idea why he wanted her coming to a strange address in a costume she felt more like torching than wearing. The only reason she would pull herself off this couch and go to the foreign address was because there were things that needed to be said between them. Things that involved her yelling and him cowering in the dirt like the no-good bastard he was.

She would go, and she would wear the costume, and when she left, he would be sorry he'd ever agreed to be in Mike and Molly's wedding, let alone come on that dance floor and make her want him.

The sound of tires crushing gravel filtered through the open windows of Brendan's home. He stood and hurried to the door. It might have bothered him that he was so anxious to see Jilly, if he hadn't already accepted the truth where they were concerned. However this night went, before it was through Jilly would know exactly how much he cared about her.

She stepped out of her car. He squinted against the late afternoon sunlight glinting off the front door's small glass inlets. She'd worn the witch's costume, though she didn't look any too thrilled about it. Her lips were pinched together and temper filled her eyes. She glanced from side to side, taking in her surroundings as she made her way up the front walk. Slowly, the annoyance in her expression gave way to wonder.

When he opened the door, Brendan expected the first words out of her mouth to be far from friendly ones. At the very least a comment on his pirate outfit and the fact he'd asked her to wear a costume, as well. Instead, they were, "This is your house?"

He nodded. "Do you like it?"

"Yes. I'm just . . . surprised, I guess."

"You thought I was still living in the hotel?"

Jilly shrugged as if she hadn't given the matter any consideration. The truth was in her eyes. She didn't expect a man with his reputation for bouncing from place to place and woman to woman to own a permanent residence. If that surprised her, the rest of this night was going to shock the hell right out of her. "Let me guess, I don't seem the homeowner type because of my reputation for getting around."

"I didn't say that."

"But you meant it. As much as I valued my freedom, and in many ways still do, I also appreciate the worth of having a place to call my own."

Her lips firmed again. "Why *valued?* What's changed?"

Brendan bit back a laugh. She had to know the answer, was guessing by now the whole office knew. It was simple; one word. One woman. "You."

Shock filled Jilly's eyes, quickly subsiding as she fisted her hands at her hips. While the witch's costume was far from flattering, it was still a hell of a lot more formfitting than the clothes she wore to work, and her action had the black gown pulling tight across her breasts. "I haven't changed, Brendan," she grated out. "You might have people believing I have, that I'm some kind of warm, tender woman they'd be honored to call their friend, but I haven't and I won't. I'm still the same callous woman I've always been."

He pulled his attention from her chest and met her gaze, which wasn't cold the way her voice had suggested, but devoid of emotion altogether. She was attempting to block him out, to make him believe she was unfeeling. The effort was futile, and one he wasn't about to let her get away with.

Mindful of the plastic hook attached to his right hand, he reached out with his left and caressed his knuckles over the soft rise of her cheek. She flinched with his touch, but otherwise remained still. His strokes continued, the mossy green shade of her eyes darkening. He grinned with the acceleration of her breathing.

If she was unfeeling, then he was a saint. "You're such a bad liar, sweetheart."

"Why do you call me that?"

"Because you are." *Sweet. Kindhearted. Warm. Mine.*

Jilly jerked her face away and narrowed her gaze. "No, I'm not. The only thing I am to you is a coworker and . . . a lover."

"Are you still?"

Indecision flickered in her eyes, but then she nodded. "Yes."

Brendan sighed. Her answer to that question was liable to change before this night was over, but for now it was everything he needed to hear. He raised an eyebrow and said in a terrible excuse for a Caribbean pirate accent, "I was hoping ya'd say that, me pretty. In case ya haven't noticed me clothing, I'm feeling quite jaunty, like finding me some sweet young thing to plunder. Avast, the sweet young things have run thin, so I'll have ta make meself happy with a witch."

He reached out with his right hand and slid the curved end of the plastic hook between the row of buttons that started at her throat and ended midway down her torso.

Indignation flashed over her face. She took a step back, knocking his hand from her dress. "I didn't come here to have sex with you, Brendan!"

As if she really thought a few terse words would sway him.

She knew him better than that, just as he knew her. The one and only guaranteed way to draw the real Jilly out, and hopefully get her to listen to him, was physically. "Then when did ya change yer mind, me pretty?"

"I haven't."

"Ar, but ya have." Brendan grabbed hold of her wrist and pulled her into his arms, up against his chest. He slid his left hand between their bodies and filled his palm with the softness of a breast. She squeaked out a gasp.

He lowered his mouth to hers, hovering centimeters from the lushness of her lips, already imagining their sweet taste. "You can't lie to me, Jilly. I know you better than that. Better than what you want anyone else to know you. I know the feel of my hand on your breast, stroking over your nipple, makes you wet." He released his grip on her breast and drew her nipple between his fingers, toying with it as best as her clothing allowed. "I know when I rub my tongue over this spot beneath your ear," he bent his head farther and licked the spot where her pulse beat hard, "it makes you squirm. I know that when I move my hand lower and cup your sex, it makes you want to scream." He freed her nipple from his fingers and brought his hand to her mound, cupping her in his palm. "You want me, sweetheart, just like I want you. And I know you're going to let me take you, because as much as you want to, you can't tell me no—"

"No," she breathed out frantically.

Brendan chuckled and pressed his hand harder against her pussy. Wet heat permeated through the thin material of her dress. His cock throbbed to life. "I wasn't done, Jilly. I was going to say, 'You can't tell me no and mean it.'"

"I do mean it. I don't w—want you."

He smiled against her neck, hearing the way her voice broke when he moved his hand beneath the hem of the gown and caressed the softness of her inner thigh. She wanted him every bit as much as he wanted her, and not just in the physical sense. "What was that? I couldn't quite understand that one word. What don't you want, sweetheart?"

"I don't want th . . . is."

He moved his hand higher until it met with the damp crotch of her panties, then went beneath that barrier. He slid his fingers through her curls to tease the outer edges of her pussy lips. Her breathing grew faster, her breasts thrusting against his chest with each ragged inhale. His balls drew tight with the sound. His heart accelerated. Inhaling the heady scent of her arousal, he plunged two fingers into her cream-filled sheath.

The breath cruised from Jilly's mouth with a low cry. Brendan turned her in his arms and rubbed his stiff cock against her ass. "I can tell you don't want this," he rasped in her ear. "You're not wet at all. Your pussy isn't contracting around my fingers, begging me to push them in even farther. Your breathing isn't coming too fast. Your nipples aren't hard, throbbing with the need for my mouth." He pulled his fingers from her, ceased his grinding and stepped back. "Since you don't want me, I guess there's no reason to invite you inside."

She spun back. Fury and passion blazed in her eyes. "You . . ."

"What? What am I?"

"You're a bastard." Her tone held no bite, only acceptance. "I hate you for making me feel this way."

He could guess how she felt by her expression, like she'd lost both control over the situation and whatever else it was she'd hoped to gain by keeping her real self from him. Still, he wanted to hear the words. He needed to hear one thing come out of her mouth that was the truth. "How do you feel, Jilly? Do you want to run away? Do you want to go home to Ginger and cry because the big bad pirate took advantage of you?"

"I want . . ."

"Yes?"

"I want to make you pay." Her eyes glimmered with challenge. She was on him in an instant, her hands pushing at his chest, knocking him back inside the doorway.

Brendan swaggered with the surprise of the attack. The feathered captain's hat fell from his head to the floor. He righted himself and caught her in his grip as she came at him a second time. He grabbed hold of the ugly black gown and pulled her flush against him. She tipped her head back and eyed him with need, with desire. With a longing he knew only too well.

They'd spent one night apart—one goddamned night—and he wanted her so badly his dick felt ready to burst from its skin. "Is this how I pay, Jilly? You plan to punish me with sex?"

In response, she licked her lips and rubbed her breasts against him. The action was completely un-Jilly–like—or at least un-Jillian–like. While he'd planned to reach the real Jilly by way of her body, he hadn't planned for it to be aggressively. He'd wanted a slow, sweet seduction. That was not what she appeared to want. He was willing to meet her on her own terms.

His cock growing harder, his heartbeat faster by the moment, he crushed her mouth with his. She met his tongue with frantic strokes of her own while her hands pushed past his waistcoat to work free the buttons of his ruffled shirt. She tugged until two let loose, and then her palms touched down on his bare chest. She greedily licked at his mouth, and he met her thrust for thrust. Her short fingernails nipped into the muscles of his chest. He burned to have his hands on her as well.

He released her for an instant, long enough to free his hand of the hook, and then recaptured the bodice of her gown and gave the material a yank. The sound of ripping cotton filled his ears followed by Jilly's startled cry. Then the gown was gone, pooled on the floor at her feet. His hands touched down on the softness of her bra and, beyond that, her smooth, supple skin.

Brendan stepped away from her. Always when he'd come to her before, part of her body had been concealed, whether it be by clothing or the shadows of night. Only her black bra and panties and thigh-high stockings obscured his view now, and he wanted them gone as well.

"Undress," he growled.

Jilly's eyes widened and she shook her head. "No."

"Yes! It's an order. I order you to undress. If you can't handle it, get out." It was a test. One he knew she'd pass. She wouldn't leave him. She wanted him, needed him, trusted him. Cared about him every bit as much as he cared about her.

Anger took over her expression and she fixed him with a burning glare. "Who the hell do you think you are? You can't order me around!"

And he wouldn't in the future. Just for tonight, until he uncovered the real Jilly. Just until she listened to what he'd brought her here to say. "It was part of the deal, remember? We play by my rules. If you want me, Jilly, then take off your bra and panties. You can leave the stockings on."

"Such a fucking gentleman."

The words were laced with loathing, but her fingers went fast to work, unhooking the back clasp of her bra and sliding the straps down her arms. The bra fell to the floor and the pale globes of her breasts sprang free, her nipples dark pink and fully aroused. The panties came next, down her long, slender legs. Then she was standing before him in his foyer, naked aside from the sheer stockings.

He moved forward and tugged her hair from its ritualistic knot. The honey-blond waves fell around her face to halfway down her back. The breath snagged in his throat. "You're beautiful. Perfect."

The resentment melted from her expression. Traces of the real Jilly shimmered in her eyes, in the softness of her face. She murmured an unsteady, "I'm not perfect."

Brendan took a leisurely tour of her body, over the gentle

swell of her breasts, down her waist to the treasure of damp curls covering her pussy. All the blood in his body jetted to his groin. His heart threatened to pummel out of his chest.

She *was* perfect. If not in character, then in appearance. Perfect for him.

He couldn't stand here another moment not touching her, not taking her. He had to have her. Had to make the real Jilly come out completely and make her his for now and forever.

He jerked her into his arms and carried her to the nearest room with a flat surface, the kitchen. He set her down on the table and, gripping the globes of her buttocks, pulled her toward him until the wet heat of her sex brushed against the bulge of his cock through his pants.

He looked into her eyes, pouring every bit of the emotion he felt into hers, needing her to see the truth in his words. "You *are* beautiful, Jilly. Beautiful, warm and mine."

She started to speak and he covered her mouth with his fingers. He shook his head and made a shushing sound as he pulled his hand away. He stepped back, far enough to work the pants and boxers down his thighs, then returned to her and pulled her flush against him again.

"You thought I was joking with you that first night when I said *Peter Pan* was one of my favorite movies. If the Captain Hook costume doesn't speak loudly enough, then read my lips: I wasn't joking with you, Jilly. It is. Along with a number of other classics *Jillian* probably thinks are too immature for a grown man to watch."

She bit down on her lower lip and a thousand emotions he could never grasp raced through her eyes. "L-like *Cinderella*."

"Yes. Like *Cinderella*. I love fantasies. How there are so few rules, so few expectations. How people can just be, just do what they want without having to face the firing squad for their actions. I used to think those movies were just fantasies. That two people who seemed different in so many ways and yet so much the same could never meet and fall in love in such a short amount of time. Or that someone who wasn't looking for love or even believed it existed could magically find it all the same. I know now that they aren't just fantasies, that things like that really do happen.

"I know that, Jilly, because you've taught me love does exist. It's sitting right in front of me. I love you, Jillian Lowery, and whether or not you're ready to admit it, you love me, too."

Brendan was conscious of the tremor that shook through her, of the words she tried to speak. Before they could work their way out, he regained his hold on her bottom and slid her onto his shaft. Jilly's mouth parted in an O and a stream of hot air whooshed from between her lips.

It was the real Jilly he held now, and he wanted to keep her this way forever, speechless and yet so expressive it took his heart away. He couldn't do that. He could only do his best to convince her that his love was genuine, and hope after he'd told her the truth about the job that she'd be able to move past her disappointment and accept he'd never meant to hurt her.

He lifted her from the table and, relying on the strength of his thighs, thrust deeply into the silky moistness of her pussy. She started to speak. Once more he covered her mouth, kissing her hard while he milked her body with the force of his own.

Using his grip on her ass, he worked her up the length of his cock, then quickly back down, ensuring each thrust put pressure on her clit. The sudden widening of her eyes, followed by a breathy moan against his lips, told him how close she was to climaxing. It was a good thing because he was about to topple over that edge himself.

He quickened the pace, reveling in the sound of slick flesh slapping slick flesh. The spicy tang of sex filled the air. Each of her moans was met with an answering one of his. The pace became erratic, beyond his control. Shudders trembled through her and the muscles of her cunt contracted around his cock, pulling until he couldn't hold back any longer. He gave into the pressure sizzling through his body, drawing his balls near painfully tightly and his blood to a frenzied state, and cried out first his love and then her name as he came inside her.

It hit Brendan like a fist to the gut that he truly had come inside her. He hadn't even thought to use a condom. If this thing between them ended the way he wanted, it wouldn't matter. But if it didn't and their actions led to pregnancy, Jilly would have his head on a platter. Or possibly his balls.

Weak-limbed, he set her on the table and then fell into a wooden chair beside her, struggling to regain normal breathing. He wasn't going to bring up their little oversight just yet. He had way the hell too much else to tell her first.

Jillian wasn't sure she could breathe, and, as much as she'd enjoyed the sex, it wasn't because of that. It was from Brendan's admission of love. How could he honestly believe it? He'd guessed at the real her, but he had no way of knowing if his assumptions were accurate. "You can't."

He looked up at her and nodded. "Yes, I can. I do. I love you, Jilly."

"Oh, God, you don't even know me!" Clearly she hadn't known him. Never in a million years would she have believed a man with his reputation would be into children's movies. Would actually go so far as to dress up as a pirate and invite her over for fantasy sex. Where had he even gotten the costume? From the same box hers had come from would be the logical answer, but why had they been at Neilson's in the first place?

Brendan stood. "I just told you I do, sweetheart. I showed you. How much more proof do you need? I love you."

Jillian's heart gave a fierce bump. She blinked back the emotions that stormed up her throat and into her eyes. Why did he keep saying that? Why did he sound like he meant it? "Why?"

He chuckled. "You haven't exactly gone out of your way to

make yourself likable, have you? Maybe that's why. Maybe because for the first time in my life I've found a woman who doesn't want me, and I'm infatuated by her."

"I never said I didn't want you."

"You ordered me out of your house the moment I tried to get close to you, Jilly. I'd say that speaks for itself."

She had done that, but she hadn't wanted to. At least, not in retrospect and never deep down. "I was scared, all right. You're not exactly known for getting to know the women you sleep with. When you wanted to know about me, I thought it was for the job. That you planned to somehow find a way to ruin my chances at winning the position."

"I'll be the first to admit I haven't always been a saint, but how the hell could you think I'd sleep with you, let alone want pillow talk, for the sake of the job? I told you my first day at Neilson I'd win it fair and square."

Jillian laughed at the confidence in his words. The way he'd sounded as if he'd already won the job. He was so arrogant, so damned sure of himself. And as much as she didn't want to admit it, he was also right. "I just . . . Things have happened."

He smirked. "No shit they have."

"I mean in the past. I didn't want to make another mistake. I've worked so hard the last four years. I want that job so badly. I was afraid to mess up again."

Brendan's look softened. "What happened? Tell me. Please."

It was time to do just that. If she was to believe him when he said that he loved her and believe the way he affected her own heart, then she had to trust him. "I will, but first I want to tell you other things. You're right about me, Brendan. I'm not cold the way I pretend. I dress that way, act that way because I have to in order to make people respect me. But sometimes it makes me want to scream. Sometimes I feel like I might explode if the real me doesn't come out."

"Like at the reception?"

"Yes. That was the real me. At least until you mentioned you were moving here, and then I panicked. I was worried our paths would cross and you'd bring up my actions that night, that Larry would somehow find out."

He frowned. "That makes no sense. Larry would be thrilled to know the truth about you."

"No, he wouldn't. He doesn't like the wilder me. He depends on me being strong, reliable. The one person who doesn't turn soft under pressure."

"That isn't how he feels at all, sweetheart."

Jillian met his frown with one of her own. The conviction in his words was too strong for guessing, for even arrogance's sake. It sounded factual. "Why do you think that?"

"Because he told me so. He thinks . . . he thinks you're stiff, Jilly. That you hold people at too much of a distance and it affects the way they look at you, the way they treat you." Something akin to remorse passed through Brendan's eyes, and her body tightened with inexplicable anxiety as he continued. "He doesn't believe someone with your personality would work well in a position of authority."

Her belly knotted with his fast-fading tone. "What do you mean, 'A position of authority'?"

"Someone who would have others reporting to them."

He'd gone even quieter with those words, his look guiltier. She fisted her hands at her sides, struggling to remain calm when all she wanted to do was fling herself at him and pound her fists into his chest. What was he holding back? "What are you trying to tell me, Brendan?"

"I'm trying to tell you . . . I love you. I know you don't want to believe it, but I do. Nothing I say or do will change that."

She believed him, but that he even had to add those last words worried her beyond reason. Her heart sped. She gritted her teeth and curled her fingers tighter. "What in the hell are you saying, Brendan?"

"I'm saying that . . . I'm saying Larry gave me the job, Jilly. He gave me Donaldson's position."

Her frantic heartbeat died and she closed her eyes and breathed a sigh. He was teasing her. She felt ready to explode with anxiety and the big idiot was teasing her. "Nice try, but the proposals aren't even due until Friday morning."

Brendan's guilty look grew with her playful tone. He shook his head. "I'm not joking. He didn't wait for the proposals. At least, not yours. I turned mine in last Tuesday. Apparently, Larry approved of it. He pulled me aside last night and told me not to share the news yet, but that he was giving me the job. It's the reason for the costumes. They're for a party this weekend, a costume party that will give *the Wild Side* management a chance to mingle with the staff of—"

"No! I don't believe you." It was just a bad joke. It *had* to be a bad joke. "Larry wouldn't do that to me. He's a fair man. He would at least give me a chance. I've worked for that company for more than six years. The least I deserve is a chance." Jillian's voice shook as reality slammed into her and turned the knotting in her belly to painful cramping.

Oh, God, he wasn't teasing her! Larry really had given him the job. "I deserved a chance. But he didn't give that to me, did he? Instead he picked someone who's worked for Neilson for less than a month. He'd rather have a damned outsider than me."

"I'm sorry. I didn't want it this way. I never meant to hurt you, sweetheart. Never."

He started to reach for her. Jillian batted away his hand and shot to her feet. Wet warmth gushed between her thighs. She acknowledged what the liquid was with an inward laugh. God, he had her head so messed up she hadn't even noticed they'd forgotten to use a condom. It wasn't a big deal since she was on birth control. The fact he didn't know she was on the pill and had yet to speak up about the misstep, however, *was* a big deal.

Her emotions strung tighter than ever, she narrowed her gaze at him. He looked lost. As if he truly was sorry. She knew better, knew he wasn't sorry. He didn't know the first damned thing about the word. "You didn't want it this way? If you didn't want it this way, why did you even apply for the position? You wanted it, Brendan. From the moment you walked into Neilson's boardroom and saw me sitting there, the one woman in your life to actually turn you down, you wanted it. The thing is, so did I. Enough that I was willing to do anything to win, including sleeping with the competition on the off chance I might learn a thing or two about his game plan.

"That's why I was so afraid you'd use the things I revealed against me, because that's exactly what I was doing with you."

The sorrow in Brendan's eyes fled in an instant, cold fury taking its place. "Bullshit. You're lying again. You did not fucking sleep with me for the job."

He was right. It had never been about the job. She'd slept with him in the beginning because she'd needed a chance to let the real Jilly out. That hadn't been the reason she'd kept accepting him back into her home, though. That reason she'd never fully accepted until right now, as she realized how fickle his love and her own stupid heart were.

She crossed her arms over chest, suddenly too aware of her nakedness. "Not this time, Brendan. This time I'm telling the truth. I did do it for the job. If you don't believe me, ask Tawny. It was her idea. Enjoy the ride, she said, and if I happened to get close enough to learn a thing or two about your plans to win the position, wouldn't that be a nice side benefit? Only, it didn't work. I didn't learn a thing outside of the fact that you're a demanding bastard no woman in their right mind would sleep with unless she had an ulterior motive."

A muscle ticked in his jaw and his eyes darkened to near black. Her breathing grew hampered with the idea that he might grab her again. He didn't move, but said in a ragged voice, "I don't believe you, Jilly. I won't. You're too caring to do something like that. Too honest. You love me, just as I love you."

She blinked with the effect of those words, the pain they squeezed at her heart. Some small part of her wanted to agree, wanted to say to hell with it and return to his arms—the part that hadn't spent the last four years hiding her true identity in the hopes of repairing her past mistakes.

Jillian squared her shoulders and prayed her voice wouldn't tremble. "If that's what you want to believe, then believe it. Either way, I guess congratulations are in order. Way to go, Brendan. I wish you the best of luck. Now, you'll have to excuse me. Ginger's hungry and you know I hate to keep her waiting."

6

The last thing Jillian wanted to admit was that Brendan had been right about Larry. She'd been too tired and emotionally drained to bother with her dowdy clothes and severe hairstyle this week. She'd gone to work as herself. And Larry had complimented her on the change, not once but every morning when she'd arrived. Tawny encouraged her, too, as well as a handful of her other coworkers. And Brendan . . .

Brendan didn't say a word. He didn't even look her way.

People noticed. Even if she hadn't seen the sidelong looks, she had ears. She heard the rumors. They thought Brendan had grown tired of her and moved on to his latest sexual conquest, and now she was dressing and acting differently in an attempt to get him back. They couldn't be more wrong.

"I don't want him back."

"Right. You don't, girl, and I enjoy spending my weekends home alone, reading romances and watching reruns I've seen a hundred times."

Jillian jumped at the sound of Tawny's voice. She spun in her office chair to find her friend sitting on the opposite side of the desk. She looked as dejected as Jillian felt. "You go out on the weekends."

"Sometimes, but more often than not I only wish I did."

"Oh." She frowned. "Why didn't I know that?"

"I didn't think you needed anything else to worry about. You've developed this mindset about the two of us the last few years. You're the steady one, the rock. I'm the wild one who lives by the seat of her pants and never thinks twice about doing something—I just do it."

Jillian couldn't help but laugh with the irony in the words. "We used to be exactly the opposite, didn't we? I was the wild one. You were the rock. What changed?"

"You."

The one-word response tightened Jillian's belly, and the emotions she'd done her best to move past pushed at the backs of her eyes as tears. It was the same reply Brendan had given for his changes. How could she be responsible for the way so many others acted? "Why would you change because I did?"

Tawny shrugged. "We've always balanced each other out. I guess I wanted to keep it that way."

They *had* always balanced each other out. From the moment they'd met in college, they'd been there for each other, keeping each other's lives on track. At least, they used to be there for each other. These last years Jillian obviously hadn't been there for Tawny. If she had, she would have known that the vivacious woman her friend acted like was nowhere near to her true character, just as Tawny had known the truth about her.

"So what do you plan to do now?" Tawny asked.

Become the person she used to be. Take the time to pay more attention to those around her. Focus on the job she had instead of the one she'd convinced herself she wanted. Tawny had been right about the job, as well. She hadn't wanted it; she hated managerial-type work. Somewhere along the way she'd convinced herself that attaining the high-up position would bring her absolution from her past mistakes. If Larry's reaction to her wardrobe and hairstyle change was a sign, she'd been absolved long ago. At least, by everyone but herself. "Be happy with who I am and what I have."

Tawny smiled. "Good for you, but I actually meant about Brendan. What happened there, Jilly? Was it just about the job? He got it, so you gave up on him?"

Jillian stared at her in stunned silence. Was this the same woman who'd warned her that Brendan wasn't the kind of man to want long-term and that she should never care about? "I figured you'd be happy I quit seeing him."

"I might have been once, but that was before I had a chance to get to know him past his reputation. The rumors are wrong. He loves you, and it's obvious to anyone who looks beyond his bogus smile that he's miserable without you."

Jillian's breath caught. Brendan was miserable over her? It seemed impossible, but Tawny wouldn't make up something like that. "I don't know what happened. I did blame him for my not getting the job. He told me it was my own fault because of the way I acted. I didn't want to believe it, but . . ."

"You do."

"Larry's been treating me so differently this week. Almost everyone has. For the first time in years I feel like a part of this company, of its people. I feel happy. Almost."

"I hate to say it, but you're the only one keeping that *almost* from becoming a *completely.*"

She was right. It was something Jillian had been slowly accepting. Because of his reputation and because of how much her feelings had been wrapped up in things, she'd jumped to conclusions with Brendan and had been too quick to accuse. She'd screwed up, and in doing so had lost the best thing that ever happened to her, the man who'd made her see the truth about herself whether she wanted to or not.

Only, if what Tawny said was accurate and Brendan was miserable, then maybe she hadn't lost him yet. Maybe he was just waiting for her to make his fantasy come true.

Brendan laughed at the remark made by the woman in his arms. It was a hollow sound that anyone who knew him would know was feigned. This woman didn't know him enough to suspect anything was wrong.

Something was wrong. Jilly hadn't come to the costume party.

He was willing to accept her coolness toward him at work and do his part by keeping his distance in return. He couldn't accept her risking her job to avoid him. Larry had ordered that all account specialists and higher-ups attend this party for the Wild Side. That she hadn't come wouldn't go unnoticed.

"This party is a marvelous idea. What a wonderful way for everyone to have a chance to mingle and get to know the faces behind the names."

He smiled down at his dance partner and nodded his agreement. As concerned as he was over Jilly's absence, he couldn't let it show, particularly to this woman, the senior manager for the Wild Side. "I'm glad you're enjoying—"

"Forgive my rudeness, but I need to cut in."

Brendan stopped short at the sound of Jilly's voice. He wouldn't miss that husky yet authoritative tone anywhere. The woman in his arms stepped back to look at Jilly. Brendan swiveled to take her in as well, and the air came to a standstill in his lungs.

A sparkling silver band pulled her hair back from her face. Her cheeks were speckled with matching silver sparkles, her eyelashes coated in a dark green that matched her short green, strapless dress perfectly. Wings sprouted from her back. Fairy wings tipped in shimmering silver and green. "You look . . ."

She smiled. "Like a fantasy come to life?"

Like he wanted to take her home and show her exactly what happened when Captain Hook got Tinkerbell alone. His cock stirred to attention. "Yes," he said thickly.

Jilly's smile stretched into her eyes, warmth exuding from her to an extreme she'd never before allowed around him. He started to reach for her, when he remembered they weren't alone.

He turned back to Doreen Popple. "Doreen, this is Jillian Lowery, Neilson & Sons' finest account specialist. Jillian, Doreen is a senior manager with the Wild Side."

"The Wild Side," Jilly repeated, her voice a whisper, her smile gone. She looked to the other woman and regret filled her eyes. "Oh, God. If I'd known who you were I never would have cut in like that. I'm so sorry. Please don't let my unprofessional actions shape your opinion of Neilson & Sons. This company is wonderful. Brendan is the perfect person to see to your nee—"

Doreen's laugh cut her off. "Relax, dear. I would never let my opinion of an entire company be shaped by one employee. Even if I was, you have nothing to be concerned about. A woman is entitled to dance with her man whenever she wants."

Doreen made her way off the dance floor. Jilly watched her go with wide eyes and a slack jaw reminiscent of the fish-face look she'd given Brendan that first morning in the boardroom.

What the hell was going through her mind? As usual, he had no idea. "Jilly? Are you okay?"

She turned back to him. "I . . . I thought I did it again. I thought I lost another account for Neilson."

"Another account? You've done it before?"

She nodded, her stunned expression fading. "Yes. Four years ago at the company New Year's party. Tawny and I drank too much. When I drink, I can get very friendly. I ended up kissing this guy; it was a surface kiss, but his wife didn't care about that. She was the proprietor of a hotel chain I was marketing a grand-scale presentation to. She was about to sign with Neilson, but . . . she didn't after that. She told Larry I was incompetent, and that if he was smart he'd get rid of me before I lost him the rest of his business. I thought . . ."

The dread that had overtaken Jilly when she'd learned who Doreen was suddenly made sense, as did every other thing about her. The reason she'd acted the way she had for so long, why she'd believed Larry liked her better cool. Even the way she'd attempted to distance herself from Brendan. "You thought you did it again."

"Yes."

Relief assailed him. He grabbed hold of her hand and pulled her into his arms. "You didn't, sweetheart, so you can relax and dance with me. Doreen expects it. I wouldn't let her down."

She shook her hand free and pushed at his chest. "Brendan. Please. I need to—"

"Go?" he finished, not missing the return of her anxiety.

He'd thought her behavior before had been solely because of Doreen. Now he realized otherwise. She hadn't come here to make amends, but merely to show him what he'd never again have. His gut lurched. He pushed the sensation aside and pulled her tightly to him. There was no reason to fear she would feel his erection; that had gone the moment he'd realized he wasn't wanted. "Let me have this one dance, Jilly. After that you never have to talk to or come near me again."

"*What?*" she squeaked out, tipping her head back to reveal panic in her eyes. "But I want to! It's the reason I came here tonight. The reason I dressed the way I did. You were right, about everything. I thought Larry hated me after what happened that last time. That I had to earn his and everyone else's respect all over again. And maybe I did have to, but I took it to extremes. I made myself so cold I didn't even like me. It's the reason that lately I've felt like I would explode at every turn, because I couldn't handle not being me any longer. This week I came to work as the real me and it was great. I feel like I actually fit in again. I'm happy for the first time in years."

Brendan shook his head at her rambling words, at the fact she'd admitted to his being right. At the reality she truly had come here for him. She did want him. And he wanted her, too. Wanted to crush her to him and never let go. Instead he loosened his hold. "You're completely happy?"

"Well, almost."

"What would it take to make you completely happy?"

Her lips curved into a naughty smile. She dropped her attention to the vicinity of his mouth and rubbed her pelvis against his. This time it wasn't just his cock that stirred to life, but the soul-deep hunger for her he'd spent the past days doing his best to forget. "A kiss wouldn't hurt, for starters. Then you could tell me that you love me six or seven hundred times. That is, assuming you love the real me and aren't just infatuated with the heartless-witch version."

He chuckled and allowed himself to pull her close again. The heartless-witch version of Jilly had its moments, but the warm, soft and sensual version had a whole lot more. "A kiss? In front of all these people? Do you really want to admit you're that taken by the competition?"

"You're not my competition anymore. I got what I needed most. I got myself back. And you got what you deserved."

"But what about what I want?"

"What do you want?"

"You to admit that you love me."

Her eyes twinkled and she glanced around them. "In front of all these people? But what about your reputation? Are you really ready to say good-bye to your bad-boy ways?"

"Sweetheart, just because I plan to spend the rest of my days with one woman doesn't mean I plan to stop being a bad boy. In fact, I already have some wicked thoughts underway about how I plan to show Tinkerbell everything Peter Pan forgot to." He accentuated the words with a playful pump of his hips.

Jilly laughed and moved her hips against his in return. "Are you going to tear off my clothes again? Because I have to tell you, I'm pretty partial to this costume. It makes me feel special, like I can do anything without having to worry about pleasing others."

Brendan glanced down the front of her dress, at the perfect view of her cleavage his height provided. Between the thought of filling his palms with her lush breasts and the carnal way she rubbed against his aching dick, he was more than ready to rush her to a dark corner and rip off the dress. Only, if he did that, she wouldn't be able to wear it again. As partial as she claimed to be to the Tinkerbell costume, he was even more so. "The costume stays intact, but only if you say the magic words."

"I love you, Brendan Jordan. I was wrong and you were right. Happy now?"

More so than he ever believed he could be after hearing a woman speak those words. "Yeah," he said teasingly, "but the magic words I had in mind were actually *please* and *thank you.*"

Jilly swatted his arm and laughed. "You drive me crazy. Now stop messing around and get to work. You owe me a kiss."

"You've got it, sweetheart." He lowered his mouth to hers slowly, thrilling in the expressions that soared across her face. He touched down on the softness of her lips for an instant, then glanced back up at her eyes and grinned. "Ar, prepare to be plundered, me pretty. . . ."

Night Secrets

1

"You really have to learn to keep your mouth shut."

Stuffing a runaway red ringlet back into her ponytail, Tawny Madison frowned at her reflection in the bedroom mirror. Shimmering hot-pink lipstick layered her lips and a matching low-cut shirt molded to her breasts, thrusting the better part of her cleavage into prime viewing territory. It was amazing she could breathe for how tightly her jeans fit.

She looked like the brazen, wanton woman she'd built herself up to be, at least in the public eye. At home she wasn't that woman. Only, tonight she had to be, and that's exactly why she should have kept her mouth shut.

Considering it had been ten months since she'd shared more than breathing space with a man, she ought to be happy for tonight's events. So her evening plans lacked the ingredients that made up a hot date—namely the hot part and the date part—but spending the night helping out a guy in need had to be more entertaining than her typical Monday night routine of a mud mask and solo scrapbooking session. Since her best friend Jilly was in the process of settling down permanently with her fiancé, most every other night was just as pathetically boring as Mondays. At least she had Wednesdays. The weekly book-club meetings offered the chance for mingling. She was even becoming friends with Joyce Donovan, the quiet bookstore manager who organized the meetings.

Tawny smiled at the thought of the petite blonde. It was a shame she wasn't awaiting Joyce's arrival. Helping the woman conquer whatever fears kept her from speaking her thoughts had to be a whole lot easier than helping Andrew Korben accomplish the impossible.

Andrew Korben. A recent hire at Neilson & Sons, the Atlanta-based advertising firm Tawny worked for. Andrew Korben. The information technology specialist who could talk for hours about bits and bytes and a whole bunch of other technical mumbo jumbo she couldn't even begin to comprehend. Andrew Korben. The computer geek who expected her to work miracles.

Thanks to her ridiculous *I'm every man's wet-dream woman; hear me roar, scream and pant* guise, Andrew thought she was a social butterfly with a full date book and a heavily notched bedpost. He believed it wouldn't be hard at all for Twany to bring him to that same level of sexual magnetism by way of an extreme makeover. Tawny couldn't perform miracles. If her lack of bad dates—let alone the ones that ended with mutual orgasms and twisted sheets—was any sign, she wasn't even a social moth.

If it weren't for her big mouth and inability to say no to those in need, particularly one in so great a need as Andrew Korben, she would never be in this predicament.

But her big mouth had done its usual thing, and she was in this predicament of teaching enticement skills she didn't even possess to an honest-to-god computer geek. Judging by the ringing of the doorbell, the computer geek—er, Andrew—was right on time.

With a vow to never agree to anything so foolish again,

Tawny made her way to the front door. Smiling broadly, she opened it. Light from the houses that surrounded hers in the subdivision splintered through the darkness of late fall to showcase Andrew wearing a smile of his own. Really, it wasn't such a bad smile. For sure something she could work with.

She stepped back and gestured for him to come inside. "Great! You're right on time. Punctual's always a good quality." Unlike perky. A little perky here and there had its moments. Playing the quintessential perky woman 70 percent of the time was enough to drive a person bonkers.

Andrew stepped into the entryway that connected to the living room and looked around. Long seconds passed as his gaze shifted from one corner to the other. There wasn't that much to take in, just the standard living room setup: TV, sofa, rocker, coffee table. A slight frown tugged at his lips. Tawny's own smile drooped. She forced it back into place. Obviously, conducting a thorough study of every person's home he visited was part of his nerd MO.

Another few seconds and he looked back at her, all trace of frown gone. "Thank you for agreeing to do this, Tawny. I know it has to cut into your nightlife."

"Trust me, it's my pleasure." Liar. But it was a whole lot better of a response than, "What nightlife?" Not about to dwell on her sad lack of a sex life when she had someone else's to ponder over, she took Andrew's faded tan trench coat and indicated for him to have a seat on the sofa.

She hung the coat in the front closet, then sat cross-legged in the rocker across from him. The tightness of her jeans grew with the position. Thank god she'd opted not to wear the miniscule pink thong that matched her gaudy shirt and lipstick. The scrap of lace that made up the rear of the panties would be buried so far up her ass cheeks it would take an extra-large winch to pull them back out.

"So, how do we start?" Andrew asked.

Good question, and the answer likely had nothing to do with a thong or a winch. Tawny made a picture frame with her thumbs and forefingers and looked at him through it. "Hold still and let me take you in."

Dark eyebrows winged together behind black frame glasses with lenses thick enough to be doorstops. "You've seen me every day since I started working for Neilson three weeks ago. Do you really think I'm going to look any different now than all the other times?"

"I've seen you, yes, but I've never really looked at you as a man."

"Oh."

She winced. His response might as well have been, "Ouch," the injury to his pride came through so clearly. She dropped her hands back at her sides. "I didn't mean that like it sounded. I just meant . . . at work my mind is on whatever job I'm doing, not my coworkers' appearances."

"Oh."

This "Oh" sounded more positive, so Tawny returned to her task of taking him in sans the picture frame. What she saw wasn't as bad as she'd feared. Maybe not even impossible to make over. He had a decent face—straight nose, clean shaven, strong jaw and, as she'd already noted, his smile was decent. His eyes were a nice shade of hazel, even if the color was a bit distorted behind his glasses. His hair was a bit long and basic brown, but, then, there had been many a day she would have killed for boring brown hair instead of the mop of bright red curls she'd gotten stuck with.

The biggest problem was his personality. Outside of computers, technology, and anything associated with the two subjects, Andrew didn't have much to talk about—unless he was different away from the office. But if he was, he wouldn't be here now.

"What do you find attractive in a man?"

"A pulse." Tawny gasped at her automatic response. She hadn't been expecting the question, let alone to have an answer for it.

"Excuse me?"

No, by all means, excuse her enormously huge mouth. "Impulse," she improvised. "You know, like, spontaneity."

Blowing out a breath, he ran a hand through his hair and sank back on the sofa. "Uh, yeah, I'm not very impulsive."

Covered in gray slacks that looked more appropriate for his grandfather, Andrew stretched out his legs. It had to be a universal male position, because every guy Tawny had ever known sat that way at some point in time. Even the geeks.

She really had to stop thinking of Andrew that way. Not all IT guys were geeks, even if this one did happen to have the fashion sense God gave a goat.

Fashion could wait for another day. Tonight was about the basics and brevity, which was why she hadn't offered him a drink. He'd be out of there before he could even realize he might be thirsty. "Don't worry if you're not naturally impulsive. It's pretty easy to learn, or at least fake."

"Okay, so what else?"

"A nice body never hurts." Unlike her mouth. The damned thing appeared to be set on high tonight. Clearly a guy like Andrew didn't have a nice body hidden behind his burgundy cardigan and seventies slacks.

He straightened and nodded. "I think I'm okay there. I've been working out."

"Running?"

"I generally do a mile or two after the weights."

Chalk one up to the mouth because Tawny couldn't stop another gasp from coming out. "You lift?"

He smiled. "Does that surprise you?"

"Well, yeah. It does." A lot like his smile did. She'd thought it was decent upon opening the door, but nothing like the one he aimed her way now. This smile was genuine and brought a dimple to his left cheek and warmth into his eyes that even foot-thick lenses couldn't hide. There was definitely hope for this guy.

"I go to Mark's Gym three mornings a week," he said.

"So do I. I wonder why we've never seen each other?"

He shrugged. "The place is pretty big. Statistically, the odds we'd run into each other aren't as good as what you would think."

And just like that all his newfound potential was gone.

Tawny sighed. She didn't want to think of him as a geek, she really didn't, but he'd brought statistics into what should have been a perfectly normal conversation about exercise, for God's sake.

Andrew nodded. "Okay, so we have impulsive and a nice body. Anything else?"

"A good sense of humor never hurts." Maybe he had one. Maybe he'd been using it a second ago, when he'd dragged out that statistics comment. Right. And maybe she'd wake up soon and discover her agreeing to help him out was nothing more than a bad dream.

"That could be a problem. I'm not funny."

Yep, the bad-dream angle was definitely her only hope. "You don't have to be funny, Andrew. You just have to know when to laugh."

"And you can teach me that?"

He looked hopeful—too hopeful for her to discourage. "I don't see why not."

"What about sex?"

"You want me to teach you how to have sex?" And he'd said he wasn't funny!

He laughed, and the smile that warmed his eyes and dimpled his cheek returned. "What should my feelings be on it? It seems like most of the guys my sisters bring home want it as soon as they can get it. I've never been one to push for it too early, but maybe—"

"Don't push." *And please don't tell me about your sex life.* It was more than enough to know he'd found his handful of past experiences and the women he'd shared them with lacking, which was the reason he'd enlisted Tawny's help. "It's okay to be a little forceful at times, but only when you know your partner's comfortable with it."

"So I should wait until the woman says she's ready?"

"Not if you want to come across as a master of carnality." Ick, wrong word choice. It made her think of sex and handcuffs and Andrew reciting statistics while he wielded a flog. Not a pretty picture.

She struggled to maintain a serene expression. "Give her a half dozen dates, feel her out, and if she seems cool with you and like the sort of sexually adventurous gal you're after, try making a move."

"Define making a move. Do you mean kissing or groping?"

"Definitely groping." And they were definitely back to a subject she didn't want to discuss with him. "We're talking about a modern woman. If she seems like she's into you by the end of the first date, there's no reason to hold off kissing any longer. I'm not suggesting you play tonsil hockey the first night. Give her just enough to make her want more. Something else you might consider is your name."

His eyebrows came together and he frowned. "What's wrong with my name?"

Guilt struck Tawny for pointing out all those things that stole from his potential dream-lover image. She pushed it aside. He wanted her help and no matter how much the truth might sting, she had to give it to him.

Sinking into her brazen persona, she rolled her eyes.

"Exactly how many studs do you know named Andrew? They might really be named that, but they go by something else, like Andy or Drew. I could see you as a Drew."

Andrew looked thoughtful and then nodded. He repeated the name a few times. "Yeah, I like it. It has a certain ring." He picked up the cordless phone that rested on the end table at the head of the sofa and ran his hand over the mouthpiece. "*Ring.* You know, like a phone."

Uh, was that a really bad attempt at humor? She didn't know and wasn't about to ask. Instead she clapped her hands and stood, breathing a sigh of relief when the waistband and seat of her jeans gave way slightly. "Wonderful!" She moved to the closet. "That's your lesson for the night, Drew. I know it isn't much, but I don't want to burn you out on the first day. There's a whole lot more to be learned."

"That makes sense," he agreed, sounding like he didn't think it did at all. She grabbed his trench coat and turned back to find him giving the phone another peculiar rub. Sending her a sheepish look, he set the phone aside and stood. His tone brightened a little as he said, "So, should I start applying what I learned immediately?"

"Sure, if you're comfortable with it." As if he actually thought he could find someone to try it out on tonight. Just in case he did . . . "Not the actual dating part, but I don't see how the rest can hurt to try."

"Gotcha."

"See, that right there was a start." Tawny moved to the front door. "You don't normally use slang."

Andrew joined her at the door. Taking his coat, he shrugged into it. "Mmm . . . maybe not. I guess I've never really paid attention to the way I talk."

"You should." Along with the way he dressed, she thought, giving the faded coat a last once-over.

She hadn't wanted to bring up his far from fashionable wardrobe so soon, but maybe tomorrow night they could cover it. If she got home from work early enough, she could pull some pictures out of the *J. Crew* catalog as an example.

God, how sad was that? Her life was so pathetic, she had nothing better to do than plan tomorrow night's lust lesson with Andrew.

They reached the door and Tawny opened her mouth to ask what time tomorrow worked best for him. Not a single part of that question made it out, which probably had a lot to do with the fact that Andrew's mouth was covering hers. He had her pinned against the wall and she couldn't even remember him moving.

His lips moved against hers stealthily, testing, teasing, nibbling. His hands coasted along her back until they were firmly cupping her ass. The sides of his coat parted, and the press of his chest against hers as he used his grip on her bottom to haul her up his body ensured he hadn't been lying about the weight lifting.

He felt solid, strong—nothing like an IT guy should. Sure as hell nothing like a nerd liable to start talking statistics at any given moment. He also felt hard. The swollen length of his cock against her belly was undeniable. Shockingly, so was the moisture that gushed in her panties.

She had to stop this!

Andrew was nowhere near to her type—she might not be a brazen bad girl who saw a man she wanted and demanded he come to her, but naughty-thinking bad boys were the type of guys she went for. No matter how good of a sexual education she gave him, Andrew would never be that type, and she shouldn't lead him on for so much as a second. Tawny knew that. Yet the instant he slipped his tongue into her mouth and along her teeth, she was powerless to do anything about it.

He tasted of mint and male. As his tongue found and tangled with hers, the part of him that was most male twitched against her stomach, as if anxious to get past her tight-fitting jeans and bury into her sheath.

It had been months since she'd had anything more substantial than battery-operated plastic inside her body. Clearly, too many. With a single stroke of his fingers against the rear of her sex, her pussy pulsed with hungry need and a sound that was half moan, half sigh erupted from her throat. Andrew's tongue went wild, lashing out, stabbing deep, daring hers to do the same. She'd never been good with peer pressure. It seemed she was going to fall victim to it this time, too, because her tongue obeyed, darting, feasting, consuming.

Heat rushed into her face and down to her groin. Her breathing came in harsh pants. She wanted more. So much more.

Tawny reached past his coat for the waist of his cardigan, needing her hands beneath it, on the hard muscles of his abdomen and chest, and then in far more intimate places. She wanted to feel the strength of his cock throbbing in her fist, taste his essence on her tongue. She had to have—

"So how was that?"

An arrogant look claimed Andrew's face as he released her and stepped back. On any other man and at any other time, the look would have either heated her further or cooled her off completely. On Andrew, it had Tawny's mind screeching to a halt and her common sense returning with a jolt.

What in the hell was she doing?

It wasn't enough that she'd allowed the kiss to continue after telling herself not to lead him on, but she'd thoroughly enjoyed every minute of it, would still be taking part in it and quite likely much more if he hadn't stopped her.

The arrogant look faded and he tipped his head to the side. "Hey, are you okay? You look sort of strange."

Not surprising, since she felt a whole lot strange. Strange in a way that had everything to do with lust. Strange in a way that had her nipples hard and her pussy pulsing with cream. The real question here should be, why wasn't he acting strange, too? Unless he did this sort of thing a lot—grabbed a woman and kissed her senseless. If he did, then they seriously need to think about changing roles in this whole *learning how to fill your date book and notch your bedpost* experience.

"Tawny?"

Right. He expected an answer. "Uh, it was . . ." Shocking. The last thing she'd expected. And yet amazingly good.

"Impulsive? Or did I totally misunderstand what you meant by that?"

What she'd meant by . . .

Oh! He'd kissed her as a way to try out being impulsive, not because he was attracted to her and hoping to get somewhere. And she sure as hell wasn't attracted to him, even if for a few seconds there she was pretty sure her heart had stopped. As for the stimulated body thing, it was a fluke. One brought about by sexual deprivation. One she wasn't going to think about a second longer—a lot like his unexpectedly clever tongue and the impressive length of his cock against her belly.

Tawny pushed forth a broad smile and willed her voice not to give away her heated state. "I'd say you have the impulsive thing down well. Some lucky woman's bound to be naked, sweaty and tangled in your sheets before you know it." She meant every word in a way she never would have meant a half hour ago.

Andrew—make that Drew Korben—might be a computer geek, but he also knew a thing or two about kissing a woman until her knees were weak and her panties wet. It was a good thing she wasn't going to waste any more time thinking over the way he'd all but gotten her socks off with that kiss, because if she did, she might wonder what else he was good at getting off.

"Whadda you got for me?"

As he drove away from Tawny's subdivision, Andy popped

a mint in his mouth and grimaced at the sound of his brother-in-law Rick Donovan's voice coming through his cell. He'd never cared for the man—something about his personality was off—but Andy's sister Joyce loved him. For his sister, he abided by Rick, and for his sister's welfare, he was providing his PI services to the man free of charge. Rick believed that Joyce's naive nature had allowed her to befriend a woman who was using Joyce to attain inside information on the business strategy of Rick's fledgling advertising company, and then sell that information to a higher-up at Neilson & Sons. The woman in question was Tawny.

Andy had spoken with Tawny a number of times since hiring on at Neilson under the pretext of an IT specialist. At work she came off as a hardworking, fast-talking, barely clothed babe. He'd believed spending time with her and seeing her in her natural environment might hint at an immoral side. So far the only thing she'd done that even came close to immoral was succumb to the kiss of a guy she thought was a complete nerd.

A kiss that could've led to more if he'd allowed it.

He'd been tempted. Damned tempted to tear off that flimsy little breast-hugging shirt, right along with those indecently snug jeans. The way she'd responded to the simplest squeeze of her ass and touch of her sex, he had no doubt he could be inside her house right now, screwing her gorgeous brains out.

Instead he was en route to his home, fighting off a major hard-on and talking to one of his least favorite people. Yeah, that was some kind of trade-off.

"Not much," Andy said, adjusting his erection while reminding himself he didn't mix business with pleasure. "Her home's in a decent neighborhood, but nothing she couldn't afford on her salary at Neilson. From what I could see in the living room, she doesn't have any new appliances. TV's only a twenty-inch and the furniture's pretty well used."

"Then she's saving the cash, banking it for a trip to Hawaii or a boob job or some shit like that. C'mon, Andy, you gotta find me something to work with. I know my gut, and my gut isn't wrong on this one. This chick's got something to do with the info leak; the timing of her making friends with Joyce is too convenient."

"I don't know. I'd say her biggest concern, outside of putting everything she has into her ad designs, is what guy she's going to bag next." Whoever that guy was wouldn't be thinking she needed to invest in a boob job, either. He'd seen plenty of her breasts, felt them pressed up against him. They were real, firm and plentiful.

"So she dolls herself up nice. That's gotta cost some bucks."

"I wouldn't say nice. Trashy maybe." In a way that spoke directly to his dick. His shaft, which had only begun to relax, threatened to harden again at the thought of her scanty clothing and spicy cinnamon scent. Had they met under other circumstances, she was exactly the kind of woman Andy went for. The sort of bad girl who knew what she wanted and wasn't afraid to go after it.

Rick's snort reverberated through the phone line. "My sister used to say it costs a lot of money to look trashy. She's already worked her way through three ex-husbands' settlement checks, so I'd say she knows a thing or two on the subject."

Andy remembered the man's sister Amanda. Her version of trashy went to a whole different degree than Tawny's. Amanda reeked of sleaze. Tawny reeked of . . . hell, sex appeal. The kind that made a man want to toss her up against a door and bury his tongue in her mouth.

Shit, he really shouldn't have done that, but the opportunity had been too much to let pass. And he'd pulled it off well enough. Left himself with an aching cock because of it, but still . . .

He shook his head free of the vision of Tawny standing before him, her eyes dark blue with lust and her nipples erect and stabbing into his chest. The only place an image like that would get him was in a cold shower, giving himself a hand job. It might have been a while since he'd taken time out of his schedule for sex, but he wasn't quite ready to resort to masturbation.

Andy turned down the street that led to his apartment complex. One thing he'd learned in his eight years of being a PI: Going along with the client's claim until fact proved otherwise was easier. "I planted a mini recorder on her phone that'll pick up her calls and any conversation that happens within thirty feet of the receiver." And, as fast as his hands were, had damned near been busted before he could get the cover back on the mouthpiece. "If the cash is going to her looks, we'll find out soon enough. I need to get going. I'll check in later in the week."

"You do that. And this time have something. The company can only stand to take so big of a cut before investors are gonna start getting nervous. I need those investors, Andy. I need this info leak taken care of now, by whatever means necessary."

The sudden chill in Rick's voice stirred Andy's temper. He might not care for the guy, but he'd never come across as aggressive before. Andy would likely say something similar, were he the one in Rick's shoes, but the idea that Rick might use that tone with Joyce had Andy's temper flaring to high.

His sister was too trustworthy. It was the reason he'd bought into Rick's claim of her talking about his company to a near stranger. It was the reason he'd be lucky to get any sleep tonight, for worrying over how Rick might take the loss of company profits out on his wife. Hell, it was probably better that Andy didn't sleep. He had a sinking feeling that the moment he closed his eyes, his mind would be filled with thoughts of a brassy redhead and exactly what she could do with those delectable, tasty lips of hers.

2

"This is all your fault." Glaring, Tawny sank down in one of the two chairs Jilly kept on the other side of her office desk for visitors.

Her friend stopped typing and looked over from her computer screen. The hair she'd kept trapped in a bun for years in an effort to make others respect her as a cool operator now hung in loose blond waves. A green three-quarter-length sweater with a loud jungle pattern that would look tacky on anyone else brought out the soft green shade of her eyes. The same shade was interwoven with vivid blues and yellows throughout the office decor, giving off a cheery atmosphere.

Jilly smiled and leaned back in her chair. "Morning to you, too, sunshine."

Several months had passed since Jilly had shed the witch's wardrobe and breezy attitude she'd acquired upon nearly losing her job over a moment of drunken foolishness. Still, her laid-back appearance had Tawny conceding to a smile of her own. "Morning. You look great, by the way. Is that what having a sex life does for a person?"

"Please. Brendan kept me up so late last night trying out a new tongue technique that if it weren't for downing a half pot of coffee, I'd be a zombie."

Just one of the many things Tawny had missed during Jilly's witchy years: the way she freely shared information on her sex life. "A new tongue technique?" She shook the question away. Living vicariously through her friend and the woman's fiancé had its moments. Now wasn't one of them—not when she hadn't been able to stop thinking about tongue techniques since Andrew left last night.

Her response to him had been about the length of time she'd gone without anything hot, hard and male between her legs. She knew that. But that hadn't stopped her from wondering, from wanting, and her pussy from aching so badly following his departure that she'd finally given in and broken out her favorite vibrator. The orgasm had been good. Too good. And that was damned depressing, because at the moment of climax Andrew's face had been filling her head.

Tawny groaned. "Never mind, I don't want to hear about it. I'm already depressed enough."

Concern replaced her friend's smile. "Why? And how is it my fault?"

With Jilly, Tawny didn't bother with the perky or brazen act. She laid out the wretched truth. "The only kissing or groping I've done in months was last night with the IT geek himself, Andrew Korben. And it's your fault because I spent the last few years leading everyone to believe I was some red-hot wild woman to offset your black-widow routine."

Jilly's eyes widened. "Oh, god, you hooked up with Andrew?" Her stunned look faded. "Not that it's a bad thing. I mean, he's not exactly Mr. *GQ*, but I'm sure he's a nice guy, though not what I'd call your type. What happened to dropping the wild-woman act? You said you changed to maintain balance in our friendship when I changed. I changed back, and thought you were going to do the same."

"I'd planned on it, but then Andrew asked for my help getting laid and I just couldn't say no. It's my mouth. Lately every time I open it something evil comes out."

Gasping, Jilly straightened in her chair. "You're planning to sleep with him, and a little kissing and groping has you concerned?"

"Hell, no!" Tawny winced at the shrillness of her response. The office door was closed and still the words were bound to carry to everyone on the sixth floor of the advertising firm. Another prime example of her mouth behaving badly. Her mouth wasn't the only part being naughty, either. Just the mention of sex with Andrew and her nipples beaded with anticipation.

"I'm not going to sleep with him," she said, as much to her overzealous nipples as to Jilly. "I'm going to teach him what it takes to catch a woman who thrills in wild-monkey sex." She snorted. "After all, I'm such the aficionado when it comes to the horizontal mambo."

Jilly relaxed in her chair. "You know danged well that's your own fault. You put off waves that make it seem like you know what you want and routinely go after it. All you have to do is put those waves into action. You've done it before."

That had been years ago, and, more often than not, when liquid courage was involved. "I don't know, girl. All those other times were in college. Any man I've dated or even slept with since has approached me."

"So, let him approach and take over the driving from there."

"Yeah, good thinking. I'll give it a try at the next book club meeting," Tawny said dryly.

Jilly shot her a sympathetic look. "I know the bar scene's a drag, but if all you're after is a one-night, get-you-off-and-go man to end your dry spell, give it a spin."

Tawny nodded, aware of what her friend's response would be before she voiced her next words. Ever since Brendan had come into her life, Jilly's nights were occupied. And that was great; if anyone deserved to be happy, it was Jilly. It just sucked ass for Tawny. "Fine. Saturday night. Pick you up at eight."

"Oh, I can't. I have plans with Brendan."

"I know, and that's half the problem. Back when I used to have men in my life—men I picked up, and not the other way around—we were both single and not pretending to be someone we aren't. I need you for sex, Jilly!"

"Now, there's something every man wants to hear." Brendan appeared next to Tawny's chair, wearing navy slacks, a white polo shirt and a devilishly sexy grin that made it easy to see why Jilly had first been attracted to him. He raised a dark eyebrow and looked from Jilly to Tawny. "So, we making it a threesome, or am I watching from the sidelines and making sure the camera keeps rolling? Wouldn't want to miss any critical footage."

"Sicko," Tawny said. Then, because she knew his words were spoken in good humor, laughed. Before he could round Jilly's desk and start in with the midmorning make-out session, Tawny stood. "Allow me to leave you to your tongue games."

To the sound of their laughter, Tawny moved out the door, closing it behind her. Brendan and Jilly weren't really the type to drool over each other at the office—at least, not in public view—but right now even the thought of seeing them exchange a surface kiss tightened her stomach. No way would she go on with a bellyache over her friends' happiness. She would end it exactly the way Jilly had recommended, by spending Saturday night at a local club, putting her wanton image to the test.

She could do it. No, she *would* do it. She had to take care of this ache that had everything to do with lack of sex before she did or said something too inane to reverse, like take a certain IT geek for a test drive around her bedroom.

Tawny returned to her corner cubicle and the ad design she'd left up on the computer screen. The new–e-mail icon flashed at the bottom corner of the monitor. Settling into her chair, she clicked on the icon to open her in-box. The screen turned white, camouflaging her layout. She frowned, clicked the icon again and waited. Ten seconds turned to twenty, and finally her e-mail opened to reveal a new message from Larry Neilson, the company CEO. She clicked on the e-mail maximize button and the white screen reappeared.

"No! I don't need this on top of everything else."

God, she hated computers. They were like vibrators—great until they stopped working, right at the moment of climax. She'd been minutes from completing that ad, dammit.

Tawny clicked the e-mail icon again, but the white screen remained. And that meant she was screwed. The primary IT specialist was out on maternity leave, thereby bringing about the need to hire a fill-in. Also, thereby assuring that only one person could help her now—the temp in question.

She really didn't want to see Andrew. She'd made it a point to veer away from him when he'd approached the break room this morning, wearing his typically nerdy attire and carrying an enormous coffee mug that sported the slogan SAVE YOUR HARD DRIVE, GET A JUMP.

For the sake of the ad, she would call Andrew for help. She would not, however, think of the man and the word *jump* in the same sentence. She didn't want to jump him, or ride him around her bedroom. She didn't want to do a thing with him but carry through on her promise of helping him become a sex god.

She picked up the phone and punched in his number. He answered on the first ring. "Hello, this is Andrew Korben. May I help you?"

A shiver chased through her at the deep timbre of his voice.

She shifted in her chair as that shiver came to a rest between her thighs and had her clit tingling.

Oh, man, something major was wrong with her. He'd answered his phone as straight-laced as one could. That wasn't a reason to get aroused.

Perky, she reminded herself. Perky, bold Tawny was the expectation here. "I need you, Drew." Okay, so that hadn't sounded perky. More like she was lying naked on her bed, fingering herself while she breathlessly awaited his arrival. The tingling spread throughout her pussy and moistened her panties. She curbed the urge to shift again. She would get laid soon and take care of this strange reaction to Andrew; until then, she had to focus on work. "My computer's spazzing."

"Spazzing computer. Right. Doesn't sound good. I'll be there as soon as I can."

She hung up the phone and drew long, deep breaths meant to alleviate her stimulated body. Knowing Andrew's penchant for punctuality, he'd be at her cube before the minute was up.

Less than sixty seconds later, he knocked on the wall of her three-sided cube. Not about to turn around when, despite her attempt to dislodge them, thoughts of lying on her bed, fingering herself filled her mind, she put forth her best perky attitude and nodded at the screen. "So here's the prob: It's all white. I have a design under there somewhere and my e-mail's open. Assuming a computer gremlin didn't eat them, that is."

Andrew moved next to her chair. His elbow brushed against the outer swell of her breast as he reached for the keyboard. Tawny's breath dragged in while heat zinged from her womb to her pinkie toes and her nipples hardened with throbbing awareness. She inhaled instinctively, the smell of mint filling her senses.

He tasted like mint, she remembered. Mint and male. A heady combination she never would have guessed at. And he kissed . . . oh, how he kissed. Her sex pulsed with the memory of the primal way he'd pinned her against the door and taken over her body and soul. Last night she'd called what he'd done to her kissing, but it had been far more. Definite groping had been involved.

His fingers moved over her keyboard, opening the control-panel folder in search of something. She had no idea what that something might be because she couldn't take her eyes off his hands, the graceful glide of his long fingers. He was tall. She'd noticed that last night when he'd lifted her up the length of his body. And more than a little endowed. She'd nearly found out the exact size of his cock. She could have begged him to pull her back to him. Could have told him it was an important part of his education, learning about untamed sex from firsthand experience with his teacher. If she had, she wouldn't be sitting here, imagining how much better it would feel to have his fingers moving inside her body than her own.

"Have you defragged lately?"

Tawny trembled as the warmth of Andrew's breath caressed her ear. He was so close. . . . He could nibble on her neck, lick her overheated flesh, tongue the shell of her ear. Her head lolled to the side. "It's been almost a year." Ten months. Ten long, unbearable months since she'd felt this rush of desire, this need to give in to his every carnal demand. To feel his hard sex pushing inside her, pulsing.

His fingers lifted from the keyboard. He drew back, his elbow brushing her breast once more. "In that case, I'm amazed you're still running at all."

She closed her eyes, waiting for the return of his elbow—another quick, delicious brush. "Some days, so am I."

"If you let me get closer, I'll see if I can fix things."

Oh, yeah. Closer. Right where she wanted him. "Mmm . . . closer."

"Tawny, you need to move back so I can look at your computer."

Her eyes snapped open with the firmness of his words. His

serious expression brought warmth into her cheeks. No dimple-revealing smile. No hint of arousal behind those thick, black frames. What a dork! Not him, but her. Here he was being the congenial coworker, and here she was getting ready to lift her skirt, pull down her panties and skewer herself on him.

"Um, yeah. Right." So much for perky, bold Tawny. She sounded more like rambling, geeky Tawny. Maybe they were right for each other after all.

No, they were *not* right for each other. She wasn't a geek and she certainly didn't go for geeks or nerds or even IT specialists who claimed they were sexually inept but kissed like Greek gods.

She wheeled her chair back a couple feet. Andrew squatted in front of the computer. Ignoring the agile movement of his fingers as they stroked over her keyboard, she attempted to flush all thought from her mind. Thinking was not safe where Andrew was concerned.

"Doesn't seem to be anything wrong on this end," he said after a minute. "Let me check the wall connections."

He moved onto his knees, unblocking her view of the computer screen to reveal her ad design back in place. Happiness over seeing that the computer gremlin hadn't eaten her work was replaced with shock the moment her gaze drifted below the keyboard. The breath caught in her throat.

"Ohmigod!" What an ass.

His charcoal slacks might be old-fashioned, but the way they hugged his tight buttocks was 100 percent now. Her fingers itched to reach out and grab a handful of delectable cheek.

"What's the matter?" He turned back, but his attention never reached her face. Instead it zeroed in on her slightly parted thighs. He was at the perfect height and angle to see her panties beneath her impossibly short, black leather skirt. The panties growing damper with every whisper of his hot breath on her thighs.

Tawny fought the reaction to cross her legs. If she did that, it would be obvious she'd caught him in his stare. He would stop looking on his own soon. Hopefully before her panties resembled a swimming pool and the scent of her juices perfumed the air. "I, uh, just remembered something really important that I look for in a man."

He rocked forward, bringing his face less than a foot from her thighs. Her sex grew wetter. She bit her lip to quell the moan threatening to break free. Maybe his looking away wasn't such a good idea. Maybe he could move a tiny bit closer.

"Okay," he said quietly, without looking up, "but we agreed not to talk about that at work."

At work. Where they were currently. She'd selected the corner cubicle because the open side faced a wall instead of another cube. The odds of someone spotting them or, for that matter, hearing them, were still high. No way could she keep quiet were she to give in to the sudden urge to grab hold of his ears and tug his mouth to her crotch. One lick of his talented tongue beneath her panties and she'd be crying out. One single thrust between her pussy lips and she'd be on the edge of orgasm.

Tawny shook her head at the crazy thoughts. Sexual deprivation couldn't be completely at fault. There had to be some other reason she was responding this way to Andrew. A reason she would consider later. "Uh, yeah, sorry. You're right." She didn't want to call him on the ogling, potentially embarrassing him, but they couldn't stay this way a moment longer. "Andrew? What are you doing?"

"Thinking."

Laughter bubbled up in her throat. Of course he was thinking! He was a geek, not a bad boy out to take advantage of the situation. He probably hadn't even noticed her parted thighs or her damp panties, he was so busy considering her computer problems.

"I was thinking about underwear."

The unreleased laughter died with a harsh gulp. Okay, so maybe he *had* noticed her damp panties. Maybe he was contemplating how to get beneath them. Right now it wouldn't take much more than a "please" to gain access. Or hell, he could forget the "please" and just dive in, tongue first.

"Briefs or boxers?"

Panties that were miniscule enough they might as well be a thong. Did he need a stronger prescription? How could he miss the tiny triangle of damp yellow silk that covered her mound?

Andrew looked up. His eyes were no longer void of emotion, but dark hazel and thick with the same lust cruising through her blood stream. "Which does a woman prefer, briefs or boxers?"

Naked was good. Naked on her wraparound desk, where she could climb on his stiff cock and shout out her ecstasy as she rode him. And then scream out her mortification when the entire sixth floor came to investigate.

Work. She was at work. With Andrew. The nerd. It was important she concentrate on the particulars. "I thought we said we weren't going to talk about that here."

"Right. We aren't. Sorry." With a last glimpse at her panties, he turned around and bent back under her desk.

Tawny's belly flipped with the return of his ass. It was wrong for a geek to have such a fine behind. Wrong, wrong, wrong.

Andrew backed up after a half minute. He pushed the glasses farther back on his nose as he stood. "It looks like it's going to take more than wiggling a few cables. Whatever is going on, you should be okay so long as you stay working in the current program. I'll come back after you leave for the day and look into the problem some more."

After work? But what about his lesson? She'd never gotten around to suggesting they continue his training this evening, but she still planned on spending the night with him. And not in bed, either, but sitting on her couch. Which was just as good a place to get horizontal and sweaty. On second thought, he should spend tonight working. "Um, okay," she said hesitantly, her body not quite convinced by her mind. "That shouldn't be a problem. I'll be gone by five thirty."

"Great. I'll do my best to see that it's running good as new tomorrow." He turned to leave.

She opened her mouth to say thanks. Instead, out came, "If fixing my computer doesn't take too long, we should continue your education tonight. Shopping."

"Shopping?" Andrew spun back to give her a look that suggested he was as excited by the idea as he might be to jab razor blades under his fingernails.

"Clothes really do make the man, and yours are a little outdated. You have way too fine of a body to hide it behind vintage." Oh, man, had she just said that? It didn't have to be a big deal that her huge mouth had taken over yet again. Not if she made it sound factual, like something that would naturally come from brazen Tawny. "Don't look so surprised. You said you've been working out. Obviously, it's paid off. If you wear the right clothes, many a wild and willing woman is going to take note. Let me help dress you, Andrew."

The smile appeared, sparking the yummy dimple in his cheek. His eyes glimmered with naughtiness. "As opposed to undressing me?"

"*What?*" And had she thought of him as both yummy and naughty?

"Sense of humor . . . I was working on it."

"Oh. I knew that." Pasting on her best *Tawny knows all* look, she assured, "Trust me, shopping is a must-do event. We can pick up some new boxers and briefs while we're at it."

"Both?"

"Of course! Women want both. One puts what you have on display, the other hides it just enough to make us curious." Not that she meant to include herself as part of that "us" factor, or to drop her gaze to his crotch. She'd wondered if he could see how damp her panties were. If the obvious bulge of his groin was a sign, the answer was a big yes. One big, thick, long, hard yes.

Desperate to get her mind out of his briefs, or boxers, or whatever it was he wore beneath his grandpa slacks, Tawny looked up and said, "Just not both at once."

Andrew chuckled, the sound surprisingly deep and rich. Like his ass, his kiss and so much more, the sound shouldn't have belonged to a nerd. "Right. I should be done working on your computer by six thirty. Is it okay if I pick you up at seven?"

"It's a date. A shopping date," she amended quickly. She hoped it was fast enough to stop him from believing she wanted a date of any other kind. It hadn't been even close to fast enough to stop her from wondering how a real date with Andrew, the nerd who seemed less and less like one with every moment, might end.

Andy had endured the shopping trip, much of which had to do with the fact that his true taste matched Tawny's well. He wasn't making any promises about lasting through the movie. She'd suggested they take in the ten-o'clock show since they were already out, and the obvious place to take a woman on a first date was a dark theater. Plenty of opportunity to get his arm around her shoulders, or even better, his hand on her thigh.

Sitting in the last row of the nearly empty theater, directly behind a couple who'd passed the necking stage and were now into the under-the-clothes, fondling and moaning stage, he didn't want his arm around her shoulders or his hand on her thigh. He wanted her naked beneath him and crying out his name.

Shit, he had to remember she was a potential felon. He'd

used her morning absence from her computer to rig it to freeze up and require assistance to fix; he could have gone in the back way and networked to her system from his own, but didn't want the tracks leading back to him. While she'd seemed hesitant about his looking at her computer while she was away, he hadn't found anything to suggest suspicious activity, just file after file of design work. His gut said he'd find the same lack of evidence when he retrieved the mini recorder from her phone.

Rick would be pissed when he reported in next, but Tawny wasn't shaping up to be a criminal. From the way he'd observed her interacting with Jilly to the many pictures set about her living room of her with who looked to be her parents and brothers, he could guess the only thing she wanted out of Joyce was friendship. Between Joyce's timid nature and Tawny's out there attitude, it seemed an unlikely match. But then, so did Tawny and an IT geek, and she'd been plenty attracted to him earlier today.

With his face inches from her spread thighs, the scent of her arousal had been difficult to ignore. The sight of it darkening her skimpy panties had been damned impossible. The slick sounds and heavy breathing coming from the couple in the row in front of them was more than impossible to ignore. Only one thing made that sound: a finger pumping into an aroused pussy.

Hot breath caressed Andy's ear and he turned far enough to realize that the couple in front of them weren't the only ones breathing hard. Tawny's focus was riveted on the pair, her breath coming out in uneven waves.

He should remember she was hands-off material and leave her alone. Only, the thought of toying with her was too much to resist. He leaned toward her until her springy red curls tickled his nose and his lips feathered along her earlobe, and whispered, "Is that the kind of thing you had in mind for my first date?"

Observation was a key part of his PI job. Despite the darkness, he didn't miss the way she shivered or the rough edge to her quiet laugh. "Not even close. That's just—"

"Exciting?" He didn't bother to stop his stimulation from reflecting in his tone. Even nerds got horny, right?

Tawny jerked her face toward him, their lips almost brushing. She pulled back a few inches. "Is it to you?"

Andy leaned in closer, greedily inhaling her electric scent of spicy cinnamon. Kissing her wouldn't be wrong, not if he did it for the sake of the assignment. He found her mouth in the dark and quieted her startled gasp with his lips. He rubbed once softly, then retreated far enough to murmur, "Call me a nerd, but, yeah, hearing the way she's panting, knowing his fingers are inside her cunt, fucking her until she's so wet and hot she can't hold back any longer, that's exciting."

"I've never heard you talk that way, Drew."

She sounded breathless. Not nearly breathless enough, though. He wanted her needy, hungry, aching for his touch— that's the way he'd been since turning back to find himself face-to-crotch with her this morning at the office. He'd have her that way in a heartbeat if it wasn't for the fact that he was working a case and that he'd already pushed his luck with his words. "Sorry, it slipped out. I guess I overheard one of my sisters' boyfriends talk that way. I didn't mean to offend you."

"I wasn't offended. Just . . . surprised."

"Maybe I'm naturally impulsive after all." And maybe the longer they sat there whispering about sex in the dark, the more he wanted that very thing.

Adjusting his cock so that it didn't feel so liable to split his boxers and slacks, Andy straightened and focused on the movie screen. He grabbed a mint from his coat pocket and popped it in his mouth, well aware that the cool taste would never be enough to calm his hard dick. Then again, he didn't have to calm his dick—just make Tawny not want it.

NIGHT SECRETS / 133

On the big screen, the guy in the hero role took out a high-tech gadget that resembled a souped-up Palm Pilot and proceeded to use it to track the whereabouts of the villain. Andy worked with and researched surveillance equipment regularly enough to know that the device didn't exist in the real world, but Tawny wouldn't know that. "No way, he has the new GeoMac V7," he said, as if it was the best thing since cleavage. "I'd kill to get my hands on one of those things." He glanced at her. "Do you have any idea the capabilities that thing has? With its speed and unlimited storage, you'd never need another hand-held again."

Her mumbled, "Uh, yeah," response assured he'd accomplished his goal of firmly resettling his geek hat and eliminating any chance he had of getting his mouth back on hers or anywhere else on her shapely body.

"No kiss?" Tawny bit her lip to keep from calling herself an idiot out loud. So Andrew had walked her to her front door in a fashion that made their night out seem like a real date—that didn't mean she wanted a kiss. She *didn't* want one. She hadn't even wanted the one he'd given her in the movie theater.

Right, and she also hadn't been so stimulated by the sounds of the guy in front of them fingering his date, she'd probably left behind a cum stain on her seat.

It was strange and inexplicable and something she never saw coming in a million years, but she wanted Andrew's kiss. Wanted his touch. She wanted to drag him inside her house and live up to her wild-woman image again and again. And it wasn't just because she'd gone so long without getting any that she deserved a Born-Again Virgin label. If that was the case, any man would do. But any man wasn't looking good right now. Just one. The nerd standing in front of her.

His eyebrows pulled together behind his glasses. "Do you think I need the practice?"

"Honestly?"

He nodded, and she smiled. Too bad for him that honesty wasn't on the menu tonight. Not that he would be suffering from what was on the menu. "You weren't that bad, but your technique could use some fine-tuning."

"I guess we'd better have one then."

"Great!"

His look said he was shocked by her enthusiasm, and she quickly added, "I want you to be as ready as possible to face your next sexual conquest."

"Ah, gotcha. How's this?"

Andrew brought his hands to her forearms, lightly rubbing as he bent his head and brushed her lips with the same soft kiss he'd given her in the theater. Unlike in the theater, he didn't stop with the subtle rub, but slid his hands down her hips and around to her bottom. Palming her ass, he tugged her to him and sank his tongue between her lips. Kneading her buttocks, he licked over her teeth and found her tongue with his. The taste of him exploded in her mouth, while the maleness of him burst to life against her belly.

With each lap of his tongue against hers, his cock rubbed harder and grew longer, thicker against her stomach. Tawny sighed into his mouth, her fingers anxious to move between them and stroke his hard length. She'd accepted that she wanted him. There was nothing stopping her now. Nothing but the fact that they were standing on her front porch in a well-lighted subdivision and she'd told him that all this would be about was a kiss.

Andrew lifted from her lips. Frustration unleashed within her over the idea that he was finished. Screw their audience—if anyone else was even up after midnight on a Tuesday night. She reached for him with the intention of tugging him back into another kiss. He moved his hands beneath her short, snug skirt and planted his lips on her neck before she could make a move.

His tongue came out, licking at her hypersensitized skin. She sucked in a breath, and then a deeper one as he moved his hands beneath the waistband of her panties and cupped her naked ass. Like the night air, his hands were cool in contrast to her heated skin. The contact as he slid his hands lower and rimmed her sex from behind was too amazing to deny.

"Yes, Drew! That's exactly right. Keep going."

His tongue lifted from her neck, his mouth quickly replacing it. Nibbling on the damp flesh, he brought his hand around and fingered her from the front, running his hand along the length of her slit. Tawny's pussy pulsed and she bit her lip to keep from begging him to go any farther. Seconds later, she learned that begging wasn't required.

One long finger pushed into her sheath and she cried out with the rapid entry. "Don't stop now. You're doing so well."

His mouth moved upward to her ear, first nibbling on the shell and then dipping its tongue into the center. She shivered as gooseflesh rose on her skin, and then whimpered as he sweetly worked his finger inside her wet, aching body. He pushed in and out, eliciting the same slick sound they'd heard in the theater. Those sounds had Tawny aroused beyond reason. These sounds, accompanied by the magnificent feel of Andrew fucking her with his finger, had her pussy afire and her legs quaking.

He added a second finger and pumped them inside her dripping cunt. She closed her eyes at the force of pleasure building within her. Orgasm was just around the corner. Orgasm that crashed over her the instant he used his thumb on her clit. One brush and tremors sliced through her. Heat consumed her and her heart constricted so tightly, it bordered on pain.

"Just like that, Drew. Oh, man, just like that!" she shouted as her sex contracted around him.

Cream gushed around his fingers and soaked her panties. He continued to push into her, milking her sopping cunt with fast thrusts until the last of the juices drained from her body. Letting go of her ear with his mouth, Andrew stepped back to give her a thoughtful look.

What was he thinking? Tawny silently questioned as she righted her clothing and struggled for sane breathing. No way in hell about statistics. Maybe about underwear, though. About the fact that she'd allowed hers to become drenched in plain view of her neighbors and anyone who might be driving by. Thank God she had her brazen image to fall back on.

"So," he finally said, "how was that?"

That was his thought—or, rather, concern? She was lucky to still be standing in the aftermath of her orgasm, and he was afraid he hadn't been good enough? If he wasn't sure of how good he'd been, why tell him and ruin her chances of getting a second helping? "You're nearly ready. A few more practice runs and I'm sure you'll be at the top of your game."

A grin settled on his face that was almost cocky. Without a word, he turned and started for his car. He turned back after a few steps. She held her breath with the idea he might give her that second helping immediately. Could she be so lucky?

"Tawny?"

"Yeah?" Please ask to stay. Please.

"Thanks for the lesson. I already feel more confident about finding the right woman to next warm my bed."

"Right. The lesson." That's all tonight had been in his eyes. If it wasn't, he already would have found that right woman. He would see that she was standing in front of him. Only, she wasn't, because Tawny was not his type any more than he was hers. Now, to convince her turbulent hormones and aching pussy . . .

3
_____

"How goes the manhunt?" Jilly asked, entering the sixth-floor ladies' room and capturing Tawny's gaze in the mirror that extended the length of the double-sink basin.

Tawny stopped applying her signature hot-pink, *you know you want to do me* lipstick to frantically glance around the room.

Jilly laughed. "Relax, already. We're alone. And since when have you cared if someone hears us talking about sex? Unless you've finally dropped the love-goddess charade." She cast a meaningful look at Tawny's second-skin attire: knit black pants and a low-cut red sweater made complete by three-inch black heels. "Judging by the clothes, I'm guessing not."

Tawny should have dropped the act. She should have told Andrew from the beginning that she wasn't the brazen woman she made herself out to be. But she hadn't, and now she was trapped into keeping up the charade until Andrew's lust lessons were complete.

Right. Trapped. Ending last night with his masterful hands up her skirt had been such a hardship. Orgasms always were.

Tawny rolled her eyes, hoping Jilly would take it as a "whatever" expression. "I don't care if my own supposedly breathtaking sex life is put on display. I just don't want Andrew's name being brought up and people thinking there's something going on between us."

"Is there?"

Last night, after the way he'd left, Tawny had been sure the answer to that question was no. Then she'd lain awake for hours, recalling the feel of his erection cradled against her belly, and the hungry way he'd kissed her. Those weren't the signs of a man using her solely for sexual education. They were the signs of a man who wanted to get her naked and sweaty as badly as she ached to have him the same way.

God help her, she was going bonkers with lust for the geek. "I told you, I'm giving him lessons on how to get sex with other women. It has nothing to do with me."

"Mmm . . ." Jilly caught her lower lip in her teeth, looking as though she didn't believe Tawny. She released her lip and turned back to the mirror. Relocating a few errant strands of blond hair, she said, "So, I know I can't be there Saturday night to help find your new stud man, but what do you say I come over in the afternoon and help you get ready?"

Saturday night?

Tawny recalled yesterday's conversation and grimaced. At the time, landing a one-night lover had seemed the only cure to her Andrew craving. Now, despite the fact that her Andrew craving was stronger than ever, it was the last thing she wanted to do.

She shot her friend a "get real" look. "Do you honestly think I would go to a club on my own?"

"Brazen Tawny would."

Oh, that was low. Throwing her alter ego at her. "Yeah, well, open your eyes, girl, because I'm not brazen Tawny."

A knowing smile in place, Jilly glanced at her snug attire.

"Could have fooled me." She sobered. "In fact, you did fool me. As you might recall, even I bought into the whole wild-woman routine for quite some time."

"You were preoccupied." Jilly had been so concerned with keeping up her cool-operator persona that she'd missed Tawny's transformation from everyday girl to bad girl with too damned much perkiness. That didn't change the fact that Tawny wasn't a bad girl. Or perky. Take now, for example. She didn't feel perky in the least—more like doing bodily harm to her big fat mouth for getting her into this situation.

"The point remains—"

"That I have a design due to the marketing heads in less than an hour," Tawny finished for Jilly and started for the ladies' room door. She couldn't have this conversation now. Not when she wasn't convinced Jilly didn't have a point. The way she'd acted last night, shamelessly offering herself to Andrew in public view, was something brazen Tawny would do, but never the real Tawny. Unless the real Tawny and brazen Tawny were becoming one.

Refusing to ponder the possibility, Tawny stepped out into the hallway. Or so she thought she had. The sudden pain that exploded between her temples suggested she'd actually plowed into a brick wall.

"Whoa!" Two strong hands grabbed hold of her forearms, setting her back a ways and stabilizing her. "You okay?"

"No kidding," Jilly's voice came from beside her. "I thought you were going to rebound off him and take me out."

Tawny gave her head a shake. The pain that had come with the collision of her nose into what she now realized was a man's chest turned to a shallow throb as that man's face came into focus. Andrew.

The memory of the last time they'd seen one another washed over her. Heat spread up her neck and fanned into her cheeks. A glance at those long, capable fingers wrapped around her arms had her sex tingling. He'd held her this way last night, right before he'd proceeded to kiss her, stroke her and rock her world.

Moisture damped her panties. She opened her mouth to thank him for catching her, praying it would be enough to get his hands off her. Nothing came out. Nice. Either the crash had injured her vocal cords or she'd officially turned into an idiot.

"Nod if you're okay," Andrew suggested.

She did so quickly, sighing when he released her. A slight smile tugged at his mouth. "Well, that's a relief. Your nose is so red, I was afraid I'd broken it." She lifted a hand to rub her nose, and his smile turned to the sexy smile.

Sexy? Yeah, she'd admitted she wanted him, but to think the nerd was sexy? Okay, so that dimple was pretty damned hot in a way that made her tongue move over her teeth with the urge to lick the dimple.

"You sure you're okay?" Jilly asked.

Tawny glanced at her friend's concerned expression. Enough playing mute. She had a design to get out, and so long as she stood here having naughty thoughts of Andrew, she would never get the design wrapped up on time. "Fine," she said as energetically as possible, while starting to turn toward the other end of the hallway. "Geez, girl, it was just a little crash. No biggie. Hey, thanks for rescuing me, Drew, but I seriously have to run. I have to get a job done by noon or Larry's going to freak."

"It was my pleasure."

The response was formal; the look in his eyes anything but. Tawny's breath caught at his wolfish expression. Did he realize how he was looking at her? Could Jilly see it?

"So, how's it going, Andrew?" Jilly asked, acting like Tawny was already gone. "Great shirt, by the way."

Needing to look away from his face before she questioned his expression aloud, Tawny focused on his shirt and once more found the breath lodging in her throat. She'd never expected him to start wearing his new clothes immediately, or to the office at all. The soft, greenish-brown cotton matched his eyes perfectly. And the way the material hugged his molded pecs . . . Her mouth watered while her pussy grew wetter.

Oh, man, he had better have been trying out the sense-of-humor thing again last night when he'd walked away from her as if she was nothing more than his teacher. If he showed up wearing that shirt to tonight's lesson, she'd never be able to keep her hands to herself, whether he wanted her or not. She'd be the impulsive one this time. She'd have him pushed up against the door before he could say hello. Have her tongue in his mouth and her fingers wrapped around the rigid length of his cock.

". . . you're okay? Tawny?"

With a groan of displeasure, Tawny surfaced from the hedonistic vision filling her mind. Jilly stood next to her, alone. Tawny looked down the hallway and spotted Andrew walking away. Andrew, who'd not only worn a new shirt, but also new pants. The way the casual tan Dockers hugged his taut ass was pure perfection and incredibly unfair. She ached to let go a wolf whistle, but couldn't see even brazen Tawny doing that while on the job.

"Something you forgot to mention?" Jilly questioned.

"What do you mean?" Tawny asked absently, unable to look away from Andrew's retreating backside. He *so* did not look like a geek from this angle.

"That Andrew got a little more than a kiss."

Her attention shot back to Jilly, and Tawny just managed to stifle her gasp. Talking about Andrew in the privacy of the bathroom was one thing. Out here, when her friend wasn't even attempting to lower her voice, anyone could overhear. She whispered, "Why would you think something so ridiculous!"

Jilly's gaze narrowed shrewdly. She grabbed hold of Tawny's arm and pulled her back into the ladies' room. When the door closed, she said, "The way he looked at you. Not to mention the way you couldn't stop looking at his ass when he walked away. I have to admit it looks better than I ever would have believed possible in those Dockers, but good God, woman, I thought I was going to have to call 911 for the jaws of life to pull you free of your stupor."

"I haven't slept with him," Tawny retorted defensively, and winced. The big mouth was at it again. An innocent person would never have made such a claim.

"But you want to, and he wants you just as badly."

Then she'd seen the hot way he'd look at her? Tawny nearly laughed at the anticipation filling her. Whoever would have believed Andrew Korben could have her so tied up in lust knots? Hell, just two short days ago she'd been fighting off images of him wielding a flog while reciting statistics. Geek he might be, but from what she'd experienced so far, he was quite capable of keeping his nerdiness at bay long enough to get her hot and bothered and dripping with desire.

Tawny feigned a disgusted look. "You know, at moments like this, I seriously miss the Jilly in witch's clothing."

Jilly laughed. "Oh, come on. I know I haven't been around as much as usual lately, but we're best friends. If you can't come clean with me about your Andrew obsession, who can you come clean with?"

"It's not an obsession." That would entail much more than the yearning to strip him naked and lick him from head to toe. Tawny shivered over the idea and the resulting twinge of longing it shot between her thighs. "It's just . . . strange. We're so different—night and day—and yet there's something there."

Jilly nodded understanding. "That makes you want him. If you remember, there was a time when I felt the same way about Brendan, like the two of us could never mesh beyond a few nights of sex, and the safest thing I could do was avoid him at all costs. I was wrong, and so might you be."

"You're suggesting that me and Andrew could work out in

the long run?" Tawny asked incredulously. "Short-term maybe, but long-run, no way." Even short-term was presuming that he wanted her as more than a teacher. She couldn't guess at that. She shouldn't. Okay, so there was that possibility, upped by the wolfish look he'd given her moments ago. Just in case there was a chance of the possibility becoming reality, she'd be sure to have on her best thong when he arrived for his nightly session.

The thought of the red and black number riding the crack of her ass merely because she'd sat down while wearing too-tight jeans brought tremors of distaste. The thought of Andrew tugging it between her butt cheeks and over the aroused lips of her sex had shudders of a whole other kind traveling through her.

He probably didn't want her, but she couldn't stop the trickle of liquid desire at the idea that maybe he did.

"This is going to be so up your alley."

Andy glanced over at Tawny as he followed her directions into the heart of downtown Atlanta for some destination she'd yet to reveal. She sat looking out the passenger-side window of the economical sedan he'd rented as part of his nerd guise. She shifted in her seat as exuberantly as a kid at Christmas. "Sounds like it."

"We're almost there."

The grin she sent him was full of excitement, and didn't even come close to belonging to a criminal. It did, however, have the power to stir his cock. She was always a knockout, but when she was grinning over something that truly excited her, she was drop-dead, *test his willpower to keep his hands to himself* gorgeous. As if his willpower hadn't been tested enough from the moment he'd picked her up.

Tonight she'd didn't wear a tiny skirt, breast hugging top and do-me pumps. Tonight she wore sensible jeans, a sweat-shirt and tennis shoes. Her vivid red ringlets were pulled back in a low ponytail. Even her cinnamon scent had been replaced with a sedate vanilla. She was nothing like the siren he'd come to know, and for some twisted reason it made him want to get her naked all that much more.

There would be no getting her naked. Just like there would be no more kisses or climaxes. He'd been reckless last night, egged on by the couple in the theater and his building lust to get into Tawny's panties. In his line of work, recklessness could get you killed. While he didn't believe Tawny could harm him more than she could a fly, he wasn't about to leave anything to chance. If that meant ending the evening home alone, giving himself a hand job to still the rampant want she inspired in him, that was the way it would have to be.

At Tawny's command, Andy braked at a four-corner stop. Tawny's hand shot out, grabbing his forearm and his attention. Her grin was so huge his shaft stood no chance of softening any time soon. "Ta da! Are you excited yet?"

Growing more so every time he looked her way. She focused back out the window, and he followed the direction of her gaze to the small corner shop on the other side of the street. All thoughts of sex died as alarm pummeled him in the gut. "A bookstore?" And not just any bookstore, but the one his younger sister managed.

He glanced at the dashboard clock. Eight thirty. Joyce typically left by six. He could only hope that today was a typical day. He and Rick had decided it best to keep Joyce in the dark about checking out her new friend's potentially nefarious behavior. Now would be a hell of a time for her to find out, and reveal all to Tawny in the process.

"Yes and no," Tawny said. "It gets better. Find a spot to park and I'll show you."

Andy parallel-parked a few shops up the street from the bookstore. Wariness ate at him as he got out of the car and came around to open Tawny's door.

Remembering his disguise, he frowned. "That probably wasn't the right thing to do. A bad boy would never open the door for a woman, right?"

She climbed out and hoisted the strap of a plain beige satchel over her shoulder. Right about now she looked innocent enough to be a schoolgirl. "We're making you into a sex magnet, not a bad boy. Either way, opening the door is a great touch."

"Why not a bad boy?"

She smiled sympathetically. "You're doing great with the lessons and being impulsive and everything, but the bad-boy image is a little much to aim for."

"What would it take to make you change your mind?" He happened to know he was the bad boy every bit as much as she was the bad girl. That she thought otherwise meant he was playing the nerd role far better than he'd guessed.

Tawny sent him a contemplative look as they started down the sidewalk for the bookstore. They'd nearly reached the front steps when she stopped and said, "It's all about attitude. You don't have the bad-boy attitude. I don't think it's something you can learn, either. Sorry. But, honestly, it doesn't take away from your appeal." She blinked as if she hadn't meant to say those last words, and then looked toward the bookstore. "Here we are. Better hurry and get inside before things start."

"Things?" It wasn't what he wanted to ask. No, that would be exactly how appealing she found him, and if she was as painfully aroused after he'd left last night as he'd been. Only, those questions wouldn't be asked. He was done having thoughts of her and sex, starting now.

Tawny grabbed his hand and tugged him up the steps to the door of the Book Shed. Bells jangled merrily overhead as they moved inside the store, but those bells had nothing on her smile as she turned back to say, "After dragging you shopping last night, I figured I owed you a night of being yourself. Tonight's

146 / *Jodi Lynn Copeland*

for you, Andrew. I guessed coming here would be the perfect way to start things out. After this, whatever we do is up to you, no matter how boring you think I might find it."

Andy forced a smile of his own, while inside his gut felt like it was made of lead. Dirty, rotten lead. She'd dressed the way she had and brought him here, somewhere she obviously wouldn't go on her own, to give him a night off from his sex lessons. He never would have guessed that such a kind action could make him feel like complete shit.

As she led him to the back of the store, guilt speared him for the lies he'd told her since the day he'd begun working at Neilson. Lying was a part of his job, and, until tonight, had never bothered him. Was it that no one in the past had ever done anything quite so selfless before? Why the guilt now, after years of working as a PI?

He didn't have the answer. He only knew that he wanted to drag her into a deserted aisle and confess all, including that he didn't have any wild sisters who dated even wilder men. He just had a meek sister he hoped to hell wouldn't be getting the rough end of things once Andy had a chance to speak with his brother-in-law and tell him to try another source for his information leak, because Tawny wasn't it.

"Andrew? What are you doing here?"

Dread hit Andy hard at the unmistakably soft sound of his sister's voice. He looked up to find Joyce standing a few feet away in front of the store's door. Voices came from inside. He realized in a flash where Tawny had been leading him. The book club meeting his sister held every Wednesday night. Damn, how could he have forgotten?

Tawny sent a surprised look from Joyce to Andy. "You know each other?

Joyce nodded. "Yes. He's my—"

"Best customer," Andy cut her off. "I'm always in here checking out the latest technical magazines." Realizing that Tawny still held his hand, he shook it free and said to Tawny, "I just re-membered I owe Joyce for a book she mailed me last month. Go on inside and I'll join you as soon as I pay for it."

Tawny frowned. "But the meeting's going to start in a sec."

"I hate being late on stuff." Christ, he sounded whiny. Fighting off a grimace, Andy laid the whine on even thicker. "If I don't pay it off now, I won't be able to concentrate enough to enjoy the meeting. Besides, it can't start without the coordina-tor." He glanced at Joyce. "Wouldn't that be your job as the store manager?"

Her blond eyebrows winged together in confusion—the ac-tion and shared eye color the only traits that marked the two as siblings. "Yes. It is. I can take care of the charge now."

"Great." He beamed at Tawny. "Get us a good seat. I'd hate to get stuck in the back after you picked out such an ideal place to start off my night."

The frown still clung to Tawny's lips, but she nodded. "All right. I'll see you guys inside."

The moment Tawny was out of sight, Joyce asked, "What was that about? And how do you know Tawny?"

Andy glanced around for eavesdroppers. Finding no one in listening distance, he looked back at his sister. "Is there some-where we can talk?"

"The stockroom, I guess." She hesitated. "I should get the meeting started, Andrew. I don't want anyone being upset if there's a delay."

He cursed under his breath. That was his sister, always con-cerned about the rest of the world. When it came to herself, she didn't put forth nearly enough effort. He couldn't bring the confidence to her life in the next few minutes that twenty-six years hadn't accomplished, so he focused on what he might be able to achieve in that time. "They can wait a minute. Please, Joyce, this is important."

"All right." She moved to the meeting-room door and

ducked her head inside. "I'll be just a couple minutes and we can get started. Help yourself to juice and cookies while you wait."

Andy shook his head as she returned. "You're too nice."

She cast her attention to the carpet, but not before he caught her sheepish look. He wanted to grab hold of her hair and force her head up high. He couldn't instill confidence in minutes, but the thought of her acting so subservient at home, around Rick, twisted his guts.

"The stockroom's this way," Joyce said softly. Several seconds later they stepped into a musty-smelling storage room overflowing with books and magazines. She shut the door and swiveled back, bringing her attention up from the floor. "So, are you and Tawny dating? She doesn't seem like your type."

"She's exactly my type," he said too briskly. He added in a sedate voice, "But, no, we aren't." They were just . . . not lovers. Last night they might have come close to that, but that was as far as things would ever get. He forced himself to concentrate on the matter at hand. "What I have to tell you is confidential, Joyce. I need your promise that you won't tell a soul; not even Rick."

Her lips pressed together. She hesitated several seconds before nodding. "All right. Unless he asks. He doesn't like my keeping secrets."

The concern Andy had felt over his sister's safety since hearing the threat in Rick's voice two days ago escalated. He was tempted to ask if her husband had ever showed signs of violence, but couldn't bring himself to do it. Joyce was a delicate woman, but also one he trusted to come to him if the need was there. He hoped to God there was never a need.

"I'm undercover," he said, opting for half truths over a complete lie. He had no choice but to show a false face to the suspects he came up against. He would do anything to avoid showing that face to family. Or to Tawny. Right—as if he had a choice. "Tawny's a suspect in a case I'm working."

Joyce's eyes went wide. She brought a hand up to cover the gasp that slipped from her mouth. "Oh, my gracious! She seems so sweet. What did she do?"

"Nothing. She's not guilty. I don't think she's guilty," he amended, knowing that stating the words as truth was based more on hope than facts. The facts were there, as well—just not as strongly as the hope. "I can't tell you anything else. I just need you to play along. I know she's sort of your friend, but for now I need you to lie. No, not to lie, just to agree with me. Act like I'm a customer of yours. A nerdy one."

The wide-eyed look faded. She laughed into her hands. Letting her arms fall at her sides, she looked at him through amused eyes. "You have her believing you're a nerd?"

Andy chuckled at how ludicrous the idea had to seem. She'd met many of the women who'd come through his life, and knew about the rest. He could guess she didn't approve of the casual way he treated relationships, but admitting to that was something Joyce would never do. In this instance, at least, he was glad for her timidity. "Apparently so. She said I could never be a bad boy; I don't have the attitude."

She giggled some more, this time not bothering to cover her mouth, but letting the sound roll out freely. Tears of amusement filled her eyes. Andy's heart warmed. How long had it been since he'd seen Joyce's true smile, heard her honest laughter? He didn't know the answer and it brought his concerns over Rick's treatment of her back to the forefront of his mind.

He'd turned a blind eye on his sister's two-year marriage, mostly because he wanted to believe she was happy. He couldn't bring himself to keep turning that blind eye. Once he had Rick convinced that Tawny had nothing to do with the information leak at his ad firm, Andy would take on a case for himself. One he prayed revealed that Rick was an ideal husband deserving of Joyce's love.

"This is really beautiful, Andrew."

Andy looked from the starlit sky to the woman leaning against the hood of the sedan beside him. "Call me Drew. I like it."

"Drew," Tawny amended, a smile curving her lips. "So, do you come here a lot?"

Whenever he was hoping to get lucky. Something about the atmosphere and the throwback to parking as a teenager never ceased to get the women hot in a matter of minutes and naked nearly as fast. He shouldn't have brought Tawny here, for those exact reasons. After leaving the book-club meeting, which had turned out to be only partially the drag he'd imagined, she'd suggested they go to his favorite place. The clearing in the center of the heavily treed metro park sprang to mind and was out of his mouth before he could stop it. "I come here quite a bit to observe." He lied about the first part, but not the second. "I'd once hoped to be an astronomer."

Instead of answering indifferently, the way she did when he was acting the nerd, she leaned toward him and her smile grew. "It's an intriguing subject. I took a few courses when I was in college. It started as a Greek mythology fetish. When I learned that most of the gods can be found in the constellations, I had to see it firsthand."

Greek mythology? Now *that* he'd never have guessed from this woman any more than he'd have believed she would attend a book-club meeting on her own. Only, she had to have, because in hindsight he remembered Rick telling him that's how Joyce and Tawny met. He'd done a fair share of research on her before going to work for Neilson. That research had obviously left out a good deal, including the way her expression could go from friendly to hungry in two seconds flat.

Tawny's gaze went to his mouth. Her tongue slipped out, rimming her lips. Tonight they were unpainted. He'd guessed that he would prefer the hot-pink lipstick she favored to au naturel. He'd been wrong. Andy had vowed not to think about sex where Tawny was concerned. Apparently he was about to be wrong about that, too. "Do you have any more of those? Fetishes?"

She nodded, her attention never leaving his mouth. "Kisses," she murmured. "I have a thing for kisses." She leaned closer until her hip rubbed against his.

His shaft hardened with the subtle brush and her almost innocent actions. Whether her reserved behavior was part of making tonight about his supposedly natural self or something else entirely, he couldn't stop from giving into the moment. "It makes sense. You're good at it. Me, I'm not so good."

"Do you need more practice?"

"Yeah." He slipped an arm around her waist. "A lot of it."

Tawny's arms came up, wrapping loosely around his neck. She tugged gently, as if encouraging him to come into her arms. Andy went, but—he could guess—not in the way she'd expected. Catching her around the waist, he lifted her onto the hood of the sedan and moved into the cradle of her thighs. The hard ridge of her mound brushed against his cock through their clothing. With a low moan, she squirmed. The pressure against his shaft increased with her wriggling, and he covered her mouth with his before he could speak the sort of carnal words she'd question coming from Andrew the geek.

Her usual cinnamon scent might not cling to her tonight, but she tasted every bit as spicy hot as the woman he'd kissed the past two nights. The restless way she returned his kiss, sliding her tongue between his lips and rubbing his with demanding strokes was the brazen Tawny he'd come to know. The needy way her hands moved from his neck to his waist and then up under his shirt to coast over his abdomen and pectoral muscles suggested she was that brazen woman for certain.

"Women like to touch." She pulled back from his mouth as if she thought he required step-by-step instruction. "Especially when a guy has a body as good as yours."

She could give all the instructions she wanted, particularly if it meant she'd be talking dirty, but he planned to give a few of his own. He slid his hands under the hem of her sweatshirt and up beneath the silky cups of her bra. The night air was cool; the feel of her nipples as they beaded beneath his palms hot as hell. His balls drew tight to his body, commanding more space than what his briefs allowed.

"Men like to touch, too," he said roughly, not bothering to hide the effect caressing her bare breasts had on him.

"Yeah, they do." Her head fell to the side as he drew her nipples between his fingers and twisted. Her eyes closed with a husky mewl, her hands stilling their exploration beneath his shirt. "Oh, man, you have amazing hands, Drew. Strong with long fingers, perfect for cupping a woman's breasts or sliding inside her body."

Andy's pulse spiked with the thought of fingering her, feeling her sweet cunt creaming around his fingers the way it had last night. She'd been so fucking hot, so open to anything he'd wanted regardless of the fact that they were in plain sight. She was that way again now, and he couldn't stop from asking questions he was certain would never leave geeky Andrew's mouth. "Do you like to be touched that way? To feel a man's fingers inside your pussy, bringing you to climax?"

He plucked at a nipple. The breath wheezed from her mouth, fanning warmth into his face. She arched against his touch, her hips shifting once more and wreaking havoc on his aching dick. "I'm sure all women do," she said breathily.

He released her nipple and traveled his hands down her stomach. Leaving one to play at the dip of her surprisingly unadorned belly button, he brought the other to her crotch and rubbed her sex through her jeans. Tawny's eyes flickered open to reveal a building inferno of desire. He knew that need, felt it reflected in every part of him.

Applying a bit more pressure, he stroked the length of her slit, smiling wickedly when she squirmed. "How many fingers do you like at once?"

"It depends on the guy. On the situation." She whimpered and opened her legs wider, making it clear how anxious she was to have him beneath the fabric. "The two you had inside me last night felt perfect. But maybe I'm remembering wrong. Maybe you should try it again. I'd hate to give you bad guidance."

"That would be awful." Stifling a chuckle, he helped her to her feet. He ached to rip the jeans from her body and follow suit with her panties, stripping away the layers until her pussy was bared to the moonlight—even better, to his tongue. Instead, he stepped back and watched dry-mouthed as she unzipped her jeans. She pushed them and her panties down her legs, revealing a triangle of dark red curls and an arousal that mingled with the pine scent of the woods and the clean smell of the November air.

She toed off her sneakers and kicked aside the clothing. Lifting herself back onto the hood, she yelped upon contact of her bare bottom to the cold metal. "Chilly."

"I'll heat you up," he promised, returning between her thighs.

"Excellent. Confidence is the key to everything. Make the woman see how badly you want to please her, and she'll want to please you just as much in return."

Andy grinned. Confidence, she wanted? That he could give her in spades.

"Lean back," he ordered.

She hesitated an instant, but then did as he asked, leaning back on the hood. He lifted her legs up, positioning her knees so that they were bent toward the night sky. Her pussy was open to him now, and glistening in the moonlight with the juices of arousal. He was tempted to taste her, but that would be going against her instruction and ruining this game they played. If she even thought it was a game. Maybe to her this was all about fine-tuning his sexual education. For his sake, he hoped to hell not, because he had a feeling one night with Tawny would never be enough.

Inhaling a sharp breath at the potential implications of his thoughts, Andy slipped a finger past her damp curls and into her sheath. Hot, wet warmth surrounded him. His cock twitched. He pushed aside his own need and focused on hers. He worked his finger in and out of her cunt, bringing forth more cream.

His grin intensified when her hips bucked up and a throaty moan lit the still night. Though he could already guess her answer, he asked, "Is one enough?"

"Good." She sounded winded. "But I want another."

Eagerly, Andy added a second finger alongside the first, fingering her with long, hard strokes. The scent of her arousal grew stronger, obliterating the scents of the woods and the air. His nostrils flared. His tongue moved in his mouth with the urge to lap at her juices. He settled on working his finger faster, fucking her with vigor. "Better?"

"Oh . . . yeah," she breathed. "Better. Much better."

"Am I moving too fast?"

"No. Not fast enough. I need more. I want to feel more than your fingers this time. I want to—"

"This?" The temptation was too strong to ignore. He couldn't stand here, inhaling her heady scent, and not taste her. Grabbing hold of her thighs, he buried his head between her legs and sank his tongue into her sex.

Tawny's hips bucked up against his face. Her hands shot to his head, her fingers pushing into his hair. The breath panted from her lips. "Ohmigod! You . . . you've been studying."

He chuckled against her pussy and she shivered in response.

Studying was overrated. Firsthand experience had a definite appeal, as did feeling her come around him while he tongued her. He wanted to feel her orgasm, taste her essence as it dripped from her quaking body, more than he'd ever wanted to fuck a woman in his life, orally or otherwise. The thought urged him on, had his lazy licks turning to quick nibbles and darting thrusts. For long seconds he held on to her legs as she writhed beneath him, moaning, mewling, squeaking out words he couldn't understand. Then guilt grabbed hold of him by the throat and he pulled back his head and let her thighs go.

Shit, he couldn't do this. He couldn't have her this way when all she knew of him was lies. He couldn't because he truly did want her more than any woman before her. He wanted the woman who'd volunteered her nights to help a nerd get a better sex life, and the one who looked just as hot in street clothes as she did in barely there ones. He wanted her beyond tonight and beyond every single one of his lies. "This is wrong."

Tawny bolted up on her elbows. She shook her head wildly, loosening her ponytail. "No. No, it isn't. You were doing it exactly right. The only way to do it wrong is to stop once you've started. Don't stop, Drew. Please, don't stop permanently."

Damnit, he should. He should order her to get up and get dressed and then tell her every detail of his life and the lies between them. Only, he couldn't, not when she was looking at him through the vee of two of the most stunning legs he'd ever set eyes or hands on, begging him to continue.

"Sorry," he mumbled, apologizing not for stopping but for the fact that she would eventually despise him for the way he treated her tonight. Somehow he'd make it up to her, make her see once this whole ridiculous case was over that he wasn't a nerd, but a man who was seriously into her. A man who wanted her so damned badly, his dick felt ready to explode.

"Don't apologize. Think confidence. Think—"

He pushed his head back between her legs and plunged his

tongue into her sex. Catching her clit between thumb and fore-finger, he pulled at the swollen pearl, twisting until she bowed up and cried out.

Tawny's fingers threaded back through his hair, yanked. "Oh, hell, Drew!" she cried out, then added amidst ragged breaths, "You . . . learn . . . so . . . fast. . . ."

She released his hair and fell back against the hood. The air wheezed from her lungs. Tremors shook through her body. Around his tongue, her pussy lips contracted and released. Hot juice trickled onto his tongue and down his throat. The taste of her was alive in his body, in his mind. His cock throbbed. His heart hammered. He pulled from her sex as her orgasm reached a crescendo.

He had no right going further than what he already had. No right at all. But, fuck it, he had to have her.

Stepping back a few feet, he fumbled with his zipper, cursing when the tab refused to budge. Shit, he was acting like a pimple-faced kid on prom night, or, rather, a true nerd.

"Drew?"

He looked up to find Tawny sitting upright on the car's hood, eyeing him. He'd missed his opportunity. Tonight's lesson was finished and he'd be going home with a hard-as-hell erection and only his own hand to take care of it. Served him right. "Sorry, I just—"

"Let me help." She pushed off the car and came to him, seemingly mindless of her half-naked state and the fact that she looked like a seminude Eve padding sock-footed through the Garden of Eden.

Drew wasn't mindless. Liquid desire dribbled down her inner thighs and the tips of her nipples were so hard they looked ready to stab through her sweatshirt. He sighed as her words caught up with him. She didn't want him to stop, just to offer her help, because he was acting like a geek who'd never had a hard-on before. Arrogance attempted to raise its head, and make him say he could do it on his own. The thought of Tawny's warm fingers snaking into his pants and around his shaft stopped those cocky words from reaching his lips. "Thanks," he said instead.

"My pleasure."

No—Andy knew the moment she'd worked his zipper free and started his pants and briefs down his thighs—it was definitely all his. Her gasp as his cock sprang free was that of pure carnal delight. The eager way she fisted his shaft and pumped him spoke of raw want. He knew that want, had kept it caged far too long. It raged to get out, and it would take a better man than him to stop it.

Grabbing her around the waist, he lifted her up his body and growled, "Hold on."

The moment her legs locked around his middle, her arms around his neck, he took her mouth in a deep, wet kiss. Stroking her tongue with urgent licks, he bent for the wallet in the pocket of his discarded pants. He jerked out a condom with one hand, not caring what else fell out in the process, and then tossed the wallet aside. Consuming her with his kiss, he brought them both back to the car hood. This time he sank against it, using it for support as he brought a hand between their bodies and rubbed the slick head of his cock against the lips of her sex.

"You're hot, babe. Hot and wet. I can't stand not fucking you a second longer."

The shock over his coarse words was in Tawny's eyes, and then was quickly replaced by that of elation as he rolled on the condom, reared back and pushed into her. Cries of ecstasy tore from both their mouths. Her pussy lips gave way, sucking him in greedily, taking him all the way to the glorious hilt.

"How do you want it? Fast? Slow? Fast is my preference." Next time they'd go slow, presuming there was a next time. More likely she'd find out what a lying bastard he was and demand he never come within a hundred feet of her again.

"Fast." She used her grip on his shoulders to lift herself up his shaft and slam back down again. "Oh, yeah," she cried. "Definitely fast."

Lying bastard he might be, but right now that wasn't stopping Andy from either finding or giving pleasure. Holding her with one hand, he moved the other between them. As he pumped into her with long, firm strokes, he found and fingered her clit. He circled the tight pearl, quickening the pace with each thrust into her slick sheath. Tawny's erratic breathing and the pummel of her lush breasts against his chest had that pace hastening all the more.

Next time he'd have her breasts bared. He'd take his time sucking each delicious nipple, laving it, loving it. He'd have her wild mane of hair free to tickle and torment him. He'd have her in his bed, right where she belonged. And there would be a next time. They were too damned good together for there not to be.

"I can't . . . hold back . . . any longer," Tawny panted.

"Me neither, babe," Andy assured as his balls hugged his body with the savage need to release. "Come with me," he ordered, giving her clit a last tug.

Her sex convulsed around him, milking his shaft with urgent strength as climax washed over her in rippling waves. His orgasm followed quickly behind. As it tore through his body, shaking him to the core, Andy knew tonight's lesson was one neither of them would forget anytime soon.

4

Tawny paused outside her front door. Neither she nor Andrew had spoken more than a few words since he'd pulled from her body. As if by some silent agreement, they'd dressed and climbed into the sedan. Now here they stood, back in her light-brightened subdivision, on the verge of saying good night.

She didn't want to say good night. She wanted to yank him inside her house and tug off his clothes until he was standing naked and proud and ready for her. She wanted him to do the same, to strip away her jeans and sweatshirt and to utter more of the coarse words he'd used back at the park.

He'd either spent time around his sisters' rowdy boyfriends these last couple days, picking up on their explicit dialect and behavior, or he'd been skipping his morning exercise routine to study *The Kama Sutra*. Aside from a slight problem with his zipper, he hadn't been a fumbling nerd unsure of how to proceed. He'd been the bad boy she'd claimed he could never be. She'd been wrong, and she wanted that bad boy back.

But did that bad boy want to come back?

She still had no idea if he thought of her as anything more

than an instructor. The purpose of taking him to the book club meeting, wearing clothes that for once didn't expose more than they concealed, had been to show him she wasn't always the wild woman he believed. She was that woman to some extent— a larger one than she would have guessed a few short days ago— but also one who appreciated the simpler things in life. One who appreciated his geeky moments almost as much as his sexy ones.

Tawny leaned back against the door and found that now was one of the sexy moments. The way Andrew looked at her, his dark gaze smoldering in the fluorescent glow of the porch light, made it clear that he hoped for at least one more lesson tonight. Likely he believed that lesson would come in the form of a good-bye kiss. She had other plans.

She reached out and stroked a lone finger across the hard wall of his chest through the soft cotton of his shirt. Fluttering her lashes in a completely tacky way only brazen Tawny could pull off, she gave him her best naughty smile. "Sometimes bad boys spend the night."

"Are you sure?"

The roughness of Andrew's voice suggested he wanted to accept her offer. So, why the hesitation? Did he fear even after she showed him her tamer side that they were too different to last beyond a few days?

And had she implied that she wanted to be with him longer than the few days it would take to sate her sexual appetite?

She'd told Jillian that the two of them in the long run was improbable. But then he'd turned out to be so much more than she'd expected. Not a nerd who recited statistics in the heat of the moment; rather, one who heated her up all the more with his unexpectedly rough language.

As for his behavior the rest of the time, he wasn't too shabby there, either. Yeah, he had his computer and technology obsessions; man, she thought he might come on the spot when the hero dragged out that advanced-looking Palm Pilot at the theater last night. Orgasming over techie gadgets aside, he'd almost seemed to enjoy their shopping excursion, and his taste in movie selection was right on course with hers. Though she had yet to run into him during her early morning gym sessions, he said he liked working out—she'd more than witnessed the proof of that in his hard body and scrumptious ass—and while his sisters and their choices in men seemed wilder than she could ever imagine, he obviously cared a great deal about his family. All those things were biggies in her book, but were they big enough?

She shrugged off the question. There would be plenty of time to contemplate their relationship later. Right now all that mattered was showing him how badly she burned for him. How much more she wanted than a good-bye kiss.

Tawny closed the short distance that separated him. She rose on tiptoe to brush his mouth, her nipples rubbing against his chest and hardening to erect points in the process. He'd popped one of the mints—she noted he consumed mints the way most women did chocolate—into his mouth during the drive from the metro park to her house. The cool, crisp scent drifted from his lips, inviting her to slip inside.

She would be there soon, just as soon as she had him in her house; better yet, in her bed. A quick nibble at either corner of his mouth and she pulled back to breathe, "I am the teacher here. Haven't you ever heard 'teacher knows best'?"

The dimple shot to life in Andrew's left cheek. His hands came to her back, tugging her more firmly against his body and revealing that his cock was once more at full, gloriously hard attention. "I have heard a thing or two about that."

Moisture settled in her panties as she remembered the feel of his hard sex slamming into her. Whether it had to do with the length of time she'd gone without getting laid or simply his talent, he'd had her on the edge in seconds. She wanted to move slower this time, explore every inch of his delectable body, taste his silky essence sliding over her tongue.

Her heart beat faster with anticipation. Reaching behind her, she twisted the doorknob and pushed in the door a few inches. "Come inside. Let me introduce you to my bed."

"I want that."

And he wanted her. No way could he still think this was about making him into a sex magnet. She liked him just the way he was. Different yet quite possibly perfect for her.

Tawny stepped free from his hands and back through the doorway. From the dimly lit shadows, she reached to the hem of her sweatshirt and pulled it up and off. She cast the shirt aside and brought her hands to her breasts, toying with the nipples through the red silk of her bra. The breath snagged in her throat as a delicious sensation shot from her pebbled tips to her pussy. Never had touching herself felt so erotic. But, then, never before had she done so in front of another. Wanton Tawny had truly taken over.

She dragged one cup of her bra down and pulled a tight nipple between her fingers. "Tell me, how bad do you want it, Drew?"

His attention fixated on her breasts. His hands fisted at his sides, as if it was the only way he could stop from reaching out and touching. "Really bad," he said thickly. "Oh, babe, do I ever want it."

"Show me."

She expected more talk out of him—possibly hesitation. The breath huffed from her mouth as he took two steps forward and hoisted her into his arms. His mouth came down on hers hard, taking, demanding, devouring her whole. His tongue slipped between her lips, first stroking over hers and then pulling back to play a wicked game of dart and retreat that hinted at the blissful things to come.

Andrew kicked the front door closed. He moved through the dark living room as stealthily as if he had the vision of a panther. He paused when he reached the hallway, lifting from her lips to growl an impatient, "Bedroom?"

The animalistic sound reached down inside her, stoking to life a fire of need greater than anything she could accomplish on her own. Greater than anything she'd experienced at another's hands. Her bad boy was back and she ached to get her hands and mouth all over him.

"Down the hall," she said shortly, and nearly swore as her big mouth added, "But I need to use the bathroom first." God help her bladder, but she'd drunk a lot of coffee during the book club meeting, and now it was having its revenge.

With a grunt of protest, Andrew set her down. She reached for the wall switch. Bright light flooded the hallway and bled into the living room. She blinked like an owl and silently cursed her bladder. Really, was there any worse way to kill a moment than saying, "Put me down, I gotta take a pee?" Okay, so she hadn't said those exact words, but the implication was there.

Tawny glanced from the bathroom doorway to Andrew's face. Hunger shot from his eyes, impatience from the suddenly hard line of his mouth. Guilt for the impatience flooded her. She'd make up the short delay to him and then some.

Rising on tiptoe, she speared her tongue past his lips. Feeding from his mouth, she found his erection through his pants. She stroked his cock with two quick rubs she mimicked with her tongue, then stepped back, panting. "My bedroom's the last door on the right. I promise to be fast."

Andy wanted to forget that Tawny was a suspect in a case he was investigating and spend the time until she emerged from the bathroom getting naked and familiarizing himself with her bed. But she was a suspect. An innocent one as far as he was concerned, but that didn't change the facts. He was in her bedroom and he had to make use of that opportunity.

Quickly, he moved about the room, opening drawers and shuffling through papers, looking for anything that might hint at her involvement in taking information about Rick's ad firm and sharing it with others. The closet revealed a shitload of clothes and shoes; the filing cabinet next to her bed, paperwork on her car and financers. The brightly colored selection of bras and panties that filled her top dresser drawer had his mind threatening to roam back to the physical. His time was almost up, and that meant he had to keep his thoughts away from the ache in his dick a few seconds longer.

Andy dove to the floor and searched beneath the bed. Along with the expected collection of dust bunnies and cobwebs, several boxes revealed old photographs, items he recognized as scrapbooking material from the times he'd seen his mother creating the pages, and a short tub filled with racy lingerie and sex toys.

His cock throbbed over the plethora of toys. Handcuffs, dildos, whips, enough lubricant to last a lifetime . . . Rick wouldn't be happy with his findings, but Andy couldn't be more pleased.

The bathroom door opened with a *snick*. He shot up from the floor, grabbing from the tub a pair of fuzzy pink handcuffs and a thick black vibrator, and tucking them under the sheets near the head of the bed. The bulge was obvious, but then he had no plans to give Tawny the time to wonder over it.

He was through playing PI, through playing the nerd. It was bad-boy time.

Tawny entered the room. She'd freed her hair of the ponytail, and loose red ringlets spilled wildly about her face, framing a siren's smile. "Was that fast enough?"

His gaze went to her breasts. Pale, lush cleavage dotted with freckles spilled over the cups of her bra and invited his hands to come closer and fondle her nipples the way she'd done in the foyer. He accepted that invitation gladly, moving to her and filling his hands with the mounds. Her nipples strained against the red silk. He pushed the material down and rubbed his thumbs over the swollen tips. A breathy sigh slipped from her lips. Her head lolled to the side, sending tendrils of hair dancing over her chest and his hands.

If she thought he would let her off that easy for keeping him waiting while she freshened up—or did whatever else it was that women did in preparation for sex—she had another think coming. "Not even close to fast enough." He captured both nipples between finger and thumb and pinched. "You took too long. It's punishment time."

Her eyes snapped open. "P—punishment time?"

Her voice may have trembled, but he could see the excitement alive in the deep blue of her eyes, feel it in the heat that shot from her nipples. Laying a hand at her waist, he moved behind her and pulled her tightly against him. Through her jeans, he pressed his dick against the seam of her ass and whispered into her ear, "Punishment time."

Tawny trembled in his arms. Before she could speak, he lifted her against him and moved to the bed. He placed her onto her stomach and straddled her waist with his thighs.

She squirmed beneath him, attempted to push herself up. He grabbed a wrist and brought it to the headboard. Securing it in place with one hand, he found the fuzzy pink handcuffs with the other. He twined them around the center limb of the headboard and, to the sound of her stunned gasp, shackled one of the cuffs to her wrist.

Her breathing came in loud pants as she wriggled beneath him again and tucked her free hand under her body. "Drew? W—what are you doing?"

Chuckling, he easily pulled her hand from beneath her and shackled it alongside its mate. "Showing you how important punctuality is to me. After this I guarantee you'll never keep me waiting again."

"But . . . where did you get the cuffs?"

He brought his mouth to her back and ran his tongue the length of her spine, smiling when she shivered. "Under your bed, with a whole lot of other naughty things. You're a bad girl, Tawny. A very bad girl. I might just have to spank you."

"You were snooping," she accused, but didn't sound upset. More like thrilled at the prospect of feeling his hand paddle against her ass.

A guilty woman would sound upset, Andy thought, and then chased away the idea to come up on his knees beside her. He pulled her into the same stance. Nibbling at her neck, he undid her jeans and started them down her thighs. "You're glad."

And he was fucking overjoyed. Wedged between the firm slopes of her ass was a thin string of red silk decorated with shiny black pearls. At the metro park she'd undressed herself, removing her panties and jeans in one quick move. He hadn't known this scrap of delectation existed. Damned good thing. Had he, they never would have made it all the way back to her house without him fucking her a second time.

Andy reached around to her front and touched down on the tiniest patch of silk he'd ever had the pleasure of laying hands on. The tiniest, wettest patch. One that he had every intention of getting wetter yet.

He caressed part of her slit through the thin material and then slipped beneath it to push a finger into the wet heat of her pussy. Her sex shuddered around him. Her whimper coasted over her stimulated nerves, tightening his balls with painful pleasure. He worked his finger in and out of her slick body, coating it with her cream.

Pulling it free, he returned to the string. He dipped his finger beneath the edge, drawing back on the string and letting it return to her crack with a soft slap. Tawny's hips reared back. Her breath hitched out.

His own breathing heightened. His heart pounded. He ached to thrust into her this instant while her sweet ass waggled in his face. Only, her punishment wasn't finished. "Did you wear this for me, in the hopes that tonight's lesson would lead to this?"

"I . . ." She started in a tone that spoke of denial, but then quickly changed it to one of acknowledgement. Vibrant red hair brushed along her back as she nodded. "Yes, I wanted this. I've wanted it from the first time you kissed me. From the first time I leaned against you and felt your cock, hard and ready."

"It's hard again. Hard and aching to get inside you. But it's not the only thing that wants in."

"What else—" The words died with a gasp as he worked his wet finger into her puckered hole. She twisted in her bindings, pushing her buttocks farther onto his finger. Bringing his mouth to her ass, he kissed each cheek, then tugged the string aside and licked the silky length of her crack.

"Ohmigod, Drew! Ohmigod!"

"Andy," he corrected, drawing back from her ass to further part her bent thighs with a nudge of his knee. "Drew's my sex-god name. Andy's my bad-boy one." And he *was* a bad boy. Just in case she wasn't convinced of that yet, he drew his finger out of her body and tugged the beads of the thong into her crack. "Be a good girl and hold still and I'll think about letting you go."

The breath choked from her lips. He tightened his hold on the string, stretching it to the rear of her sex and grinding it against her pussy lips and deep into her buttocks. Cream leaked from beneath the thong, drizzled onto his fingers and perfumed the air. Tawny went wild, tugging at her bindings, struggling to clamp her thighs together and bucking her sweet, curvy ass in his face. "I can't . . . hold still . . . when you're . . . doing that."

"Then I'll just have to punish you more."

"No. No more," she pleaded. "I can't take . . . any more."

"Oh, yeah, you can." Continuing to grind the beaded string against her ass and pussy with one hand, he reached for the vibrator with the other.

She had to have closed her eyes, because she didn't say a thing as he pulled the thick black beast from beneath the covers. As he moved the patch of material at her mound aside and hit the ON switch to the vibrator, she said something, though.

One strikingly loud, "If you stick that thing in me, I swear I'll come so hard you'll think you have a waterfall on your hands."

Laughing, Andy brushed the head of the vibrator against her sex. The tip buzzed along her clit. Her back arched and her thighs shook. "Oh, man. . . . I'm warning you, Andy. I'm talking Niagara Falls here."

"You like it better than me? Is that what you're saying? You'd rather feel battery-operated plastic fucking you than my dick? I think my pride's hurt." He grinned wickedly, letting naughtiness come through in his tone. "Do you know what that means, Tawny?"

"Hell, no!" She yanked at the cuffs, groaning when they refused to budge. "No more punishment. I don't like it better than you. I wouldn't even want it if you weren't operating it. You drive me crazy. You make me too hot to bear. Too wet. I want—"

The words died with a blistering moan as he buzzed the vibrator back over her clit, circling it around the swollen pearl. Juices trickled from her opening, darkening the thong and glistening on the black rod. He bent his head and licked at those juices, up the length of the vibrator and over the lips of her sex. Her hips jerked, her pussy shifting against his tongue, welcoming it inside her body. He slipped inside for one long, lusty lick, then retreated to fill her with the black beast.

She screamed as he loved her with the rod. His cock jerked against the metal teeth of his zipper, aching to get out and take part in the action. Unable to play the part of the spectator any longer without risking coming in his jeans, Andy reached for his zipper, relieved this time when he was able to pull it down without fumbling. He slid his jeans and briefs partway down his thighs. Yanking the wallet from his back pocket, he retrieved a condom and quickly rolled it on.

Tossing the vibrator aside, he lowered against Tawny's back and nudged his shaft between her thighs. Into her ear, he breathed, "Ready for the real thing, babe?"

Her laugh sounded near painful. "Am I ready? If you don't fuck me this minute I'm going to explode."

He moved aside the wet silk and slipped into her, groaning as her pussy gripped him tight. Filling his hands with her breasts, he teased, "Feels like to me you already did. Yeah, I believe we have Niagara Falls happening down there."

She turned her head to the side and narrowed her eyes playfully. "You haven't seeing anything yet, buddy."

"Then I'd best keep trying."

Claiming her mouth in a openmouthed kiss, he reared back and thrust hard into her sheath, setting a tempo that wasn't nearly as wild as the one they'd shared earlier and yet had his balls hugging tight to his body in seconds. The sac slapped against her ass, ringing out a melodiously carnal tune. Sweat gathered on his brow. Warmth radiated through his body. Tawny's tongue stroked his with erratic fervor, her cunt clamping and unclamping, signaling how close she was to her waterfall of a release.

He let free a breast to finger her clit. He circled the pearl once, twice. Her tongue stilled against his, and she released a puff of hot air into his mouth. He circled a third time. Her sex constricted, tightened. Wetness flooded him. Lust exploded in his veins. His blood sizzled, his cock throbbed.

"Andy!"

A deluge of hot, sticky juices followed his name. His real name this time. One less lie between them. One less reason to fear she'd despise him when she learned the truth.

Her pussy gripped him hard as orgasm crashed over her. Thoughts of names, lies and everything else faded away as climax shuddered through him. With a savage curse, he rode the turbulent currents of his own personal waterfall.

The moment lust lifted and sanity returned, Andy undid the handcuffs and pulled Tawny into his arms. Both of their pants were still hooked about their ankles and they fell together into a tangle of naked, sweaty limbs.

Tawny pushed off from his chest, laughing. Her eyes twinkled with merriment and warmed his heart with hope. He hadn't cared to consider tomorrow with any woman before her. From the moment they'd arrived at her secret destination of a book club meeting, he'd hadn't been able to forget the idea. For tonight he would keep things light, continue the cat-and-mouse game of pupil and instructor they'd begun. Soon, though, he had to take things seriously, both by telling her the truth and acknowledging exactly what it was he hoped to get out of this relationship beyond great sex.

Toeing off his pants, he rolled onto his side and brushed his finger along the soft rise of her cheek. Pale red freckles dusted her nose. He prided himself on taking in details, no matter how insignificant; blame it on the fact that he couldn't get his mind off his dick when she was around, but until tonight he'd missed the freckles. They were endearing in a way he never expected to care about.

Light, Andy reminded himself. Keep it light. "So, tell me, teach, did I pass?"

She frowned. "Pass?"

"Am I a master of carnality?"

A smile tugged at Tawny's lips. She kicked off her jeans and pounced on him. Devilment shone in her eyes as she grabbed the handcuffs and then his wrist. "No, but you're a bad boy. A very bad, very naughty boy who obviously was studying up on his sexual technique without me. It's punishment time, naughty boy."

Andy's cock leapt as she moved off the bed and pulled the box of lingerie and toys from beneath it. She pulled out a whip and a second set of handcuffs. Her smile grew wicked as she climbed back on the bed and proceeded to shackle his free wrist and ankles. Passion burning hotly in her eyes, she moved up his body, dragging her damp sex and the soft flared tassels of the whip against the sweaty skin of his inner thighs, eliciting shivers of hedonistic delight.

She set the whip aside and carefully removed his geek glasses, placing them on the filing cabinet beside the bed. "Things are about to get rough." She picked the whip back up and cracked it against her palm. "I'd hate to break anything."

If her idea of rough punishment meant being laid out spread eagle, watching her beautiful breasts jiggle in his face while she taunted him with sex toys, then Andy could say only one thing. "Bring it on, babe. Bring it on."

Irritation ate at Andy as he listened to his brother-in-law rant through the phone line. He padded barefoot from the kitchen to his apartment bedroom while Rick droned on.

"Fine." The reluctance to agree reflected in Rick's voice. "It isn't the chick getting information from Joyce and selling it off to some big gun at Nielson. Somebody else has found a way to get their hands on my shit. I'm betting that somebody works for Neilson. I want copies of everything going in and out of that office. E-mails, faxes, meeting minutes, design plans. Whatever paperwork's floating around, get it and get it fast. Things are getting shaky here. The backers are gonna start jumping ship. I don't have any more time to sit on my ass and wait for this leak to wash out."

"It's a shitty situation you're in"—Andy scrubbed a hand through his hair; he had far better things to do than coddle a cranky Rick—"but what you're asking is illegal."

He snorted. "Yeah, and I just bet you've never done anything illegal."

Bugging Tawny's phone line and snooping through her computer system and home hardly qualified as legal. That was small potatoes compared to what Rick wanted. If Andy screwed with a corporation the size of Neilson and got caught, his life was as good as over. "Not to the extent you're suggesting. Besides, I'm a one-man operation. Securing all the information you're after would require a team and time."

"I told you we don't got time."

"*You* don't have time," Andy corrected, letting his irritation bleed through the line. "If you're seriously convinced that someone at Neilson is to blame, I suggest you take this thing to the cops."

"And get stuck in the system for months while the company falls apart? No fucking way, man. You're all I have, Andy. All Joyce has. Or do you like the idea of your sister living in poverty because you were too much of a candy ass to make a few copies."

Andy glared at the phone. What a low fucking blow. Joyce was the only reason he'd agreed to help his brother-in-law. He wouldn't continue to help for her sake. If worse came to worse and Rick's ad firm bit the dust, he'd see to his sister's welfare. Hearing the fury in Rick's voice, he'd as soon have her living under the safety of his roof than with her husband. "I've done all I can. You don't want to talk to the cops, you'll have to figure out another way."

"Yeah, I guess I will. Thanks for nothing, dickhead."

The connection went dead with a slamming at the other end of the line. Andy considered calling Joyce and asking her to come stay with him immediately, at least until Rick's problems passed. Only, his sister didn't know Rick had problems, and it wasn't his place to interfere in their marriage by telling her about them.

He went to the dresser and grabbed a pair of socks. He had to flush thoughts of his sister and her husband from his mind. He was due at Tawny's any minute for their nightly session. While they'd admitted Thursday morning that what they wanted from each other was more than a teacher/student relationship, they had yet to speak on exactly what it was they did want. He also had yet to reveal the true reason he'd come into her life—that he wasn't a nerd at all, but a guy who knew about and appreciated technology for the ways it helped him with his investigations.

If he said to hell with his ever-present desire to get her into his home and bed—both of which were decorated in ways a computer geek would never appreciate—he could risk not telling her the truth. But knowing she was at least casual friends with Joyce, the odds of her finding out on her own weren't in Andy's favor. Even if they had been, he wasn't taking the chicken-shit way out. He owed her the truth. He just hoped the right amount of groveling would make her understand that they had more than lies between them. They had something good, something real. He'd be damned if he'd lose that something for so much as a day.

Knocking on her front door brought an expectant smile to Tawny's face. Andy was here. At least, she hoped it was her bad boy. The way she was dressed and laid out on her bed, if Andrew the nerd showed up, he'd probably come in his pants.

If Andrew the nerd even existed.

Considering how quickly he'd become sexual adept, it seemed he'd never been a true nerd at all. Just a bad boy who'd momentarily gotten confused about his talents and confidence. And had she ever been confused. She'd thought she wasn't the brazen, wanton Tawny. Thought all those toys and risqué out-fits she'd bought during her sister-in-law's sex party two years ago would become victims of the dust bunnies beneath her bed. The past three nights and mornings, every last one of the toys had been dusted off and put to use, and she'd thoroughly en-joyed every screaming, quaking minute of it.

"Tawny?" Andy's voice came from down the hallway.

Heat chased through her body and her pussy dampened. She'd broken out the most risqué of the outfits for tonight's les-son. No, not lesson: lovemaking.

She smiled. Was she falling for him? She hadn't investigated her feelings fully yet, but the way her heart sped up and the happiness that filled her every time she saw him, at home or the office, it seemed she might be. "In here."

"I was starting to think you weren't—whoa!" He stopped short in the bedroom doorway. His gaze drifted from the black lace teddy that revealed her hard nipples through precisely cut holes, to the open crotch splayed wide by the bent positions of her legs, to the black fuck-me stilettos digging into her comforter and mattress. She'd realize at the time of lying down how drastically the black contrasted with the pale pink of her comforter. Contrasted and gave her that much more of a naughty thrill over greeting Andy this way.

"I missed you today." She clamped her mouth shut at the unexpected words. Maybe she was falling for him, but she didn't know where his feelings lay and didn't need her big mouth scaring him off.

Tawny glanced down, between her spread thighs, where her sex glistened with her essence. She batted her heavily made-up lashes. "She missed you, too."

His eyes darkened from hazel to deep brown as they met hers. His throat worked visibly. "I, uh, came over hoping to talk—"

"But you've changed your mind." She stroked the bed beside her. "We can talk later. Now I need you to fix me."

"You don't look broken from where I'm standing. Hot as hell, but not broken."

"I am broken, though. And it's your fault. I had this water craving today at work and my supply of bottles is fresh out. I thought I'd snag a glass from the water cooler. But you were already there, bent over, filling your mug, teasing me by waving your tight ass in my face. After that I didn't need water. I was already dripping with wetness. I have been ever since."

She reached between her thighs and dipped a finger into her slick pussy. Her eyelids flickered to half-mast as erotic sensations shot through her sex and deep into her belly. "Oh, man, am I ever wet."

She worked her finger in and out of her sheath, heating up further with the slick sounds. "I could sit here and play with myself for hours and it would feel good." Andy's nostrils flared; loud, rapid breaths escaped his slightly parted lips. "But it wouldn't feel as good as your fingers inside me, as your cock filling me up and taking me over the edge. I need you, Andy. Come love me. Or fuck me, if you'd rather."

"Love you. I'd rather love you."

Tawny's heart constricted with the passion that clung to his words. That same passion vivid in his features, Andy moved to the bed, shucking his clothes in seconds to expose a massive erection she ached to get her lips around. He came down between her thighs and slid a finger into her body beside her own. He moved them together, stroking into her heated flesh and making her burn all the more.

"I've never walked in on a woman as hot as you wearing so damned little." He rose up to run his tongue over a nipple while he continued to pet her dripping pussy. "It's an experience I plan to repeat again and again."

"Just where do you plan to find all these hot women?" She bit her tongue. Damn, she'd sounded jealous, like he wasn't entitled to sleep with other women. They had no commitment to each another. But he'd sounded like he wanted to love more than her body, like he might already love her.

Amusement entered his eyes as he rose farther up her body and rubbed her lips with his. "As much as it does wonders for my ego hearing the jealousy in your voice, I was planning on finding her right here. In this bed. Or in my bed, so long as the woman in question's you."

Relief charged through Tawny, and a breath she didn't know she was holding eased out. She pulled her finger from her body and pushed against his chest. He lifted from her and frowned. "Did I say something wrong?"

Shaking her head so that the curls floated righteously around her face, she grinned. "Uh-uh. You said something right. Lie down for me, Andy. On your back."

His look faded to one just this side of arrogance. "You plan to have your way with me again, is that it? What do you have in mind for punishment tonight? Whips? Feathers? Rope?"

She moved between his feet. "Tongue."

"Tongue?"

She nodded and bent between his legs. Resting her hands on his thighs, she licked her tongue across the weeping, dark purple tip of his cock, down the length of his hard sex. "Oh, yeah. And mouth, lots of mouth."

"Oh, fuck, yeah," Andy agreed harshly as she returned to his tip, took him completely into her mouth and suckled.

Fondling his balls, she loved him with her lips, thrilling in his salty-sweet taste, the feel of his silky fluid against her tongue, the scent of his arousal thick in the air. He grew incredibly harder in her mouth, hotter. Wetness pulsed in her cunt. He reached down and captured an erect nipple between his fingers, fondled it. Sweat gathered on her forehead. Cream leaked from the open crotch of the teddy to trickle along her thighs. She closed her eyes and let sensation take over, more than eager to go on sucking him forever.

Loud chirping pushed through Tawny's subconscious. With effort, she stopped sucking and glanced in the direction the sound came from, somewhere on the floor.

"My cell's in my pants pocket," Andy bit out. "Ignore it."

She looked up at him and found his eyes intent on her, intense. Knowing he watched her every move brought a fresh course of wetness between her thighs. She returned to sucking him, watched his expression change, his lips part and breath push hotly out as ecstasy worked its way through his body.

The cell phone stopped ringing. Andy released her nipple and pushed his fingers through her hair, pulling roughly in a way that spoke directly to her pussy. The phone rang on the filing cabinet beside her bed.

"Go away," Andy grunted. His tone turned husky yet elated as looked back at her, affection shining in his eyes. "Not you. You don't ever go away."

The bedside phone quit ringing. Tawny focused on his words, on the fact that he wanted her in the long run. She wanted him, too. She knew it with heart-pounding certainty. Wanted him and loved him.

She smiled around his shaft, sliding her tongue over the rigid veins that ran the length of it as she worked her mouth and hand in opposite directions. She stopped licking to hum against his shaft. With her free hand, she reached behind his balls and fingered the sensitive spot between his testicles and anus, dipped her finger into the puckered hole and applied pressure.

"You little devil," Andy ground out.

His cock throbbed in her mouth, pushing between her lips automatically now. His fingers bit harder into her hair, fisting, yanking. His thighs tensed around her body, clamping her in place. A last thrust between her lips and hot cum shot into her mouth, coasting over her tongue and down her throat.

Tawny moaned and kept sucking, wanting to savor every last bit of his essence. Low music started up from somewhere behind her. She recognized it as her cell-phone ring tone. Someone obviously wanted to speak with her badly. The same someone who'd called Andy's cell? Did he have the number on file at work? If so, who would be working this late? Whoever was calling, it had to be important.

Reluctantly, she lifted her lips from his sex. "Do you think it's the same person?"

"Shit, I don't know." His expression conveyed how upsetting he found the interruption. "You'd better answer it, just in case."

With a last teasing lick over the head of his cock, she darted from the room in search of her cell phone. She found it on the end table in the living room. Hitting the TALK button, she grabbed the phone to her ear. "Hello?"

A frantic female voice came through the line. "Thank goodness you're home. Is my brother with you?"

She frowned as she recognized the caller. "Joyce, what's the matter? You sound upset."

"I need to speak to my brother," she retorted with a conviction Tawny had never heard out of the soft-spoken woman. "Rick's on his way over. I overheard him on the phone with someone. I don't know who, but he was shouting and swearing, and he said . . . he said he was going to make you two pay for ruining his plans." She rambled on in a ragged tone. "Oh, my gosh, I'm so sorry. I had no idea he could want to hurt you. I didn't even know he knew who you were beyond—"

"Slow down." Tawny started back to the bedroom. In her panic Joyce had obviously called the wrong person. Still, trepidation tightened her belly. "Joyce, this is Tawny you're speaking with. I don't know anyone named Rick and I've never met your brother."

"You know Andrew," she exclaimed as Tawny reached the bed. "Rick is my husband. He's on his way over there to—"

"Andrew's your brother?" The words left her mouth with a gasp while the impact of them hit her in the stomach like a physical blow. Two nights ago Joyce and Andy had been at the book club meeting together. Two nights ago they'd acted like nothing more than casual acquaintances. Two nights ago they'd lied to her.

Sickness eating at her belly, Tawny looked at Andy. He sat on the side of the bed, his dimpled smile nowhere to be seen, only guilt. The meaning behind that guilt gripped her to the core. She felt suddenly naked, dirty. Like she'd been nothing more than a pawn in some game she didn't know the name or reason behind.

"Rick's angry, Tawny. Really angry. I tried to stop him and he hit—"

Andy stood and jerked the phone from Tawny. "Joyce? Slow down and tell me what's going on. What's Rick going to do?" Several seconds passed and his expression went from guilt to disgust. "Shit. Listen to me, honey, you need to calm down. I can take care of myself and Tawny. I promise he won't hurt us." He hesitated an instant, then, "No, I won't hurt him either. Not if I can avoid it. I'll call you back as soon as I can."

"Who are you?" Tawny's words vibrated out on a wave of frustration and hurt the moment he ended the call. "Not a nerd, that's for damned sure. How could I have been so stupid to fall for that act? You don't kiss like a nerd. You don't look like one outside of the mile-thick glasses and the clothes you used to wear." She realized now that he wasn't even wearing his glasses. She'd been so drunk on lust, she hadn't even noticed. And it was lust. No way in hell did she feel love for this lying asshole. This stranger.

God, did she even know Joyce? She'd believed they were developing a friendship, but had she been wrong about that, too?

Wrapping her arms around her too-exposed chest, she narrowed her gaze. "Did you ever really want me, or was this all just some game to you and your sister?"

Andy took a step toward her. She took one back and he halted. "Yes! Hell, yes, I wanted you. I'll always want you, and my sister is as innocent as they come. This is no game, Tawny. This is serious." He dragged a hand through his hair and swore.

"My brother-in-law's on his way over and he's angry. I've never been around him when he's volatile, never guessed he could even get that way until a couple days ago. From the fear in my sister's voice, he gets that way. According to Joyce it isn't just temper he's packing either."

Andy hurried into his clothes, growing more upset with each passing second.

Shit, he'd royally screwed things up, with his sister and with Tawny. He couldn't reverse the hostile words and the slap Joyce told him Rick had given her upon learning she'd been listening in on his conversation. He could only protect her from further hurt. As for Tawny, he didn't know where to begin.

Had he stuck with the plan and told her the truth the moment he'd arrived tonight, or any time in the last week, she might not be glaring at him now, like she was torn between staying put in the bedroom as he'd asked or making a break for it. He hadn't stuck with the plan. He'd arrived at her home, taken one look at her barely clothed body dripping with anticipation, and let his dick rule his mind.

Maybe it was too late for the truth, but it was all he had to give. "Rick hired me to investigate you." He talked fast as he yanked on his shirt. "He claimed you were using Joyce to learn inside information about his ad firm and then selling that information to someone at Neilson. I knew you—"

"Investigate me?" Tawny stopped tugging on a pair of jeans to look at him incredulously. "You're a rent-a-cop?"

"Private investigator, and I knew from nearly the beginning that you were innocent. What I didn't know is that my brother-in-law's guilty. If what Joyce heard is true, then there never was an information leak at Rick's firm. His company's struggling to survive. He set us both up in the hopes I'd bring back information from Neilson that he could use to make a profit and get his financers off his back."

Her glare turned lethal. "You prick. You're not the victim here. Don't even pretend like you are."

"Not to the extent you are," Andy agreed, wishing he had the time to choose his words carefully. The last thing he wanted from her was pity. He deserved every ounce of her anger. "I'm sorry about this, Tawny. I swear I came over here tonight intending to tell you everything. But then you—"

"Acted like the sex-driven woman with the uncontrollable mouth you were counting on me to be." She shook her head, self-ridicule filling her eyes. "I made it so easy on you—let you into my home without question, into my bed. My life. Tell me, what exactly were you hoping to learn by fucking me?"

Temper burned through Andy. He knew he'd hurt her, but he'd be damned if she'd stand there and demean what they had shared. He crossed to her and pulled her against him, locking her arms beneath his. She wriggled and kicked, coming centimeters from doing serious damage to his groin. He held fast, determined to make her understand how much more they had between them than lies. How much he cared. "Nothing. Not a goddamned thing. And it wasn't fucking. It was—"

Heavy pounding came from the front of the house. "Open the door!" Rick's shout reverberated through the walls. "I know you're in there, Korben, screwing the chick responsible for destroying my business."

Son of a bitch. What timing. What bad damned timing.

Andy bent his head and slanted his mouth over Tawny's, kissing her despite her continued attempts at escape. One quick rub of his tongue against hers, one quick taste of her spicy-sweet flavor, and he released her. She retreated fast, backing herself into the corner between the bed and her closet. Rage and fear warred in her eyes.

Christ, he was no better than Rick, handling her in a way that frightened her. Rick's shout came again, followed by fierce knocking that silenced Andy's attempt at further apologies. If he left the man to his devices, Rick would be breaking in by any means possible.

"Call the cops and then stay put. Unless you hear gunshots." The color washed from her face. She'd always been so vibrant, so loud and out there. Now she looked timid, and he hated himself for making her that way. He wanted to pull her back into his arms and tell her everything would be okay. He ignored that want, and instead nodded at the window that faced the street. "You hear gunshots, climb out the window. Find a house or car to hide in and don't come out until the cops arrive."

Andy went to the bedroom door. With a last look at Tawny, he moved through, closing it behind him. He yanked open the front door just as Rick's pounding started up again. He forced a serene expression, when all he wanted to do was put his fist in the man's face for hurting his sister and invading Tawny's life. "Rick, what's all the shouting about?"

Hatred shot from the man's dark eyes and turned his mouth in a sneer that was nearly eaten up by the overgrowth of his blond beard. Ruddy color stained his cheeks. "Don't play stupid with me, Korben. I know she's here." He elbowed past Andy and started through the living room.

Andy grabbed the sleeve of Rick's jacket, jerking him backward. Violence wasn't something Andy supported. At the same time, he was trained to fight and to win. He was also trained to keep cool in intense situations and, at the moment, was doing a shitty job of it.

Andy inhaled a calming breath. He had to make this thing impersonal, separate his feelings from his actions and words. He'd failed to do that last week, and look where it had gotten him: pissed-off-at by one person and looking to get his ass kicked by another. "Leave Tawny out of this. She has nothing to do with your company being in the red. Joyce heard you on the phone. She heard that you lied to me about the info leak. There never was a leak, was there?"

"That sniveling bitch."

So much for keeping things impersonal. Fury pushed at Andy. He balled his fists, unable to contain the heat in his voice. "Talk about my sister that way again and I promise you won't be standing."

"Oh, yeah, what you gonna do?" Rick pushed his hand inside his jacket pocket and returned with a 9mm. He pointed the nose toward Andy's chest. "Take on a loaded gun?"

Apparently Rick was looking to do more than kick his ass. Joyce had warned him Rick was packing. He'd hoped she'd been mistaken. Andy had left his gun at home, not wanting to risk Tawny finding it and panicking. Hand-to-hand combat, he could beat Rick. Bringing a gun into the equation, particularly when the gun was held by a man motivated by financial desperation, upped the odds in that man's favor.

Fear that Rick would do something stupid trickled through Andy. He shrugged it off and tossed a cocky smile at his brother-in-law. "Wouldn't be anything I haven't done before. Little hint, Rick: Those guys I took down in the past are in prison, right where you're going to be if you don't hand over the gun."

Rick shook his head. Dirty-blond hair stuck to his cheeks and forehead. As little as a few months ago, Rick had been in decent shape, clean looking. His looks now were as revolting as his expression. "Think again, dickhead. I'm not going to jail. Joyce'll never talk. She'll just crawl into the same pathetic shell she always does. You, you'll be six feet under, alongside your trashy girlfriend."

Andy had been the one to suggest Tawny was trashy. He'd meant it as a misguided compliment. Rick made it sound like she was a five-dollar-an-hour whore. The urge to put his fist in the man's mouth returned to riot through him. The gun Rick waved at his chest stopped him. Three feet away, the weapon looked small. Andy knew better. He'd seen the brunt of its impact, the deadly holes left behind in the victims. Raising a hand against Rick without some form of distraction was out of the question.

Andy searched the room for a weapon. "Fine. No jail time. Get the hell out of here and we'll forget everything."

"I'm not going anywhere without the chick."

"She's not going—"

"I'll go." Tawny stood at the end of the hallway that led into the living room from the bathroom and bedrooms. Her hair was pulled back neatly in a ponytail, and not a trace of the fear he'd witnessed in the bedroom could be found in her eyes. Just steely hard resolve, the kind Andy wished he could feel. Any other time, any other case, and he would feel that way. This case had messed with his head, his heart. This case he'd never had a clue who the bad guy was until it was too late.

Hands in the air, Tawny moved slowly toward Rick. "Whatever you think I've done, I'll go with you and admit to it. Just leave Andy alone. He did what you asked, lied to me to find your answers. Slept with me to learn more of the same." Her gaze shifted to Andy and hurt passed through her eyes. "He was good to his word. A regular seek-and-destroy prick. Let him go."

Snickering, Rick pushed a hand through his hair, knocking the greasy strands back in place. "Your devotion's amusing, but

I don't think so, sweetheart. Neither of you's leaving." He pointed the gun at Tawny, then back at Andy. "Get over there with him, and don't try anything stupid. Unless you want a hole in that pretty forehead."

Tawny crossed to Andy, shrinking away when her arm brushed his. "You can't keep us here forever."

"Right on, sweetheart. I can't. Not alive, anyway." She gasped and his lip curled in a derisive smile. "Don't worry, I'll aim for a place no one's ever gonna see again. Makes you feel better, I'll take care of lover boy here first."

Enough. He'd had enough of Rick's twisted mind. Andy had told Joyce he wouldn't hurt her husband if it could be avoided. It couldn't be avoided. Before this thing was over, one or both of them was going to get hurt. "Put the gun down, Rick. You don't want to end your life this way."

Rick's eyes glimmered with amusement as he turned them on Andy. "Who said anything about ending mine, bro?"

"You really think I'll let you hurt us?"

"I'd like to see you stop me."

The second-to-last thing Andy wanted was to give Tawny another reason to hate him. The last thing he wanted was for either of them to die tonight. Time and groveling might earn Tawny's forgiveness; neither would accomplish a damned thing if one or both of them were dead.

He stepped a few inches forward, far enough to get Andy's attention, and gave Tawny a hard shove in the side. With a shriek, she flew toward the wall. The thud of her hitting either it or the floor registered in Andy's mind and then was quickly forgotten as he charged at Rick. The man's gaze ratcheted from Tawny to Andy. His eyes bugged as Andy rammed into him. Andy grabbed Rick's weapon hand, twisting the wrist so that the gun faced away from everyone. He'd never wrestled with his brother-in-law. The man was chunkier than he'd been months ago, and still stronger than he looked. Either that, or adrenaline made it seem that way.

"You fucking idiot," Rick spewed, slamming a fist toward Andy's ribs and connecting before he could block the blow.

Pain exploded in Andy's gut. He winced at the idea that his sister might have felt that same fist pounding into her. The thought fueled his strength, had him twisting harder at Rick's gun hand and bringing his free arm up around the man's neck. He clamped down, constricting his grip on Rick's throat.

He expected Rick to drop the gun, to claw at the arm stealing his breath. Instead, Rick's free hand reached for his own weapon hand. Placing that free meaty hand over Andy's, Rick pried the hands fighting over the gun around until the gun pointed inches from Andy's side. The soft *snick* of a bullet engaging slid through Andy's mind, followed by the metallic ring of release and the sting of tearing flesh and muscle.

"Son of a bitch." White-hot pain sliced through Andy's middle.

Tawny yelped and came into view as a charging blur of red. She crashed into them, sending a fresh course of ache through his body and disengaging his arm from Rick's neck. Rick staggered and went down in the process releasing the hand that had covered Andy's. Ignoring his pain and Tawny's shouts to run, Andy leapt on his brother-in-law and once more captured the man's gun hand. He used his advantage from above, jabbing a knee into Rick's gut as he pried at the gun. Rick wriggled like the slimy worm he was. Andy believed the move to be a last-ditch effort at escape. As Rick's legs came up, fastening around his middle, he realized otherwise.

Rick thrust his weight to the side and rolled them over until he straddled Andy from above. With a snicker he dug his fist against the wound in Andy's side. Blood seeped out, staining Andy's shirt and the floor with crimson red. His vision wavered; spots danced before his eyes.

"Not a smart move, bro," Rick mocked. "Now you're gonna die."

Death wasn't an option—not when he knew Tawny and Joyce would be the next to feel the effects of Rick's rage. Andy shut out the ache and the oily sensation gathering at the back of his throat. He turned his strength on the hand still holding Rick's. Grunting with the effort, he managed to bring the gun around, but only far enough to have it pointing at his own head. Damn, he'd never be able to get it on Rick.

Red filled Andy's blurred vision. Red he guessed to be blood filling the backs of his eyes as death worked its way over his body. Any day was a shitty one to die, but knowing Tawny hated him made this one all that much worse.

Somewhere above him, metal crunched against bone. Rick's cry filled the air. Andy struggled for one last chance at escape. He dug his fingers into his brother-in-law's wrist and gave it a final twist. Rick's body lurched and then jerked toward him. The hand holding the gun went limp, followed by the rest of his big, beefy body. Rick toppled over him, stealing the breath from Andy's lungs and shooting shards of razor-edged pain dancing through his middle.

"Oh, god, I killed him!"

Tawny's panicked words registered. He moved his head to the side and forced his eyes to focus through the haze of hurt shrouding him. Her hand shook as she brought it to her mouth. Wide-eyed, she backed up. She slammed into the couch from behind and a shadeless lamp fell from her hand to the carpet. "I didn't mean to kill him," she whispered. "I didn't mean it.

"Tawny?"

Her gaze flew to Andy's face. As panic was replaced by concern, she hurried to his side and helped roll Rick off. Her throat worked visibly as she focused on the red soaking through Andy's shirt and onto the carpet. Tears glistened in her eyes as she brought her eyes back to his own. "Andy . . . you're not . . . ?"

"I'm fine. He . . . nicked me." Rick had done more than nick him, but for her sake he played at strength. Pressing a hand over his wound to staunch the flow of blood, he commanded his voice not to waver and give away the severity of his injury. "You sure he's dead?"

She glanced at Rick's prone body and shivered. "I don't know. I'm afraid to touch him again."

"Then don't. The cops should be here any second; go wait for them. Tell them we need an ambulance immediately." He laughed, hoping the sound would belie his next words. "Better make that two."

She stood, backing up slowly. "Okay. Okay, I can do that."

"Tawny?" Keeping the waver from his voice was no longer possible. Talking hurt like a bitch. Just in case he bled out before an ambulance arrived, he risked the pain. "We had more than lies. We always will."

She licked her lips, her eyes conveying that she wanted to trust him. Sirens wailed in the near distance. She nodded slowly, whispering, "I'd like to believe that, Andy, but I don't think I can," then opened the door and stepped out into the night.

Tawny pulled aside the curtain and peered through the window next to the front door. Her heart sped at the sight of the man who'd filled her thoughts for days now. Andy stood on the front porch, his eyes imploring her to forgive him while his mouth asked her to let him in. She wanted to forgive him, wanted back the happiness he'd unexpectedly brought into her life. But how could she forgive him when he'd lied to her yet again?

He'd claimed Rick had only nicked him. In truth, the bullet had missed the lower lobes of his lungs and his spine by millimeters. He was lucky to be walking after a week of recovery time, let alone to be alive.

Emotion rose in her throat at the thought of him being dead.

She couldn't turn him away. He tried to protect her against a madman. For that he deserved to say whatever he'd come to say.

She opened the door and fisted her hands at her sides. He wore no glasses now, no nerdy clothes. His hair was cut and styled, still basic brown and yet somehow so much richer and thicker. He looked too damned good for words. Her sex moistened, her nipples beaded. Tawny ached to tug him into her house and forgive him with her hands and mouth. Instead she said a cool, "What do you want, Andy?"

He smiled, the dimple sparking to life in his cheek and making her tongue move in her mouth with the need to lick over it. "You already know the answer to that. I want your forgiveness. I want you to believe me when I say it wasn't just lies between us. You had to feel the truth when we kissed, when we touched, when we made love. And it was lovemaking; don't you dare say otherwise."

Damn her aching heart, but she wanted to believe him now just as badly as she had a week ago. But how could she? She'd blindly opened herself up to him, let him into her life, let him rule her behavior. She'd become brazen, wanton Tawny for him, not just in actions but in truth. And she'd loved being that confident, sexual woman. Loved the power that charged through her when she made Andy shiver and tense with climax, loved laying her hands all over his lean, virile body.

His body which, beneath his T-shirt and bandages, sported a hole. A wound that could have killed him. Tears pushed to the backs of her eyes. He deserved a lot for his lies, but not death. Never death.

If anyone deserved to die for their actions, it was Rick. He'd survived her lamp attack with a concussion and a lump and now awaited trial in a jail cell. The odds of him getting off were slim. Not only did he have three people ready to testify against him, but the mini recorder Andy planted on her phone had caught the entire struggle and lead-up conversation on tape.

On second thought, it was good Rick hadn't died. Not only would the knowledge she'd killed him haunt her, but she'd know she was to blame for Joyce's heartache. Tawny had seen Joyce once in the last week, long enough to know she planned to stand trial against her husband but at the same time grieved over him. Bad as Rick turned out, Joyce had given him her heart two years ago. That love couldn't be expected to die overnight.

"I love you. Doesn't that matter?"

Andy's words seemed to mock Tawny's thoughts and throw them back at her. She'd given Andy her heart. And she had to admit, if only to herself, that she still loved him. Maybe in time they could try again, start over without the lies between them. Or maybe that was just another foolish hope.

"Tawny, speak to me." He reached for her hands, pulling them into his own before she could stop him. "I don't care if it's just to say you hate me. I need to hear your voice. I need to know you're okay. I'm trained to deal with the sort of situation Rick put us in last week; you're not."

He was as good as his word. The concern in his voice and his expression confirmed it. Hell. Not trusting her big mouth to speak without revealing every emotion that raged through her, Tawny pulled her hands from his and shook her head. Slowly, she closed the door. Her heart stampeded the moment his face was no longer visible. He was out of sight, the way he'd been for the past week. The way he could be for the rest of her life if she chose it. She could fall back into the routine she'd lived before meeting him, the Monday night mud mask and scrapbook session, Tuesday night pedicure, Wednesday book club meeting . . . where she'd see Joyce . . . and think of Andy, and how stupid she'd been to let him go.

He wasn't the only one who'd lied. She'd led him to believe she was some wild woman who could teach him sex from kiss to climax, who could fill up his date book until he had to turn women away. With Andy, she'd become that woman. Before him she'd been living a dreary existence, deriving her greatest pleasure by reliving the sexual exploits of her best friend. She didn't want that life back. All she wanted was her bad boy.

Tawny yanked open the door. He was already getting into his vehicle—not an economic sedan, but a gas-guzzling duelie extended cab. Her body heated with the thought of the evenings they'd share in the cab of that truck, making out like teenagers. She wanted that, wanted to throw away her nonexistent social-butterfly black book and notch her bedpost with this one man alone.

"Andy!" she shouted, stepping out onto the porch.

He climbed back out of the truck and, closing the door, came around the front of it. Hope waged in his eyes. "Yeah?"

She smiled, not wanting to give into him so easily, but unable to stop herself—just as she was unable to stop herself from hurrying to him and flinging herself into his arms. Brazen Tawny, it seemed, was destined to floor her neighbors with her naughty antics.

Rising on tiptoe, she wrapped her arms around his neck and kissed him long and hard, reveling in his minty-fresh taste. His cock hardened against her belly, and she pulled back sighing. Oh, man, how she'd missed him. "It matters. All of it matters."

Cupping her face, Andy looked into her eyes; sincerity and an affection that warmed her through filled his own. "It was never just about the case."

"It was never just about teaching you lust lessons, either."

He grinned and lowered his head to rub her lips. He nibbled gently, then pulled back to eye her soberly. "I love you, Tawny. Always. Forever."

Her head spun. Her pulse went mad. She wanted to jump up

and down and giggle like a little girl with a newfound kitten. She forced her feet to stay planted on the ground and settled on squeezing him tighter. Andy winced, and she realized his wound still bothered him. Apparently she should have stuck with the jumping up and down and giggling. "Sorry."

"Don't be. I'm a big boy. I can handle a little pain." He took her hand and started for the house. "Does this mean you forgive me?"

Tawny cast her gaze along the length of him, taking in his honed body clothed in a black T-shirt and jeans, instead of some seventies geek getup. She leaned back and whistled at the way the jeans hugged his taut ass. Her fingers tingled to touch. She gave into that urge with an impish smile, first swatting his backside and then cupping it. "I'll work at it, but I can already tell you there's going to be some serious punishment involved. You can consider it your last lesson: Love hurts."

He raised a dark eyebrow. "Is that your way of saying you love me?"

"I probably shouldn't, considering what a bad boy you are, but, yeah, I love you."

She squealed as he lifted her into his arms, carried her through the front door of her house and kicked the door shut. His mouth came down hard on hers, demanding, possessive. She'd felt removed from herself in the week since Rick invaded her home, numb. With each brush of Andy's tongue against hers, the numbness left her body until she felt whole again, complete, like letting him carry her to bed where she could jump his bones.

She remembered his injury then and swatted at his arm. His lips lifted from hers only to drop on her cheek and work their way downward in a hot, wet path. She wriggled against him, struggling to escape. One of them had to be logical here. He held firm, catching her ear between his teeth and nibbling as he moved through the living room en route to her bedroom.

Tawny shivered as desire rocked her to the core. She fought

to remember why she wanted out of his arms. Oh, yeah. His injury. "Put me down, you idiot! You're hurt."

"I thought that was part of your lesson," Andy said, sliding his tongue into her ear. He moved through the bedroom door. Laying her on the bed, he came down over top of her.

Tawny reared back and pushed at his chest, fighting to get away before the ache in her core overpowered her common sense. "The lesson can wait until you're healed. You might deserve it, but I still won't have you hurting over me, not really."

Andy's mouth lifted from her ear and he sent her a pained look. "Then stop your wriggling, babe. You have me hurting something fierce and it isn't from my injury. My cock's been aching to feel your sweet pussy around it for days. My lips to run over your body, brush against yours. My tongue's not going to be happy until it's inside you, loving you, making you come undone."

He moved to the end of the bed, between her legs. She hadn't changed since meeting Jilly for lunch. He took advantage of her short skirt, pushing it up and out of his way. Sliding her legs up so that her knees pointed at the ceiling, he blew on her damp panties.

Her sex shuddered, famished for the swipe of his tongue. "I guess a little oral lesson couldn't hurt much."

A wicked laugh drifted from his lips. He bent his head and nipped at her pussy through her panties. She pushed her fingers into his hair and urged his mouth to press harder, to go beneath the thin layer of cotton. As if he could read her thoughts, he pulled the panties aside and plunged his tongue deep into her sheath.

Tawny released his hair and dug her fingers into the comforter as orgasm built fast and furious, flaming her need to fever pitch. Yeah, oral sex definitely couldn't hurt his injury. In fact, it felt like just what the doctor ordered.

Night Illusions

1

She'd never been witness to such a massive orgasm in her life.

Just looking at the word, decked out in bold red and standing two inches tall, was enough to have Joyce Donovan's hands shaking and the urge to crawl under her desk almost too great to bear. Her cheeks stung as she read the book's full title aloud, *"Indulge Yourself: Achieving the Ultimate Orgasm."*

"Can you believe someone actually has the balls to buy that?"

Joyce slammed the book back on her desk as Tiffany, the blue-haired college student who worked part-time at The Book Shed, came into her office at the back of the store. Tiffany propped a generous, leather-clad hip on the edge of Joyce's desk and ran a black fingernail the length of the ten-inch penis that decorated the book's spine.

Her face ablaze and her inner thighs tingling, Joyce covered her discomfort by pushing her glasses up her nose. Gracious she felt like a voyeur, watching the young woman stroke that huge thing. Did penises even get that large? If so, she hoped she never had the misfortune to experience it firsthand.

"I mean, yeah," Tiffany continued, "I can see getting it mail-order, but to walk into a store and pay for it where everyone can see you—like, wow, that takes some big *cojones*." She ceased her stroking to eye Joyce curiously. "So, who's it for?"

Me.

At least it *had* been for her, before the book arrived and she realized exactly what she was getting herself into.

Two weeks ago, when she'd overheard a couple of the Wednesday night book club participants discussing the sex manual after the conversation on a far tamer book had ended, it had struck a chord. What better way to attain freedom from her naive ways than by making herself a self-indulging sex goddess? According to the women, the book accomplished that and more.

Her chord must have been playing off-key that night. Now that the book was here, in all its explicit color and details, it couldn't possibly be the best route to conquering her naïveté. But if not through this book, then how?

At twenty-seven, she was too darned old to be afraid to share her opinion on general topics, much less touch herself in the name of pleasure. It wasn't just age prompting her to change her timid ways—her gullibility was dangerous. She could blame her gullibility for falling in love with the first man to look her way with seduction in his eyes. The very same man who'd become verbally abusive days after they'd said "I do." Eight months ago Rick had taken that abuse to the next level, hitting her and then going after her brother Andy and his girlfriend, Tawny, with murder on his mind.

That horrible night had ended the best way possible, with her brother and his girlfriend alive, and Rick in a jail cell. Though it had turned her emotions upside down, Joyce had filed for divorce three weeks later. It had been the first step toward her new life. A life that was lonely at times, but never ruled by the desires of another. A life where she was a strong, outgoing woman who saw what she wanted and went after it. A life she'd shape to perfection via *Achieving the Ultimate Orgasm*.

Reading the book and admitting she was the so-called ballsy owner were two different things. She never lied, but now it seemed the only answer. "Gosh, I'm not sure who ordered it."

She opened the book and turned to where she'd randomly tucked the customer invoice. *Ménage* was spelled out in bold, black capital letters on the left page. Beneath the word, a two male/one female trio illustrated the technique. A large nude black man pushed his penis into a kneeling woman's bottom, while a second, equally large, nude white man sucked at a hard-tipped nipple and filled her from the front. Ecstasy drew the curvaceous brunette's mouth into an O, her eyes to half moons, and telltale wetness glimmering on her inner thighs.

Joyce shifted in her seat as moisture dampened her panties. Good gracious, the book had to be good if just looking at a picture heated her up more than her ex had been able to accomplish from start to finish of their lovemaking.

Remembering she wasn't alone, embarrassment flooded her. She had to get past this mortification over talking and thinking about sex around others. She was an adult on the verge of breaking out of her repressed shell. She had to think confidence. To live it. She ought to start today by owning up to her purchase.

Only, tomorrow sounded like a much better day to begin.

Joyce lifted the invoice and scanned it. "Here it is." She held her breath as she read the buyer's name, one that was a combination of her middle and maiden names. "Caitlyn Korben."

Tiffany tipped her head to the side and pursed lips rimmed with black lipstick. "Sounds familiar. She a regular?"

In the beginning, the young woman's appearance had been a bit frightening. Joyce's belief that there was good in everyone prompted her to give Tiffany a try, and she'd turned out to be sweet, if not overly bold at times. Then again, compared to Joyce a turtle was assertive.

No, compared to the old Joyce. The new Joyce was as assertive as one could be, or at least she would be once she had a
chance to read and reap the benefits of her new book. Maybe
beginning her transformation process today was a good idea
after all.

She glanced down at the book to find her fingers running the
interior length of the spine. The same penis that covered the
outer spine skimmed beneath her fingertips, growing harder,
thicker, longer. She gulped and slammed the book closed.

"I don't think she's ever been in the store." The words
rushed out as Joyce pushed the book to the side of her desk.
She needed help beyond that attainable through a how-to manual if she believed a painted phallus was turned on by her
touch. "As I recall, she called in the order and asked me to hold
it for her until she could get to this part of town."

"I bet she's working up the nerve to come in."

"Maybe." Or maybe she should rethink the whole "in over
her head" thing.

Joyce looked down at her prim white, sleeveless blouse and
navy pencil skirt. Was it even feasible that she could convert
from reserved bookstore manager to self-assured sex siren by
way of an orgasm manual? "It has a two-week, satisfaction-
guaranteed return policy, so I'd, uh—she'd better not wait too
long . . . to pick the book up, that is."

Tiffany laughed. "What a guarantee. If she doesn't 'come,'
the book goes. So is it okay if I take my lunch break? The place
is, like, dead."

"Yeah. Go ahead." Before she caught on to Joyce's blunder.
Better yet . . . "Take the rest of the day off. The jazz street festi-
val has most of the downtown blocked off. I was hoping it
would bring in some foot traffic, but apparently listening to
music and reading don't go together."

"In that case, I'll see you tomorrow. Ciao."

"Have a wonderful night."

Joyce stuck out her tongue at the singsongy quality of her own voice. Along with conquering her repressed ways, she had to get past being so terminally nice. Andy often said it was a great quality, but one that made people take advantage of her. The way Rick had sweet-talked her with kindness and generosity, only to show his true selfish colors months later, proved her brother accurate.

The tinkling of the bells that hung over the store's front door announced Tiffany's departure. Joyce pulled the book back in front of her. Rick was no longer the man in her life. Some other man was out there waiting, some temporary lover who would lavish her with orgasm-inducing attention without quashing her heart and spirit. With the aid of this book, she'd hunt him down and rope him in. Either that, or she'd discover just how far beyond help she was.

"Confidence," she scolded herself. "Think confidence."

Joyce stared at the thick, lengthy penis on the spine, urging her cheeks not to warm. Becoming a sex goddess meant being able to look at the male anatomy without risking a hot flash. She counted to thirty, chalked nonflushed penis-ogling up to one challenge met and turned to the table of contents.

The chapters weren't laid out by number, but by letter, from O to M, or, rather, *Outliving Your Expectations* to *Masturbation*. She'd already outlived her expectations by ordering the book, but she turned to Chapter O all the same.

Outliving Your Expectations.
Whether you want to bring new life to an old relationship, start a new one, or just find the confident sex goddess in you, the first step to achieving your goal is to surprise yourself. Take that one thing you've always wanted to do, but were too afraid, and put it into action, girlfriend. And don't tell me you don't have a secret desire hidden away in that heart of yours.

Did she have a secret desire? She'd always sort of wanted a tattoo, one that was small and practical. The few times she'd mentioned the idea to Rick, he'd told her she was crazy and that if she got one, she'd end up dying of ink poisoning.

"Pooh on Rick." She was an assertive woman now, one willing to chance death by needle.

The visual of a foot-long needle digging into her skin and spurting forth blood filled her mind and tightened her belly. Focusing on the needle was a bad idea. She'd think about the tattoo itself. A nice butterfly or kitten. Something to show her independence, yet not make her look like a biker chick with a needle fetish. Perfect.

"You sure you want that tat, lady? You seem like more of a page–twenty-four gal to me."

Joyce focused on the good-looking guy who'd introduced himself as Ernie. After picking out her tattoo from a thick portfolio full of what he'd referred to as "flash designs" in the front of the store, he'd led her to a curtained-off, bathroom-sized room in the back. He stood next to her chair, pointing at a transfer of the tattoo she'd chosen.

She squinted, trying to decide if he was really good-looking and potential new short-term-lover material. It was hard to be certain without her glasses on if his long black hair was thick and shiny or thin and greasy. She'd come to the tattoo parlor directly from work, before her courage could falter. Dressed as conservatively as she was, wearing her glasses into the place seemed a definite no-no. She'd left them on the dashboard of her car and shaken her hair out of its typical twist in the hopes she'd look like she wore the prudish clothes for the sake of the job and not by choice.

If Ernie's tone was to be believed, losing the glasses and letting her hair down hadn't been enough of a change. Or maybe it had. Maybe page twenty-four was where all the wild women chose their design from.

She sat straighter and inclined her chin at what looked like a vivid black and orange monarch butterfly. She tried at an assertive tone. "I paid for it and I want it. It's perfect for me."

He brought a hand to his jaw and rubbed. "Mmm . . . coulda fooled me, but it's your body. So, where do you want this thing?"

Good question. Since finishing chapter one of *Achieving the Ultimate Orgasm*, Joyce was anxious to change her after-hours persona as quickly as possible. At the same time, she wanted to get her customers used to the idea slowly. That ruled out placing the tattoo anywhere visible when dressed. She'd overheard Andy's friends saying how much more sensitive, and therefore painful, it was to get one on skin located directly over bone. "Somewhere fatty."

He looked the length of her. "That rules out everywhere but your ass or your breasts. Let's see what kind of rack you have hiding under that shirt."

She stiffened. Rick had used coarse language often, but she'd never heard it directed toward her out of a stranger's mouth. And what exactly was that stranger asking her to do? "You want to see my chest?"

"This tat ain't getting on your body by magic, lady."

"Oh, right. Sorry. I'm new to this." Why hadn't she realized that getting a tattoo—or tat, as seemed to be the correct term—would entail her getting naked?

"You don't say," he said sarcastically.

Potentially good-looking or not, this guy was not of short-term-lover quality. His tone reminded her of the belittling way Rick used to talk to her. Those days were past. She was a smart thinking, independent woman now who didn't take flack from anyone and had no qualms about undressing for a stranger.

Joyce stood and unbuttoned her shirt. She tossed it to the brownish looking stool a few feet away, wrinkling her nose when it fell on the floor instead. Too darned bad. Without her glasses, her depth perception was way off. She inhaled a nerve-fortifying breath as she popped the front clasp of her sensible white cotton bra, aimed for the stool a second time and once again missed.

Ernie murmured, "Nice. Much more to work with than I'd guessed."

Her breath drew in sharply. She forgot all about the missed shots and fought the urge to cover her breasts. It was early July in Atlanta, the temperature in the high nineties outside and close to the same inside the shop. Gooseflesh rose on her skin all the same. She sank onto the chair, grasping for conversation. "Uh, thanks."

"It wasn't a compliment, lady. Just gonna make my job easier. Now sit back and relax. The less tense you are, the better."

He pulled on a pair of latex gloves and brought the transfer sheet to her right breast. The heat of his hand melted through the gloves and the sheet as he rubbed the temporary tat on. The back of his hand grazed her nipple. She swallowed a gasp as carnal sensation shot from the tip directly to her sex. The rubbing moved inward, centimeters from her nipple, tightened her nipple to a hard, straining bud. Wetness gathered in her panties. She bit down on her lower lip and fought the urge to squirm.

Ernie glanced up. "You cold, lady?"

No. She was embarrassingly turned on by this guy who had a nasty habit of speaking down to her and, for all she could tell, was toothless and dirty. It had to be the hours she'd spent reading about orgasms. She'd passed the nonflushing penis-ogling test, but there was a heck of a lot more in that book than just penises. Detailed pictures covered every position and sexual scenario imaginable and quite a few she was pretty sure were impossible. Each one had had her a little more aroused than the last. She'd left the bookstore feeling incredibly naughty.

This was neither the time nor the guy with which to act on that newfound naughtiness. "I'm a little chilly," she lied. "Will that mess up the design?"

"No. But I can turn up the heater if you want."

The offer was unexpected. He'd turned this place into a sweatshop for her benefit. She offered him the first real smile since walking through the door. "That's okay. I can handle—it!" The smile died with a squeal as a needle prick of pain sliced through her breast. "Oh, my gracious!" It felt like he was jabbing a million tiny toothpicks into her boob. Maybe Rick had been right. Maybe getting a tattoo would be the death of her.

"Just do your best to hold still," Ernie advised. "You won't feel much soon. The pain gets so intense after the first minute or two, the area turns mostly numb."

After the first minute or two? Was that to say it was going to get worse before it either numbed up or she passed out?

Joyce's eyes watered as he continued to work the needle across her breast, inking in the design with black. She closed her eyes and counted slowly, waiting for the numbness to settle in. It took far longer than predicted, but finally she could feel only dull pokes.

Minutes dragged on as Ernie worked in silence, adding orange and yellow to the blurry black outline. Voices carried into the small room from out front, hinting at more customers. One wouldn't dare come inside when she was half naked, would they? With his concern over her warmth, she'd accepted the idea of Ernie looking at her bare boobs from a professional standpoint, but she wasn't liable to handle an audience so well. "Does it always take this long?"

"You picked a decent-sized tat. Lotta color and detail." He set the needle aside several minutes later and nodded. "All set.

Looks good. Still not sure it's right for you, but whadda I know?" He handed her a mirror.

The tat looked like the same blurry blob of orange and black when reflected as it did when looking down at it. Smiling, she handed back the mirror. "It's bright. Nice. I like it."

"That's all that matters." He applied a thin layer of ointment and then bandaged the area. Reaching to a small table loaded with ink and other supplies, he grabbed a sheet of paper and gave it to her. "This'll tell you how to take care of it. That bandage should come off in a couple hours. After that, keep it exposed to the air and lotioned up good."

Joyce stopped scanning the instructions as his last words repeated in her head. She looked at him, incredulous. "You're saying I can't wear a bra, or even a shirt?" And just how the heck was she supposed to get home?

"No bra for a bit. Loose shirts, like the one you wore in, are fine."

"What about sex?" Oh, gosh, had she really asked that? She turned her attention back on the instructions in the hopes Ernie wouldn't detect her discomfort.

"Sex is fine, just so long as your guy won't be licking your tits too much. Too much moisture'll ruin the tat."

He'd spoken crudely again, but in such a professional-sounding voice, she couldn't even work up a blush. Maybe that's all there was to using coarse language—doing it with the right tone. Storing away the information for later, Joyce stood and smiled. "I'll be sure to keep that in mind. Thanks for being patient with me."

"Come back any time and we'll fix you up with a matching bike for the other side."

As she exited the room, she laughed at his joke, an obvious play on the fact that he thought she didn't belong in a tattoo parlor getting a tat of any kind. A woman worked the front desk now—either that, or a man who looked like a woman through her poor vision. Joyce nodded at the person and then hurried out to her car.

She slipped on her glasses, anxious to see the design as more than a vivid blur. Carefully, she peeled at the bandage. Color crested where once her breast had been pale white. Thick, black whiskers extended from the side of the cat's head.

Wait. She'd gotten a butterfly, not a cat.

Frowning, she peeled the bandage down further. Two round circles tinted with pale yellow came into view. They weren't the markings of a monarch, but the distinctive wheels of a bike. The front spokes circled her nipple. Headlights beamed toward the center of her cleavage. The air left Joyce's mouth as a disbelieving gasp.

Holy Hades! There was a Harley on her breast.

Chapter O hadn't gone so well, but Joyce wasn't going to let it get her down. So she had a Harley on her breast. That spoke of confidence, of independence . . . of being foolish enough not to wear her glasses when being branded for life.

She wouldn't be making that mistake twice. She'd picked up disposable contacts this morning and had even braved sticking her finger in her eyes to put them in. Glasses or no glasses, she could see, and that meant no more stupid moves.

Joyce shook her head as she pulled into the light-brightened parking lot of *Dusty's Backroom Bar*. No negative thoughts, only confidence. The last two days, she'd breezed through Chapter R, which entailed reading up on dirty talk and the latest words for male and female body parts, and was now on to Chapter G: *Getting Your Man*.

She hadn't planned on literally roping in her short-term lover. Since she'd opted to put her new personality to the test thirty miles outside of Atlanta, at a small country bar where she'd be unlikely to see anyone familiar, roping might well come into play.

She opened the driver's-side door of the canary-yellow Mustang she'd leased that morning. Stepping out, she surveyed the lot. For a Monday night, the place was busy. There had to be plenty of guys to choose from inside. And plenty of them would be looking at her. For once it wouldn't be because she was dressed like a no-figure dud, but as a curvy, if not a bit on the short side, blonde poured into the smallest outfit she could find. The jeans skirt seemed to fit the bar's theme. The snug navy tank top had been picked for the built-in cotton-shelf bra and the fact that it pushed more of her tat out than it held in. She'd do whatever it took to avoid going back under Ernie's needle for touch-up work.

Sticky air rife with cigarette smoke and loud twangy music assailed her as she cleared the bar's front door. Conceited as it might be, she'd honestly expected everyone to stop what they were doing to look at her. Through the low lighting, a few patrons glanced her way, but most kept up with the dancing, chatting and pool shooting. Not feeling half so out of place as she'd guessed she would, Joyce stepped onto the hardwood floor and threaded her way through the crowd to the bar.

She pulled out an empty stool centered between a group of laughing woman in business suits and an old man in a faded black Stetson. From his gnarled, tan skin to his worn jeans and boots, he looked like he might be a real cowboy.

A big-haired brunette in a black T-shirt with DUSTY'S written in sparkling silver across her generous chest dropped a coaster on the bar in front of Joyce. She leaned on an elbow and smiled. "What'll be, stranger?"

The woman on Joyce's left stopped laughing to nod at the bartender. "We need another round of Blow Jobs when you have a sec, Jen."

Blow jobs? For women? And they gave them sitting right at the bar?

Joyce's nerves stretched tight at the thought of everyone in the place watching as she received a blow job from a stranger. As much as he'd demanded it for himself, Rick hadn't given her oral sex once in the two years they'd been married. He hadn't even given her an orgasm outside of their first few times together, and they had hardly been ultimate. While she wasn't one for skipping ahead, the next chapter in the book was *Audience Participation*, or, rather, the thrill of being watched while having sex. The idea had given her gooseflesh when she'd read about it, but it might not be so bad. Bad or good, she had to try it. The success of her assertive, sex-goddess status depended on it.

She inclined her head at the woman, who'd resumed the animated conversation with her friends, and then at Jen. "I'll start with what she ordered." Her tongue stuck to the roof of her mouth as she attempted to get the words out. Heat tinged her cheeks. *Remember, it's all about attitude.* She stuck out her chin. "I'd like a blow job, please."

Jen's smile grew; amusement lit her eyes. "Don't take it personally, hon, but you look more like a Cosmo girl to me."

Cosmo, Joyce knew. She'd read several issues just last night. But why was that relevant? Or was "Cosmo" more than a name for a magazine? Was it another kind of oral sex? *Achieving the Ultimate Orgasm* hadn't said a thing about it.

Remembering the way Ernie had tried to change her mind on the Harley tat for one from page twenty-four, which was likely where the butterflies and kittens frolicked, she nodded. "All right. I'll try a Cosmo."

"It's a good drink. Little fruity for my taste, but I think it'll be perfect for yours."

The heat returned, pushing into Joyce's cheeks full blast. She'd ordered a drink, not oral sex. What a dunce.

Jen returned thirty seconds later, setting a large fluted glass filled with pink liquid in front of her, and cute little shot glasses of something cream-colored in front of the group of women at her left. Blow Jobs, Joyce realized, and felt twice as dim-witted.

Wiping up with a white bar rag the liquor that had dribbled from the shot glasses, Jen said knowingly, "Let me guess, new to the area?"

"No. Well, sort of." Oh, who was she kidding? No matter what she wore and how many Harleys she stuck on her boobs, she wasn't a sex goddess in-the-know and probably never would be. She frowned. "No negativity" was tonight's theme, but darned if it wasn't hard to follow. "Is it that obvious?"

"This tends to be a locals bar. A stranger stands out."

It wasn't her behavior that the other woman questioned— she just didn't recognize her. Maybe there was hope yet. Maybe there was more than hope . . . if she could work up the nerve to voice the thoughts in her head.

Joyce lifted the Cosmo to her lips and took a sip for courage. The taste was surprisingly sweet and went down easy. She took another sip, then pasted on her best confident face. "Do you know everyone here?"

Jen glanced around the bar. "Yep, pretty much. Looking for someone?"

Think attitude. Think assertive sex goddess. Oh, heck, just say the words already. "A short-term lover to worship me."

The bartender let out a robust laugh. "Aren't we all, hon." Her gaze returned to Joyce's face, and something in Joyce's expression must have hinted at her sincerity, as the woman sobered and asked, "What's your taste? What kind of looks do it for you?"

Rick had been blond with nearly black eyes, and, toward the end of their marriage, covered in a straggly beard. She wanted as far from that as possible. Taking a sip of her drink, Joyce scanned the dimly lit room. From their closeness and the intimate way they moved, most couples on the dance floor were either married or already planning to go home together. She continued on to the pool tables, coasted over a middle-aged redhead in a ball cap, moved on to a nice-looking guy who was far too blond, and then stopped abruptly on a tall, sandy-haired man with a golden-god tan.

He bent over the corner table and drew back on his pool stick. Faded blue Levi's pulled taut across his bottom, accentuating the play of a deliciously firm behind. He straightened to reveal a strong profile. Clean-shaven jawline. Nose with just a bit of a hook. The too-blond guy said something to him, and gentle laugh lines creased the corners of his mouth and eyes, making him look approachable yet sexy.

Butterflies of lust flapped wildly in her belly while her heart pounded with excitement. Yes! It was him. "He's nice."

"And unavailable," Jen put in from behind her.

The butterflies slowed. Dangit. She'd found her short-term lover and he was already taken.

"Married?" Joyce asked, unable to take her attention away from the graceful flow of his long legs or the way the upper half of his arms corded with mouthwatering muscle as he sank a ball and proceeded to line up another shot.

"Divorced, but not looking. Then again, you said you were only after a fling. Colin hasn't been with a woman in some time that I'm aware of. He might be willing to let you pick him up."

The butterflies regained strength. She smiled widely. She had a chance, and she'd be darned if she wasn't going to take it. Right after she had a couple more drinks.

2

"Why don't you go over there and say hi before she falls off her bar stool from the weight of all that drool?"

Colin Hart sank the 2 ball, then glanced up at Dusty Marr, his best friend since middle school and the owner of the bar. Though Colin had made it a point not to look directly at her, he knew whom his friend referenced. The hot blonde sitting backward on a stool at the bar, talking to Jen over her shoulder while she watched his every move. "Not my type," he said absently.

"Tight ass, nice legs and ripe tits that look ready to pop out of her shirt at any second." Dusty snorted. "Yeah, man, she's a real eyesore."

Colin leaned in for another shot, sinking the 5 in the corner pocket. "Too short."

"I bet you a beer you're going to say she's too blond next. I know you aren't looking for love—hell, if you *were* after the way Marlene screwed you over, I'd kick your ass—but is there something wrong with letting your dick have a little fun?"

Colin miscued his next shot when the word *dick* left the

other man's mouth. Not that he had a problem talking about his anatomy in public—he'd just made it a point to ignore his sexual urges since the day he'd caught his now-ex-wife screwing her boss. Considering he'd never been able to make her happy, the man had done him a favor. That didn't mean Colin was ready to accept the past seven years as wasted time and move on to the first woman who sent fuck-me eyes his way.

If Blondie was giving him those eyes purely for the sake of a one-night fling, that was all well and good. But if she had anything more on her mind, like hopping into his bed and staying there for the next fifty or sixty years, she could turn her attention elsewhere. Hell, if he was lucky, she already had.

With Dusty preoccupied lining up his shot, Colin glanced toward the bar. Blondie was right where she'd been the last time he'd looked. Only now her tongue wasn't in her mouth, but rimming her empty martini glass. The pink tip dipped into the center, thrusting toward the bottom, then jerking back to slip between her candy-apple-red lips. His cock hardened, pushing against the constraints of his zipper at the idea of her damp tongue tackling his body the same way. Only, she wouldn't be thrusting into him, but wrapping that plump mouth around him and licking his shaft from tip to base.

Her gaze connected with his before he could look away, and lust hit Colin in the gut like a sucker punch. The lighting might be low, the air heavy with smoke, but there was no mistaking the desire smoldering in her eyes. She wanted him in a big way.

It was possible Dusty had a point. If all Blondie wanted was one night, then why let his dick suffer another nine months of abstinence?

He set his pool stick against the wall and grabbed the empty beer bottles from the ledge. "I'm due for a refill. Maybe I'll say hi while I'm at it."

To the sound of Dusty's laughter and shout of, "I don't want to see your ass back at this table tonight," Colin started over to the bar. Blondie had broken eye contact to turn on her stool and talk to Jen. She swiveled back when Colin reached the halfway point, a full drink in her hand. She took a sip, her eyes lifting over the rim of the glass. They went wide the moment they met with his, something akin to shock slipping through them. But, nah, there was no way in hell a knockout like her would be surprised to get a response to her sensual invitation.

She brought the glass back from her mouth. Moisture must have stuck the coaster to the bottom, as it fell from the glass and onto the floor. Color burst into her cheeks. Quickly, she set the glass on the bar and bent for the coaster.

Colin's wonder over her blush died the moment her jean skirt rode up to reveal her ass hanging out. Smooth, pale flesh that had clearly never seen sunlight winked at him in all its naked glory. No panties. No fucking way. His cock twitched with the urge to push into her tight behind.

Did she know the show she was giving him and most of the rest of the bar?

Poor old-man Jenkins, who sat on the stool beside her, eyeing her shapely rear, looked like he had the first hard-on since his wife passed, and was ready to keel over because of it. Either that or he was planning on bending down and planting a long, wet one right on her sweet ass.

Blondie jerked upward, slapping the recovered coaster on the bar. She looked at Jenkins, who had the good sense to bury his ogling behind his whiskey glass, then at Colin. Her tongue came out, taking a leisurely journey over her full red lips. Hunger darkened her hazel eyes.

Oh, yeah, she knew what she was doing. Luring him in just a little bit more in case the bait hadn't been enticing enough from afar.

He'd started over with the intention of bypassing temptation in a scantily wrapped package and moving on to the open section of the bar to order a beer. Nine months of pent-up testosterone and the enduring image of one fine, round ass raged through his body and boiled his blood. Colin set the empty bottles on the next table he passed and headed straight for Blondie.

In his early twenties, he'd been known for his ability to meet a woman and get her into bed within the next half hour. He was thirty-three now and hadn't used those seduction skills in damned near eight years. With the blatant way she was looking at him, he might not need to worry about seduction. She might just open her legs and let him plow inside.

He didn't stop moving until his thighs brushed up against her bare knees. She shifted on the stool, parting her thighs and wordlessly inviting him into their vee. He didn't go with his body, but his gaze accepted the offer. A glimpse of pale blonde pubic curls, damp with juices and a musky scent that curled into the moist air and wrapped around his nostrils, assured him that the ass shot hadn't been off in suggesting a lack of panties. She was bare beneath that skirt. Bare and wet. He definitely wouldn't be needing seduction skills tonight. Minimal conversation, a gratuitous dance or two and he'd be hilt-deep in warm, dripping cream.

Colin brought his gaze back up her body, pausing at the pale but plentiful breasts that plunged above her tank top. "Nice headlights."

Her eyebrows winged together. "Uh, thanks, but there's only one."

The better half of a Harley was visible on her right breast, its headlight flowing over into the slit of her cleavage. That wasn't the headlight he'd had in mind. "I was talking about your breasts."

"Oh. Right." She looked him up and down, settling her attention on his crotch. "Nice bulge."

He chuckled. Not exactly the most articulate of women, but then he wasn't looking for an English professor, just someone warm, willing and guaranteed to be gone minutes after the fun ended. "What do you say to a dance?"

"Let me finish my drink."

Blondie reached behind her, with a hand tipped by short, blood-red nails, to reveal a glass nearly full. He frowned. She'd been sipping her drinks all night. No way was she going to start guzzling them. Taunting his dick by giving him that ass shot or not, she'd obviously lost interest the moment she'd seen him up close. "I'm a big boy, cupcake. I can take no for an answer."

Her eyes went wide, almost ingenuous. "No," she gasped. "I mean, I want to dance. Just give me a second to finish my drink." She proved his guzzling theory wrong, swallowing the drink back like a fish desperate for water. With a smile, she slammed the empty glass on the bar and stood. "Okay. Ready now."

She moved forward before he could step back and her breasts rubbed teasingly against his chest. The shelf-style bra did nothing to hide the tenting of her nipples. Her hands came up, grasping his forearms, and warmth radiated from her body hot enough to singe. Her hips pushed against his groin, rotating sinuously.

He'd been right about her height. She was petite, barely over five feet. Dusty had been right on every other account. She was a sexual bottle rocket just waiting to go off, and he had the good fortune to get to be the one to light her fuse. She continued to move against him, her sex grinding against the swollen head of his cock, and he realized he wouldn't be lighting anything, just stoking a fire already in progress.

"What do you say we take this onto the dance floor?" Or back to his bed. His truck would work just as well. It'd be a little crowded in the cab, but they'd manage.

Blondie giggled, then hiccuped. Releasing his arm, she stopped moving and brought her hand to her mouth. "Oh, my gosh! I guess I drank that last one too fast."

With a second hiccup, she freed his other arm and took his

hand, pulling him onto the dance floor. Toby Keith's "Whiskey Girl" thrummed through the overhead sound system. If the color of her drink was to be believed, Colin had a Cosmo girl on his hands tonight. A Cosmo girl who twirled away from him only to fly back into his arms and nearly knock him and several other dancers onto their asses.

Her laughter mingled with the music. "Oops. I haven't been dancing in a while."

More like she hadn't been drinking in a while. The way she was acting now, he'd say the liquor had gone straight to her head.

He moved back, intending to put some space between them. No matter how happy his shaft was over the idea of sinking into Blondie's compact little body, he wouldn't be doing it while she was under the influence. Her arms wrapped around his neck before he could move. She rose on tiptoe and shifted her hips against his, circling with a fast, carnal rhythm that had his balls snugging tightly to his body.

She tipped back her head and implored him through heavily lidded eyes. "Maybe if we dance close enough, I won't go flying off like that again."

Her attention lowered to his mouth, hovering there as she thrust her body against his and shimmied her hips. The ridge of her mound rubbed over his erection, chafing the sensitized head through his jeans. He grunted. "Keep it up, cupcake, and you're going to get a lot more than just a dance."

Her gaze flew to his. She smiled—not with a hint of naughtiness, but rather as if she were both stunned and pleased with her efforts. "Really? You want me?"

The return of her suggestive moves had seemed too practiced for drunken behavior. The artlessness of her questions now had him confused as hell. Was she plastered, or was it all just part of an act?

Only one way to find out.

Colin mimicked her movements, pressing his throbbing cock into her pelvis and swiveling his hips. "What do you think?"

Her smile curved higher, and a trace of the expected naughtiness entered her eyes. She lifted her right hand from his neck and crooked a finger. Intrigued, he bent down. Her lips brushed his ear. Her voice as liquid as warm honey, she purred, "That your great big cock can't wait to get inside my pussy."

Colin's pulse picked up with the dirty words, and the way she punctuated them with a thrust. No way was she plastered. And that meant all signs were go for a well-deserved lay.

Continuing the circling and thrusting rhythm she'd begun, he slid his hands down the curve of her spine to rub her ass through her skirt. He knew she was wet for him, had seen the evidence of that excitement dampening her pubic curls, scented it on the air. He wanted her more so, aroused to the point of near pain—the same way he felt—before he took her out to his truck and sank into her heat. "It *is* pretty anxious."

"Is it the headlight?" Her lips moved along his neck, feathering barely there kisses and making his body burn to fever pitch. Nine months was too damned long to go without sex. He would never feel this close to splitting his jeans otherwise.

He wasn't coming yet. Not until he had her begging for release.

"All three of them. And the skirt. What there is of it." He slid his hands beneath the jean skirt. Warm, supple flesh filled his palms. He sighed at the feminine softness. Nine months was also too damned long to go without holding a woman in his arms, even temporarily. "This ass isn't too bad, either." He squeezed her bare buttocks, pleasuring in her answering sigh. "Forget to wear your panties, cupcake?"

Her mouth returned to his ear. Hot breath caressed his damp skin and a shiver racked through him. "Panties are overdone. So, you want a blow job?"

The air stuck in Colin's throat at the abrupt change in topic.

His dick pushed hard against his zipper. If she honestly thought he'd say no, then she had to be plastered. "That all depends: How much have you had to drink tonight?"

She pulled back to give him a questioning look. Realization seemed to settle in then and she shook her head. "Oh, gracious, I don't mean the shot. I mean oral sex."

Odd. She was acting odd, but not in a drunken way. Not in a way that suggested he should remove his hands from the silkiness of her ass. "You're going to give me oral sex right here on the dance floor?"

She glanced around, then back at him. "There must be an alley."

"You want to give me a blow job in an alley?"

"Don't you think it sounds exciting, being there, where anyone might see us?"

Fuck, yeah. "And dirty."

"Dirty's good, though, right?"

The kind of dirty she had in mind, but he'd been thinking in regard to germs. Christ, he'd softened up since bringing on enough employees to handle the fieldwork for his landscaping business. There was a time he'd loved the feel of moist dirt sliding through his fingers. Now he had a hot blonde ready to go down on him and he could only think about the bacteria that dirt carried.

Softer he might be, but he was also healthy enough to risk any germs that lingered in the back alley, particularly when it meant Blondie's red-hot lips would be wrapped around his dick.

"Yeah, dirty's good." With a squeeze, he released her ass and grabbed her hand. "C'mon, dirty girl. Let's see if we can't find us an alley."

Tonight was supposed to be about getting her man and then getting an orgasm from that man. Instead, Joyce was about to go down on her knees in the name of someone else's pleasure. It was exactly the way sex had gone in her marriage, and yet something was different about tonight. Maybe because she'd done the instigating. It wasn't Rick pushing her to her knees and sticking his penis in her face, demanding she suck on it. It was her short-term lover leading her into a dark alley—but only after he'd made certain she wanted to be there.

Colin pulled her into a partially shadowed area and pushed her back against the wall. Sticky night air rank with the scent of the dumpsters washed over her. The setting should have been the furthest from what she wanted for her first assertive, sex-goddess adventure. The way he shoved his hands into her hair and slanted his mouth over hers in a hard kiss made it seem perfect. It also made her darned glad she'd had the foresight to pop the stick of gum from her pocket into her mouth on the way outside. She tucked it into her cheek, wanting to taste fresh for him, but not share her gum.

His tongue speared between her lips, roving over her teeth, tangling with hers and stroking greedily. Sensation spiraled in her belly. Shards of wicked delight arrowed direct to her erect nipples and damp sex. Her head spun as she kissed him back, exerting a want she'd never let show in the past. Heck, that she'd never experienced.

His hands pulled from her hair to move down her body and mold to her breasts. Cupping their weight, he pushed them up and out of the shelf bra, exposing the mounds to the gentle breeze and anyone in viewing distance.

Joyce sighed with the first lick of the sultry breeze over her pebbled nipples, and then froze. Despite what she'd said about it being exciting to get caught, she wasn't ready for an audience to see her naked boobs. It was bad enough she'd mooned the bulk of the patrons inside when she'd only been trying to cover her coaster fumble. She'd forgone panties in an attempt to feel sexier. Instead, she'd felt like an idiot.

Colin's hard thigh moved between her legs. His knee pushed up against her tingling sex, and rivulets of liquid desire jetted through her body, heating her blood. His thumbs rubbed over her nipples, pressing at the straining buds. A throaty cry filled the night.

Oh, my gosh. Was that her, sounding like a wild animal in dire need?

It might well be, because suddenly she didn't fear getting caught with her breasts hanging out. Suddenly she could only remember her mission from inside. To get his cock inside her mouth, where she could run her tongue over the weeping head and drive him crazy with her *read about if not yet practiced moves.*

Liquid courage had emboldened her into standing from her bar stool and all but climbing into his arms. The Cosmos were fast losing their effect. She didn't need them. Not when she knew the golden rule of being a sex goddess: attitude.

Joyce pulled from his mouth and went down on her knees. Gravel jabbed into the soft pads of knee flesh. She ignored the bite to look up at him and bat her lashes. "Ready for that blow job?" she questioned in the best X-rated whisper she could manage.

She reached to his groin and stroked his hard length through his jeans. Nerves tightened her belly when her fingers continued on for inches. Too many inches.

She jerked her attention to the bulge her hand caressed. What if he was really big—a hot, solid replica of the penis from the sex manual's spine? What if she couldn't fit him into her mouth without gagging?

Colin's cock jerked beneath her hand. He groaned. "Christ, cupcake, you have me ready to explode and we're not even naked yet."

The nerves disappeared. Silent thrill coursed through her, power to think she'd made him want her so badly. And, extra big or not, she wanted him. Wanted her mouth on his shaft and wanted it there now.

She tugged at his zipper, whimpering when it refused to budge. His hands came over hers, blocking further attempts.

Joyce's heart skipped a beat. Oh, gosh, no. He hadn't changed his mind.

The agonizing thought had her looking up. Lust vivid enough to light up even the darkest shadows of the alley rallied through his sea-green eyes. Her own need pitched higher. The ache in her sex intensified. She felt practically liquid with her longing. Such unfamiliar sensations, the tightening in her belly, the restless throb in her core, and yet something she wanted to experience again and again.

His voice edged with roughness, he asked, "Do I get to know your name first?"

Did he? *Achieving the Ultimate Orgasm* hadn't said anything about names. Common sense suggested that giving her name would make this moment about more than just sex. At the same time, she knew his. Giving him a name in return might be the only way to get his zipper down. Tossing out more dirty words probably couldn't hurt, either. "Caitlyn. With a C, as in 'cock.' Do I get to suck on yours now?"

He grimaced as if the question had pained him. "Don't you want to know mine?"

"Colin. Which also starts with a C, as in 'cock.'" She wiggled her hand beneath his, licked her lips. "About that suck . . ."

"Are you in a hurry to get this over with?"

"Not at all."

Or was she?

Maybe desire didn't egg her on. Maybe she secretly wanted to get this first adventure over with and prove she was more than a timid bookstore manager. But if that was the case, would her nipples be hard? Would her sex be heavy with wetness and aching for something inside it?

No. She didn't want to get it over with. She wanted this tall, sexy, wondrously built stranger because she hungered for him, and not because she'd been coerced into having him. "I want to taste you. I want to feel your cock sliding between my lips. I want to feel you coming in my mouth."

Uncertainty flashed through his eyes, quickly replaced by carnal appetite. He lifted her hand from his zipper and pulled down on the tab. Bringing her hand back to his fly, he set it over the swollen bulge of his cock. "Then I suggest you get my dick out and start sucking on it. A few more strokes and there won't be anything left to swallow."

Joyce's face warmed as she pushed into his jeans and past his underwear. Her fingertips met with wetness and she ordered her hands not to shake. There was no reason to act timid now, not seconds away from getting her tongue on him.

He pushed his jeans and underwear down lean hips to his knees. His shaft sprang free, directly into her hand. She gasped at the sight of it rising from a tangle of sandy-brown pubic hair. So long, so thick, so incredibly warm and male. Covering her gasp with a sigh, she leaned forward and settled her lips around the dark pink tip. Gingerly, she tongued the ridge that surrounded the sensitive head.

"Ah, hell, cupcake, that feels even better than your ass in my hands."

Satisfaction filled his voice and stoked her courage. Pre-cum wept onto her tongue. Eagerly, she sucked in his towering length, moaning over his salty-sweet taste in a way she'd never moaned for any man. Not that she'd been with any man other than Rick.

Joyce ordered the thought from her mind. This wasn't about her ex-husband, this was about her short term lover. About bringing him ecstasy he'd repay with benefits until she was quivering and soaking wet with the ultimate orgasm.

Taking the base of his erection into her hand, she pumped

his sex. His hips jerked toward her face, his hands burying in her hair and pushing her down, urging her to take him farther inside. She wanted to do that. She wanted to take every inch of his luscious cock into her mouth, until the head brushed her tonsils and his seed filled her throat. Her pussy leaked juice with the wild thought, and she moved her hand faster, sucking his cock as if his essence were her life force.

Heavy moans came from above—the electrifying sound of Colin losing control. He gripped her hair and tugged. "I can't hold back any longer. I'm going to come."

She understood what he was telling her, to move her mouth away before it was too late. She clamped her lips tighter. Let it be too late. For the first time in her life, she thrilled in the idea of sucking a man until he was bone dry.

His shaft pulsed hotly between her lips. His fingers gripped her hair hard. This was it, her last chance to back away. She slid her hand lower and found his tightly drawn balls, fondled the sensitive sac as she met his eyes.

He looked at her as if she was his savior—the best thing to come into his life in ages. And then his mouth opened and out came a growl so feral it stroked her from womb to pussy lips. With a last driving thrust, he pumped his cum into her mouth. She lapped at him, licking, sucking, wanting this moment to go on forever, wanting this feeling of power, of naughty delight, to last until the sun rose.

Too soon, the pumping of his hips and the trembling of his big body slowed, then ceased. His fingers left her hair. A grin tugged his lips into a smile sexy enough to make her heart stutter. "That was good, cupcake. Damn good."

She was good.

Joyce's heart swelled with pride; tears pricked at the backs of her eyes. She wasn't hopeless. She was a sex goddess in the making.

Smiling with triumph, she started to lift from his cock. A

splotch of bright pink amidst his pubic hair stopped her. Was he tattooed down there or—

Oh . . . my . . . gosh. . . .

No. Not when she'd accomplished so much. Not another stupid move. Not her gum matted in his hair.

She dabbed her tongue into her cheek, praying the gum was still there. Her stomach dropped when she encountered nothing but the soft tissue of the inside of her mouth. Maybe it had fallen out and onto the ground. She glanced at the cement. There were a number of cigarette butts and scattered pieces of trash, but not a single speck of pink.

She looked back at his groin and winced at the now unmistakable wad. Darnit, it was her gum.

Hoping he hadn't quite yet returned from his trip to orgasm land, she slipped her lips back around his shaft. Sticking her tongue out, she buried it in his springy curls and attempted to pry the gum free. It didn't budge. Crud.

"Keep it up, and you're going to get seconds."

After this she'd be lucky if he even thought of her as good any longer. She pulled back and murmured, "There's just, um . . . there's a little problem."

"What kind of little problem?"

I decided to become a sex goddess when clearly all I'm capable of is being a hopeless flake. No negativity. Think confidence. Attitude. She could still turn this around. Somehow. "I, uh, lost my gum."

"I'll find you some new inside."

"But I didn't actually lose it. It's just . . . stuck."

"Stuck?"

She moved back. He looked down. Her belly knotted as his expression went from blissful to furious. "Ah, hell."

Joyce fought the urge to flinch. Just because he sounded angry didn't mean he was going to become volatile. Even if he did, it would probably only be verbally. She'd endured Rick's verbal abuse for two years. A few minutes of listening to Colin belittle her wouldn't hurt anything.

Her face burned all the same, her hands curling into nervous fists at her sides. She looked to her feet. "Sorry. You distracted me and I forgot I had it in my mouth. I was hungry and Jen gave me beer nuts, and they were so salty and I figured didn't give me the best breath, and . . . and you're upset. It's okay to yell, I can handle it."

Tension bunched her shoulders. She waited for the swearing to start, the blame. Colin's hand came to her chin, gently cupping it and lifting up her face so that she had no choice but to meet his eyes. They weren't stormy with rage, but gentle, understanding. "I'm not going to yell, cupcake," he said softly, a slow grin turning up the corners of his mouth. "I'll take care of it later. Now what do you say we head back inside before your girlfriends start worrying about you?"

She shivered with his compassion. How could he be so gentle after what she'd done? "I c—came here by myself." She winced when her voice shook. Dangit, what happened to Caitlyn the sex goddess?

His smile fled. Vehemently, he warned, "Don't you ever tell a stranger that when he has you alone in a dark alley."

He looked upset again, but continued to cup her chin. She saw in his eyes it wasn't anger but concern that made him say those words. First kindness and now concern. How unexpected. It gave her the strength to rein in her lost attitude, put on a wide smile and point out, "But we aren't really strangers. I sucked your cock."

"And shared your gum." A teasing glint entered his eyes and a lazy smile returned. "Agreed, we aren't strangers. Just promise me you won't tell anyone else you're here alone."

"I won't. I—"

"Col? You out here, man? I thought I saw you come out with that—"

"We're over here." Colin's smile disappeared and he hurriedly pulled up his underwear and jeans. "Everything's fine. Caitlyn needed some fresh air."

The blond guy who'd been playing pool with him came into view just as Colin finished zipping up. "Nothing quite like that dumpster air to refresh a person, eh?"

Joyce's sex tingled as the man's gaze slid over her body, lingering on her breasts and making her overly conscious of the fact that because of him she hadn't gotten to experience an orgasm. One more night without climaxing wouldn't kill her. She'd just have that much more to look forward to tomorrow.

"I need to leave," she said to Colin. "Thanks for the dance. If you want another one, I'll be at Club Sensation tomorrow night."

His eyes narrowed, little lines crinkling at the corners. "That's a clothing-optional bar. Anything goes on the dance floor, and I do mean anything."

"I know. Audiences are supposed to up the sexual stimuli that lead to the ultimate orgasm." She blushed, not having meant to reveal so much. It was the way the blond kept staring at her chest, reducing her to the nervous Joyce of old. "I'll be there at nine."

Colin hesitated a few seconds, then, "Make it nine thirty and I'll meet you at the door."

She rose on tiptoe and gave him a kiss on the cheek that hardly seemed enough of a good-bye, considering what they'd shared. Before they hadn't had an audience. Tomorrow night, at the most provocative club in Atlanta, they'd have couples, trios and groups dancing naked and doing far more than that all around them. They'd also have a massive audience if they chose to partake in the risqué activities.

She'd worry about that tomorrow. Now she wanted to get home and celebrate tonight's small victories.

Joyce pushed her chin forward and let her voice slip into a

sultry purr. "See you tomorrow then. I'll be wearing black. On the outside. On the inside, I think you can figure that one out for yourself."

Feeling decisively naughty for her words, she started for the bar's back door. When she reached him, the blond lifted his attention from her chest to raise an eyebrow. "Feeling better?"

"Much, thank you. Have a good night."

"You, too." He looked at Colin and grinned. "Or maybe I should say an even better one if the fact that your tits are hanging out is any sign."

What had he been thinking when he agreed to meet Caitlyn tonight? Colin questioned as he settled at the kitchen table with two pieces of toast and jam and strong black coffee. It wasn't the weekend and he wasn't a kid. He was a man with responsibilities. He'd been trying to make a go of his landscaping business for damned near five years. Hard work and long days had accomplished more than pushing Marlene out of his life—the time he dedicated to work was just one of the reasons she'd given for cheating on him—it had him on the precipice of seeing the business a success. If things continued the way they were going, the end of this fiscal year would show a profit for the first time. No way he'd risk it over a quick screw.

A quick, amazingly good screw at the candy-apple-red lips of one hell of an intriguing woman. He didn't want to wonder over Caitlyn, beyond how snug and tiny the black number she planned to wear tonight would be. Yet he couldn't stop from remembering the way she'd morphed from aggressive and outspoken to fragile and timid after discovering her gum was tangled in his pubic hair. He hadn't been exactly thrilled about it, had been even less thrilled when he tried to cut it out only to end up having to shave the hair off altogether, but he'd had no plans to reprimand her. Her anxious words and the fear in her eyes before she looked at her feet suggested she expected shouting and more. And that suggested someone had raised their voice, possibly their hand, at her in the past.

If Colin found out who that bastard was, he'd make sure it never happened again by way of several well-placed fists.

Before he could question the thought, Elizabeth bounded into the kitchen with all the sinful energy of the devil, considering it was barely after seven. Grabbing a piece of toast from his plate, she sank into a hardwood chair across from him. His sister studied him through the eyes of their father as she chewed— dark blue and assessing in a way that seemed to look right through you. Her cropped black hair came from her mother, the woman their father married nearly a decade after divorcing Colin's own. Apparently their father hadn't endured enough pain with his first deceitful wife.

Then again, look who was talking. Colin had walked into marriage expecting everlasting love despite growing up aware that his mother and stepmother had both cheated on his father, One by emptying his bank account and running off in the dead of night, the other by leaving their six month old daughter in his care while she took off to be with another man. If it weren't for the eyes and her loudness and obstinacy—both traits passed down from their old man—Colin would have thought Liz was the byproduct of another man's sperm.

Liz set the half-eaten piece of toast on the table and brushed the crumbs from her hands. "You look different this morning. Younger or . . ." Knowing filled those damned astute eyes and she grinned. "You got laid. 'Bout time, bro."

He took a long drink of coffee. Thanks to ceaseless thoughts of Caitlyn, he'd slept little last night. He'd woken before six and pushed himself into a hard workout. Normally, working with the weights helped ease away his tension. This morning the routine had left him strung tighter than ever and he needed all the help he could get to deal with his sister's flamboyant morning personality. Hell, her flamboyant anytime personality.

"I didn't get laid, Liz, and even if I had, I wouldn't be talking to you about it."

She pouted. "I tell you when I get laid."

"And I ignore every word. It's not right for a girl to share her sex life with her brother." They'd had this conversation twenty times since she'd moved into his house following Marlene's departure. The two-story seemed too big for one person. In hindsight, maybe it wasn't too big. Maybe it would've been just right.

Liz's eyes narrowed, stubbornness alive in every line of her body. "I'm twenty-three, almost twenty-four. Hardly a girl. And you obviously did get laid or you wouldn't try to change the subject. If your charming personality's any sign, she must have sucked."

"She didn't suck." At least, not in the way his sister meant.

Colin's cock hardened at the thought of Caitlyn's lush lips sucking on him, her talented tongue running the throbbing length of his erection. Months of buildup had him coming hard and long, and she'd taken in every last drop like a champion.

Liz laughed. "Told you you got laid."

He blew out a breath. Five minutes before heading out the door to work was not the time to be fighting a hard-on. "I didn't get laid. I got a blow job. And I have better things to do than have this conversation." Willing his shaft to relax, he stood and handed the remainder of his coffee to Liz. Never mind there was a full pot five feet away—she'd still snag his the moment he left. "See you tonight. Try not to burn down the house between now and then."

"I'll have you know that with this class I'm taking, my cooking has greatly improved. If you'd been here for dinner last night instead of eating another charred burger with Mr. I'm So Good I Can Barely Stand Myself and getting your rocks off, you'd know that." The loathing that always came into her voice whenever Dusty entered the discussion faded to interest, "So, do you have plans to see this woman again?"

Colin grabbed his keys from the ring by the kitchen door. He considered questioning what it was about Dusty that rubbed her so wrong, but then he'd probably get the same dumb look and no-response answer as always. He shrugged curiosity aside and opened the door. Sunlight filtered in followed by humid, heavy air that suggested it would be another scorcher. Caitlyn wouldn't dare risk wearing much to the club.

He grunted. No more thoughts of Caitlyn. Tonight he could think about her long enough to supply the orgasm he'd planned on giving her last night before Dusty appeared. Liz didn't need to know about tonight. "It was a one-night thing."

"Then you'll be home later to try out my Mud Pie Bliss?" she asked in between sips of coffee. "I have to work until nine, so I'm going to make it for a late-night snack."

His stomach turned as he recalled some of her past recipes. Knowing his sister, this latest really was made out of mud. He'd rather endure her taunting then risk his life to her cooking. "Fine, it's a two-night thing. I told Caitlyn I'd meet her at Club Sensation tonight, but that's it. You know where I stand on the relationship front."

"Right where everyone should," she said, making her jaded outlook on the topic clear. "For the record, it's easier to keep things on a sexual level if you don't call the person by their real name. I do like her name, though. It goes well with yours. Colin and Caitlyn. Caitlyn and Colin." Amusement filled her eyes and she started in a singsongy voice, "Colin and Caitlyn sitting in a tree, K-I-S-S-I-N-G."

He glared at her. He'd never cared for that fairy tale as a kid. And it was a fairy tale. Babies didn't follow marriage. The arguments did. The lies. The catching your wife being fucked by a man old enough to be her father. "Good-bye, Liz," he said irritably, then tacked on a gentler, "Annoying little twerp."

"You know you love me for it. Hey, that reminds me of a song: First comes love. Then comes . . ."

3

Contacts in. Check. Gum out of mouth. Check. Boobs inside shirt. Check.

Joyce gave her reflection a last look in the visor mirror, noted that her mascara hadn't run or her Revlon Volcanic Red lipstick faded and drew in a breath for valor. Everything was in place—or, in the case of the gum, out of place—and now all she had to do was get out of the car, go inside the club, and meet up with Colin . . . and their audience.

Butterflies winged through her belly. Gracious, she wasn't ready for an audience. She'd been so sure after studying all those explicit pictures in *Achieving the Ultimate Orgasm* that she'd be ready to be the naked one. The one bent over and being taken while strangers ogled her jostling breasts and dripping sex. But then Colin's friend had caught her with her boobs hanging out and she'd been so embarrassed, it was all she could do to get out to her car before breaking out in a hot flash to rival all those before it.

She stuck out her tongue at her reflection. "Quit being a baby and get in there."

With a shaking hand, she tucked her driver's license and a small wad of cash between her breasts. She winced at the scrape of the bills against her soft flesh. When women did that on TV or in the movies, it always looked sexy. It felt sexy in a way. An itchy, sort of painful way.

Chalking it up as a price she paid for being a sex goddess, she exited the Mustang. The outside of the club resembled a huge warehouse set down in the bustling heart of the city. The only things to offset the sedateness of the aluminum-gray siding were flashing yellow and red lights that announced the club's name over the top of a windowless door. A huge black security guard sat on a bar stool to the right of the door, arms crossed and showcasing a mountain of muscle.

Maybe she'd get lucky and he wouldn't let her in.

Joyce scolded herself. She would get lucky tonight, but with Colin and in a completely gratifying way. Her insides warmed with the thought of seeing him again. Would he kiss her hello? The short time they'd kissed last night had had her hot, wet and tingling for more. The time he'd spent with his cock in her mouth and his fingers desperately gripping her hair had her becoming a different woman. Caitlyn the confident. A sexual predator ready for anything.

"ID?" the big guy asked when she reached the club's entrance.

She fished it from her cleavage and handed it to him. Audiences be danged, her short-term lover was in there waiting for her and suddenly she couldn't get inside and find him fast enough.

"Nice picture." He smiled, revealing white teeth so large it was probable they could chew through her arm in a single bite. "Makes you look like a schoolteacher."

She considered throwing out a touch of Caitlyn attitude to combat the words, then changed her mind. She liked her arm right where it was.

Joyce grabbed her ID and tucked it back between her breasts, grimacing as the bills resettled to accommodate the license. He opened the door for her. "Enjoy yourself."

"I have every intention."

She stepped through the door and into a world from another time, one where clothing was optional and the norm was to go without. Unable to keep her mouth from gaping, she moved into the black-lit club. The hypnotic throb of blaring music rocked through her body and pounded between her temples. A stage rose several feet in the air to her left. Strobe lights cut through the purple haze of darkness and glided across the dancers—if what they were doing could be called dancing. Body parts were visible everywhere. Naked breasts, torsos—

A hand clamped around her wrist, jerking back and stealing her breath. She spun into the wall of a broad, muscled chest. Exhilaration shot through her as the man's mouth came down on hers, openmouthed and possessive. Colin. His tongue pushed between her lips, his hands beneath the short hem of her snug, black, spaghetti-strap dress. Fingers gripped her buttocks, bit into her flesh. The kiss turned wet, sloppy, gross. He tasted like something from the bottom of the sewer. Ew!

Definitely not Colin.

Joyce pushed hard against his chest, hoping he'd take the hint and release her. His tongue continued its soggy assault, his fingertips fast heading toward the rear of her sex. Panic coursed through her.

Rick. He reminded her of Rick.

Her stomach pitched. She raised her knee, ready to use it on him the way she'd learned to do in the self-defense class she'd taken a few months prior. Before she could make contact, the foul-tasting stranger lifted from her lips and released her bottom. Strobe lights flickered over them to reveal his eyes wide, pained looking. She saw the hand at his neck then, grasping his throat, cutting off his circulation.

A chilling voice shouted from behind her, "Get the fuck out of here, or next time I won't let up." The hand released the man and he scrambled away with a stagger that suggested he was plastered as well as perverted.

That dark voice came at her next, warning, "That's exactly why you don't go out to a bar alone."

"It's a club," Joyce said automatically. Panic had fled along with the drunk. It returned now as she realized she had no idea who her savior was and what he hoped to get in repayment for his services. She could stand there and cower, or she could face him. The Joyce of old would cower.

Sticking out her chin, she turned around, and warmth radiated from her ears to her toes. Colin. Her short-term lover. Her savior. "Thank goodness it's you."

She moved into his arms, rising on tiptoe to show her gratitude with a kiss. She'd intended a brush, but the nearness of his rock-hard body, the memory of how good he felt beneath her tongue, assailed her. She sank her tongue deep, licking at his warmth, relishing his masculine flavor. Sliding his hands down her back, he returned the kiss, thrusting and tangling with her tongue, ravaging her senses until her head spun with giddy sensation and the music wasn't the only thing throbbing.

She lifted from his mouth, stunned by the way he affected her. Her pulse chased wildly, her heart pounded. Arousal had to be dripping down her thighs in thick, creamy rivulets. Never had Rick made her so hot, so wet with a kiss or his lovemaking from start to finish. But then, she knew now that what Rick had done to her wasn't lovemaking but the kind of hurtful handling the drunk had tried.

Thank goodness for Colin.

She smiled. "Thank you. He had really smelly breath and his hands weren't so great, either. Nothing like yours." His hands dipped lower, cupping her ass and squeezing the way they had in her dream last night. Her very first erotic dream. She'd woken up damp and breathing hard and craving Colin's touch. "I dreamt about your hands last night."

He looked like he wanted to say more about her being there alone, but caved to a salacious smile instead. "Did you? And what exactly did these dreams entail?"

"You touching me." Joyce sighed. Not nearly bold enough. Think attitude. Dirty words. Think about that ultimate orgasm just waiting to be had. "I dreamt about the way your fingers would feel inside me, loving my pussy, making me scream." She moved a hand between them and found his cock through his jeans, already so hard, so ready for her. "I thought about this all day. About how it would feel pushing into me, taking me. I thought about the hot sounds you make when you come."

Screams of ecstasy exploded to her right, sounding out above the hammering music. Colin spun her in his arms and pulled her back flush to his front. His breath fanned warmth into her ear as she followed his gaze toward the owner of those screams, a voluptuous platinum blonde standing naked and spread-eagled against a railing.

"How do you want me to take you, cupcake?" His hot words teased her ear as his hard sex pressed into her bottom. "From the front or the back? Tongue or cock? Watch, and tell me which one excites you more?"

Nipples straining into hard aching buds, sex letting forth a gush of wild juices, Joyce watched rapt. The woman's hands were cuffed to the metal bar at her back and her legs splayed wide, parting her shaved pussy lips to a redheaded man kneeling on the floor in front of her and her butt cheeks to a second man behind her. Fully clothed, the redhead held her thighs in his hands and used his tongue to push up the hood of her clit. He drew the swollen pearl between his lips. The blonde's tongue came out, licking at the sweltering air. Her hips thrust forward, burying his face in her mound. The large, raven-haired man at her back held her long hair in one hand while he reached around to squeeze a heavy breast with the other. Unlike his friend, he wasn't clothed, but naked from the waist down. The blonde's hips went wild and her frenzied screams came again as the man thrust forward then quickly jerked backward, revealing a long, thick cock glistening with juice.

Ménage. She knew the word, had seen the pictures in her book, but never could've guessed at the naughty thrill of watching one unfold. The bouncing strobe lights and grinding music made the scene seem that much kinkier.

Unable to steal her gaze from the thrusting trio, Joyce's own scream filled the air when Colin's big hand cupped her sex. A lone finger drove upward, stroking her dripping slit through the thin material of her dress. She'd risked all and went without panties again. Closing her eyes as that long, bold finger rubbed against her aching clit, she smiled her gratitude.

Tonight she wouldn't be an idiot. Tonight she would be a sex goddess coming undone with the ultimate orgasm.

The hair was lifted from her nape and his warm mouth nuzzled her neck. She shivered as he trailed moist kisses from her nape to the spaghetti strap of her dress. Teeth bit into the tiny strap, tugging it down her arm. Those teeth gave a yank and sultry air licked over her breast, against her painfully tight nipple.

Joyce's eyes flared open. She looked down to find the Harley on her right breast had zoomed out of hiding, its vivid colors gleaming in the bouncing glow of the strobe lights. Colin's teeth tugged on the other strap. One large hand flicked across her chest, brushing her nipple and retreating far too quickly. Her left breast came into view, exposing an aroused, deep pink areola. His hand returned, this time bringing its partner. They covered her breasts, palming, squeezing, tugging at her nipples while his mouth worked a wicked wet path down her spine.

She moaned with each damp, teasing kiss, reclined into his

touch completely. Liquid desire pumped hotly through her veins, deep into her sex. The dress slid lower over the softness of her belly to the tilt of her hips. Pale blond pubic hair flirted into sight. Good gosh this was it; soon he would have her naked, fully exposed to every patron in the club, and there were hundreds of them.

Could she let it happen? Could she be so daring?

One hand lifted from her breast, moved beneath the hem of her dress and rimmed her swollen pussy lips. Joyce's head fell back with a lusty sigh, the ends of her hair tickling her naked, sweaty back. Hedonistic delight thrummed from the tips of her erect nipples to the center of her aching sex. Her heart pounded in time with the pulsating beat surrounding them.

"Is this how you want it, cupcake?" A lone finger pushed into her sheath, milking her.

She cried out. Oh, gosh, did she cry out. Heat rushed into her face. Her legs shook. Her belly tightened. Was this it? The ultimate climax? Was she building up to it? If so, then this was how she wanted it. "Yes. I want that. I want more."

"How many more?" Colin added a second finger, pushing up into her creaming body. He came around to her front. Watching her through intense, hungry green eyes he lashed his tongue across a nipple. He added a third finger, stretching her, pushing her ever closer to the edge. She closed her eyes with a moan as his mouth took in her nipple, his teeth scraped. Fire ignited in her loins.

This was it. This had to be it.

The wet, sucking warmth of his lips lifted. He pulled his fingers free of her body. She whimpered at the heavenly loss.

No. Please no. Don't stop now.

Joyce opened her eyes, ready to protest, ready to demand that he return to her. Speech failed her, breath failed her. She could only stare as he pushed the dress to the floor, fell to his knees and fit his mouth over her sex.

His tongue skewered into her center, thrust deep into her slick cunt. Shivers shook her to the core. Words left her lips as senseless sobs. His hands wrapped around the apex of her thighs, his thumbs spread her pussy lips wide, wider, until she was splayed like the woman from the ménage.

Joyce looked over, expecting to find the blonde cuffed and screaming. The woman was gone, but the men were there, both naked now, mouths fused and hands stroking each other's erect cocks. The kiss ended and the smaller of the men, the redhead, went to his knees. He guided the other man's erection toward his lips. She gasped as his tongue came out and lapped at the fluid glistening on the head of his partner's cock, then gasped again as Colin twisted his tongue inside her body.

Tremors sliced through her. Her limbs shook so forcefully she feared she might fall. Something hard pushed up against her, supporting her from behind. The tremors increased, stealing her breath, her sanity. She closed her eyes and gave into heady sensation. Hands closed over her breasts, fingers toyed with her aching nipples. Colin's tongue pulled out. Tugging at her clit, he thrust back in and twisted both finger and tongue. The hands at her breasts plucked at her nipples, squeezed hard.

Fever gripped her belly, her mind. She screamed as she came, pulsing hot, flowing cream into Colin's mouth. One hand left her breast to grip her hair and pull her head back. A tongue pushed into her mouth, ate at her. Not Colin's, her mind registered somewhere through the tremors of ecstasy. But she was powerless to do anything but ride out those tremors, to give into the kiss and bask in the glow of the ultimate orgasm.

Through a rapturous fog she was aware of Colin's hands leaving her thighs, his tongue pulling from her body. The tongue pulled from her mouth, as well, the hands from her hair and breast. Shouts sounded around her.

The yelling lifted her from her haze. She opened her eyes to find Colin standing in front of her. She smiled, ready to tell him how good he'd been. How incredibly, amazingly good. His dark look stopped her. She thought him angry last night. He hadn't been then, but he was now.

Rage compressed his lips and narrowed his eyes. A muscle twitched along his jawline. He seemed taller than she'd ever realized. Towering over her, emanating a storm of dark, furious passion. "I guess you didn't want the front or the back, did you, cupcake?" he mocked loudly in a tone cold as ice. "You wanted both."

Trembling with the accusation, with the cruelty of his look, Joyce darted for her dress. She tugged it on with shaking hands and wrapped her arms around her chest. She didn't want to be afraid. She didn't. But she was. "W—what do you mean?"

"Did you enjoy his kiss?" he snapped. "Did you like the way his hands felt on your tits? I hope so, because he's the only one you'll be going home with tonight."

His? The other man. The one she'd heard arguing with Colin. The one who'd had his hands on her breasts, his tongue in her mouth. Her insides crawled. "Oh, my gosh. I didn't realize. I didn't know. I—I don't want him. I want you. I swear I do."

He smirked, no laugh lines present now, just cold, hard rage. "Do you? For how long? Just until you get my dick in your ass and then you'll move on? How about I give it to you right now, and you can still go home with him."

Colin was at her back before she could blink. His arm banded around her middle like a metal vise. His free hand yanked at the hem of her dress, exposing her buttocks.

Tears pricked at her eyes. No, he wouldn't take her this way, not when she wasn't ready. Not when fear held her in its crippling grasp. "C—Colin. Stop. Please stop! I don't like you like this. You—you're scaring me."

Long seconds passed. She fought for strength. The arm at her waist loosened. The hem of dress slipped back down. The warmth and hardness of his body left her. Joyce turned to find him shaking his head, looking deflated. Defeated.

Remorse filled his eyes. "Shit!" he shouted above the music. "I'm sorry. I didn't mean to scare you. I thought we came here tonight to be together. If you want someone else, fine, but don't expect me to take part."

"But I don't want anyone else. I want you." Fear was gone now, replaced by soul-deep desire the moment she'd witnessed his regret.

He wasn't Rick. Nor the drunk who'd manhandled her when she'd first entered the club. He wasn't a man to fear, but one to give and receive pleasure.

She stepped forward. Laying her palms on the hard planes of his chest, she rose on tiptoe and brushed his cheek with her lips. "Let me show you how badly I want you."

His eyes reflected his need to experience that. But he lifted her hands away and shook his head. "I've already overstayed my visit."

"Take me home with you then," Joyce pleaded. This wasn't just about pleasure any longer. This was about more. Not forever. But maybe about faith. About trust. About showing him she wasn't the type of person to taunt another with her actions or her words. "I promise you won't be sorry. I'll do anything you want. You can do anything to me. Don't leave angry, Colin. Please."

"I'm not angry, just disappointed."

"Let me make it up to you. Let me show you how much I didn't want him. How badly I want you. Only you. Take me with you."

Indecision warred in his eyes. She held her breath; he expelled his, long, hot and hard. "All right. Let's go."

What the fuck was he thinking, bringing her home with him?

Colin killed the engine on his truck. Headlights flashed from behind, and a car pulled in the driveway and shut off. Caitlyn was here, expecting him to take her up to his bed and give her a screaming orgasm that Liz would overhear and never let him live down.

Or maybe Caitlyn didn't expect an orgasm. Maybe she expected him to make her give him another blow job and anything else he desired in exchange for what happened back at the club. The past made him anxious to find her guilty and send her packing. The expression on her face as she apologized for letting that other guy touch her had him wanting to buy her every word. She'd looked upset when he'd started shouting, fearful the way she'd been last night in those moments following the gum incident. She'd admitted to the fear, told him he was scaring her. That was the reason he'd brought her home, because—asinine of him or not—he believed her. He believed she was genuinely sorry and that she'd been so into the moment she hadn't realized another man was touching her until it was too late.

Hell, he shouldn't care if her apologies were genuine. He shouldn't be wondering over the bastard responsible for putting that fear in her eyes in the first place. Shouldn't even give a damn if every man in that club stuck his tongue down her throat and his dick in her ass. She didn't mean a thing to him. Come tomorrow, she'd be gone, nothing more than a memory. His comeback fuck.

Colin grunted. He'd never feel this way over a comeback fuck. Shaken up inside and confused as hell by the way Caitlyn could be scorching hot one minute and timid as a mouse the next.

He got out of the truck and went back to her car, a Mustang so brilliant yellow it nearly glowed in the dark. The perfect car for the blond bombshell who'd beckoned him to her side last night. It wasn't the bombshell inside the car, though. That woman would be bounding out of the door and into his arms. This woman sat motionless, looking ahead as if he'd frightened her into having second thoughts.

He opened her door. The dome light filtered out into the darkness and lit up her face as she looked at him uncertainly. He smiled. Someone needed to get this thing back on the solely sexual track it belonged. "You plan on staying in there all night?"

"I shouldn't go inside. It's your home. Your personal space."

That should be his concern alone. Unless she was having as many problems keeping her thoughts on the physical as he was. "I want you to come in. If what happened back at the club is stopping you, forget about it. I reacted badly."

Her eyebrows drew together and she frowned. "I would never taunt someone that way, make them believe I wanted them when it was another guy I was after. That's just awful. I honestly didn't even realize he was there at first, and then I couldn't think. You had my mind spinning." A smile touched at her lips and warmed her hazel eyes. "You were really good, Colin."

Conceit spiked through him. When was the last time a woman told him he was good? Marlene sure as hell hadn't. She'd spent her days making sure he knew how bad he was—at sex, at marriage. Even with his job. She never thought he stood a fighting chance getting the landscaping business off the ground and into the black.

For the sake of keeping his mind on work, he should say good-night to Caitlyn. Good-night and good-bye to all the questions she raised. He should, but he wanted her to come inside too badly. Her words belied his ex-wife's claim that he was a lousy lay. Still, he ached to show Caitlyn the magnitude of his skills as a lover, for the sake of his ego, and, hell, because he'd slept alone for too damned long.

"Trust me, cupcake, that was nothing." He extended his

hand to her. "Let me show you how good I can be. I promise not to scare you again."

Her tongue slipped out, moistening her lower lip. He groaned, wanting his own tongue on that plump lip. Wanting to burrow inside her mouth and remove all taste of that other guy. Possessiveness shook through him. He had neither the time nor the heart for anything lasting, but for tonight she could be his. For tonight he could take her to his bed and remember how incredible it felt to sleep with a woman's warm, soft body spooned against his own.

Her tongue pulled back in. She nodded. "All right. If you're sure."

"I am."

She reached for his proffered hand. The heat of her fingers against his as he helped her out of the car sent a shiver coursing through him. That shiver grew as he led her up the walk to the front door and turned the knob. He'd bought this home for Marlene, for the family they'd have together. It seemed wrong to bring another woman here. Wrong to want to take that woman to his bed. But it couldn't be wrong. He hadn't been the unfaithful one who destroyed his belief in marriage and love once and for all. He couldn't live in the past with shattered dreams forever. He pushed open the door and guided Caitlyn inside.

Light bled from the crack beneath the kitchen door. Switching on the living room light, he led her to the wraparound staircase on the opposite side of the room. "Go on up. My room's the second one on the right. I need to do something real quick."

He'd intended to leave it at that. Send her to his room while he dealt with the light in the kitchen, or, rather, Liz, who was inside cooking up her latest special, Mud Surprise. The coy way Caitlyn's blond lashes fluttered against her cheeks made walking away without a good-bye kiss impossible. If he had only tonight to invest in her and her night-and-day personality, he would see they both enjoyed the next several hours to the fullest.

She'd started up the stairs in anticipation of him following. One step up, her mouth was mere inches below his. Colin leaned forward and bent his head, slanted his mouth over hers. Her lips blossomed, parting to release her warm, damp tongue. She sank into his mouth, explored with slow licks, unsteady rubs. The moves were shy, almost virginal, and affected him more than her fast, lusty kisses ever could.

He pulled her against him and rocked his hips into hers. Hers responded with a slow, rolling thrust. His cock hardened, pulsed with need. Her hands feathered through his hair, toying with the strands, tickling his ears. Needful in a way he'd never experienced—a burning that started in his mind and scorched a hungry path to his groin—he closed his eyes and took control of the kiss. Slipping his tongue between her lips, he explored with the same slow licks and unsteady rubs that she had. She whimpered against his mouth and sweetness exploded on his tongue, goodness that came from deep within her.

Christ, who was this woman and how could she affect him this way? He didn't do slow kisses with his eyes closed. He didn't stand in the living room making out while his sister was one room away.

Colin eased out of the kiss with the reminder of his sister's presence. The last thing he needed was Liz discovering them. He opened his eyes to find Caitlyn's still closed. Her lips pulled into a soft smile. Slowly, she opened her eyes.

"He didn't kiss me like that," she said softly, dreamily, like she was coming down from her own personal cloud nine. "No one's ever kissed me like that."

Who was she? he wondered again, and then shook away the question. Regardless of who she might be to others, to him she could be nothing more than the woman who'd share his bed tonight.

Colin grinned while melancholy gripped him hard. So he'd have an empty bed come morning. So the fuck what? He was a big boy, he'd deal with it.

He looked up the stairs, then back at Caitlyn. "Get your sweet ass moving before I do you right here on the staircase."

She laughed huskily. "I might like that. It sounds like a great deal of fun."

Now *that* sounded like the Caitlyn he'd first met. Ready to try anything, ready to give him a blow job in the back alley of a bar. His dick twitched. He spun her around and gave her bottom a whack. "Go. Now. That's an order."

"Yes, sir." She hurried up the staircase, her short dress fluttering with her steps and flashing peeks of her supple white ass.

That's what she represented for him. A fine piece of ass.

Repeating that thought, Colin went to the kitchen door and pushed it in. Liz glanced up from putting the finishing touches on a lopsided heap suffocated with chocolate frosting. Or mud. One or the other.

Licking some of the alleged frosting from her thumb, she gave him a sympathetic look. "I heard you drive in. Sorry the date blew."

"Yeah, well, I wasn't hoping for much." He wasn't hoping to get away without his sister knowing he had company, either, but maybe tonight he'd be getting lucky in more ways than one. "I'm going to bed early. Work's been taking a lot out of me."

"But what about the Mud Pie Bliss? I just finished it."

Colin feigned a yawn. It was better than giving into the shudder that threatened at the idea of sticking a fork in that dark brown heap and shoveling it into his mouth. "I'm seriously whipped. I'll have a piece for breakfast."

"Yeah, right. I'll believe it when I see—" The floor over their heads creaked, and she stopped short to narrow her eyes and swat his arm. "You dog. You brought her home and weren't even going to tell me."

He shrugged. "The walls aren't that thick. I'm sure you would've figured it out on your own."

She tipped her head to the side and studied him. Her perceptive eyes gave him the urge to bolt before she opened her mouth and said something he had no longing to hear, tonight or ever. "You really like her, don't you?"

Shit. Too late. "It's just for the night. That's it."

"Uh-huh."

"I mean it. And I promise to have some Mud Heap—uh, Pie Bliss in the morning." He moved to the door before she could ask any more questions he refused to take the time to consider. Pushing the door open, he called over his shoulder, "Good night."

Liz laughed. "Let's just say it's not half as good as yours is going to be."

4

Joyce stood in the center of Colin's bedroom, taking in the warm blues and greens of the decor and the king-size bed in the center, while her mind repeated one thought: She shouldn't be here.

Home was personal. Home was where you went to learn about someone. She couldn't learn about him. Not without risking their relationship becoming about more than sex; her heart wasn't ready for more than that. But, darnit, she also couldn't allow Colin to believe she was the kind of girl to be with one guy while she lured in another. He was all she needed—more than enough.

Not need in the traditional sense, either. Need as in burned for his touch. Just the thought of his tongue pushing into her sex had her clit tingling. Gracious, how sexy he'd made her feel, how undeniably naughty and desirable. Right up until the moment they'd been interrupted by an unwanted third party.

That he not only believed her apologies but gave those of his own for the harsh way he'd reacted said so much about the man. He was both compassionate and trustworthy. The kind of guy a girl could get used to.

Joyce pulled from her silent stare to look at a picture of a small lake surrounded by lush green grass and a plethora of vibrant, multicolored flowers hanging over the bed. No more thoughts of Rick and for sure no more thoughts of getting used to Colin being in her life. Just thoughts of the physical. Of redeeming herself as a sex goddess in his eyes. She'd let traces of the old Joyce slip out too many times tonight. She had to erase those traces from his memory.

Showering was the next chapter in *Achieving the Ultimate Orgasm*. Cleansing your partner with your hands and mouth while keeping the rest of your body in sight but off-limits was supposed to have both of you desperate for release. When climax came, it was said to be mind-blowing. The climax she'd had earlier had been staggering, but, then, she didn't have anything worthwhile to compare it with. Maybe it hadn't been ultimate the way she'd believed. Maybe it had only been good.

Shivering over the idea that an orgasm could be better, she moved into the bathroom connected to the bedroom by a doorway. She flipped on the light switch and quickly stripped off her dress. She paused to inspect her naked reflection, pleased when the sting of embarrassment didn't heat her cheeks.

An extremely late bloomer, she'd never been comfortable with her body. She'd been teased over it and her dry personality too many times as a kid and a teenager. She wasn't either now, nor was she trapped behind a bad personal image built up by her ex-husband. She was a confident, appealing woman with a Harley streaking across her chest. A woman about to have really excellent sex.

Smiling because for the first time she truly believed in herself, Joyce moved to the bathtub. She pulled aside the navy-blue shower curtain and turned the faucet handles. Hot water sprayed from the nozzle and steam raised thick in the air.

"Joyce?"

Colin's voice drifted in from the bedroom and froze her on the spot. He'd called her Joyce. Not Caitlyn, but Joyce. No. He couldn't have learned her secret. Not now.

Her shoulders sank. Every bit of confidence drained away. She turned off the water and wrapped a towel around her. "In here."

He stepped into the bathroom doorway. His gaze slid over her body, lingered on her breasts straining against the towel and returned to her eyes to reveal lust burning in his own. "Very nice. Planning on sharing?"

"Y—you still want me?" Dangit! He still wanted her even after learning what a dud she used to be, and she was doing her best to ruin it by stammering. Boldness was needed here. Assertiveness and attitude.

She unwrapped the towel and let it drop to the blue-and-white-checked tiling. Her nipples hardened instantly, her sex moistening as Colin's potent gaze zeroed in on the strip of trimmed blond curls covering it. He'd seen her naked back at the club, but it hadn't been light there, not the way it was now. Here he could see every little part. Every little imperfection.

Her heart hammered as she waited for his next words.

On second thought, why wait? A sex goddess would never wait. A sex goddess would take matters into her own hands, literally.

Joyce brought her hands to her breasts, cupping their weight and rubbing her thumbs across the sensitized nipples. The breath dragged in between her lips as pleasure shot to her womb. "Still like what you see?" She didn't have to fake the breathiness of her tone. She'd never touched herself this way. It felt incredibly sensual.

"You know I do, cupcake." His lips curved into a sexy smile, bringing gentle laugh lines to the corners of his mouth. "Just in case you need further proof . . ."

His hands went to his zipper, parting the fly and pushing the jeans and underwear down his muscular thighs. The tail of his shirt hid his cock, but she could tell its erectness by the way it pushed against the material. It wasn't enough. She wanted to see all of his big, buff body the way he was seeing hers.

"Take the rest off."

The demand in her voice stunned her. She nearly retracted the words when Colin responded with a mock salute and a teasing, "Yes, ma'am."

He pulled the shirt over his head, tossing it aside. Her mouth went dry as she took in the solid width of his sculpted chest and the crisp, sandy-brown hair that lined it. In the beginning Rick had pretended at being a snuggler, but truthfully that wasn't his nature. He'd preferred to have sex and then roll over to sleep without so much as a good-night kiss. She prayed Colin wasn't that way, because the idea of curling up against his warm, hard body, legs and arms intertwined, had her anxious to get the sex part over with.

Joyce shunned herself for the thought. This wasn't about snuggling. It was about the physical, and a true sex goddess would never want to rush things. Of course, once they had their hands on each other's bodies, neither would she.

As her nerves fired with the restless need to touch him, she traveled her gaze down his body, past his defined abdomen to his groin and gasped. "Oh, my gosh!" His pubic hair was gone. His cock seemed larger, his balls heavier as they hung naked between his thighs. "What happened to your hair?"

He looked down. "Damnedest thing. I was blowing bubbles a little too close to my dick. One of them got stuck and I had no choice but to shave the hair off to get it out."

She frowned, not believing his joking tone. He had to be upset over his hairless state, and it was all her fault. Her and her idiocy. "The gum wouldn't come out. I'm so sorry, Colin."

He looked back at her and smiled reassuringly. Trying to comfort her yet again. What a man. He shrugged. "Hey, no big deal. It'll grow back."

"I hope so."

"Does it bother you?"

"Does it bother you that my real name's Joyce?" She held her breath.

"Figured you just like your middle name better. While I still had some blood left in my brain, I put your driver's license and cash on the end table by my bed. I grabbed them when I was undressing you earlier."

Heat chased through her at the reminder of the way he'd stripped her at the club, his long fingers and teeth working her dress off until she was naked and aching and frantic to feel him inside her. That heat turned to sweet relief as she realized the meaning behind his words. He didn't know anything about her past. He only thought she went by a different name than her given one. She was still a sex goddess in his eyes.

A sex goddess eager to bring her short-term lover to his knees with pleasure.

Joyce stepped forward and caressed the freshly shaven skin that surrounded his erection. His shaft jerked toward her hand and her sex tingled with heady awareness of the way she made him want. As unexpected as it was, she liked him hairless. It made him seem so much more open to her. Closer somehow. It also made his cock easier to grip, to wrap her lips around.

She went down on her knees and flicked her tongue across the arousal-reddened skin at the base of his sex. Cupping his balls, she massaged the sac, studying it with interest and not even a hint of the embarrassment she would have felt days ago.

"This is really erotic," she breathed against his groin. "I've never seen a man so naked before. It makes my lips anxious to kiss you. My mouth to suck on you." The hunger thick in her voice made her hot, wet. Nipples throbbing, she ran her tongue up the length of his shaft, seeming to go on forever before she reached the soft, ridged head. "Gracious, you have a really big cock."

"Haven't you heard size doesn't matter?"

Oh, gosh, had she offended him? She liked his large size. Really, she did. "I didn't mean that it's a bad thing. I thought I might choke on it at first the other night, but I didn't. I was fine." Joyce's cheeks heated over the rambling admission. Before she could say anything else foolish, she opened her lips and sucked in the dark pink tip of his shaft. She suckled at the head, savoring the silky fluid that leaked onto her tongue. So male. So potent. So very, very good.

Rubbing the ridge at the underside of his erection with her thumb, she looked up at his face. She swirled her tongue over the head, dipping into the tiny hole at the end, and murmured her delight. "Mmm . . . better than fine."

Colin's features tightened, his mouth firming and his eyes going to half mast. Thickly, he said, "You're the one who's better than fine."

Electrified by the words, she drew him back into her mouth, this time taking him in as far as he could go. Wrapping her hands around the thick base of his cock, she twisted in opposite directions while applying pressure with her lips. His hips shot toward her mouth and his fingers pushed into her hair.

He groaned. "Ah, hell, cupcake. I'd like to let you go on sucking for hours, but I'm not going to last that long. And this time when I come, it's going to be with your body loving me."

Joyce's lips stilled on his shaft. Her heart beat fiercely. Loving him? Had he meant to call it that? No. She was reading something into words spoken out of lust. There was no love here, and there shouldn't be. Couldn't be.

254 / Jodi Lynn Copeland

She concentrated on the physical, on driving him wild. Ignoring his words, she continued to milk him with her mouth and hands, twisting, licking, sucking until a moan erupted from his throat and his cock pulsed hotly between her lips.

Slowly, she eased back, his sex pulling free with a pop. She stood and staggered, her hip hitting against the sink basin. He wasn't the only one she was driving wild. She was more than a little light-headed, and cream dripped from her pussy down her inner thighs. His eyes opened fully, falling on the rivulets of arousal. His nostrils flared while his look turned primal, predatory. He started to reach for her.

Heart pounding, she stepped back. He wanted to have her now. If she didn't make her next move this instant, he would take her. And she wouldn't stop him. Couldn't. Not when every cell in her body sizzled with the need for his touch. "Shower time," she said tightly, turning toward the bathtub.

"Looks to me like you're already wet enough."

The coarseness of his voice scraped along her nerves, already so bunched with sensual tension. She forced herself to focus on preparing the water, turning on the faucets and adjusting the temperature. She couldn't stop her tremble as she lifted one leg over the bathtub ledge. "All ready."

"You can say that again, cupcake."

Colin's strong hands wrapped around her arms from behind, lifting her against his aroused, solid body before she could move another inch. Holding her to him, he climbed into the tub. Hot spray pulsed between her shoulder blades as he lifted her arms, bracing them, palms down, on the tiling above her head. The position was incredibly subservient. It should have scared her. Instead, carnal delight shot through her, stripping the last of her nerves until they were so raw with want, it was all she could do not to beg him to take her now.

One hard knee pushed between her thighs and rubbed

against her swollen sex. His lips brushed her ear. "Hold still while I get you clean."

"But I'm supposed to—"

"Be a good girl and do what I say. Remember, you promised."

Back at the club she had promised to do whatever he wanted, but that was in total conflict with her plans to drive him wild. He held the reins of control now. She had no choice but to give in to him and prove her word was good. "I'll behave."

He reached past her for the bar of soap on the corner ledge. Bringing his arms around her, he rubbed the bar between his hands until suds sloshed to the tub floor and the scent of sandalwood lifted into the air. Gliding the soap over her body with one hand, he filled the other with a breast. He massaged the throbbing mound, rubbing the nipple into a painful, aching bud, then gave the same treatment to the other. The hand that held the soap skimmed over her belly and down the top half of her thighs.

Joyce giggled as he brushed it over the back of a knee. "Sorry, but that tickles."

"Does this tickle, too?" He guided the soap up between her thighs and across her slit. She shuddered as the hard edge scraped over her clit, then sighed as he rasped the short side back across her lips and applied pressure.

The hand at her breast moved to her mound, threading through the tight curls to part the slick folds of her pussy. Her sex pulsed, and she whimpered in expectation of the soap filling her, fucking her. Instead, he dropped the soap and grabbed the showerhead, disconnecting it from the base. He brought the head between her legs. The steady stream of hot water pounded against her swollen clit and pushed forcefully into her opening. She writhed as pressure built in her belly. Her legs shook uncontrollably. Heat consumed her chest, her face. Her pulse raced.

The whole point of showering together was to prolong the pleasure, to make it the best climax either of them had ever had. If Colin kept touching her this way, kept stroking her with the steady flux of the water, she'd be coming in seconds.

"Tickling yet?"

He nibbled at her earlobe. She reared back and cried out when his stiff cock caressed her ass. "Not tickling. Too much."

"Nuh-uh. Not nearly enough, cupcake." His voice rasped wickedly. He turned the showerhead's dial to the next setting. The steady stream of water turned to dozens of little jets, all pulsating against her juicy sex, all threatening to drive her mad and straight over the edge.

Pushing his thumb and first finger into her opening, he parted her sex so widely that pleasure pain sliced through her. The jets thrummed against her cunt, blinding the subtle ache, drawing forth sensation greater than anything she'd ever known. He angled the showerhead in varying directions until every inch of her sheath was afire with the need to explode. And she was going to explode. There was no more holding back. She couldn't stand it a second longer.

Colin replaced the showerhead in its base. The pressure in her sex tapered off, orgasm slowly receded.

Joyce cried out her disbelief. "What are you doing? You can't do that." It wasn't nice to build her up and leave her hanging. And he was a nice guy. Wasn't he?

He chuckled, not sounding nice at all, but downright sinful. "You told me I could. You said I could do anything I wanted to you." His tone became lower, tighter, eager. "I still need to clean your mouthwatering ass."

One hand remained at her mound, cupping her sex, teasing a finger back and forth across her clit. The other moved to her lower back, rubbing the rise off her buttocks. Two fingers journeyed down the slope, stroked the cleft. A single finger dipped between the cleft and pushed into the puckered hole.

Joyce swallowed hard. She closed her eyes, expecting pain. She'd seen pictures in the sex manual, had witnessed that woman being taken from behind at the club, but it didn't seem possible that such a thing could be pleasurable. It was pleasure, though, that erupted between her thighs as he pushed his finger farther inside her anus and wiggled it. White-hot pleasure that leaked juices down her thighs, thick and creamy, to mingle with the streaming water.

"Do you like it in this end, cupcake?" He pulled partway out and milked her hole with a slow, thrusting rhythm. She cried out and arched back, wildly desperate for more, wanting all of him. "Please . . ."

His laughter fanned hotly against her sweaty flesh. "I'll take that as a yes."

"Yes," she managed, her thighs trembling, pressure sizzling through her once more, building up even greater than before. "It's so . . . so good. You're so . . ." He added a second finger. Ecstasy crashed through her. "Oh, gracious . . . so good."

"Just good?"

"Amazing. You're am—" The breath left her as his fingers pulled out quickly and his cock pushed into her hole. Her eyes watered at the magnitude of him filling her ass, so strong, so sturdy. So deep. Thrusting a finger into the slick valley of her sex, he pushed deeper still. "Holy Hades, Colin!"

She reared back. He pistoned his hips, meeting her thrust with one in the opposite direction. The pressure was too much, the tension all-consuming. She screamed as orgasm toppled over her, near blinding with its intensity.

"Okay?"

Colin's rough voice pushed through the tempest of ecstasy. She forced out, "O—kay," as spasms continued to ripple through her.

His moan blistered her ears as his seed pounded into her buttocks in a hot spray that almost brought her to her knees.

His arm wrapped around middle, locking her in place. The breath raged from his lungs as his hips pivoted, emptying the last of the cum from his body.

Seconds passed in a daze of unspeakable bliss. His words broke the silence. "I think you almost killed me."

Joyce laughed at the incredulousness of the statement. He was the one who'd nearly pushed her past the point of consciousness. She thought he hadn't been nice when he'd put the showerhead away, leaving her on the brink. He *had* been nice. Incredibly, wonderfully, ultimate-orgasmically so. "That was . . . so . . . Rick could never make me come like that. Not even in his dreams."

The arm around her middle tightened. "Rick?"

Bliss left her in a deflating sigh. No. She hadn't just pulled the most inane move ever and brought up her ex-husband. Only, she had. "He's no one important."

"Important enough to compare me to."

The rapture was gone from his voice, replaced by a tightness she understood well. He believed she was involved with another man and sleeping with him on the side. Dangit, she thought she'd convinced him earlier she would never do something like that. Maybe he didn't trust her after all. But then, maybe he had good reason not to. She hadn't been truthful with him. For the sake of bringing back the thrill of the moment, she found herself admitting, "My ex-husband. I never see him anymore. He's in prison."

Colin should have relaxed. Instead, his entire body stiffened against her back. "For abusing you, right?"

"*What*?" Why would he think such a thing?

He spun her in his arms and eyed her soberly. "Did he hit you?"

The urge to look at the floor was automatic. She forced her gaze to steady, not to show or feel fear. She was stronger now.

She could stand up to the truth. "Just once, I swear. It was the night he went to prison, and, no, it wasn't for abusing me."

Sympathy filled his eyes. He pulled her tightly against him. Brushing the hair back, he kissed her forehead. "He yelled a lot, made you feel like you were less of a person. Made you feel scared. I'm sorry, cupcake."

Joyce wanted to stand up to the truth with a bold front, to be confident, self-assured, as if the past were long forgotten. But she couldn't when he was holding her so compassionately.

Tears welled in her eyes. She hid her face against his chest. He was so darned sweet. So much more than she'd expected to find in a short-term lover. But that's what he was. What he had to be. A short-term guy who wouldn't be messing with her heart or mind. That meant she couldn't say any more on Rick. It meant she soon had to tell Colin good-bye. "I don't really want to talk about him. I'm tired."

"Okay," he said after a moment's hesitation. Tipping her face back with a finger under her chin, he gave her a comforting smile. "Just remember, the way he treated you wasn't your fault, Joyce. He was the messed-up one. The fact that he's in jail says that much."

Her own smile came with the confidence he exuded. She could practice a lifetime and never be that sure of herself. "It must be nice to be so strong."

"How do you mean?"

"You would never let anyone make you feel like less of a person."

His lips fell flat and he stepped from her arms out of the shower. Grabbing a towel, he mumbled, "That just goes to show how much you don't know me."

"No, I don't." But she did know one thing. She hadn't kicked her naïveté.

She was just as gullible as ever to believe she could be with a man as kind and warm as Colin and not have her heart get involved. The lack of his arms around her, and the lack of his presence in the shower, hurt more than Rick's cruel words or even his fist had. The thought of never getting to know him better, let alone seeing him beyond a few more days, made her feel lonelier than she'd been in her entire life.

Standing naked in Colin's bathroom, following a morning shower for one that reminded her too much of last night's explosive shower for two, Joyce rubbed lightly at her tat. She stuck out her tongue at the Harley. Rubbing was pointless. The tat wasn't looking any better. The thing was just as dry and flaky as its owner. Only, as she recalled from the care instructions, this was just a stage along the way to the tat's completion. Her own dry flakiness was permanent.

Last night, for such a long while, she'd been self-assured, in control and loving the power that confidence wrought. After convincing herself it was for the best that she and Colin had no future, she'd pushed her inner sex goddess back to the forefront and joined him in bed for another round of mind-blowing sex. Everything was good. Back on track. Then morning had come and he'd left for work with nothing more than a fleeting smile and hasty good-bye kiss.

No talk of another liaison. No exchange of phone numbers. Nothing but cold, hard reality returning to nip her in the bottom and call forth her inner flake—that naive little dunce who'd run her life for far too long. That gullible woman who in less than ten seconds had reversed every amount of last night's self-convincing that she was better off without Colin. Now she didn't feel better off. Now she ached for him to return home and tell her that he never should have left so casually because the way he felt for her was anything but casual.

Oh, pooh. Why did he have to be such a nice guy?

She should have dirty-talked Ernie into being her short-term lover. The tattoo artist wouldn't tease her over blowing bubbles into his pubic hair. He'd yell, just the way she deserved. All right, so she didn't deserve to be yelled at, but he wouldn't have made a joke over it the way Colin had. He wouldn't hold her close and offer comfort when he learned about Rick's ill treatment of her.

"Waky-waky time, Col. You're going to be late for work and both of us know what an ass you'll be if that happens. Besides, your Mud Pie Bliss is ready."

Joyce stiffened, her heart slamming against her ribs at the sound of a woman's loud voice. Who the heck was she? According to the bartender at Dusty's, Colin was divorced. The way he acted when he thought she wanted another man made it improbable that he could have another lover. Improbable, but not impossible. Maybe he wasn't such a nice guy after all. Maybe he was every bit as low-down as Rick.

"Colin?" A knock sounded against the bathroom door. "Col, you in there?"

Joyce grabbed her dress from where it had been left in a heap on the floor last night and tugged it on. Holding her breath, she darted her gaze around the room. A window, just above the sink, thank goodness. Barefoot, she climbed up on the basin. The window was small, but, then, so was she. She could fit. She had to fit. She pushed open the window and nearly wept to find no screen. Then nearly screamed as she took in the sheer drop down. She could handle a two-story fall. Suffering a broken arm or leg would be far better than meeting the girlfriend of the man she'd slept with last night. Wanted to sleep with again right this minute.

And that proved how truly flaky she was, Joyce thought as she stuck one leg out the window. Here she was, risking life and limb because of Colin's infidelity, and all she could think about was getting back into his arms. Bracing her palms on the sink basin, she stuck her other leg out the window. A warm morning breeze lifted her skirt and she grimaced. Imagine if Rick could see her now, starting out the day by escaping an about-to-be-scorned girlfriend and mooning the neighbors.

A second round of knocking started up. Joyce jolted; her arms trembled. Her palms slid forward on the slippery sink basin. She screeched as the faucet came into up-close-and-personal view, followed by the tiled flooring. Pain shot through her hands and knees as she skidded to a stop, inches from the door.

"Caitlyn?"

Joyce shook the fuzziness from her head and checked her body. Lots of ache, but nothing appeared bloody or broken. Nothing but her sanity. Her name registered, then, followed by the concern in the woman's voice. Whoever stood outside that door knew who she was. That ruled out a girlfriend. Which meant she'd nearly killed herself for no reason. Unless it was Colin's mother. What if she knew about the gum incident and that he'd had to shave off his pubic hair because of it?

Heat pushed into her cheeks. She stood and, ignoring the ache that shot through her limbs, straightened the skimpy black dress as best as possible. She didn't want to face his mother this way, but she wasn't risking that window again.

She counted to five, willing the embarrassment of the situation away. It didn't leave. Maybe she'd get lucky, and if she responded, his mother would go. "Um, yeah, I'm in here. Everything's okay. I just . . . thought I saw a spider."

"Is Colin with you?"

"Um, no. He had to go to work. He said I could sleep in and use the shower and stuff when I woke up. I have the day off work." Now go away. Please.

"Me, too." Her tone turned conversational, like she had no plans to go away any time soon. Crud. "Well, sort of. I have a cooking test tomorrow, so I have to spend the day trying to figure out how to make a soufflé."

"My mom has a great recipe." Joyce bit her tongue. Dangit. She really hadn't meant to say that.

"It sounds killer."

"It's excellent. I could teach . . ." Close your mouth. No matter how kind Colin's mother sounded, she could not teach her how to make a soufflé. That would mean spending the day with the woman, and that would be even worse than sharing information on her ex-husband with Colin. "I'll write it down for you." If she could just find a pen, she could jot it on toilet paper and slip it under the door.

"You cook a lot?"

Oh, gosh, she sounded excited about the idea. Was there even a chance of her getting away sight unseen? Maybe the window was worth a second try. She glanced at it, saying absently, "When I have time."

"Unless you have other plans for the day, can I hire you to teach me?"

Joyce spun back to the door and gasped. Beyond the assistance she provided customers at the bookstore, no one ever asked for her help. Warmth swelled in her chest. She smiled and opened the door before she could stop herself. A tall woman with short black hair and vivid blue eyes stood on the other side. She wasn't nearly old enough to be Colin's mother, but closer to Joyce's own age. "You honestly want my help?"

"I could really use it. Colin will tell you what a terrible cook I am."

The warmth wavered. She forced the smile to stay intact. "We're not close like that. We're just . . ."

"Sleeping together?"

Embarrassment returned to flood her. Joyce shifted, struggling to keep her attention from the security of the floor.

"Oh, please do not get all antsy and act like you shouldn't be telling me these things. Colin does that, too, and it drives me nutso. We're adults here. Talking about sex is not taboo. By the way, I'm Liz and I owe you a huge thanks. My brother was in major need of a lay."

"Colin's your brother?"

"Yeah. What, did you think he was my boyfriend?"

"Only at first." Just long enough to try to break her neck.

Liz laughed, then offered a wide smile. "Col's as single as they come. He hasn't even been with a woman since Marlene left. Well, he hadn't been before last night. Okay, the night before last, but I hardly think a blow job counts as real sex—even a good blow job, which apparently you gave him."

Joyce tried to shut out the woman's words—they were far more than she needed to hear. But she couldn't. She could only bask in the glow of knowing the blow job she'd given Colin was good enough to mention to his sister, and wonder over his ex-wife. If she stuck to sexual matters, asking a few questions would be okay. It wouldn't make her feel any closer to him.

Think attitude, she reminded herself, then asked, "Was Marlene good at blow jobs?"

"Marlene was a heinous bitch he never should have married. She had us all fooled at first, acted very sweet. But she wasn't even close to that. I hate that Colin had to find out she was cheating by walking in on her doing her old fart of a boss, but he never would have believed it otherwise. He's a huge believer in love and marriage. I'd say it's the reason he's put off sex for so long. But enough about my brother, let's hear about you and this excellent soufflé recipe of your mom's."

A huge believer in love and marriage? Then why was he wasting time on her? He'd made it clear last night that she didn't know anything about him and never would. Joyce's belly tightened as she remembered the aloof way he'd spoken those words.

She should leave immediately, not listen to another word about Colin or his ex. But Liz seemed so nice, not to mention anxious for cooking advice. Staying just a while longer couldn't hurt. Hopefully.

* * *

Sitting on a barstool at the kitchen counter, Colin stabbed a bite of soufflé and brought it to his lips. If he died for being nice enough to Liz to taste it, there would be real hell to pay. He swallowed hard and shoved the forkful into his mouth. Flavor exploded over his taste buds. And not the flavor of dirt, either. Really good flavor.

"Holy shit. I don't believe it." Stabbing another forkful, he looked at Liz, who leaned against the other side of the counter, beaming. "This is incredible. If you weren't my sister, I'd marry you and make you cook this for me every day."

Her smile widened. Her eyes twinkled. "Then I've got good news for you. I didn't cook it."

Pleasure over the soufflé's superior taste forgotten, he set the fork down on his plate. He knew that look. It was Liz's way-too-happy face. She only got it when she was up to no good. "Who made it?"

"Caitlyn."

"Caitlyn," Colin repeated, his stomach roiling.

He didn't want to think about her. He'd already endured thoughts of her—as well as thoughts on Liz's comment that he really liked her—all day when he should have been concentrating on work.

Fuck, yes. He did really like her.

When she looked at him not through the eyes of the red-hot siren, but as the cautious woman who'd obviously endured as messy of a divorce as he had, he wanted to reveal all. He wanted to show her that he understood her fears because he'd been in similar shoes. Marlene had never raised her hand at him, but she'd made him feel like less of a man on a daily basis.

No matter his wants, he couldn't share that information with Caitlyn. It would mean making things between them about more than sex, and he wasn't prepared to do that for any woman.

"She had the day off and just happened to have this killer

soufflé recipe of her mom's in her head. And, well, it turns out she's quite the cook."

"You spent the day together." It wasn't a question, but a statement that further irritated his stomach. How much of his past had Liz shared with Caitlyn? Knowing his big-mouthed sister, it was every sordid detail.

"Not the whole day. She had to meet up with someone tonight. She left around four. By the way, she said to tell you that you're a god in bed and you can call her any time." She nodded at the notepad next to the phone at the far end of the counter. "Her number's on the first page."

Who was she meeting with tonight—another man? And why the hell would she bother if he was truly a god in bed? Shit, he shouldn't care what she did with her time. Last night had been it for them. End of the road. Still, Colin couldn't help but ask, "She said that?"

"Not in quite those words, but it was pretty clear."

It was also pretty clear he should end this discussion. Only, he couldn't. Liz looked more energized by the second. She no longer leaned against the counter, but stood back and shifted foot to foot, as if she had something big to tell him. "How?"

"The way she blushed whenever I would bring up your name," she rushed out. "It's really cute. Kind of in a gag-me-sick way, but still cute." She stopped her shuffling and lowered her voice. "There's just one small problem."

Colin sat forward on the bar stool and steeled himself for the worst. "What?"

"She isn't taking this just-sex thing so well. I'd say she's already half in love with you. I definitely wouldn't use that phone number she left behind, because if you see her again she's going to fall harder and eventually you're going to break her heart."

He grabbed on to the counter ledge for stability as the impact of the words hit him. Liz had to be mistaken. He'd witnessed a softer, almost insecure side of Caitlyn by accident. He couldn't imagine she would show that side to his sister. "Are we talking about the same woman here? *My* Caitlyn?"

Liz tossed back her head and let out a boisterous laugh. "Normally I'd say possessiveness doesn't become you, but in this case, I think you might have something. 'Your Caitlyn.' That's just so cute."

So cute it curdled his gut.

What if she was right? He'd owe Caitlyn a chance to explain that they couldn't work out. Any other woman he wouldn't care to say good-bye to, but she wasn't any other woman. She wasn't just his comeback fuck. She was a woman he could relate to, and for that reason, if no other, she deserved a proper good-bye.

If Liz was right.

"One question and then I don't want to hear another word about her. Who did she really leave her number for? No bullshit now."

Liz glanced at the notepad, then back at him. "Oh, fine, you old bore. She left it for me. I asked if I could call her if I needed cooking tips."

"What about the rest? Was the rest of what you said legit?"

She stuck up her hand, extended her fingers and folded in her thumb and index finger. A fresh smile twitched at her lips. "Sorry, Col, but count 'em: That's a total of three questions. You said I couldn't talk about her after the first one."

"Answer me!" Damnit, he hated raising his voice when it was unwarranted, but Liz's teasing was more than he could handle.

Her lips fell flat. Soberly, she said, "Yes. Everything else I said was for real. She's sweet. She's gaga for you. And for such a little thing, she's really loud in bed. I swear, I had to break out my vibrator, I was so keyed up after listening to you two go at it half the night."

Colin shook his head, his temper fading with the highly unwanted information. For better or worse, it was impossible to keep a bad mood going around Liz. "No. No discussion on your vibrator. I'm your brother, for Christ's sake."

"That's okay. I already told Caitlyn all about it."

And what about Caitlyn? Did she have vibrator stories of her own to recount?

An image of her pale, curvy body splayed out on a bed, her legs spread wide and her sweet pink pussy dripping with juices around the long, thick shaft of a vibrator filled his mind and hardened his dick.

He groaned and shifted on the bar stool. She might have plans tonight, but come tomorrow he'd meet up with Caitlyn a last time and say his good-bye. He had to do it and soon, before she wasn't the only one thinking they had something more between them than sex.

5

Joyce answered the knock on her apartment door with a trembling hand. Colin had called just before midnight to ask if it was too late to stop by. She'd gone to bed shortly after arriving home from the weekly book club meeting. Regardless, she'd wanted to blurt out that it would never be too late for him to come over. The tension in his voice stopped her from speaking those foolish words. Something was wrong.

She opened the door. A plain white T-shirt lovingly hugged the sculpted muscles of his arms and torso. Frayed jean shorts displayed a drool-worthy pair of long legs made all the sexier by a dusting of sandy-brown hair. Heat zoomed into her belly and warmed her inner thighs. Good gracious, he was turning her into a nympho.

Fisting her hands so she wouldn't give in to the urge to touch, she met his eyes. They weren't friendly sea green or weighted with lust. They were cool jade and distant, as was the rigid set of his mouth. The sizzle between her thighs tapered. Something was definitely the matter.

"Come in." She stepped back, anxious to demand to know

what was going through his mind. It wasn't her place to ask such questions and she had to remember that. She was nothing to him. Nothing but a temporary lover.

Sorrow threatened. She pushed it back to cross the entryway and sit on a faded tan sectional couch. He would talk when he was ready.

Colin sat in a recliner several feet away. He looked around the small sitting area, which opened up into an even smaller kitchen and dining room, then back at her. "This place doesn't seem like you."

What did he expect? An apartment swathed in red and black with strategically placed whips and chains and Harley signs trimming the walls? Somehow Joyce didn't believe she'd played the part of sex goddess that convincingly. Even if she had, it didn't explain the comment. A man who didn't want her beyond the physical shouldn't bother to put any thought into her tastes. Unless Liz was accurate about him being a love-and-marriage kind of guy.

"It was my brother's place," she explained before hope she shouldn't want to feel could take flight. "Andy moved in with his girlfriend a couple months ago. Since he still had a lease on this place, I sold the house I owned with my ex and moved in. I haven't had much of a chance to redecorate."

Questions filled his eyes. He didn't ask them, but stood and paced to the open window. He looked out into the dark muggy night for several silent seconds, then moved on to a photo collage hanging on the wall several feet away. His fingers stroked over a picture of a dark-haired man with a laughing redhead sitting on his lap on an old wooden swing.

Moisture settled in Joyce's panties as she recalled exactly how incredible those long, graceful fingers felt stroking over her body, into her heated sex. She pulled her attention from his hand to focus on the day the shot had been taken. She smiled. "My brother with his girlfriend, Tawny. I never thought I'd see the day Andy would settle for just one woman, but they've been together for almost a year and seem really happy."

Colin dropped his hand from the collage and sent her a doubtful look. "Yeah, well, hopefully it'll work out for them."

She stood and thrust out her chin, called forth the strength to act casual. What he'd come here for was now clear. He'd come to prove his sister didn't know him any better than Joyce did. He'd come to tell her he wasn't a relationship kind of guy and to say good-bye. Despite the way her marriage ended, the last few days had proved she was a relationship kind of gal. For his benefit, she lied, "I hope so. Me, I have no desire for another relationship. They take too much out of you. Straight sex is easier. All the pleasure without any of the complications."

His skeptical look intensified. She expected him to call her bluff, tell her just how complicated things could become. Instead, a smile touched at his lips. "Hate to break it to you," His eyes darkened, turned intense and he took a step toward her, "but you miss out on some of the best parts when it's just about sex."

"Like w—what?" She closed her mouth around the stutter. The last thing she wanted was to relapse to the Joyce of old. He wasn't making that task easy. She felt suddenly breathless, trapped in the heat of his gaze.

He continued toward her, his pace unhurried, his voice intimate. "Curling up together on cold winter nights. Laughing at each other's stupid jokes. Looking forward to babies and old age." Colin laughed, a low, rough sound that stoked the fire kindling to life in her sex. Stopping two feet away, he shook his head. "But, then, I don't do relationships anymore, either. I'm not even sure where that stuff came from."

"You said you had something to tell me?"

His smile faded. "Yeah. I . . . Like I was saying, I don't do relationships. Too much time. Too much effort. Work's the thing for me."

"You came to tell me you don't want to have sex again?"

Joyce might not be completely rid of her naïveté, but instinct and the lust in his eyes said he *did* want her again. Just as she ached to have him.

"No," he said soberly, then quickly added, "but, hell, yes, I do." His gaze moved to her breasts. Her nipples steepled beneath her tank top, pouting for his mouth. He grunted. "Fuck, I can't stand here and see the way I affect you and not want you." His arms opened to her. "What do you say, cupcake? One more time?"

"Heck, yes!"

Laughter followed her response. Moving into his arms, she rose on tiptoe and cut it off with a gentle brush of her mouth over his. The passion that erupted the moment his tongue pushed between her lips and stroked over her gums was anything but gentle.

Colin's tongue found hers in a demanding caress, and a storm of wild need flashed to life in her belly. His hands slid over her back, pulling her against his hot, hard body. She buried her own hands in his hair, wanting him closer still, his stiff cock thrusting inside her, pushing her over the edge and into one last ultimate orgasm. Clinging to his solid strength, she feasted on him, consumed his masculine taste, committed every single texture to memory.

His hips rocked against hers and he moaned into her mouth. She repeated the sound with a hungry, husky one of her own. She rolled her pelvis, and the hot, thick length of his shaft pushed against her mound. Restless ache clawed at her from every direction.

Holy Hades, she had to have him. Had to have him now.

Panting, Joyce lifted from his lips. "I need you." But, no, she couldn't allow him to think that. "I want you," she corrected.

She stepped back a half foot and grabbed the hem of his T-shirt, tugged it from his shorts. Pushing up the shirt, she placed her hands on his bare abdomen. Shudders rippled through her with the longing to feel his entire mouthwatering body naked and pressed up against hers, skin on sweaty skin, limbs tangled and hips pumping. "I'm going to strip you."

"Not if I do you first." Challenge glimmered in Colin's eyes. Wicked challenge she thrilled in.

His hands moved to the bottom of her tank top, fisted and yanked. The untamed sound of ripping cotton filled her senses and sent her pulse into a frenzied dash. Juices of anticipation spilled into her panties. Hastily, she reached for his zipper and gave the metal tab a tug. His hands came over her breasts, cupping, squeezing. He bent his head and his mouth latched on to a nipple, sucked hard. Her attempts at freeing his cock were momentarily forgone as ecstasy tore from her lips with a ragged sigh.

He freed her throbbing nipple to tease, "I thought you wanted me naked."

She did want him naked. Wanted his hard length buried in her dripping sheath. His shorts she might be able to manage. The shirt he was too tall to get off without assistance. Ripping it off the way he had hers sounded more than a little appealing. Since she wasn't that strong, Joyce settled on a more direct route.

Taking a step back, she flung herself at him. Her body rammed into his and she wrapped her legs around his ankles. Colin went down with an "oomph." For once her tactics proved successful. He didn't land on the floor and crack his head open on the end table. He landed on the sectional, with her splayed over top.

He puffed out a breath. "Nice move, Rambo."

She grinned and ducked her head to nip at his erection through the open vee of his shorts. His shaft jerked beneath her lips, fueling her desire all that much more to get him inside her. She slid down his legs, her pussy flaming with the hard press of his thigh against her clit. She grabbed hold of the legs of his shorts and pulled. He lifted his hips. The shorts and underwear slid down easily and his cock leapt free.

Tongue out and at the ready, she grabbed hold off the thick base of his shaft and licked over the weeping head. His taste assailed her, masculine and heady.

"I love the way you taste." Joyce retracted her tongue and stood, pushing her own shorts and panties quickly down her legs. "I love the way you feel even more."

Colin's mouth opened. Before any words could make it out, she came onto his lap and consumed his cock with her body. His pubic hair was starting to come back in, and while it probably itched to him, to her the short stubble was the most incredible friction ever. Erotic sensation shot from her slippery sex to her curled toes. She tossed back her head and lifted herself up and down the length of his erection. A tidal wave of pleasure coursed through her with each move—pleasure that nearly had her climaxing with the first of his hard thrusts.

He shifted beneath her, his pelvis positioning to scrape against her aroused clit. He rotated his hips and the breath snagged in her throat. Her eyes watered. "So good . . . you're always so good."

"It's all you, cupcake."

His tone was tight, as if he hung on to control. He had more willpower than her. Joyce couldn't contain the pressure building inside her a second longer. Orgasm rippled through her, sheer and intense. Spasms gripped her pussy. His cock shuddered within her. Before those shudders could turn to an explosion, he pulled out. Fisting his cock, he pumped his seed onto her belly.

The bliss of release died the instant the reality of what he'd done filled her hazy mind. "Why?" She shouldn't ask it, but darnit, she had to know. Was this his way of saying good-bye? Denying her the last chance to feel him climaxing inside her?

He tucked his finger under her chin and smiled. "Not because I didn't want to feel your pussy dripping honey on my cock. I didn't have a chance to put on a condom before you jumped me."

"Oh. Right." How inane of her. She should have known he was thinking about her well-being. That was Colin. Compassionate to the end. She smiled impishly. "Sorry. I was a little excited. Next time . . ." The words died with a sharp intake. Heartache pressed at her ribs as she realized this truly had been the end. There would be no next time.

Her smile vanished. She eased from his body and stood. Retrieving her ruined tank top from the floor, she used it to wipe the cum from her stomach. When she looked back at Colin, it was to find him dressing.

The tab of his zipper slid up with a foreboding hiss. The look of finality in his eyes wasn't any better. "I should go."

He should. It was for the best. Neither of them wanted a relationship. At least, he didn't. She shouldn't. Joyce grabbed the throw blanket from the back of the sectional and wrapped it around her body. The urge to hide her unhappiness by looking at the floor was almost too great to deny. She did so with the reminder that she wasn't that weak woman any longer. She could face the future looking ahead, even if that future was destined to be a lonely one.

"It is l—late." Darn, her trembling voice. She drew a steadying breath. "I have to work in the morning and I'm sure you do, too. What do you do anyway?" Not that it mattered. Nothing about him mattered.

He looked at the door, but then responded. "Own a landscaping business."

"That explains why you're so good with your hands." Two minutes ago she'd been riding him like a sex goddess extraordinaire. Now she couldn't stop her blush over the inappropriate response. She sank down on the sectional, dismissing the words with a shrug. "It has to be a lot of work to own a business. I just manage a store and it takes enough out of me."

"What kind of store?"

"A bookstore. It's not half as boring as it sounds." Sometimes exciting books were ordered in. The kind of how-to sex manuals that lured in an incredible guy. A guy who clearly wanted to leave and was only sticking around asking questions out of kindness. "See you, Colin. It's been fun, but I really do need to get to bed."

Something flickered through his eyes. Some emotion that made her heart skip a beat with hope. He returned to her and leaned down. She swallowed hard, waiting, praying to feel his lips on hers. He brushed her cheek with a hasty kiss and straightened. "Good-bye, Caitlyn. Thanks for everything."

Joyce, she opened her mouth to say. One more time she wanted to hear her real name on his lips. The tears that welled in the back of her throat stopped her from saying a word. Through blurry eyes she watched him turn and walk out the door.

Ten days spent hundreds of miles away doing a solo landscaping job for a friend should have been enough to make Colin forget about Caitlyn. If not the time and distance, then the nights out. More than one suntanned honey who called the West Coast home and attended night clubs wearing little more than a string for a skirt had sent fuck-me eyes his way. Despite heckling from his friends and his own fervent desire to move on, he couldn't get his dick even a little bit interested in those honeys.

It wasn't just his dick, either. His head wasn't into doing some other woman. His damned heart wasn't.

Grunting, Colin stepped out of his truck. He should have called Liz and told her he'd be taking a red-eye flight home tonight, and to leave the porch light on. Since he hadn't called, he relied on the faint light bleeding through the slits in the living room shades to guide him to the front door. Cursing his bad luck for ever meeting up with Caitlyn, he pushed open the door. The curses died with a hard gulp at the sight of a naked ass waving at him from the living room floor. A naked ass that gave way to a slim female back, which led to a long neck and a crop of short black hair. The bare legs attached to that ass straddled another pair of legs, these ones unmistakably male in their shape and hairiness.

The woman's head bobbed. The man released a guttural groan and pushed his hands into her short dark locks. Colin's stomach bottomed out.

He'd been convinced that getting another woman stuck in his head after what happened with Marlene was a shitty thing to have happen. Walking in on his sister giving a guy a blow job topped that and then some—his sister who continued her merry sucking, as if she didn't have a clue he was standing here.

"I'm home!" he yelled, to be sure she could hear him over her happy slurps.

Liz's head ceased its bobbing. She shrieked and dove for the heap of clothes on the floor several feet away. She tugged a shirt too big to be her own over head, then shot him a scathing look. "Jesus, Col. Haven't you ever heard of knocking?"

"To come inside my own house?" he asked incredulously.

The urge to send her to her room, and her companion on his way with a well-placed fist, hit Colin hard. Only, his sister wasn't a kid anymore, and her companion . . . He turned his attention on the guy, who now stood with his hands planted on his hips and his stiff cock aimed right at Colin. He did a double take over the man's face. No fucking way. This wasn't happening. Not Dusty. But it was Dusty. Only his friend would have the balls to shoot him a cocky smile while standing naked and erect with his dick glistening from the moisture of Colin's sister's mouth.

Not about to let that visual build, he looked back at Liz. "What the fuck—I thought you hated him?"

She turned her glare on Dusty. "I do. His ego's a freaking mile wide." She glanced accusingly at Colin. "I thought you weren't coming home until tomorrow."

"I caught a red-eye. And if you hate him so damned much, what are you doing with his cock in your mouth?"

"She came up to the bar for a burger," Dusty offered calmly.

"I challenged him to a game of pool," Liz added, just as casually. "Winner got a free round of oral sex."

"You lost?" Colin guessed.

"Actually, I won that game." Her lower lip came out in a pout. "I lost the next one. He still owes me my win, so if you don't mind . . ." She crossed the room and grabbed hold of Dusty's cock.

"Easy, chick," Dusty warned. "You break it, you pay for a new one. One this big won't come cheap. "

Liz rolled her eyes. "In your dreams it's that big."

Colin fought the urge to shut his eyes, turn around and walk back out of the house. It was *his* house, damnit. He shouldn't have to be witness to his sister's twisted sexual exploits, or hear them, for that matter. He gave Liz a stern look. "You're not taking him to your bed."

She fisted her free hand at her hip, stubbornness shooting from every line of her body. "I am. If you're lucky I won't share the details in the morning."

"If you're lucky I won't kick your ass out—"

"Relax, man," Dusty cut him off. "I get that she's your sister, but she's a big girl." His gaze shifted to her chest, and he grinned and wiggled his eyebrows. "A real big girl."

Liz released his erection to hold up a hand. "Save it, Col. I get that you would rather catch me fucking some guy I plan to marry, but you ought to now by know that's never gonna happen. Not everyone's cut out for relationships the way you are."

"I'm not cut out for relationships," he retorted. And he did not want to hear her using the word *fuck* in that context.

Knowing filled her eyes. "Right. Like you haven't thought of Caitlyn every day since you've been gone. She called, by the way. Twice."

Colin's gaze zoomed to the answering machine on the coffee table. "She called?" He winced over his tone. Shit, he didn't mean to sound so anxious.

Liz laughed. "No. But the fact that you were hoping she did proves my theory. Regardless of what happened with Marlene, you can't go back to being the bed-hopping bad boy you were in your early twenties. You're a commitment man now. You need the whole love-and-marriage package. Deal with it."

Dusty nodded. "I hate to agree with her—not just because of her attitude problem, either—but you're in a hell of a lot better mood when you're involved with a woman."

Eyes narrowed, Liz swatted his arm. "Trust me, dickhead, if anyone has an attitude problem, it's you. Now get your ass moving before I decide not to give you the rest of your win." Her mouth curved in a catty smile. "Women are fickle, you know?"

Colin shut out further conversation as the pair hurried up the stairs. He didn't manage to miss the openmouthed kiss they shared at the top, or the way they groped each other as they rounded the hall and disappeared from sight. Hell, he didn't get either one of them. He also didn't get how he could feel so damned jealous. He did feel jealous, though, in a way that tightened his gut over the idea that his sister was right.

He'd tried to deny it again and again the last two weeks, but regardless of the past, he was a relationship man, one who'd been hiding behind a landscaping business for too long. The truth was, he didn't need to put in endless hours to see the business continue to thrive. He employed enough workers these days to comfortably take off for the next few weeks without worry.

He had the time to invest in a woman. The question was, did that woman have the time and desire to invest in him?

They'd never made it to Chapter M. Joyce didn't need *Achieving the Ultimate Orgasm* to tell her that completing the chapter exercise of masturbation alone would never be as fulfilling as doing it while Colin watched. But while it wouldn't be as satisfying, it might be the thing to ease the ache in her chest.

It was a sex ache. She'd gone wild with sex for three days straight. The last ten she hadn't done anything more than fantasize and dream about stripping Colin naked and running her tongue all over his big, beautiful body. As a result she was pent up and in need of an orgasm. Once she had that orgasm, the fantasies and dreams would die. She hoped to gosh the ceaseless thoughts of him would go with them.

Heat pushed into her cheeks as she sank against the headboard of her bed and spread her naked thighs. She was stronger these days, more of the confident woman she'd set out to become. Still, the idea of sticking her finger in her pussy was a bit much. Then again, she wouldn't be using a finger to get herself off. She'd be using a carrot.

Joyce grabbed the carrot from where she'd placed it on the bed next to her and frowned over its size. A vibrator or dildo would have been preferable, but she'd yet to make either of those purchases. The sex manual suggested using a cucumber. Every cuke in the produce aisle had seemed two feet long and eight inches thick. She'd settled on the carrot, lopping off a good chunk of the skinny end. The fat end really wasn't that big around. Not as big as Colin was fully erect. She could handle it.

Pulling up her knees, she reached between her thighs and parted the lips of her sex. Tremors shook through her as she eyed the red, uneven flesh of her pussy and the tiny bundle of nerves already standing at attention. She flicked a finger across her clit and gasped as sensation shot deep into her core and wetness shimmered to life on her sex. Holding the carrot firmly, she guided it to her sheath. The cool spear slid a half inch inside. Her hips bucked up and she cried out at the shockingly rigid texture. The carrot pushed farther inside with the arching of her hips. Her pussy grew moister, hungry, seemed to gobble the carrot right up, until her fisted hand brushed against her exposed clit. And, oh, gosh, did that ever feel good.

Moving the carrot back and forth within her juicy sex, she rubbed the edge of her hand over her aching clit. Heat flooded her belly. Her pelvic muscles tightened. She stopped rubbing to pull out the spear, then thrust it back inside. The breath whooshed from her lips as she watched the erotic in-and-out play, saw the shine of her cream coating the carrot, felt the blistering tug of a fast-approaching orgasm.

The phone next to the bed rang. Joyce grabbed it, pushed the TALK button and barked, "Can't you see I'm busy here?"

"Caitlyn?"

Colin's voice cruised to her ear. The carrot plunging into her became his cock. His fingers parted her folds, stroked her clit. His name came out a lusty cry. "Colin!"

"What are you doing, cupcake?"

The sudden coarseness of his tone said he knew well. She was too keyed up to deny it. "What does it sound like?"

His breathing intensified. "Are you alone?"

Why did he care? She should say no and make it seem like she'd been able to easily move on, but she was too busy to put any effort into a lie. "Yes," she panted, grinding the carrot in circles.

"So am I," he confessed, his tone low, husky. "Alone and lying on my bed naked, thinking of you. I'm stroking my dick, but it doesn't feel anything like your hand, Caitlyn. Tell me how you'd touch me if you were here right now."

The carrot ceased for a second, then started up again, pushing into her dripping pussy with new vigor. She was a sex goddess in his eyes. A sex goddess who elated in phone sex. A sex goddess who'd spent many long hours reading erotic stories the past ten days.

Closing her eyes, she rode the carrot hard. She breathed into the phone, imagining his hand fisted around his cock, pumping. "I'd be kneeling naked between your thighs, fondling my breasts and moaning over how good it felt." The moan that punctuated the words had everything to do with the quakes stealing through her and nothing to do with good timing. "I'd pull at my throbbing nipples, wet my fingers and stroke them over the tips." She brought her free hand to her mouth and sucked in the first two digits, whimpering over the salty-sweet taste of her arousal.

Pulling the fingers from her lips, she stroked them over her rigid nipples. She writhed against the warm moistness of her touch, the cool hardness of the carrot. "I'd make you desperate for my touch, so needy you'd beg."

"I'm not the only one ready to beg, cupcake." Colin's voice came through rough, yet cocky. "Your breasts are aching for my mouth. You want to feel it sucking on you, biting at your nipples. Your cunt's on fire for my dick. You're fingering yourself, but you know it's not half as good as it'd be if it were my fingers in your body, my stiff cock pushing inside you. Beg for me and I'll make it all better."

Joyce squeezed her nipple, crying out as electric sensation shot to her pussy. Her sex constricted around the carrot, her clit tingled. She slid partway down the headboard, splaying her thighs wider and forcing her mind back to the conversation. On the visual of Colin's stroking hand. "I won't give in, so you do. You can't stand to watch any longer, knowing how much I want you. I hurt with my ache. You toss me back on the bed and shove into me with a hard thrust that has us both crying out."

She pulled back the carrot, then skewered it in tight, twisting, turning. Her pelvis jerked up, her hips rising erratically to take the carrot deeper. She sucked in a breath, gasped. "You fuck me hard."

"Hell, yeah, I do." His breath wheezed in her ear. His cock glided in the circle of his fist, pre-cum coating the length and sounding through the phone line. Or maybe that was the sound of her arousal. She couldn't think clearly enough to distinguish.

"I fuck you so hard, tears fill your eyes and I can barely catch my breath." He inhaled raggedly.

She struggled for her own breaths, but found none worthy of taking. Orgasm had her in its grip. She balled her free hand in the comforter. Huffed in his ear. Held on tight as crippling tension washed through her in a tumultuous wave of ecstasy.

"You can't catch your breath," Colin continued, his words beyond tense, nearly impossible to understand. "You can't even think. You can only feel. Your pussy clamps down on my cock. Hugs it tight like it never wants to let go."

The crest of climax shook through her. Her toes curled. Her fingernails bit into the carrot. Her pussy gushed forth a flood of juices. "Oh, my gosh, Colin!"

"You start spasming. You scream. You . . ." He broke off with a penetrating moan. His hand would be moving fast now, milking his cock with every ounce of energy. "Christ, you're so good, cupcake. So fucking good."

"I—I'm coming around you," Joyce managed. "Dripping all over your big, hard cock. It's too much. . . . Y—you can't hold back any longer. You—"

"Come," he finished for her with a growl. "I come all over your sweet pussy lips, fill you up all hot and creamy. Hell, you're dripping so much. I can't stop coming." The sound of his release echoed through the phone line loud and clear. "I . . . can't . . . stop. . . ."

Colin's voice faded with a final moan. She sank into the hazy bliss of rapture, let it cloak her for a full minute. The enduring hardness of the carrot pushed into her thoughts then. Euphoria lifted in a rush. Sorrow threatened.

Tossing the carrot aside, she slid back up the headboard and frowned at the phone's mouthpiece. It was time to go. "I guess this is the part where I hang up."

"Guess so."

But he didn't sound like he wanted that. Was there hope that he'd called so late at night for some reason other than phone sex? "Can I come over?" Joyce asked quickly, before common sense outweighed the longing to see him again. "We don't have to have sex. We could just talk, or watch a movie or something."

"It's after midnight."

"Good point."

"Way too late to talk. Come over and warm up my bed."

"Yes. No." Was he serious? Didn't he realize coming over there would mean embedding him further into her mind and heart? Darnit, she wanted to go so badly. But she couldn't. She never should have suggested it. "No, I can't do it. I'm sorry."

"Never be sorry when you're following your heart. You're the only one you have to please, the only one whose expectations you have to live up to."

So understanding. Such a wonderful guy. And she would be such a flake to hang up this phone without admitting the truth. "Colin?"

"Yeah?"

"I'm not following my heart and I'm not pleasing myself, either. Well, I was, but that's not what I mean. I mean, I want to come over there. I . . . I miss you."

His heightened breathing pushed through the phone line. Five seconds passed. Ten. Her heart sank. Crud. She'd made the most foolish mistake ever. She'd spoken her heart and scared him so thoroughly, he'd never call or see her again.

Five more seconds passed and Colin's voice came through

the line, low and serious. "I miss you, too. And not just my body. Maybe I'm crazy for wanting another relationship, but, hell, my heart misses you, Caitlyn. My arms miss you."

"Joyce," she rushed out, happiness warming her through. "Call me Joyce. And I'm crazy, too, because I'm falling for you."

"The feeling's mutual, Joyce. Now get that sweet ass of yours in the car and come over so we can do something about it. Or I'll come over there."

She darted from the bed and tugged on her discarded shorts. Who needed panties? Certainly not a sex goddess like her. *Achieving the Ultimate Orgasm* caught her eye from the night-stand. Thank goodness for the power of the written word. Not to mention really explicit pictures. "Don't bother. I'm already on my way. I'll be there in five minutes."

"It's a twenty-minute drive."

"Then give me ten." She moved the phone from her ear long enough to yank a vee-necked T-shirt over her head. She *oohed* at the sensual friction of the cotton chafing against her aroused nipples, then grinned at the vivid orange and black peeking out from the vee. "I was a Harley mama in my former life and have the tat to prove it."

Colin's chuckle burst through the phone line, warming any part of her body not already ablaze from her touch. The future no longer looked lonely. It looked incredible—ultimate-orgas-mically so.

"In that case, see you in ten. And, cupcake . . . leave the gum at home."

Are you ready for one helluva wild, sexy, wonderful ride into
the future? Then fasten your seatbelt, and turn the page for a
little taste of
HELL KAT
by Vivi Anna
An Aphrodisia trade paperback on sale in April 2006

1

LOWER BC PLAINS, THE YEAR 2275

Dust devils whirled viciously around the broken remains of civilization. Buildings that once stood proud and strong were now only jagged cement shards protruding from infertile dirt and rock. The sun was a big glaring ball of light in the sky. Where it had once produced growth and warmth, it now scorched what was left of the Earth with its brutal rays.

Kat looked up into the blistering sun and wondered for the second time today what in the hell she was doing out on the Outer Rim. The fierce, arid wind whipped at her cloak and tried to tear it from her body. Sand peppered her face like a tiny barrage of bullets. Pulling her hood forward, she adjusted her tinted goggles over her eyes and continued to search the rubble for her treasure. No small feat, considering her right eye was covered by a black leather eye-patch.

She kicked at the dirt and crumbled concrete with her steel-toed jackboots. Nothing. They'd been searching for nearly two hours now. She glanced over at her partner.

"Damian! See anything?"

Damian stood from where he squatted, raising his head toward Kat, his blue eyes glinting in the sun. He held up his hand, something encased in his glove.

"Just this cute little dolly." He waved it at her grinning mischievously.

The doll, headless and encrusted in filth, rattled in his hand.

"Quit fucking around. And put on your goggles." Kat shook her head. The kid knew better. An hour under the unprotected sun produced cataracts. Cataracts usually led to blindness. She'd seen it happen more and more. Her sister had succumbed to blindness before she had died from the flu. Damian was lucky he had his hood pulled over his head.

"Yes, momsie." Damian reached around to his pack and unzipped a compartment. He came away with his tinted goggles.

Kat watched him put them on.

"Better?" He flashed a grin.

She shook her head but smiled. He always managed to make her smile. That was one of the reasons she had bartered for his life two years ago.

He had been an employee of a local junk dealer named Jones. Whipping boy, more like. He did errands for Jones, cleaned up the shop and, once-in-a-while, loaned out to friends. Loaned, as in pimped out for sexual favors. Men or women, it didn't matter to Jones. He was an equal opportunist. If the price was high enough, Damian could be bought.

When Kat first saw Damian, he was hanging from the ceiling by his hands, his wrists shackled in metal claps. Naked, except for a think strip of cloth hanging over his crotch, Kat couldn't help but notice his long, lean body. Muscles rippled as he twisted side to side, struggling against his restraint. When he managed to turn all the way around, Kat could see the long red welts on his back. She looked down at his dangling feet and saw the instrument of choice lying on the dirt floor: a horsewhip.

Although disgusted by the display, Kat didn't show it. She

had a reputation to uphold, and couldn't be seen as soft. It was hard enough just being a woman in these desolate times.

"Selling meat now, Jones?"

He glanced up from inspecting the electronic gadget she had brought him, and eyed Damian. "Caught 'im stealin'. 'E's usually a good boy, but ya can't 'ave the 'elp 'elping 'emselves, now can ya?"

"I guess not."

Damian met her gaze then. His eyes were as blue and clear as the afternoon sky. High chiseled cheekbones in a comely face with lips full and sensuous. Pretty like a woman, but as she gazed down at his body, there was no question that he was all male. His sculpted chest glistened with sweat.

Jones must have noticed her watching him. "You can 'ave a go at 'im if you like. Won't even charge ya, since ya're such a good customer."

Kat had wanted a go. She felt the sexual pull. It tugged at her insides, gathering painfully between her legs. Guilt also washed over her as she watched him hang from the ceiling. Scrutinizing his powerful body, she wondered what his skin would feel like under her hand. Wondered what his flesh would taste like if she trailed her tongue over his taunt stomach and down lower under the thin cloth. As if privy to her thoughts, he smiled at her, the cloth at his crotch beginning to twitch. She quickly looked away and left the store with her coins.

Two days later, she returned with more electronics and bartered for Damian's release. Jones didn't even question her. It was just another transaction to him. They had made a deal, sealed it with a handshake, and she had left the store with Damian in tow. He had thanked her for his freedom.

But several months later, Kat realized that he hadn't minded his service for Jones. In fact, some of things he had to do he really enjoyed. Now, he did some of those things for Kat. Lucky girl, she thought.

"I think Russell gave us a bum lead." Damian's voice broke into her thoughts.

She looked over at him as he kicked an old metal can her way. It landed at the toe of her boot.

"Yeah, maybe."

Eyeing the dirt and debris on the ground, Kat went over what she knew about the area. It had once been home to a school of some sort. The exact nature of it eluded her, but she knew that young children had attended. She also knew that children of old were taught by electronic means. They had access to all sorts of gadgets. It wasn't clear even if they had a teacher. Maybe they had all been plugged into some electronic thingy by wires coming out of their heads.

School. Kat had no concept of what that would have been like. The word and idea were as foreign to her as clean air and fresh water. The little bit of reading and writing she had learned was from her mothers before she had died. Everything else she needed to know, she learned by doing it out on the streets. Not a pleasant education for a young svelte girl with midnight black hair and big green eyes.

Russell, another junk dealer, had told her that she could find those old learning devices out here. At least a couple of steps above the shit ladder than what Jones had been, Kat didn't mind doing business with him. So far, he had been honest with her in their dealings. He never tried to skimp on her payment.

In fact, he had been feeding her tips as to where certain treasures were located. A win-win situation for them both, she got her money and he got his prize. As far as Kat knew, she was the only hunter that he tolerated.

Something glinted in the sun just under a rock-pile a few feet away. Moving to it, she bent down and pushed over one of the stones to brush away the earth. A small circle of metal, the size of a coin, lay imbedded in the dirt.

"Bring me the pack."

Damian rushed over to where she knelt, placing the bag down at her side. She opened it up and took out a large, long-handled tool, somewhat like a paintbrush. With care, she swept at the arc around the shiny metal. More metal appeared under the dirt. She took out a small chisel and hammer and chipped around the earth that imprisoned the artifact. She did it gently and expertly, careful not to damage her treasure.

"Is that it?" Damian's velvety voice broke into her concentration.

"Shut up, will you?" But Kat wasn't asking.

She dug around the metal and under it and then set aside the tools and lifted the treasure out of the ground. A flat silver disc with tiny buttons on one side lay encrusted in the earth. She rubbed at the metal, clearing away the stubborn clinging sand. The word *play* was etched under one button. Kat grinned.

"Is it the music maker?"

"Money maker you mean."

Laughing, Damian wrapped his arms around Kat. He picked her up and swung her around.

"I can just taste the thick juicy steak I'm going to have. I can almost see the blood on my plate."

"Put me down, or you'll see the blood on your face."

Damian did as she said but didn't stop grinning. He eyed her as she put the artifact carefully into the pack.

"Aren't you happy?" he asked.

"I'll be a lot happier after the coins are in my pocket and a bottle of vodka in my hand."

"You're a lot more than happy after a bottle of vodka."

His eye twinkled mischievously.

Kat grinned. "I know." She handed him the pack. "Let's go

before it gets dark. We don't want to be out here much longer. Raiders will come soon." She eyed the surrounding burnt-out buildings looking for any sign of scavengers.

Not the animal kind. The human ones. A few treasure hunters had been killed in this area, their bodies found partially eaten.

They moved quickly toward the motorcycle propped up against a ruined building. Kat glanced up at the first two stories that still stood erect. The rest lay buried under two hundred years of dirt and rock. Often, Kat wondered how any of these structures managed to sustain the damage of the nuclear blasts. The windows were long gone, blown to pieces and melted from the explosive heat. Then the whole place had burned. The fires had raged for over a year. With no water or rain to extinguish the flames, the fires ate up what was left of the civilized world. If it had been this bad out here, she wondered what remained at ground zero. If anything still stood in the Vanquished City, she'd be surprised.

A shrill call shattered the silence around them as Kat swung her leg over the machine. It was no cry of an animal. At least not the ones running on four legs.

As Damian mounted the bike behind her, she glanced over his shoulder. Swift dark movement near a large cement slab confirmed her suspicions.

"We've got company." She kicked the motorcycle over. Thankfully, if roared to life in seconds. Sometimes it was not so reliable.

Damian peered over his shoulder. "Fuck."

"Yup. Load my shotgun."

Damian fumbled for the gun strapped to the saddlebags on the bike. "We've only got two shells," he confessed while popping them into the chamber.

"Then pray there are only two of *them*."

"Done," Damian said as she handed her the gun.

"Grab the handlebars." Kat turned around on the seat as if to hug Damian, so she could see their attackers, the shotgun tucked into her side. "Let's rock."

Squeezing the gas, Damian shot the bike forward. It wobbled dangerously to the left, but he soon gained control. Two Raiders dressed in ragged cloaks and dark goggles rushed out at them. Kat kept the gun pointed, but she didn't think she'd need it. The bike's speed was no match for the strength of the Raider's legs. No human could outrun a machine from the past.

"Kat! We have a problem."

Trying to turn her head, Kat couldn't see the danger Damian's wavering voice indicated. "How many?"

"Two."

"Can you go around?"

"No. There's a lot of rock and debris. It's a straight patch right to them. If we run into one, the impact might kill him, but we'll go down for sure."

"Are they together, or on each side?"

"One on each side."

Kat slid the shotgun into the harness on the bike. Reaching under her cloak, she grabbed two star-shaped steel discs from her belt. They were four inches wide and the blades fit perfectly between her fingers.

"Should we slow down?" Damian asked.

"No, speed up."

Damian turned his head and stared at her. "What? Are you fucking crazy?"

"Are there any concrete slabs near them?"

"Tons."

"Find a good one, and take us up."

"You want to jump over them?"

"Yup."

Chuckling, Damian shook his head. "I'm going to get eaten alive by a cannibal."

"No you won't. I'll shoot you before they get to you." Smiling, Kat raised her arms, tucking her elbows into her body, the throwing stars gripped tightly in her hands.

"That's what I love about you Kat. You're always looking out for me."

Damian gripped the handle pulling the gas tight. The back wheel spat up gravel and rocks as he gunned it forward.

"Tell me when we're right over them."

"Okay, hang on!"

As the bike rumbled under her, Kat closed her eyes and muttered an oath under her breath. She would not die out here. There were many adventures she had yet to experience. She hadn't even faced her greatest rival . . . Hades. She couldn't die without first meeting him. How would it look to Hades, if she died out here like an amateur on their first hunt? It would give him too much gloating power. She'd never allow that.

Feeling Damian tense, she opened her eyes just as the bike hit a concrete incline. Within seconds, they were airborne.

"Now!" Damian yelled.

Whipping her arms down and back, Kat released the metal stars. Squeals of pain confirmed her lethal aim. As the bike soared overhead, Kat could see the two scavengers, with the steel discs imbedded into their foreheads. They slumped to the ground, dead.

The impact of the bike hitting the cement jarred Kat and she knocked heads with Damian. Pain exploded in her ear where she hit. Rocking violently, Damian struggled to keep the bike upright. Clamping her eyes shut, Kat wrapped her arms around him knowing they were going down.

The front wheel hit a rock just as Damian put on the brakes and turned the handlebar. Instead of flipping over, they skidded to a halt on the side, Damian's right leg pinned under the machine. Finally, they came to a rest against another wedge of cement.

Kat peeked on eye open and turned her head to look at Damian. He had his eyes squeezed shut, but he was grinning.

"Are you hurt?"

He nodded his head. "My leg."

"Then why are you smiling?"

"Because we're still alive."

Kat pushed out from him, and rolled onto the ground. "Not for long, if you don't get up. There are two more Raiders running this way." Bending down, she pulled on the bike so Damian could slide his leg from under the twisted steel.

Pain evident on his face, Damian managed to stand. Kat glanced down at his thigh. There was a rip in the leather of his pants, and a slow trickle of blood.

"Don't be a baby, it's just a scratch." After righting the bike, she swung her leg over it. "Get on before your blood attracts more of them."

Damian got on behind her, and wrapped his arms around her waist. "Okay, but I get hazard pay this time. I need a new pair of leathers."

"You can have a pair of leather underwear for all I care. Let's just go."

Laughing, Damian pressed his lips to Kat's cheek in a smacking kiss. "You're my kind of woman, Hell Kat."